"To kiss is *embrasser*."

"*Em-brah-say*," he parroted.

Violet usually hated the way French sounded when a non-native speaker tried it. Walker didn't pronounce the words perfectly, but he didn't butcher them, either. And somehow he made each one sexier in his own rugged way.

"How would you—*embrasser* me?" he added.

She laughed. "First I'd give you more warning than I did this morning. I'd say, *Je veux t'embrasser*, which means *I want to kiss you*." And did she ever. Nothing was more of a tease than being close enough to kiss him, wanting to kiss him, and *not* kissing him. How did he exercise such restraint? Or maybe he didn't want her as much as she wanted him.

"*Je veux t'embrasser*," he repeated, his accent a little better this time.

"That's good. You're getting the hang of it."

"No," Walker said. He let his bottom lip brush hers, and she sucked in a breath. "*Je. Veux. T'embrasser.*"

Her throat went bone dry, and she struggled to swallow. "Then *kiss* me already."

PRAISE FOR A.J. PINE

"Sweet and engrossing."

—*Publishers Weekly* on *Tough Luck Cowboy*

"Light and witty."

—*Library Journal* on *Saved by the Cowboy*

"A fabulous storyteller who will keep you turning pages and wishing for just one more chapter at the end."

—Carolyn Brown, *New York Times* bestselling author, on *Second Chance Cowboy*

"Cross my heart, this sexy, sweet romance gives a cowboy-at-heart lawyer a second chance at first love and readers a fantastic ride."

—Jennifer Ryan, *New York Times* bestselling author, on *Second Chance Cowboy*

"Ms. Pine's character development, strong family building, and interesting secondary characters add layers to the story that jacked up my enjoyment of *Second Chance Cowboy* to maximum levels."

—*USA Today* "Happy Ever After"

"5 Stars! Top Pick! The author and her characters twist and turn their way right into your heart."

—NightOwlReviews.com on *Second Chance Cowboy*

"This is a strong read with a heartwarming message and inspiring characters."

—*RT Book Reviews* on *Second Chance Cowboy*

Also by A.J. Pine

Second Chance Cowboy

Saved by the Cowboy (novella)

Tough Luck Cowboy

HARD LOVING COWBOY

A.J. PINE

A Crossroads Ranch Novel

FOREVER
New York Boston

Forever
Hachette Book Group
1290 Avenue of the Americas, New York, NY 10104
read-forever.com
twitter.com/readforeverpub

First edition: March 2019

Forever is an imprint of Grand Central Publishing. The Forever name and logo are trademarks of Hachette Book Group, Inc.

The publisher is not responsible for websites (or their content) that are not owned by the publisher.

The Hachette Speakers Bureau provides a wide range of authors for speaking events. To find out more, go to www.hachettespeakersbureau.com or call (866) 376-6591.

ISBNs: 978-1-5387-2711-9 (mass market), 978-1-5387-2713-3 (ebook)

Printed in the United States of America

OPM

10 9 8 7 6 5 4 3 2 1

ACKNOWLEDGMENTS

The last Everett brother is here! Thank you to everyone who's fallen in love with reading the Everett brothers' stories as much as I have fallen in love with writing them. It's because of you that I get to keep writing books, and I could not be more grateful to be able to do the thing that I love most.

Thank you, Andie, for your wonderful guidance. I'm so grateful for your help.

Thank you, Tracy, for teaching me the Dutch pronunciation of Gouda. I finally found a way to use it in a book!

And to my fabulous publishing team—super-agent Emily, magical fairy dust sprinkler (otherwise known as editor) Madeleine, and my writer sisters Lia, Jen, Chanel, Natalie, and Megan—thank you for being in my corner. I don't know what I'd do without you!

S and C, I love you to infinity.

HARD LOVING COWBOY

PROLOGUE

New Year's Eve

Walker swiped his forearm across his face, and his sleeve came away bloody. He guessed his nose was broken, but he was numb to the pain.

"What the hell?" he said. He coughed as blood ran down the back of his throat. That was when he realized he was lying down. He made a move to get up.

"Don't!" someone shouted. It was a woman's voice. "Unless you want a palm full of glass. You're paying for that window, by the way."

Window?

He was about to start asking questions again when he heard the wail of a siren. Seconds later, his vision blurred with swirls of red and blue.

A car door slammed, and boots crunched in the gravel. Or maybe that was the glass he was sprawled on.

"Gimme your hand, Everett," a gruff, male voice said. And because Walker wanted to get the hell out of whatever situation he was in, he gripped the outstretched palm and let whoever was standing above him pull him to his feet.

Walker's vision didn't clear, even when the lights were out of his eyes. But he could make out the uniform. He could tell the vehicle was a black SUV and not a white ambulance, which only meant one thing.

"Evening, Sheriff." Walker stumbled, but someone caught him by the elbow.

"Hell, Cash. This guy's a walking miracle. No embedded glass. Looks like he fell just right 'cause there's not a scratch on him...other than what looks like a broken nose." The voice belonged to a woman, but she was still standing behind him.

Whoever she was, while she'd been nice enough to keep him from hitting pavement again, she was now pushing him toward a bench. With his arm pinned behind his back.

"Walker Everett, you're under arrest for disorderly conduct, public intoxication, and likely vandalism if Nora decides she's had enough of your antics. You want to take it from here, Sheriff?" the female officer asked.

Walker sat and felt cool steel clamp around one wrist and then the other.

"Christ," Sheriff Hawkins hissed as he squatted, the two men now eye to eye. "What the hell happened in there?"

Walker leaned forward and whispered, "I'd love to tell you that, Cash, but first you're gonna have to tell *me* where the hell I am."

The sheriff winced. "Well, you smell like you're drowning at the bottom of a bottle of Jack, so that ought to give you a hint. Sorry to have to do this, Walker, but I can't help you out of this one." He straightened to his full height. "You have the right to remain silent. Anything you say can and will be used against you in a court of law. You have the right to talk to a lawyer and have him present with you while you are being questioned. If you cannot afford to hire a lawyer, one will be appointed to represent you before any questioning if you wish. You can decide at any time to exercise these rights and not answer any questions or make any statements. Do you understand each of these rights I have explained to you? Having these rights in mind, do you wish to talk to us now?"

Walker Everett had plenty to say—and ask for that matter. His brain was swimming with questions and answers and a few choice words for his friend Cash, who had the balls to arrest him. But none of his words made it to the surface. Instead the black spots dancing at the edge of his vision were a full-on blanket of dark now. The last thing he heard before losing consciousness completely was "Call his brother, Jack Everett. He'll represent him when he's ready for questioning."

To say he had a headache was the understatement of the year. Walker had been on benders before, but he'd learned early on to keep a bottle of ibuprofen in the top drawer of his nightstand. Sure, sometimes he forgot to take them, but after a while it had become habit, and no one actually forgot a habit.

But he wasn't in his bed right now. He was in *a* bed, but this wasn't his room.

"Morning, sunshine," he heard before he dared to open his eyes. "I'll call your brother and let him know you're awake. Said he wasn't posting bail until this morning as long as you had a place to sleep. Cozy, isn't it?"

Walker blinked, the tiniest movement, and hissed in a breath through clenched teeth. He guessed by the sheriff's chuckle that Cash had heard him. He pinched the bridge of his nose and saw stars. Then he caught sight of his bloodstained sleeve and imagined what the rest of him must look like.

"You're gonna need to get it set, but there wasn't much we could do without you being conscious. As long as you get to the doctor within the week, you should be good to go. Wait any longer, and they'll need to rebreak it."

Walker gingerly swung his legs off the side of the cot, his boots falling heavy onto the cement floor of the cell.

"My brother let me sleep here last night?" His mouth was drier than cotton, and he wasn't going to try to figure out what it tasted like.

Cash's feet were propped up on his desk as he sipped his coffee and stared at Walker. "I don't think I'd call what you were doing sleeping, but that's not what I want to discuss."

Walker braced his hands on his knees, head hanging between his shoulders, and blew out a long breath. "December thirty-first is her birthday. *Was* her birthday." It had been more than fifteen years, and he still had trouble thinking of his mother in the past tense.

"And it'd break her heart to know how you spent it."

Walker looked up to meet the disappointed gaze of his oldest brother, Jack. "Do you ever get tired of lecturing?"

Jack scrubbed a hand across his jaw. Dark circles rimmed his eyes. "Yeah. I do."

Walker stood, not exactly steady on his feet but enough that he wouldn't topple over. "Noted, big brother. So, this is the part where we make this all go away, right? There are advantages to that fancy law degree you got."

But Jack stood in front of the small cell with his arms crossed while the sheriff never lifted his feet off his desk.

"This isn't like all the other times. Nora's pressing charges," Jack said. "You fell through the tavern's damned window. That mess that was once your face? The wooden frame. You're lucky you still have your teeth."

"So you're leaving me here?" Walker asked, not exactly feeling lucky.

"That's up to you," Jack said. He slid a hand through the bars and held out a pamphlet. "There's a place about an hour from here. Supposed to be real nice. Program lasts two months. But you have to voluntarily admit yourself."

When Walker didn't take what was being offered, Jack's head fell against the bars.

"Please," Jack said. "I can't keep doing this. You can't keep doing this to yourself. I'm getting married the end of the summer, and—"

"And you don't want your drunk of a brother messing things up," Walker interrupted.

Jack lifted his head, and the pained look in his brother's eyes made Walker take a step back.

"I'm done making excuses for you. I'm done telling myself that you're the youngest, that you'll grow out of this. I'm done wondering when I'll get the call from Cash telling me that this time your luck ran out. I'm done, Walker. I'm—done." He dropped the pamphlet on the floor of the cell. "Just because Jack Senior drowned in the bottle doesn't mean you have to do the same." Then he started to walk away.

If Jack was finally turning his back on him, Walker's luck *had* run out.

"Wait!" he said, the panic and desperation rising.

His brother stopped, and for several long seconds he did nothing else.

Turn around, Jack, Walker thought. *Turn the hell around.*

After what felt like days, Jack turned to face him.

"Okay," Walker said. "You win. When do we leave?"

Jack's fists clenched at his sides. Then they released. "We get your face fixed up—as best we can—and then we get on the road."

"Just like that?" Walker asked.

"Just like that."

He'd do this for his brother, but it would only be a temporary fix. Walker knew it, and he was sure Jack did, too. Walker couldn't change who he was any more than a tiger could change its stripes. For better or worse—in this case he'd admit it was worse—Walker Everett was his father's son. You couldn't fight genetics, could you? Yet somehow the inheritance skipped Jack and his other brother Luke.

"It won't work," Walker admitted.

"Might not," Jack said. "But for the first time in my life, I'm asking—no, I'm begging—you to try."

And that was when Walker realized it, the one part of the equation that had always seemed to be missing.

No one had ever *asked* him to stop.

"Jenna and Luke know?" he asked his brother when they were outside in Jack's truck. No way his aunt and his other brother would be left in the dark, but confirmation was always good.

"They know if I come home without you that you made the right decision. Here." He handed Walker a soft ice pack. "Grabbed this on my way out. Cash said you'd need it. And the bottle of water in the cup holder is all yours."

Walker tore the lid off the bottle and drank its entire contents without coming up for air. After a substantial belch, he laid his head against the seat and placed the pack over his eyes and nose, letting out something between a groan and a sigh.

"You sure my luck didn't run out?" he asked Jack. "Because other than a fresh bottle of whiskey, this is about as close to heaven as I think I'm gonna get." When his brother didn't so much as laugh, let alone answer him,

Walker cleared his throat. "This isn't who I wanted to be, you know."

The only problem was, if he wasn't this—the brother who couldn't get his shit together, who nobody even expected to grow out of this kind of behavior—then who the hell was he? Because this was the only version of himself he recognized anymore.

"I know," Jack finally said as they pulled out onto the main road. "I know."

CHAPTER ONE

Two months later

"The job is yours if you want it. We leave as soon as we're done putting that addition on the bed-and-breakfast. We can use all the cheap labor we can get."

Walker held the phone to his ear for several seconds, letting the offer sink in.

"I need to stick around for Jack and Ava's wedding," he finally said. "That's not until the end of July."

Sam Callahan, of Callahan Brothers Contracting, laughed. "Yeah, I know about the wedding. Got a save-the-date e-mail and everything. We'll be heading out soon after, breaking ground on the ranch in early August."

Walker nodded, though he knew the man on the other end of the line couldn't see him.

"I gotta think on it," he said. "But I'll let you know."

"Sure thing," Sam said. "Welcome home, Everett."

Walker ended the call. He didn't have much of a response to the sentiment, not when the place he'd spent most of his life felt as foreign right now as if he'd moved to the other side of the world. It was still the place where his mother had died and where his father had gone off the rails. But it was far from home.

He slid his phone in his pocket and got back to the task at hand.

It was high noon, the heat topping out at an unseasonably hot eighty-eight degrees for early March. Walker had been using the circular saw outside the winery's back entrance for the better part of two hours. His T-shirt was soaked through with sweat, his jeans full of sawdust, and his beard was itching his neck something fierce. But when he looked at the perfectly cut pieces of crown molding ready to be stained, he considered it all worth it.

Okay, he was hotter than Satan's pitchfork in a furnace and was sure he'd sweated out fifteen years' worth of alcohol even if he hadn't had a drink in two months. Nothing was worth this kind of torture, but now that the floors were done and the entire inside of the winery painted, Jack and Luke wouldn't let the sawhorse inside even if Walker used a drop cloth.

"There's air-conditioning inside," he'd argued.

"Fresh air will do you good," Luke had countered.

"Plus Ava and Lily will have our asses if you mess up their space," Jack had added.

Leave it to his brothers to throw their respective partners under the bus when they weren't around to defend themselves *or* hear Walker's side of the argument.

"Do you know how much fresh air I had while I was gone? I've been on hikes, bikes, and"—he'd leaned close to whisper this one to Luke—"and there was outdoor yoga, man. You don't know the fucking horrors."

You'd think a guy would get some sort of recognition for two months of sobriety, yet here he was, tossed outside like his nephew Owen's Lab, Scully.

Who was he kidding? That spoiled pooch was probably in the ranch lying next to the air-conditioning vent getting a belly rub. Damn that sounded nice.

He pulled his shirt over his head, found the one dry spot left, and gave his torso a good once-over. That was when he heard the crackle of tires in the gravel out front and the distinct sound of a car door slamming not once but twice.

Excellent, he thought. *Visitors.*

As he made his way to the front of the soon-to-be Cross-roads Winery, the sound of a heated argument filled the air. At least, he thought it was an argument based on the rapidly increasing volume of their voices, but the words that floated his direction were anything but English.

"*Reviens,* Violet! *Tu sais que tu m'aimes!*"

The male, who Walker could now see was a tall, lanky guy with curly dark hair, was waving his hands in the air as he followed the woman—a curvy brunette with thick waves tumbling over her shoulders, light brown skin, and legs for days—toward the winery's front door.

"*Va te faire foutre*, Ramon! *J'arrête!*" She added a one-fingered gesture, and even though Walker didn't speak what he guessed was French, he did understand the universal language of *Fuck you.*

"We're closed, gorgeous," Walker called to her, and without a second glance, she changed her trajectory from the building's entrance to where Walker stood a couple yards to the right.

"*Est-ce que tu vois?*" she called over her shoulder to the other man as she approached. "*Il est la!*" She was close enough to touch him now—and she did, wrapping her arms around Walker's waist.

"Are you married?" she whispered. "Engaged or attached in any way?"

He shook his head slowly. "So you do speak English, huh?"

"Please," she said under her breath. "Go with this, and I promise to make it up to you."

"Mmm-hmm," he said.

She slid her palms up his bare torso and linked her fingers behind his neck. Walker didn't think, just acted. He dropped his balled-up T-shirt to the ground, pressed his hands firmly against her hips, and dipped his head so she could brush her soft lips over his. If he thought he was parched from baking in the morning sun, it was nothing compared to the insatiable thirst he felt when her tongue slipped into his mouth. He growled as she let out a soft moan. And then he took all that she gave, and damn this stranger was a giver.

His hands traveled south, and he waited for her to object, but she only kissed him harder. So he squeezed her round, firm ass as their tongues and mouths and lips spoke a language they both understood.

Need.

Sure, the tenets of his therapy strongly recommended no dating within the first six months of his sobriety, but this could hardly be interpreted as dating. He didn't even know this woman's name, only that he'd been in the desert for eight long weeks, and she was either an oasis or the best damned mirage he'd ever seen.

And working at the vineyard wasn't an issue—yet. He'd cross that precarious bridge in the fall when the vineyard officially opened. Right now his brothers were happy to let him do all the necessary busy work. After all, all work and no play meant no falling through tavern windows, right?

"*Bien!*" Walker heard the other man call, but he wasn't about to cut short whatever was happening to acknowledge him. "*Vous gagnez*. You win. You want me out of your life? *Au revoir*. Perhaps your new man would like to take you home."

His words were heavily accented and dripping with disdain.

She didn't respond, but kept up with the charade as Walker heard the car door slam, the engine rev to life, and then finally, the frantic sound of tires spinning too fast to gain purchase before finally squealing onto the main road and eventually, out of earshot.

"You gonna tell me what the hell that was all about?" he said against her lips. "Wouldn't mind your name, either."

She lowered herself onto the spikes of her heels, the shoes apparently not enough to reach Walker's six-foot-four-inch frame. Her pink lips were swollen and the copper skin of her chin was rubbed pink from his beard. She absently brushed her fingers over it as her eyes searched far down the now empty road.

"How about I start?" he said when she made no move to answer him. "Walker Everett. You seem to be stranded at my ranch."

She cleared her throat, her eyes—brown with flecks of gold—finally focusing on his.

"I thought this was a vineyard."

Walker grunted. "Depends on if those grapes out there make anything worth drinking, but I'll let my brother and his fiancée worry about that. I'm more interested in that mighty friendly greeting of yours. Not that I'm complaining."

She smoothed her fitted black skirt and refastened the button of her crisp, white shirt that had undoubtedly popped open when she was making his acquaintance. Not before he snuck a glance at the lavender lace that peeked out from beneath.

"I'm here for the interview," she finally said. "Though I realize now I've most likely already lost the job. Damn it, Ramon."

"He your boyfriend?" Walker asked.

The woman crossed and uncrossed her arms, then started looking around desperately.

"My bag!" she yelled. "He left me without my bag?"

Walker squinted, then strode past her to the empty parking area where he retrieved a tan leather tote. Her expression brightened when she saw it, but when she reached for the bag, he retreated with it still in hand.

"First your name," he said.

She blew out a breath. "Violet. Violet Chastain. I have an interview with Jack Everett for the sommelier position, and that *was* my boyfriend until a picture of him with his wife and daughter fell out of the passenger-side visor and right into my freaking lap. That kiss—I mean, what I did when I got out of the car? I guess that was my pride going into fight or flight, though I'm not sure which category my behavior falls under other than entirely unprofessional." She reached again for her bag, and this time Walker gave it to her. She pulled out her phone. "I'm going to call an Uber, and you can forget I was ever here."

As she strode to where the parking area met road, Walker's own phone vibrated in his pocket. He pulled it out to find a text from Jack.

> Running late. Supposed to interview wine expert. Fill in for me? Her references are great. She's been in the restaurant industry a long time. Just make sure she knows how to talk about and sell wine. Shouldn't be too difficult.

Walker laughed. Of the three Everett brothers, he was sure he knew the least about wine, winemaking, and what you needed to know to sell it. She could say whatever she wanted, and he'd have no choice but to believe her.

He dropped the phone back into his pocket, then retrieved his shirt from the ground. He beat as much dust off of it as he could before pulling it back over his head. Then he made his way to where Violet stood on the side of an empty road, furiously tapping the screen of her phone.

"How's that Uber working out for you?" he asked.

She groaned. "It's *not*. The closest driver is thirty miles away."

He chuckled. "Not sure where you're from, gorgeous, but you're in Smalltown, USA now. This little part of San Luis Obispo County almost doesn't exist on the map. Closest you'll get to an Uber is an Everett pickup truck or a horse. Can I interest you in either of those? Also been instructed to fill in for my brother Jack, so if you still want that interview..."

Her head shot up, and she stared at him with wide eyes. "You're kidding, right? After what I just pulled?"

He raised a brow. "Do you hear me complaining?"

"No but...I mean, you're not...Wait, now that I think of it, you did kiss me back, didn't you?"

The corner of his mouth quirked up. "I sure did."

"Thank you, by the way, for putting your shirt back on. Not that I didn't like what I saw—or felt—and ohmygod I should not even be commenting on your bare torso, but the whole being clothed thing is making it slightly easier to look you in the eye."

He looked down at his attire, then let his gaze travel up from her sleek three-inch heels all the way to her starched collar.

"I'm not exactly dressed for an interview," he said. "But Jack doesn't want to have to reschedule. So if you're still looking for a job..."

"I am," she assured him. "I most definitely am."

"Then I guess we'd better head into my office," he said, backing toward the winery's entrance. He held the door open, and she followed him inside. "Why don't you get a lay of the land while I head in back to wash up. Then we can talk about your qualifications as a..." He pulled his phone out of his pocket and opened back up to Jack's text. "...sommelier," he said.

"*Yay*," she said wincing.

"Glad you're excited."

She shook her head. "You said *suh-mel-yer*. But it's actually suh-mel-yay."

He narrowed his eyes. "That French or something?"

She nodded.

"Does it mean someone who knows about serving wine?"

She nodded again.

"Then I'm gonna go wash up. When I get back, we'll talk about your qualifications as a person who knows about serving wine."

He left her standing in the entryway as he headed toward the office on the other side of the building.

"Suh-mel-yay," he said under his breath. This woman with her fancy words and shoes and lips that were far too soft was in a league all her own. Good thing he was in the penalty box until further notice.

CHAPTER TWO

Violet watched him walk away. Stared at him was more like it. How could she not when he sauntered with all his gritty swagger? But as the backroom door snicked shut behind him, reality flooded back to greet her.

Her boyfriend—and former boss—was married. And a father. *And* he'd made a fool of her before leaving her stranded ninety minutes from home. Not the auspicious start to her interview that she'd hoped for, so naturally she'd made things even better by kissing her potential employer.

After a month of dating Ramon, she expected to be hit with a wave of heartache, but all she felt was white-hot indignation.

The score was most definitely Life with fifty bajillion and Violet at zero. How much worse could it get?

Her phone chirped, which meant a text from her mom.

Can you pick up the cake on your way here? Papa's got too much on his list already.

Sure, she texted back without thinking. She supposed she could find a car rental place somewhere in the vicinity. Or a bus. It wasn't like Oak Bluff was *that* far off the beaten path. *She'd* found it, hadn't she?

Violet gave herself a tour while she waited. The round bar was beautiful. She loved how it was the focal point of the space, right in the center of the room. The earthy tones of the travertine floor along with the warm wood panels on the walls made her feel like she was wrapped in a snuggly blanket.

Her fingers trailed the beveled edge of the bar trim.

"You like that, huh?" Walker's deep voice came from behind, the sound of it transforming her skin to gooseflesh.

"It's beautiful," she said, not yet ready to turn around. "Expert craftsmanship."

"Appreciate the compliment," he said.

Her curiosity got the better of her, and she spun to face him. "You did this?" she asked, tapping the edge of the bar.

"Yep. Not the whole structure, but that edge? All me." He crossed his arms over his chest, and she realized he was wearing a fresh white T-shirt. His blond hair was damp, too.

"Did you—is there a shower back there or something?" Then her hand flew over her mouth. "I'm sorry. That's so not a question to ask a possible future employer, whether or not he showered." She rolled her eyes at herself. This day was growing more awkward by the minute.

He grinned. "Is that your way of telling me you noticed I cleaned up? No shower. Just a sink, a bar of soap, and a clean shirt. So, tell me about being a wine expert person and why we should hire you."

She set her bag on the bar and pulled out a leather folder that held copies of her résumé, then slid one in front of Walker.

"I've been in the restaurant business since birth, pretty much. My dad owns this French fusion place in Santa Barbara. I may not have formal training in the hospitality industry, but I know more than any four-year degree could teach me. I've lived in that restaurant for as long as I can remember, and I learned everything I need to know about food and wine from him and his staff." She cleared her throat. "And maybe a bit from Ramon."

Walker scanned the document, eyebrows raising when he got to the bottom.

"This lists a Ramon Martin as a reference. Is he your—"

"Boss? Yes. I mean, he was. I recently quit."

"How recently?" he asked.

She forced a smile. "About twenty minutes ago, right before I kissed you. I did it in French. The quitting, I mean. Not the—" Oh God. What the hell had she been thinking?

The ghost of a smile teased at his lips. He scratched absently at his short beard, the one that had rubbed her chin raw.

"Look," she said. "I have never gotten involved with an employer before Ramon. I assure you it isn't a habit, and I have no intention of doing it again. He just caught me off guard with being married and all. I had to save face, you know?"

He was still reading the résumé.

"You list a former employer as Gabriel Chastain. Any relation?"

Her throat tightened. "That's my father. He had to make some recent payroll cutbacks. I didn't want him to have to fire a longtime employee, so I got another job at Ramon's."

"The job you just quit."

"Correct."

Walker looked up. "So you were going to work this job *and* your job with the French guy? I don't follow."

"Look," she said, fighting to keep her emotions in check. Ramon had already humiliated her in front of him, and then—in case she hadn't already sealed her coffin—she'd gone and kissed him. Now she had to beg him for a job. Oh, how low she'd sunk in a matter of minutes. "I need a paycheck. I was hoping to have two. Now I have none. Your brother said the winery's grand opening wasn't until early fall, that there was a wedding to plan, and whoever got hired would help prep for both and get paid, and... I know wine. I can tell you what the bouquet of a cabernet is like compared to a merlot. Want to know the perfect port to pair with a crème brûlée? I'm your girl. And don't even get me started on rosés. I could talk for days."

"Please don't," Walker said.

Violet laughed. "I've helped plan all sorts of events at my father's restaurant. I revamp his wine menu each season to account for new vintages, and I've hosted countless tastings to teach patrons the difference between a Syrah and merlot, or an oaked versus unoaked chardonnay. I will sell the hell out of your inventory when you open." She paused for a breath. "I'm doing everything short of begging here, which probably doesn't bode well as far as negotiating pay..."

Walker scratched the back of his neck. "Jack has the final say," he started. "But if I tell him the interview went well, I can almost guarantee you're hired. What happened outside, though, that can't happen again."

She shook her head. "Of course not. Trust me. I have learned my lesson. No way in hell I'm getting involved with another employer."

"Then I guess it's settled." Walker held out his hand, and she shook it. "Welcome to Crossroads Vineyard, Ms. Chastain."

She beamed. A paycheck was a paycheck. She liked wine and sure as hell knew enough about it. It came with the territory of growing up in a restaurant. It didn't matter that it wasn't her passion, only that it got her one step closer to helping her parents fund an experimental medical procedure that might make life easier for her entire family.

"Thank you," she said with as much professionalism as she could muster after having kissed her new employer until she was breathless. "Jack can contact me later with my hours. I suddenly have no conflicts. Now, if you could point me in the direction of a taxi service or maybe a car rental place?"

Walker laughed. "Closest one is at the airport, and I don't go near that place."

"What's your problem with airports?" she asked.

He shrugged. "Crowds. Bumper-to-bumper traffic with people who can't seem to drive for shit. Everyone in such a damn hurry to get somewhere else."

Violet laughed. "I'm guessing you don't travel much."

"Why leave when I have everything I want right here?" He held out his arms to gesture at the impressive space and likely the ranch beyond the vineyard grounds she knew the Everetts owned as well.

Yet there was a bitterness to his tone she couldn't reconcile, as if all he wanted was to get the hell out. For a guy probably not much older than her twenty-five years, he and his family seemed to have it all.

"Okay, well, don't car rental places pick you up if needed? I'll call Enterprise or Hertz or—"

"I'll give you a lift," he said, pulling keys out of his pocket. "A rental will cost you more than a tank of gas even if it's only for the day. Where you headed?"

She winced. "Santa Barbara?" The answer came out like a question.

His eyes narrowed, and he crossed his arms, taut biceps flexing as he did. "You mean to tell me you just accepted a job more than an hour from where you live?"

Violet chewed on her bottom lip. "Ninety-four minutes," she corrected. "In good traffic."

"No such thing," he said. "It's either open road or too many damned people."

"Wow. You really don't like being around other people, do you?"

He spun his key ring around his index finger, then caught the keys in his hand with a quick and stifled jingle. "Truck's out back. Got nothing else to do today, so I might as well drive you home."

How did she refuse such a welcoming offer? She was actually about to, but Walker pushed off the bar and began striding toward a door kitty-corner from the office. He pushed through it, and the sun shone through from the outside.

"Wait!" she called after him, then tossed her folder back into her bag. She burst through the door behind him and stopped short before tumbling over a circular saw and a stack of two-by-fours. He was standing just beyond the outdoor workshop with the saw that had almost cut her in half, leaning against the passenger side of a beat-up white pickup. As she approached—with more caution this time—she noticed the bed was filled with scraps of wood in all different shades from chestnut to what looked like a pale birch. There was also a rocking chair in need of some finishing touches, like sanding and staining, secured with bungee cords. It was rough around the edges, but she could see past it, to what it would be, and it was beautiful.

"I thought you were a winemaker," she said. "And a rancher."

"I'm a rancher by birth. Winemaker by inheritance." He knocked an elbow against the truck. "This I do for me." He opened the passenger door. "Your *Uber*, Ms. Chastain."

Violet felt the heat rush to her cheeks before she could will it away. She was not going to let his small-town cowboy charm get to her, though. This was her only job now, one she needed to keep.

"Thanks," she said, climbing into the seat. *Note to self: Next time riding in a truck, leave the three-inch heels at home.* But no one else she knew had a truck, so it was probably safe to assume this would be her one and only time. Besides, she loved her bargain-buy ombré pumps. They went with everything.

A few seconds later, Walker was in the driver's seat. He slammed the door shut and caught Violet brushing sawdust off her skirt.

"Wasn't expecting any guests today," he said.

"Or else you'd have tidied the truck up?" she asked.

"Nope." He handed her his phone, which he'd opened to a GPS app. "Punch in your address, and we'll get on the road."

She entered the address to the bakery where she needed to pick up her parents' anniversary cake. It was only half a mile from their house, so if Walker balked, he could leave her at the bakery and she'd walk from there. In her heels. Carrying a cake. It wasn't the best plan, but she felt like asking him for any more when they'd barely pulled away from the winery was not in anyone's best interest. She'd wait and see how the next ninety-four minutes went.

"Thank you," she said, giving him back his phone. "For the ride. The commute won't be a problem for me, as far as the job goes. In case you were wondering."

He pulled out onto the road but didn't offer her a response.

"Strong and silent," she said. "I get it. Not a big fan of silence myself, which is why I tend to talk. A lot."

He turned on the radio and fiddled with the dial until he landed on a country station. Then she noticed his shoulders relax.

"Okay. So you're not a talker. Message received," she said. Then, because it was Maren Morris's "Once," and she knew all the words, she hummed softly to the tune. Well, she started out humming. But once the song hit the first chorus, she was belting out the lyrics as if she was on stage herself. She couldn't help it when the music took over, and right now she was grateful for it. Strong and silent might work for him, but she'd sing herself hoarse if she had to. Anything to avoid thinking about how her mom was using her cane daily now and not only for flare-ups. Or how her dad had taken out a second mortgage on his building to cover medical bills that had been growing exponentially since Violet left school one year shy from graduating with her bachelor's degree in music education.

No way she was tacking on another year of school loans to their already mounting debt, no matter how much her parents protested. It was her decision, and she promised she'd go back when the time was right. When she didn't have to worry about the long hours Maman was alone while her father worked.

She'd sing for ninety-four whole minutes if she had to because silence was never an option.

CHAPTER THREE

Finally, after four songs, Walker broke.

"You gonna sing the whole damn way?" he asked. He realized he sounded pissed, but it wasn't at her. It was at himself for offering to give her a ride in the first place. He had plenty of shit to work on today—mainly repairing the fence between the pasture and vineyard—but hell if he didn't *want* to spend the extra time with this strange woman who had kissed him like she was suffocating and he was her only source of air.

Or maybe that was how he had kissed her back.

He needed to focus on this whole being sober situation. It was one thing to be locked away from his vices, forcing his body to enter withdrawal and somehow living through it. But it was another to keep at it alone, to *choose* to keep saying no to the bottle when saying yes would be so much easier.

He needed to focus on one day at a time—on when and if he was leaving Oak Bluff to figure out who the hell he was. Here his past defined him, but somewhere else he could be some*one* else.

Thanks to the Callahan brothers building their own guest ranch up north, there was an offer on the table to do precisely that. He didn't see much point in getting everyone wound up about what ifs, so he hadn't told anyone yet.

Right now he was fighting to not let himself get distracted by a beautiful employee who could kiss like no one's business and apparently carry a tune as well as if not better than the artists she was singing along with. Maybe she hadn't thought he was listening, but it was pretty hard not to.

She turned to face him and crossed her arms.

"If you can stay quiet for ninety minutes, that's your prerogative. But I am not a fan of silence. Feel free to turn the radio louder so you don't hear me."

Walker turned the radio off.

He was crap at conversation, but he figured the ride would feel a lot longer with all the tension that was brewing in the air.

"So you speak French," he said.

She laughed. "Is that supposed to be a question?"

The muscle in his jaw tensed. "How is it that you know English and French?"

He saw her smile out of the corner of his eye.

"My mom is Parisian by way of West Africa. My grandparents both immigrated to Paris from Senegal, so my mom is first-generation Parisian, and my dad is American. I was raised speaking both languages."

He stole a glance her way to get the full effect of her smile. Bad idea. She lit up the whole damn truck.

"So one parent was always left out of a conversation if it wasn't their native language?"

She shook her head. "Nope. My mom speaks perfect English—with a light French accent. And my dad was a French minor in college. It's how they met. He was studying in France. She was a local pastry chef, and the rest is sorta history. Tell me about your parents."

He clenched his teeth. This wasn't a therapy session, and they were employer and employee. He thought about what he could say. *My mom died and my dad turned into an abusive alcoholic, but it's all good because he finally kicked the bucket last year. Also, you know how alcoholism is hereditary? Dear old Dad was good enough to pass that on to me.* Somehow none of that really screamed small talk.

"My brothers and my aunt are my only family. Got a nephew, too," was all he said.

"Punch Buggy red!" she cried out, then slugged him in the shoulder.

He peered at her over the rim of his sunglasses with brows raised.

She let out a nervous laugh. "Sorry? It's a game my dad and I have played since I was a kid. You see a VW Bug and call out *Punch Buggy* and the color before the other person. Then you give 'em a playful little slug." She brushed her hand over the spot where he'd received his playful little slug. "I didn't hurt you, did I?" Her tone was teasing, and he bit back a grin.

"It'd take a lot more than that to cause any damage," he said.

He could still remember his father smacking his older brother Jack when he left his baseball glove on the kitchen counter. Or when Jack Senior tripped over Walker's boots on the rug inside the front door, but Jack took the blame to keep Walker from getting hit. Then there was the one time his big brother didn't get a chance to protect him—when Walker had tried to pry the liquor bottle from his passed-out father's grip only to have the man wake suddenly and backhand him across the face.

No. A little game of Punch Buggy couldn't hurt him. But it could make him remember why he'd found solace in the bottle in the first place. When he drank, the memories drowned. His sobriety breathed new life into everything he wanted to bury at the bottom of a whiskey-filled ocean.

One of the things they stressed in his *time away*—he still wasn't ready to put a label on it—was to avoid triggers. His whole life up until a couple months ago was one big trigger. It took him almost that long to start talking in his group therapy sessions. So right now, his best way to avoid triggers was to put up a wall or two. The more he kept people out of his head, the better it was for everyone, including Violet Chastain.

"How about the alphabet game?" Violet asked.

"How about we enjoy the silence?" he bit back more forcefully than he'd intended, but she didn't skip a beat. For whatever reason, when it came to car games, the woman was unflappable.

Violet bounced excitedly in her seat. "We go through the alphabet and try to find each letter on license plates, highway signs, stuff like that. I'll even throw in a bonus. I'll teach you a French word for each letter you find."

"What if I just concentrate on the road?"

"*A* in that license plate," she said, pointing at a mini-van in the other lane.

"I'm *not* playing," he insisted, even as his eyes started scanning other plates and signs.

"*B*MW!" she shouted with glee as she spotted the next letter.

"You're not going to stop, are you?" he asked, already knowing the answer.

"Nope. So you might as well join me. You know you wanna."

He sighed, rationalizing that at least if he played her game, he was ensuring the conversation wouldn't get personal. "All right, *Teach*. But we're starting over. Those first two don't count."

She clapped. "Great. Okay. *A*... where is an *A*..."

"Camry," he said as he pointed out the windshield. "Right lane, two cars up."

He couldn't help his self-satisfied grin. Once upon a time he'd had a competitive streak. Being the youngest of three brothers, he'd had no choice. It was either rise to the occasion or get left in the dust in everything from baseball, which was all Jack, to riding, all Luke. Plus, he kinda wanted to hear her speak more French.

"Very nice, Mr. Everett. You've earned yourself a word. *Agréable.*"

Her voice had a rasp that threatened to worm its way under his skin. It was even more pronounced when she sang, so he figured this was at least a bit safer.

"What's it mean?" he asked.

She shook her head. "First you have to say it. *Ah-gray-AH-bleh.*"

"That wasn't part of the deal."

She straightened in her seat and squared her shoulders, all proper-like. "It is now. You can't learn the words without practicing them."

He rolled his eyes behind the safety of his glasses. "*Ah-gray-AH-bleh*," he mumbled, feeling like an idiot. He felt too crude for a language that seemed so refined.

She smiled. "It means *pleasant* or *agreeable*. You're being *trés agréable* by playing along with my silly game, Monsieur Everett."

She said his name with an accent, the sound of it making the hair on the back of his neck stand up.

They made it through the whole alphabet twice before hitting the outskirts of Santa Barbara, and he learned quite a few words like *déjeuner*, which meant *lunch*; *jalousie*, which was *jealousy*; and *merde*, which was *shit.* He liked that one. Not that he would admit it, but he liked the game, too.

His GPS app notified them that the destination was approaching on the right. But it wasn't a residential address. It was a bakery called *Have Your Cake.*

"This is where you live?" he asked as he pulled into a parking spot.

She winced. "Not exactly. I'm heading to my parents' for their anniversary party, and my mom asked me to pick up the cake. I didn't want to ask too much of you, so I can totally walk from here. It's less than a mile away."

He put the truck in park and finally turned to face her. He glanced down at her shoes, then met her gaze. "Less than a mile in those, carrying a cake?"

"It's possible," she insisted.

"You know, I might let you try so I can drive behind you and watch."

She narrowed her eyes at him. "That would not be very *agréable* of you."

He nodded toward the bakery. "You need help with that cake?"

She blew out a breath. "I think I got it from here. Thank you. I promise this is the only stop."

She lowered herself out of the truck and strode toward the bakery door. He knew he shouldn't watch her walk away, but she was like a magnet, drawing him to her whether he wanted to be or not.

From the shoes to her pressed shirt and her perfectly styled hair, she was class and sophistication personified.

He was—well he was one fine mess. Never mind whether or not she was good for his recovery. He had no business thinking about kissing a woman like her again.

She emerged from the bakery several minutes later, and Walker chuckled before hopping out of the truck to help her carry a box over which she could barely see.

"You sure you don't need a hand, Teach? Or maybe you still want to try that *short* walk to your folks' place?"

He couldn't see her expression behind the box, but he expected she had a few choice French words for him.

"How about I open the door for you and help you into the truck?"

"Thank you," she said haughtily, and Walker grinned.

He led her to the passenger-side door, opened it, then grabbed the cake from her so she could climb in. Once she had her seat belt on, she took the cake back, holding it in her lap.

He was still smiling when he made it into the driver's seat and started the truck. He checked his window and then turned to check hers for any parking lot traffic, but all he could see was Violet's profile and the damned box.

She finally lost it and burst into a fit of laughter.

"Could you imagine"—she gasped for breath—"if I was stubborn enough to walk?" She laughed harder. "Just to prove that I could?" A tear streamed down her cheek. "Oh my God. This thing barely even fits in your truck. What were my parents thinking?"

He knew he shouldn't, but her hands were stuck holding the box. So he reached for her face and swiped at the tear with his thumb.

Her laughter trailed off. "Um...thanks," she said softly.

Walker cleared his throat. "Which way to your folks' house?"

They were on the outskirts of downtown, and based on her classy attire and her father owning what was likely a fancy French restaurant, he expected she'd be leading him to some sprawling estate with an ocean view. Despite what she'd said about her family making some financial cutbacks, this was Santa Barbara. It might only be ninety-four minutes away, but it felt like the other side of the world compared to Oak Bluff. It wasn't like the Everetts didn't own land, but their land—a vineyard and a ranch—was their livelihood. They worked every inch of it.

"Go right out of the parking lot and then right again at the first light," she said.

He did as she asked and found himself on a street lined with white stucco shops sporting red terra-cotta roofs. Impeccably dressed pedestrians lined the sidewalks, some carrying shopping bags, others with to-go coffee cups that probably held fancy drinks costing upwards of ten dollars each.

Walker had never been to Santa Barbara, and now he knew why. He fit in about as well as a watermelon fit inside a can of Pringles. Jack's hand-me-down truck must have been a sore sight compared to the BMW in front of him and the Mercedes convertible approaching from the opposite direction.

"I can't really see, but there should be an alley coming up after the coffee house on the corner," she said.

He turned down the narrow alley in between the coffee shop and what looked like some sort of fancy restaurant. He couldn't see the name of the place, but through the window he saw white tablecloths and napkins folded into intricate shapes atop the plates at a corner table.

"There should be a couple of paved parking spots with a sign that says RESIDENTS ONLY. Park in one of those."

"I thought we were going to your parents' place," he said.

"And here we are," she said. "Wanna help me out?"

Confused, because this was far from a sprawling estate, Walker hopped out of the truck, then took the monstrosity of a cake from Violet so she could exit the vehicle as well.

"Okay, so I really wasn't expecting this." She motioned to the box that he was still holding. "Since you can actually see over the top and *aren't* wearing heels, do you think you could carry it up for me? I promise after that you can wash your hands of this ridiculous day and get back to your life."

He stared at her through the lenses of his aviators, grateful she couldn't see his eyes because they'd sure as hell give away that if she wasn't an Everett employee and he wasn't fresh out of rehab, he'd be looking for any damn excuse to kiss her one more time. Even after a ninety—okay, ninety-*four*—minute drive, having to make the extra stop to pick up the monstrous cake that he now had to carry up a flight of stairs, there was still something about her he couldn't put his finger on.

It was more than the shoes, the clothes, the way she sang her heart out to every song that came on the radio, or how she could turn the letters of the alphabet into the sexiest French lesson he'd ever had—even if it was the *only* French lesson he'd ever had. More than her brown skin lit by the afternoon sun or that ridiculous cake that was nearly half her height. It was all of it, wrapped up in a stiletto-wearing package that was Violet Chastain—someone who was a damned stranger up until a few hours ago. Maybe he couldn't call her gorgeous now that they were in a working relationship of sorts, but good lord she was.

Get it together, Everett. You don't lose your shit over good-looking women.

He didn't lose his shit over anyone. He'd basically courted the bottle for the better part of ten years. This interest or infatuation or whatever it was—it was brand new. And it was with the wrong woman at the wrong time.

"Ask me in French," he said. "Then I might say yes."

She crossed her arms and glared at him, but he could tell there was a smile about to break through. "*Aidez-moi, s'il vous plaît.*"

"See?" he said. "All you had to do was ask nicely. Lead the way."

She pulled open a door on the side of the building and led him up a flight of stairs that ended at a small landing and a single door. She pushed it open, and he followed her inside.

"*Maman?*" she called out. "*Je suis là avec ton énorme gâteau!*"

She grabbed the box from Walker and set it down on a long narrow dining room table, then rounded a corner to where he guessed the bedrooms were. Walker took off his sunglasses and clipped them over the collar of his T-shirt. He ran his hand along the wood of the table—knotted pine—and spun in a slow circle to take in the layout of the apartment. It wasn't big, but it was spacious enough to not feel cramped. To the right was a living room with a large sectional and respectable big-screen television. Straight ahead was a well-lit galley kitchen. The whole space had this bright and cheery feel that made something twist in Walker's gut.

This wasn't some obnoxious mansion, but it was a *home*, a word that felt so foreign for him to even think.

He froze when he came back to the table—and to the long buffet lining the wall behind it. It was set up as a bar, lined with several liquors and two bottles of red, two bottles of white chilling in ice buckets.

His mouth went dry, and his palms dampened.

"Shit," he said under his breath.

Violet slowly emerged from the hallway with a woman who walked balancing on a cane. She was almost as tall as Violet was in her heels, but she wore flat-soled shoes. She had Violet's full lips, but her face was more drawn, cheekbones more pronounced, and skin a darker brown. Her curly dark hair was pulled back in a multicolored scarf that rested on a bare shoulder. A simple sleeveless black dress hung loose over her frame.

She squeezed her daughter's hand and smiled at him. "You've been keeping secrets from me and Papa, yes?" she asked with a mild French accent. He might not have known it was there if Violet hadn't mentioned it. "*Quelle surprise* for our anniversary to see you happily matched as well."

"What?" Violet asked. "No, Maman, this is—"

But the older woman broke away from her daughter and, despite the cane, strode toward Walker with a measured grace.

She stood before him, rested her cane against one of the dining room chairs, and cupped his cheeks in her palms. "*Merci,*" she said. "Thank you for putting a smile on Vee's face. It's been a long time since she's found a reason to do it on a regular basis." She tilted his head down and kissed both his cheeks. "I'm Camille." She lowered her hands.

"Walker Everett," he said. "And you're welcome. I quite enjoy putting a smile on *Vee*'s face, so it's really no trouble at all."

Hell. He was going to hell for lying to this woman—or at least not being the one to break first. But after the few seconds that he'd known Camille Chastain, he didn't want to disappoint her. Her daughter seemed to have a similar effect on him.

"I want to hear everything—how you met, how long this has been going on—but I have to finish getting this place set up for the party." She reached for her cane and glanced at the cake box on the table. "I see your papa went overboard on the cake. If I was feeling up to making one myself, it would have been much more sensible." She shook her head. "I'll wait for him to finish up down at the restaurant to open it together. Walker, would you take it into the kitchen for me? I can pour you and Violet a pastis?"

Now he understood why Camille nicknamed her daughter *Vee.* When she said Violet's name, she pronounced it *Vee-oh-let.*

He didn't know what a pastis was, but the fact it was something she could pour was information enough.

"Nothing for me, thank you," he said.

"But you are staying for the party?" Camille added.

Walker cleared his throat. "Of course. Wouldn't miss it."

Then he grabbed the cake and headed for the kitchen. He heard Violet's heels on the wood floor close behind him.

He stopped at the first open space and set the box down in time for Violet to plow straight into him. He braced his hands on the counter to keep from face-planting into the cake.

"What are you doing?" she whisper-shouted.

Walker exhaled slowly. This woman was trouble, and he should run far and fast—until he saw her at the winery on her first day of work. He guessed there was no real escape.

He spun to face her. "I have no damned clue. She seemed so happy. I didn't want to be the one to disappoint her."

She gave him a nervous smile. "I know. It's like she casts some sort of spell, and all you want to do is make her smile. I've been dealing with it my whole life." She blew out a breath. "I tried to correct her, but then you went along with it and I froze. Look, you've done enough already. Why don't you sneak out while you can, and as soon as you're gone I'll tell her the truth—that you're my employer and nothing else and that she made an incorrect assumption?"

He ran a hand through his overgrown hair. He needed a cut. And a shave. But then he'd look like the guy who fell through a tavern window, and he was afraid if he looked like that guy, then he'd still be him. Who was he kidding? That scared the shit out of him no matter who stared back at him from a mirror. The boy who wanted to save his mother died along with her. The man he'd become was a stranger. But he still remembered what it was like to want to make her smile—to ease her pain if only for a few minutes or an hour. Whatever he could do. He wasn't sure what Camille's situation was—what the cane meant—but Violet had that chance right here and now.

"Or maybe I eat some dinner." He shrugged. "Who am I to say no to a free meal?"

Looked like Camille Chastain wasn't the only one he couldn't say no to.

Violet's eyes softened. "Walker, I can't ask you to do that."

"Guess it's a good thing you didn't ask. It's only dinner, right? A man's gotta eat. Whatever you tell her after I leave is up to you. What are the odds of me seeing your parents again? I mean, you will be providing your own transportation to and from Oak Bluff from here on out, right?"

She huffed out a laugh. "Yes. I have my own car. Today was a onetime thing, promise."

"Then if it will help—you and me pretending for a couple hours—tonight can be a onetime thing, too." Because for the first time in too long, he wasn't itching to get home to an empty apartment and to shut the world away. He wasn't itching to say good-bye to Violet Chastain.

Walker knew it wasn't his place to ask, but if he was going to do this, he needed as much information as he could get. "Is she—sick?"

Violet's brown eyes glossed over, and she nodded. "She has MS. Multiple sclerosis. And it's hit her pretty hard in the past few years. The last thing I need is to be the one to put extra stress on her." She blew out a shaky breath. "Say no, Walker. This is a crazy, terrible idea, so please say no and force me to be straight with her."

He thought about the kiss, about the ninety-four minutes in the car with her that he actually didn't hate, and there *was* traffic. He thought about the woman who welcomed him into her home like he was already part of the family—and about the bottles on the buffet.

This absolutely was a crazy, terrible idea.

"You work for my family now," he said, stating the obvious. "As much as I enjoyed meeting like we did this morning..."

"Of course," she said. "No kissing. Strictly business. Trust me, once this party gets going, my parents won't be paying any attention to us. All you have to do is hang out, eat some amazing food, and maybe make a little small talk with my family's friends."

He shook his head. "I don't do small talk."

She waved him off. "Don't worry. I'll be your wing woman. Most of them will do all the talking anyway. And tomorrow, when they're still basking in the glow of their thirty years together, I'll tell my parents that we had a fight and broke up, and that will be that."

He narrowed his eyes. "You gonna make me the asshole in this fight?"

She laughed and shook her head. "Not a chance, not after all you've done for me. The only asshole in this scenario will be me." She was bouncing on the balls of her feet, a smile spreading from ear to ear. "Thank you, Walker. You have no idea what this means." She hugged him then, but quickly pulled away. "Sorry. Instinct. I'm a hugger. I promise that will be it as far as physical contact. Despite my impulsive actions this morning, I can behave."

The corner of his mouth twitched, but he fought back a grin. Because if she was anyone else at any other time in his life—sometime maybe in the not too distant future—he wouldn't want her to behave. Something in that kiss felt almost too right for it to be wrong.

"I just need to make a quick call," he said. "Is there somewhere I can get a little privacy?"

She nodded. "The balcony. Follow me."

Once he was outside and the door shut behind him, Walker pulled out his phone and dialed his brother Jack. He mentally prepared himself for the third degree from his oldest brother but figured it was better than the hell he'd get if he disappeared for the day without any notice. It wasn't like he had to clear his impromptu drive down the coast with anyone, but if his brother found his makeshift workshop abandoned, he'd think the worst.

"Where are you?" Jack said after one ring. "Tell me it's not at a bar or behind any."

Looked like his brother thought the worst of him no matter what, not that he blamed him.

Walker ground his teeth and took a steadying breath. "Thanks for the vote of confidence, big bro. I'm in Santa Barbara. No bars of any sort involved."

His brother sighed. "Okay, so what the hell is in Santa Barbara?"

"Long story," Walker said, "but that woman you're hiring for the know-it-all job at the winery? She lives here, and she needed a ride home. I'm gonna hang out in town a bit before heading back. Thought I'd let you know."

It wasn't exactly the truth, but it also wasn't a lie.

"So the interview went well?" Jack asked.

Walker let out a soft laugh. "Yeah. She knows her shit. And she can start as soon as we need her. I can tell her what day is best if you want."

Jack was silent for a few seconds. "Are you with her now?"

"Yeah. I just dropped her off." Every bit of information he withheld made Walker realize he was skating on pretty thin ice. His inpatient recovery included group therapy sessions with the other addicts where all that was required of him was to tell the truth. Be honest—to himself and those around him. He knew the importance of maintaining that on his own, but it hadn't been his strong suit when he was drinking, and it still didn't come naturally now.

"Ava's free Wednesday morning. How about you tell her to come in then. Ava can show her around the place, let her know what she can help out with in the months before the grand opening. We can also take care of her paperwork and make it official."

"Will do," Walker said. "I'll be back by the ranch in the morning."

"Walker... Please don't do anything stupid."

There was nothing but concern in Jack's tone, but it still sent the same message.

You're gonna screw up. It's simply a matter of when.

"When have I ever let you down, golden boy?" Walker asked. It was a dick move, and he knew it. If it wasn't for Jack putting himself at risk to protect Walker and Luke from their father when they were teens, things would have been a lot different during those five years, though he wasn't sure if he'd have ended up as anyone other than who he was.

Jack Senior laid a hand on Walker once, and that was all it took to alter him for good. Or maybe this was always going to be his path. He'd never really know for sure.

"Hey," Walker said when his brother didn't respond. But the word "sorry" sat there, stuck on the tip of his tongue.

"I'll see you in the morning," Jack said. Then he ended the call.

"Shit," he said out loud, then took a deep breath, filling his lungs with the crisp ocean air. He couldn't see the beach from here, only the white stucco of another building on the next street over. But he knew it was close, just like back in Oak Bluff. That gave him the tiniest notion of comfort.

He allowed himself a few more minutes of that comfort before heading back inside. Violet and Camille were sitting on the sectional, both with glasses of a milky-looking drink that must have been pastis.

"Everything okay?" Violet asked, looking up at him from the couch. She was no longer wearing her interview attire but instead a long cotton sleeveless dress that was white with blue flowers.

"Yeah," he said, his gaze drinking her in. "You look beautiful." The words came out without any warning, and at first he thought he might have overstepped but then remembered his role. He was the boyfriend tonight. It wasn't simply okay to say these types of things to her but was probably required.

And who was he to ignore requirements?

CHAPTER FOUR

Despite what he'd said about not doing small talk, it looked like Walker was holding his own with Thalia, Bistro Chastain's weekend hostess, and her girlfriend Liz. The three of them had been chatting since Violet left to go check on her dad fifteen minutes ago.

Guests had been filing in for the past hour, yet her father was still down at the restaurant with his chef and sous chef, putting the finishing touches on the food for the party before the place officially opened for dinner service.

She found her mother in the kitchen slicing more French bread to add to the meat and cheese platter that was already disappearing thanks to Maman's mango chutney that not even her gourmet chef of a father could replicate.

"Maman, let me help," Violet said when she saw her mother's hand shake as she held the knife—one of the telltale signs she was in pain. "Papa will be here soon with the hot appetizers."

But the other woman set down the knife and held up her hand to halt her daughter from getting any closer.

"Go," she simply said. "Do not watch over my shoulder like I am *un bébé* who cannot be trusted."

There was an unexpected bite to her mother's tone.

"Did something happen today?" Violet asked. "You seemed so happy when Walker and I got here. The party is off to a great start. I don't understand—"

"Dr. Martinez called while you were downstairs."

Violet's brows pulled together. "On a Saturday?" she gasped, her heart filling with renewed hope. "Does that mean his practice has cleared him to do it?"

Her mother's usually proud shoulders slumped, but she didn't turn to face Violet.

"*Non, mon trésor*. He cannot. His practice will not do it without FDA approval."

My treasure. Her mother always called her that when Violet was sad and she was trying to cheer her up. But now it was *she* who needed cheering.

They'd recently read about stem cell treatment for MS. Though still experimental, in some patients who were able to go through with the procedure, a transplant had slowed the progression of the disease and even offered some relief.

"It is so much money, Vee. And it might not even work," her mother had said when they first looked into it. "Do I want to make myself so sick possibly for no reason?"

But the truth wasn't that her mother, her father, or she had been afraid of it not working. They'd been afraid to hope, and apparently it was for good reason.

"We'll find another doctor, then. Dr. Martinez can't be the only one qualified."

Her mother shook her head. "He is the best in the area, and you know that. I will meet with him this week to talk about changing one of my medications. And I'm going to try some more holistic methods for relief, too. One of the cooks—his wife does acupuncture."

Violet blew out a long breath. "You can still do all that while we research more. *I'll* research more. This isn't the end of the road yet."

Her mother laughed. "Such a headstrong girl."

Violet didn't argue. But she realized she was raising her mother's hopes only to possibly have them dashed again.

She laid a hand on Maman's shoulder, and the other woman let out a shuddering breath.

"What about the doctor in Paris we read about?" Violet asked. "Maybe it's time for you and Aunt Ines to bury the hatchet so you can go back home and—"

Her mother's trembling hand dropped the knife onto the cutting board. She spun, eyes narrowed at Violet.

"Violet, don't."

"But she would want to know. So would your parents," Violet nearly yelled. "What if they could help coordinate the treatment? If they knew you were sick—"

"*Je ne suis pas malade*. It is something I have to live with. And I do not need to worry my own parents with something they cannot fix. They have their own health to deal with. The stem cell treatment was a long shot. I will fight the progression of my condition another way. End of story."

Her mother's jaw was tight.

"*Où est ma belle mariée?*" Papa's voice boomed from the apartment's front door.

Where is my beautiful bride?

"Not a word to your papa, okay? Tonight is for celebration." She sniffed and swiped at the dampness under her eyes.

Violet cleared her throat. "Okay."

Her mom kissed her on the cheek, grabbed her cane from against the cabinets, and went to greet her husband.

Violet waited for a count of ten in order to collect herself. Ten seconds to contemplate the aunt she'd never met who lived halfway around the world—the aunt who, for whatever reason, her mother hadn't spoken to in over thirty years.

The aunt who could possibly help, but Maman was too damned proud to ask her to do it.

"Headstrong woman," Violet mumbled. Then she made her way into the growing sea of people toward the corner of the living room where Walker now stood alone, sipping what looked like a Long Island iced tea.

"Can I have some of that?" she asked when she approached.

He handed her the glass.

Violet sucked hard on the straw and swallowed. Her brows pulled together. "This is just iced tea," she said with disappointment.

He raised a brow. "With three lemons. I'm living on the wild side."

She pouted. "I really need something stronger."

"How about some air?" he said, setting his drink on the windowsill. And without waiting for her to answer, he took her hand in his and directed her toward the balcony door.

His grip was firm, and she could feel the calluses on his palm. She'd normally balk at such a gesture—at someone insinuating she could be led—but she wanted to go with him, wherever he was taking her, even if it was simply across the room.

He was all rough and unpolished yet genuine and sexy as hell.

And your boss, Violet. Your. Boss.

For someone as smart as she was—and Violet considered herself an intelligent woman—she seemed to have the worst instincts when it came to men.

She blamed her parents for setting too good of an example. They made falling and staying in love look as easy as breathing. Even after her mom's diagnosis when Violet was in high school, her parents' relationship seemed to only grow stronger.

That was what she wanted. Easy, uncomplicated, unconditional love. She was beginning to think, though, that it only existed for a select few.

They slipped through the open balcony door. Without really thinking, Violet pulled the curtain across the opening, effectively closing them off from the rest of the party, if only from immediate view.

Walker dropped her hand and pressed his palms against the balcony's wooden ledge. He took in a deep breath through his nose, closing his eyes as he did, then blew it out through his mouth.

"What are you doing?" she asked softly. He seemed like he was concentrating.

He shrugged. "My aunt always thought I could benefit from the *power* of meditation." The word "power" came out with a mocking tone.

She laughed. "You don't believe her?"

He cracked one eye open. "No. I think it's a total crock. But I respect that she believes it. So every now and then I try to turn it all off, you know? The ocean air helps."

Violet mimicked his stance, hands pressed against the railing, then squeezed her eyes shut. She breathed in through her nose and exhaled through her mouth. Her hand slid left as she did, her pinky brushing his.

Walker said nothing. She felt his pinky twitch against hers, but he didn't pull his hand away.

She kept her eyes closed, hoping it would suspend them in this moment.

"Smell the salt?" he asked.

"Yeah," she said, a chill rippling down her spine. This was a moment. She could feel it. They were sharing a moment.

His pinky twitched again, and this time it landed on hers.

She sucked in a sharp breath.

"I can't get involved with anyone right now," he said, his voice low and controlled.

She nodded, her eyes still closed, and she wondered if his were, too. She was too scared to look. "And I can't get involved with someone I work for. I can't afford the fallout. And there's always a fallout."

"Here's the thing, though," he said. "I can't get this morning's kiss out of my head. And that was before I heard you sing or watched you try to carry that ridiculous cake. I can't stop wondering what it would be like to kiss you again now that you're not exactly a stranger."

"Music," she blurted. "It's why I'm not half-bad with the singing. I like the restaurant business and the wine stuff. Don't get me wrong. But I've always loved music. I don't really know anymore what I wanted to do with it—teach in a public school or maybe offer lessons out of a private studio—but I left school early when my mom's symptoms got worse and she couldn't help out in the restaurant as much. Music is my something for me. Like your chair."

He slid his entire hand over hers, his thumb brushing her skin. "You don't technically work for the Everett family yet. Jack says you can come by Wednesday to get started, but as of right now, no paperwork has been filed."

She opened her eyes to find him staring right at her, his ocean blue irises brewing with mischief and desire.

"Walker, what are you saying?"

He brought her palm to his lips and kissed it softly.

"You asked me to play a part tonight. If we're only pretending, it doesn't mean anything, right? Then neither of us is breaking any rules."

He let go of her hand, but she didn't let it fall. Instead she caressed his cheek. His beard was softer than she'd thought it was when she'd kissed him. But then the whole earlier episode was a blur. Now she was taking the time to notice him.

She ran her fingers through the overgrown blond hair above his ear.

"There's some gold in there," she said. "Maybe even a hint of red."

"Is that a good thing?" he asked softly.

She nodded.

"Well then I put it there just for you." The corner of his mouth curled up.

She rose onto her tiptoes, both hands clasping around his neck to help her balance. And maybe pull him closer.

What were they doing?

"I shouldn't want you," she whispered.

"And I can't want you," he whispered back.

"Why?" she asked without even thinking. It wasn't her business, especially if he was about to be her employer. But she still wondered. And now that the question was out there, she might as well follow through. "You pretty much know my whole story. But I know close to nothing about you other than you have brothers and an aunt and can make my toes curl with one kiss. I mean, is it more than the employer/employee thing?"

Her lips were a breath away from his, and if he decided to answer her without any words, she wouldn't object.

Instead he let his forehead fall against hers.

"It's—too soon." The words came out strained, as if they caused him physical pain to utter. And then it clicked.

"You just got out of a relationship," she said resignedly.

"You could say that." His warm breath caressed her lips.

"A long relationship?" Ugh, why was she digging for answers she wasn't sure she truly wanted to know?

"You could say that, too," was his only reply.

She cleared her throat and took a step back. She wouldn't push any further.

"Okay then. It's too soon for you, and you're entirely the wrong guy for me being my employer and all. So I guess that settles it." It didn't matter that her words made complete sense. She couldn't stop thinking about that kiss, either. Her lips didn't care about sense. Her lips had one thought and one thought only.

Devour *his* lips.

The aroma of her father's cooking filled the apartment, but out here she could smell only the salt of the sea mixed with the crisp clean scent of Walker's skin. She thought about his sink shower in the bathroom of the winery and how much she wished she was that bar of soap.

She hummed softly.

"Hey, Teach?" Walker said.

"Huh?" she responded, startled out of her reverie. "I mean, yeah?"

"How about another lesson?" He rested his hands on her hips, the simple touch doing not-so-simple things to her. "How do you say *kiss* in that pretty language of yours?"

Violet licked her lips and swallowed.

"To kiss is *embrasser*."

"*Em-brah-say*," he parroted.

Violet usually hated the way French sounded when a non-native speaker tried it. Walker didn't pronounce the words perfectly, but he didn't butcher them, either. And somehow he made each one sexier in his own rugged way.

"How would you—*embrasser* me?" he added.

She laughed. "First I'd give you more warning than I did this morning. I'd say, *Je veux t'embrasser*, which means *I want to kiss you*." And she did. Holy hell she did. Nothing was more of a tease than being close enough to kiss him, wanting to kiss him, and *not* kissing him. How did he exercise such restraint? Or maybe he didn't want her as much as she wanted him.

"*Je veux t'embrasser*," he repeated, his accent a little better this time.

"That's good. You're getting the hang of it."

"No," Walker said. He let his bottom lip brush hers, and she sucked in a breath. "*Je. Veux. T'embrasser.*"

Her throat went bone dry, and she struggled to swallow.

"Then *kiss* me already," she squeaked.

He grinned. "I guess you're the boss tonight."

She expected raw, animal hunger—expected his beard to chafe her skin. But his lips swept against hers, so surprisingly gentle she actually whimpered.

He took his time, teasing and tasting with soft flicks of his tongue. His fingertips kneaded her hips, and then his hands traveled up her sides, tracing her curves, until his fingers tangled in her hair.

She parted her lips, pulling him closer, trying to satiate her need.

His lips broke into a smile. "Have a little patience, Teach. If we're only playing these parts for one night, let's savor every bit of it."

"But if we only have *one* night," she argued, "shouldn't we get the most out of it?"

She nipped at his bottom lip, and he let loose a soft growl.

"*Patience*," he said again, then kissed her chin, her jaw, the top of her neck. His teeth grazed her earlobe, and she hummed a moan. "See?" he whispered in her ear. "Savoring is pretty damn good, huh?"

In her head she was screaming *yes, oui,* and every other affirmation that existed. But her mouth had lost its ability to form words because he'd moved from her neck to her shoulder, his hands leading the way down her body until both palms rested firmly on her ass.

He squeezed, and Violet tilted her head back and laughed.

"Didn't take you for an ass man," she teased.

He leaned in close, stopping short of kissing her again. "I'm an everything man. And you, Violet, have *everything*."

That last word made her heart swell.

It was the kind of thing her father would say to Maman. He probably had said something exactly to that effect. Maybe not while grabbing Maman's *ass*.

Yeah, she really didn't want to be thinking of her father grabbing her mother's anything.

"*Merde*," she said aloud.

"What's that now?"

She laughed and shook her head. "Nothing."

"Where is that beautiful daughter of mine?" Violet's father's voice boomed from behind the gossamer-thin curtain that covered the doorway.

Violet cleared her throat and took a step away from Walker. His playful grin fell as the curtain flew open.

"There she is!" Papa scooped her into a hug before there was any chance for introductions or to gauge whether or not their semblance of privacy was little more than an illusion.

The familiar scent of the restaurant kitchen filled her with comfort.

"You smell like *ragoût*," she said when her father let her go. Her father put a Beninese spin on the traditional French dish, substituting yams for the usual eggplant and offsetting the sweetness with the spice of his own recipe of chili paste. It was one of Violet's favorite dishes, her mother's, too. Maman said it reminded her of home—a home Violet had never known.

He grinned at her. The lines at the corners of his mouth seemed more pronounced, as did the one between his brows. She wondered how much of it was truly due to growing older compared to working longer hours after having to cut back on staff these past few years.

He was tall and broad, but his shoulders seemed to sag a bit more each day. And his once sandy hair, though still thick, was silver now, as was the five o'clock shadow on his jaw.

"Nothing but the best for my girls," he said. Then his gaze fell on Walker. Both men stood over six feet, so they were eye to eye. Walker held out a hand to shake, but her father crossed his arms, looking him up and down.

"Are *you* the best for my girl?"

Violet threw her arms in the air. "*Papa!* Come on. Be nice." The thing was, he *was* nice. The nicest man she knew. But Violet was an only child. Her mother was living with a disease her father couldn't protect her from, so Violet seemed to be his outlet. If he could protect her from any and all hurt, then maybe he'd ease up on himself for what he couldn't do for Maman.

"No, sir," Walker said. "I'm sure I'm not. But she makes me want to be the best I can, and that's gotta count for something, right?"

Violet's breath caught in her throat. *An act*...she had to remind herself that they were playing at this. Sure, there was an attraction—his hands on her behind minutes ago attested to that—but they just met. This was a game, wasn't it?

Her father extended a hand. "I appreciate a man who's not afraid of honesty. Gabriel Chastain."

Walker shook his hand. "Walker Everett. It's good to meet you, Mr. Chastain."

He gave Walker a slow nod. "Call me Gabe—for now. What do you say we all go inside so I can toast your mother and the best thirty years of my life? You a champagne man, Walker Everett?"

Even behind the beard Violet could see Walker's jaw tighten.

"Not really Mr.—I mean, Gabe. But we're thinking of trying it out for next year's harvest."

She wondered what it was about the vineyard that set him on edge.

Her father raised a brow. "A vintner, eh? We may have to talk about doing some business together. I'm always looking for new local vintages to try at the restaurant."

Walker nodded. "We don't open 'til end of summer/early fall, but we'd be happy to give you a tour, show you what we hope to have bottled by then."

"I think I'll take you up on that offer," Violet's father said. "Real soon." He clapped a hand on Walker's shoulder and led him through the open balcony door, babbling on about his favorite champagnes and what vineyard produced much of his current supply.

Violet glanced around the empty balcony and laughed. Without even trying, Walker had charmed her father into forgetting she was even there—an absolute first—but then he'd charmed the hell out of her before she even knew his name. He had that certain *je ne sais quoi,* and she wanted to soak up as much of it as she could before the night was through.

CHAPTER FIVE

Walker helped box up what was left of the two-tiered chocolate ganache cake. Despite the apartment full of people that had come and gone, there was still plenty of cake to go around. Not surprising since it was at least two feet tall and quite possibly the richest thing he'd ever tasted.

Camille placed a hand over his as he was sealing the container. "Please, take some home for your family. This will only take up space in an already overcrowded freezer."

He looked past the woman and toward the kitchen where Violet and her father washed and dried dishes while singing a duet of Johnny Cash's "Walk the Line."

Camille sighed. "*Mon Dieu*, you've got it bad, *non*?"

Walker's attention snapped back to the task at hand. "What? No. I mean, you have a beautiful daughter, ma'am." He groaned. Shit. Was she right? He didn't know what *having it bad* even meant considering he'd never truly felt anything for any woman before. And they'd only met today. But what a hell of a meeting it was.

Violet's mother laughed and grabbed a to-go container her husband had brought up from the restaurant. She held out a hand, and he gave her the cake knife. She cut and packed a piece big enough to feed him and his brothers, though he wasn't sure he'd share.

"Thank you," he said when she slid the box toward him.

She placed her hand on his. "No," she said. "Thank *you*. It is a comfort to know she has someone outside of"—she waved a bony hand in the air—"*this*. I know she gave up a lot to come home from school and help around here. It kills a small part of me each day to know she is not doing what she loves. Do you know when she's not at her paying job she's downstairs with her papa working for free?"

Walker shook his head.

Camille patted the seat next to her, inviting Walker to sit as well. He'd spent the past however many hours talking to strangers and finding every excuse in the world not to accept a drink. It had been exhausting.

He collapsed into the seat next to her, stretching his legs out under the table.

"She'll get back to school and finish up if I have anything to say about it. I never wanted her to come home in the first place, but she is stubborn." She laughed softly. "Like her *maman*."

"It's a money issue," he said quietly. He was probably overstepping, but next to small talk, heart-to-hearts were right up there on his list of things he didn't do, not to mention he was pretty shitty at both.

"Yes," was all Camille said.

He wasn't a stranger to medical bills and the strain it could put on a family. Once their father had gotten too drunk and too sick to properly take care of the ranch, Luke and Walker had moved back home despite the painful memories of the last time they'd lived in that house—of losing their mother and everything that came after. It was the only way they could manage the business, which at that point included not only the work itself, but the accounting side of things as well. Now that Jack was home, he dealt with the business end of the ranch, but back then—with the addition of Jack Senior getting sicker—they'd barely kept their heads above water. Things were better now that they'd all sunk the life insurance payout into reviving the vineyard, but they still needed to make the wine. And sell it.

"Look at you two, sitting on the job."

Violet's teasing voice came from behind him, and before he had a chance to turn in her direction, her hands were on his shoulders, massaging his tight muscles. It was all he could do not to moan with pleasure.

Walker needed to get the hell out of here before he lost all sense of reality.

He wrapped his hands around Violet's wrists, and she stilled.

"I should head out. Long drive ahead of me."

"Where is it you said that vineyard of yours was?"

He hadn't actually said it. He figured once it came out that he lived ninety minutes away he'd blow Violet's cover. But maybe it was for the best. Maybe she could use the distance as the reason for their supposed breakup. Then no one had to be the asshole.

"Oak Bluff," he said after a pause. "It's a small town in San Luis Obispo County. Probably off your radar."

Camille's eyes widened. "That's almost two hours away."

"Ninety-four minutes!" Violet blurted.

"But how in the hell are you two dating if you live in Santa Barbara," her father said, looking at her, "and you live up the coast?"

Violet's arms draped around his neck, and she planted a soft kiss on his cheek. "Because I'm going to be the winery's sommelier when they open. And don't worry. We can separate business and—*this*."

Her lips were warm on his cheek. That kiss felt nothing like a prelude to a breakup, and he was beginning to wonder how they were going to sell the end of their relationship as well as they'd already sold that they'd been dating for two months.

"You're working all the way in San Luis Obispo?" Camille asked. "What happened to Cafe Claudette? You haven't even been there a year."

Violet's teeth skimmed her bottom lip before she answered. That was her tell when she was nervous. If Walker noticed it, he was sure her parents did, too.

She shrugged. "It wasn't the right fit, you know? Not the same vibe as our place. A couple months ago I heard from a friend of a friend about the Oak Bluff job and figured it couldn't hurt to apply, especially since they weren't looking for me to start until next week. Of course I nailed my interview." She shot Walker a knowing grin, and he laughed softly, shaking his head. "I don't mind the drive. I actually kind of like the time to myself. Just me, the road, a good playlist. Doesn't get any better than that."

Walker pictured her with the windows down and the speakers blaring her favorite songs as she sang along. And even though he believed she was doing what she wanted for now, he had a better sense of what she'd given up to help someone she loved.

"I'm gonna hit the road." Walker interrupted. This was all getting too personal, and truth be told, it was none of his business. He was enough of an outsider in his own family to know he'd intruded on the Chastains long enough.

He stood and grabbed his to-go box of cake.

"Um, thank you." He held up the cake. "For this and your, uh, hospitality. But I gotta make that ninety-four-minute drive now." He shook Gabriel Chastain's hand for the second time tonight.

"I'm still not sure about you, Everett," he said. "But Violet lights up whenever she looks at you, so I'm going to take that as a good sign."

"Pa*pa*!" Violet said, giving her father a good-natured tap on the shoulder.

Walker nodded but said nothing in response. When he spun toward the door, Camille was standing. Again she kissed him on both cheeks as she'd done when they'd met.

"You're good for her," she whispered to him before backing away.

This was too damned much. Games weren't supposed to feel this real, to have stakes that involved people's lives.

He eyed the liquor still lining the buffet and licked his lips.

"Good night," he simply said before kissing Violet on the cheek.

She rested a hand on his back. "I'll walk you down."

Wordlessly, they stepped out the apartment door and down the staircase. They were still silent as they headed outside, as Walker tossed the cake onto the passenger seat, and as they rounded the bed of the truck, making their way to the driver-side door. It was dark now, well past ten o'clock, but the night was the clearest it could be—stars blanketing the sky with a moon so full it lit up the alley.

Finally he broke the spell. It was the only way he'd make it out of there alive.

"So you and your mom…" he started. "I mean, I'm just making an observation, but this is an anniversary party. Usually family shows up to stuff like this."

She huffed out a laugh, though she wasn't really smiling. "You mean why are my mother and I the only people of color here?"

He nodded.

She stared up at the apartment and then back at him with a tiny shrug. "My mother's family lives in Paris. We don't see them very much."

"End of story?" he asked, brows raised. He wasn't going to push.

She nodded. "For now."

"Okay, then. Slight change of subject. What are you going to tell them—about us, I mean?"

She winced. "I'm not sure yet. I wasn't expecting them to like you so much."

He raised a brow. "Thanks?"

She laughed. "Sorry! I didn't mean it like that. You just seemed to click with them in a way I wasn't expecting. I mean, my father is the stereotype. No one is good enough for his little girl. And my mother? She gave you cake."

"That a big deal?" he asked.

"The biggest. No one has a sweet tooth like Maman." Violet hugged her shoulders and rubbed her upper arms.

"You're cold," he said, stating the obvious. But they weren't playing make-believe anymore. It wasn't his place to wrap her in his arms no matter how much he felt the urge to do so. So he crossed them over his chest, fighting to keep from doing exactly that. "You should probably head back up."

"Yeah," she said. "You're right. We need to finish cleaning up." She rested a hand on his forearm. "Thank you, Walker. What you did tonight? I can't tell you how much it means to me. And even if it alleviated their worry only for the evening, it meant a lot to them, too. But back to our intended roles of employer, employee. I'll see you Wednesday."

Her hand slid from his arm. She lingered for a moment, like there was something else she wanted to say, but then she pivoted to walk away.

He'd finally had her all to himself—and he sent her packing. He was definitely the asshole in this scenario.

"I thought the French kissed good-bye." If he'd thought about it a second longer, he'd have talked himself out of it, but the truth was that he wasn't ready for the charade to end. They'd played their parts so well for their unsuspecting audience. Why couldn't they play a bit longer, just the two of them?

She stopped and spun to face him.

"It's more of a general European thing. Anyway, I'm not *really* French," she said, smiling. "I mean, I was born here so I tend to behave more like an American."

She was teasing him, and it only made him want her more.

"But you speak the language," he said, taking a step closer. "That's not typical American behavior."

She raised her brows. "That's true. I do speak it."

"And I'm pretty sure if one of your parents is from another country, it's okay to claim their nationality as your own."

She was the one to take a step this time. They were only a couple inches apart now.

"So what you're saying is I should act more French?"

"Way more French," he said. "You owe it to your heritage."

She hooked a finger in the belt loop of his jeans. "Walker?"

"Yeah?"

"*Je veux t'embrasser.*"

"Then kiss me already," he said, echoing her words from the balcony.

She clasped her fingers around his neck and tugged him down to her.

"Oh, thank God. I thought you were going to let me walk away, and the thought of *not* kissing one more time tonight was killing me. I wasn't sure if you wanted to because we're not really putting on our show anymore, and—"

"Vi?"

"Yeah?"

"If you stopped talking about kissing me, I could be making your toes curl right about now."

She shut up, and her lips crashed into his. There was no more time to savor, so he let her take what she wanted and gave himself permission to drink his fill. He ran his hands down her back until they rested above her ass. He wasn't taking any liberties this time, not when each step he took over the line of pretending made him want more.

As she gripped him tighter, he felt her breasts against his torso, her hardened peaks dragging slightly up and down as she stood on her toes.

This wasn't working. For one it was driving him mad, and for two, he guessed she wasn't getting everything she could out of the kiss if she was struggling to keep her balance. So he gripped underneath her thighs and hoisted her up and onto the hood of the truck.

She yelped and then started laughing.

"Figured this would be a little easier," he said, his voice rough with a need he wouldn't be able to satiate in a small alley in downtown Santa Barbara. But there was a light at the end of the ninety-four-minute tunnel called a cold shower. He could at least look forward to that.

She was slightly taller than him now, which meant when she draped her arms over his shoulders, all she had to do was dip her head toward his so their lips could touch again.

"I like it when you call me Vi," she said in a breathy voice.

"You do, huh?" He paused for several beats as he kissed the line of her jaw until he reached her ear. "*Vi.*"

She shivered, and as he leaned back, he watched the skin on her arm turn to gooseflesh. He guessed this shiver wasn't from the cold, though.

"Mmm-hmm," she squeaked.

He paid due attention to the other jaw, then let his teeth graze her other earlobe. "What about... *Teach*? You like it when I call you that? Because I sure as hell like it when you teach me how to say all those pretty, sexy French words of yours."

He was barely hanging on to the thread of his resolve anymore. He needed to touch her. Now.

"Yes," she whispered.

He slid her forward, wrapped her legs around his waist. Then he glanced up the back wall of the restaurant to where he knew the apartment was.

"What room is that window in?" he asked, noting the small glass rectangle.

"Guest bathroom. And the restaurant is closed. Employees leave out the other side anyway."

He knew from her answer—at her ensuring him of their privacy—that she was game for whatever he was suggesting.

He dropped his right hand to her leg, slid it under her dress. Then he thanked the stars for long skirts, starry nights, and a beautiful woman who knew nothing of him other than this day. This moment. She wasn't waiting for the other shoe to drop, for the next time he came to on a bed of broken glass—or worse. She saw the man he was today and believed that was who he'd always been, and with her he could pretend that was the truth.

His hand traveled up to her knee, his thumb brushing the inside of her thigh.

She sucked in a sharp breath, so he kissed her as he made his way to that sexy-as-hell place where a woman's leg met her pelvis. Suddenly he was the one finding it hard to breathe.

He'd done this before, been with women. But something was different. *She* was different. And he was...He wouldn't let his head go there right now. He wanted to be here. In the moment. With her.

This was it, the one and only time they'd do this.

His thumb snuck beneath the soft silk of her panties, and she squirmed, so damn gorgeous reacting to his touch.

He tilted his head up so his eyes met hers. "Toes curling yet, Teach?"

She bit her bottom lip and nodded.

He brushed her soft, wet, swollen center, and she gasped.

"But we're just getting started."

He pulled his hand free. Then before she could miss his absence, reentered from above, palm disappearing beneath her undergarment as one finger sunk deep inside her warmth.

"Jesus," he hissed.

She whimpered, pulling his mouth to hers as a second finger joined the first.

He kicked his resolve to the curb and let raw, animal instinct take over.

She rode his hand, and he consumed her, feasted on the taste of the rich chocolate cake still lingering on her tongue, doing his best to commit it all to memory.

Teeth clacked as her fingers tangled in his hair, and despite their dark, private corner, he wondered what would happen when he took her over the edge.

He stilled inside her, and seconds later, her body went motionless in response.

He tilted his head back, meeting her intent gaze.

"I need you to know something before this is done." One of his fingers twitched between her legs, and she let out a soft cry. "Sorry about that, Teach. I'm not exactly in control here, but I gotta say this one thing, and I need you to listen, okay?"

Not the truth of who he was or who he'd been. He wouldn't ruin the moment with that. But the truth of right now, the only damn thing he knew without a sliver of doubt.

She nodded.

"I'm not the kind of guy who lets himself want things. Probably because there's not a whole lot I deserve. But I want you, Violet. I want you like fire wants oxygen." Like a drunk wants the bottle. *Needs* the bottle. Which was exactly why he *couldn't* have her. Not when he couldn't separate the need to fill a void from simply the need for her. "So I'm making this one time count."

She opened her mouth to respond, but he didn't give her time, afraid she'd talk him into something it wasn't his right to have.

So he kissed her once more, then swirled his thumb around her pulsing bud. He took her to the edge of the cliff and then straight off it as she buried her face in the crook of his neck to muffle her cries.

Afterward, there was no official good-bye, no further discussion about how this couldn't happen again. He simply lifted her down and kissed her once more before she disappeared back into the apartment, the curtain finally closing on their very convincing performance.

The scent of her was still on him when he pushed open the door to his small apartment above the Oak Bluff antiques shop, the one he'd been renting from the sheriff's mom since she got married for the fourth time and moved to her new husband's farm a few miles outside of town.

Since Jack, Ava, and Owen had made the ranch their home, he and Luke had moved out. Luke went and bought himself a fixer-upper on a nice piece of land, but Walker hadn't been able to make the same commitment. Buying meant he was sure he'd be here for the long haul; renting meant he could pick up and leave on a moment's notice. For now he had a place to hang his hat but no place he'd call home. Nothing in Oak Bluff—the town where he was born—felt quite like home.

He strode to the cabinet above the fridge and pulled out the bottle of whiskey and his one and only shot glass, setting them both on the center of the kitchen table.

He sat and stared at his two oldest friends, then unscrewed the cap and poured an ounce of the dark liquid he knew could calm what needed calming...numb what needed numbing.

His fingers wrapped around the glass, and he swirled the whiskey slowly as he licked his lips. Then he did what he'd done the past few nights since arriving back in Oak Bluff.

He poured it back in the bottle, screwed the cap back on, and put everything back where he found it where it would wait for the next night, for the next test.

"You passed tonight, asshole," he said aloud. "But there's always tomorrow."

Rehab was one thing. He was forced to stay clean because there was nothing around to tempt him. But being back in town was another. He needed to actively *choose* sobriety each and every day—or choose to live in the fog that had made life bearable for the past ten plus years. He wanted to do the former for his brothers and his aunt. But what he wanted for himself was still a mystery. So in the meantime, he tempted fate, rationalizing that every time he did, he was that much stronger.

As much as he thought it would help, he didn't want to numb his thoughts of Violet or how it felt to be the version of himself she saw tonight. He wouldn't get to do it again, which meant the memory was all he'd have moving forward.

The memory of the way she smiled at him, the way she moved when he touched her, the way her soft lips felt against his. No way in hell was he erasing that.

He kicked off his work boots, then left a trail of clothing on the way to the bathroom.

He was still hard when he stepped under the frigid spray of the shower, as the day replayed itself in his head.

He pressed one palm against the tiled wall and let the other wrap around his shaft.

How the hell would he last one day with Violet Chastain working for his family?

"*Merde*," he grumbled.

He had the next three to figure it out.

CHAPTER SIX

"SQUAWK!"

Walker bolted up from his pillow, effectively slamming his temple into the corner of his nightstand.

"Shit!" he hissed. "What the actual—"

"SQUAWK!"

The sound was coming from the kitchen, but in an apartment as small as his, it might as well have been on the pillow next to him. He'd risen early the past three days to take care of the cattle feed and fix the patch of broken fence. It was Luke's turn for the early morning shift. So who the hell was busting into his place and cheating him out of his morning to sleep in?

He threw off the blanket, didn't bother to cover his naked form, and grabbed a two-by-four that was leaning against his wall. Small living space meant no storage space, so the whole apartment was basically his storage shed. He'd never expected he'd need to use any of his supplies as a weapon, though. And certainly not at the ass crack of dawn.

He crept down the short hallway and rounded the corner to the kitchen, wood beam raised and ready to knock the living daylights out of whoever was trying to rob him—not that he had anything of value worth stealing.

"What the hell do you think you're doing?" he roared.

The refrigerator was open, and all he could see were a pair of petite legs—a woman's legs—clad in denim.

"Squawk!"

A chicken flapped its wings and scrambled out of the sink, water spraying everywhere.

The fridge door slammed, and his aunt Jenna—the woman who'd been his guardian during his messed-up teen years—straightened with a start. Then she burst out laughing as she covered her eyes.

"Good *Lord*, Walker," she said in her lilting Texas twang. "You're naked as a jaybird, out of milk, and you scared Lucy half to death while she was taking a much needed bath!"

He still had the two-by-four raised like she was about to pitch a strike at him.

"Why the hell are you giving your hen a bath in my kitchen sink?" he countered.

One hand still covered her eyes while she gesticulated with the other.

"Because I thought I might wake you if she took her bath in the bathroom sink."

He lowered his arms and held the wood in front of his groin.

"Ya think? All exposed genitalia have been covered, by the way."

She peeked between a crack in her fingers, then let her hand fall from her face.

"We woke you anyway, didn't we?" She winced.

He raised his brows. "Yeah. You did. At six a.m. when I was planning on sleeping in. And I thought I gave you that key in case of an emergency."

She crossed her arms as Lucy-the-no-longer-bathing-hen clucked across his counter.

"Well, you *are* out of milk, so this is clearly a breakfast emergency. Plus, your door wasn't even locked. It was like an open invitation. I'd say you're lucky I came when I did." She gasped, and her hand flew to her eyes again. "Damn it, Walker. Your wood is drifting. Can you please go put something on?"

He chuckled, then readjusted his makeshift garment.

"Only if you put that trespassing chicken outside. Unless you're planning on making chicken sausage for breakfast."

Jenna gasped and shooed him away with her free hand.

"How dare you threaten Lucy. I'll have you know it was *her* idea to come here today because she thought you might need a little company before you went off to the ranch. You spend too much time by yourself, Walker."

He started toward the bedroom but called back to her over his shoulder.

"It's because I don't like most people." It was partially true, but maybe what Jenna said had some truth to it as well. He'd made himself pretty scarce the past three days—volunteering for the early morning duties so he could avoid unnecessary person-to-person interaction—and he'd planned to do the same today. Just not this early. And italicize this. Maybe he'd tell Jack to send him on a delivery. Or there were always the horses in the stable. Did they have a ranch hand working today? If not, he could give the horses a workout. Looked like a nice enough day that they shouldn't be all cooped up inside. Whatever excuse he could find, he just needed some distance from everyone and everything. Especially today. "And I don't care what you think. That chicken's not psychic."

"Yes, she is!" Jenna called back. "She walked right over to a picture of you, Jack, and Luke and pecked her beak on top of your pretty little face. So here we are. And you're welcome for the company. Because I know you like us!"

He shook his head ruefully even though she couldn't see him and decided to play along. Maybe he didn't like most people, but his aunt wasn't most people. Jenna was happiest in the company of others. And supposedly psychic animals, apparently. She raised Walker and his brothers through their high school years. For Jack that was only six months, but for Walker—after five years without a mother and losing his father to grief and alcohol—at barely a decade older than him, Jenna had been the big sister he'd never known he needed.

But he didn't need anything today other than to avoid the winery, which made Jenna's impromptu visit all the more suspect.

Ten minutes later he was back in the kitchen, this time in a gray T-shirt and his oldest pair of Wranglers. "Better?" he asked, running a hand through his wet hair. "And is that bacon I smell or did you go and turn Lucy into sausage for me after all?"

Jenna spun from the stove, her blond ponytail swinging, and placed her hands on her hips, giving him a pointed look. "Much better. But when are you gonna shave that beard? Makes you look ten years older."

He gave her a crooked grin. "And wiser?"

She rolled her eyes. "Lucy is outside, and yes, that's bacon you smell, the last two pieces you had sitting in your meat drawer. Surprisingly, it wasn't expired."

He winked at her. "Because unlike my brothers, I actually know how to cook for myself." He snatched one of the pieces of bacon from the plate on the kitchen table and took a bite. "So while I appreciate the gesture, you don't need to come over at sunrise with your supposedly psychic chicken and cook for me. I can take care of myself."

Jenna grabbed the second piece of bacon and polished it off before he could get to it.

Walker shook his head. "Taking a man's last piece of bacon? I'm not sure there is anything crueler."

She laughed. "Yeah, well, if you don't need my cooking, you don't need to eat it. You know I can't turn off the caretaker gene with you three. So it'd be nice if you indulged me every now and then."

He pulled a chair out from the table. "Sit."

Jenna's eyes widened. "Are you tellin' me what to do, nephew?"

He gave her a single nod. "Yes, but I'm also making you breakfast. So sit. *Please.*" Maybe if he proved to her that he was self-sufficient—and still sober—that gene of hers would take a rest.

She grinned and collapsed into the seat, and he ignored the little corner of his brain that asked him if he knew how to say please in French.

He knew someone who did, and she'd be showing up at the winery in a couple hours, which meant he had time to humor his aunt and figure out an excuse to make himself scarce for yet another day.

He flipped on the coffeemaker, set a pot to brewing, then threw a clean pan on the stove along with a square of butter melting in the middle of it.

"Pancakes or eggs?" he asked.

Jenna rested her elbows on the table and steepled her fingers. "Hmm... Tough decision. What if I want both?"

He raised a brow. "Then I guess that's what you're getting."

He went to work cracking eggs and mixing up the batter to the soundtrack of Lucy's squawks in the small back lot of the property.

"You're gonna make some lucky lady real happy one day," Jenna said as she rose to pour them each a cup of coffee. "Ain't nothing like a man who knows his way around a kitchen."

He lifted the pan, gave it a slight shake, and then flipped the pancake that was in it.

"Sorry to disappoint. But the two pieces of bacon should be evidence enough that I'm better off cooking for one." He followed her to the table and slid the pancake onto her plate.

"But you made me a feast," she argued.

Walker shrugged. "You broke into my apartment. Not like I had much of a choice."

He set the pan down and picked his mug up off the counter, taking a long, savoring sip.

"After this, I'm supposed to drive you over to the ranch so you can help Luke tag a couple new calves, and then I guess you're heading to the winery to pick up the new girl and take her shopping for stemware."

Jenna's words were spoken around a forkful of pancake, so it took a few seconds for what she'd said to register.

The new girl, meaning the girl who'd greeted him with the kind of kiss meant for a longtime lover—the girl who'd sat on the hood of his truck and let him touch her like they *were* longtime lovers and not strangers playing a very dangerous game.

He set his coffee down and blew out a breath.

"So this is a setup," he said as realization took hold. "Jack put you up to this."

"No. Jack simply said you'd been holed up in your apartment working on some chair or something, and I suggested luring you out of hiding with breakfast. You cooking for me is a bonus, though." She pointed out back. "Is it that rocking chair in your truck?"

He nodded. He wasn't even sure who he was making it for. He'd seen the design in a magazine during his time at the treatment center, had ripped it out, and started working on it then and there, bringing it back home to finish.

"And here I thought this carpentry thing of yours was a hobby. Walker, that chair is a work of art. You ever sell anything you've made before?"

He shrugged. "A couple things here and there. Before..." he said, indicating a time when he often wasn't sober enough to finish a project. Now that he was, he'd dived into his supposed hobby in the hopes of never coming up for air. If he could stay hidden beneath the surface, then maybe he'd make it another day pouring the whiskey back into the bottle instead of down his throat.

"There's a jam lady at the farmers market who's decorating a new house. If the chair's finished, you should bring it by next weekend and give her a look. I think she'd love it."

He raised a brow. "Jam lady?"

Jenna balled up her napkin and threw it at him. "Her name is Sylvie. She and her husband bought this rustic beach house they're fixing up room by room. Your chair would be perfect in a little reading nook or maybe out on her porch. Will you come by on Saturday or Sunday? I'll give you a discount on eggs. You're about out of everything anyway."

He took another sip of his coffee. He guessed he had motivation now to finish the thing. He could do it in a few days.

Why the hell not?

"Fine," he said. "But if she buys the chair, I'm not buying any jam."

Jenna laughed. "No one said you had to, but a jar or two would be nice. Like I said, you're about—"

"Out of everything," he interrupted. "So I've heard."

Maybe this was the start of something. He'd given a good portion of his share of Jack Senior's insurance payout to the vineyard effort. At the time it was the right thing to do, and he didn't regret it. But now he was without surplus, which meant he was stuck. This could be the way to get unstuck. He wouldn't mind a nice chunk of change before he had to tell Sam yes or no about heading up north for the contracting gig. Each day he was here, he longed more and more for that semblance of freedom—to see what life was like without the restraint of Oak Bluff and the memories it held. Seemed like now he was close to turning the idea into reality.

"Stemware?" he said after a long silence. "Didn't we buy a bunch of shit for Tucker Green's wedding last fall?" Despite the winery not yet being open, they'd already hosted a wedding in the space for Luke's best friend, which made Walker think they were all good on supplies.

Jenna waved him off. "That was inexpensive stuff your brothers found on short notice, and it was only enough for the small wedding. Y'all can keep it for backup if the good stuff breaks. But Jack and Ava's wedding is going to be the real deal. Plus this is the next family business venture. You'll want to drink a Crossroads vintage out of something with style."

His jaw tightened. "I don't think you want me drinking a Crossroads vintage out of anything, style or no style."

Her smile faltered. "Oh, Walker. Shit. I wasn't thinking. I don't know that anyone's really figured out how to reconcile, you know…"

He let out a bitter laugh. "An addict surrounding himself with the substance he abused for ten years? I've been trying to reconcile that idea for two months and counting."

She reached across the table and gave his hand a reassuring squeeze. At least, he figured she was trying to be reassuring. But no one—including himself—had the faintest idea how an alcoholic was supposed to run a vineyard.

"You'll figure it out," she said.

He cleared his throat. He could test the waters on her before mentioning anything to his brothers. "What if what I figure out is that Oak Bluff's no good for me anymore?"

Her eyes went glossy, and she pressed her lips together and nodded.

"You gotta do what's right for you, Walker. I hate to see you three boys separated now that you're finally all back together, but they'll understand. We've all got a ghost or two here. Finding out how to live with them is different for all of us. You've talked to Jack and Luke about this?"

He shook his head. "Nope. I'm still doing the figuring. But I've got an offer to do some work up north with the Callahans. They're moving up to Meadow Valley, building a guest ranch. They need hired hands and offered me a position."

She threw her hands in the air, her calm acceptance a thing of the past. "And you're taking it? You can't drop something like that in my lap and tell me to keep it to myself. I'm terrible at secrets."

"SQUAWK!" Lucy had apparently made it back up the steps.

Jenna pushed back from the table and stalked toward the door.

"See? Even Lucy knows something isn't right up here. Doesn't matter if I *can* keep my mouth shut about this, she's likely to give you away."

Walker rolled his eyes. "She's a chicken. She's not psychic, and there aren't any damned secrets. There's nothing to keep from Jack and Luke, because there's nothing to tell them yet. It's just something I'm considering. So why don't you tell me about the glasses I have to buy, and I'll forgive you for waking me at the crack of dawn."

Jenna groaned, a common response whenever she was giving up the argument. He offered her a self-satisfied grin.

"Fine. But this discussion is only paused. Not over," she relented. "Anyway, Ava found out this wholesaler her family uses for their vineyard is going out of business and is selling off all their high-end glassware at a fraction of the cost. You're supposed to take the wine girl—what's her name again?—to the wholesaler to pick out the new stuff."

"Her name is Violet," he muttered. "And why can't Ava take her to this wholesaler place? What the hell do I know about stemware?"

Jenna clapped her hands together. "Yes! Violet. That's it! Pretty name. You interviewed her, right? You liked her?"

He coughed on a sip of coffee, sending the hot liquid down his windpipe, which then sent him into a coughing fit that had his eyes watering and his lungs begging for air.

Jenna was at his side, slapping him on the back in seconds.

"You okay there, darlin'? If I didn't know any better, I'd say this girl made quite an impression on you. But it was only an interview, right?" She gave him another good whack before he had the sense to take a few steps away.

It took him several more seconds to clear his throat and take in enough air to speak. He knew his aunt was looking out for him, but he didn't miss the hint of accusation in her tone.

"What the hell else would it have been other than an interview?" Perhaps playing the part of doting boyfriend for her parents. Or maybe kissing her like it was the damned apocalypse and her lips on his were his only chance for survival. Some might say it was burying his fingers inside her until muffled cries of pleasure escaped her lips, while others would suggest that it was Walker taking a cold shower, his dick in his hand as he replayed the evening's events in his mind's eye.

Shit. What he and Violet experienced the other day was miles away from *only an interview*. He'd thought a couple days of space would have been enough to get past it, but the rigid line behind the zipper of his jeans said otherwise.

"Someone's a little defensive," she said. "I didn't mean to insinuate anything. But I know the parameters of your recovery—"

"So do I," he said gruffly. "And you didn't answer my question. This is Ava's domain. Shouldn't she be the one going on this little field trip?"

Jenna shook her head. "Ava's going to show Violet around this morning, but she has a dress-fitting this afternoon." Jenna beamed. "I can't believe Jack and Ava are finally getting married. I bet Luke and Lily aren't too far behind. And maybe, when you've put all the tough stuff behind you..."

"I already told you I'm better off cooking for one," he interrupted. "So let's leave all the relationship talk at the door. Unless you want to talk about your own. You know any guy you date needs to get clearance from me, Luke, *and* Jack, right? Anyone you want to introduce us to?"

His aunt's jaw tightened. The last guy she'd dated had hit her. Walker and his brothers didn't see eye to eye on everything, but when it came to family—to protecting their own—there was no argument. Especially when it came to Jenna, the woman who put her own life on hold to protect them.

Her gaze softened and she strode toward him, stood on her toes, and kissed him on the cheek. "Yeah," she said. "I know. But it's just me, myself, and I these days. Not quite ready to get back on the horse."

"SQUAWK!" Lucy called from where she was still waiting at the door.

Walker laughed at the welcome break in the tension of the moment. "I guess your hen agrees."

Jenna smiled. "She is a wise one, that girl."

Violet was grateful she and Ava wore the same shoe size. She wasn't expecting a tour of the vineyard and had, of course, worn heels. She'd spent the first part of the morning—when the air was still cool and crisp—in her belted red shirtdress and a pair of muddied hiking boots, thanks to last night's much needed rain.

Jack had dropped them off at the vineyard on his way to take his and Ava's son, Owen, to school, so they were now walking back to the ranch where Violet had parked.

"Careful of the—well, the piles," Ava said as they left the vineyard property for that of the pasture, the most direct line back to the ranch. She laughed as Violet rose on her toes and studied the ground beneath her feet with every step. "Don't worry about the boots," Ava added. "They've seen more than mud before. You get used to it."

Violet winced. She was a stylish shoe, hard ground kind of girl. She wasn't sure she'd ever get used to work boots and cow pies. Luckily, this tour was simply a formality. She'd be working in the beautiful new winery, not out in the fields.

Several yards ahead, closer to the barn, she could make out two men, blond hair peeking from beneath a couple of cowboy hats, one of them with his arms around the belly of a calf.

She swallowed, a lump forming in her throat. She'd expected to see Walker today, had mentally prepared herself for it on the hundred-minute ride over—*Thank you, traffic*—but he hadn't been there to greet her with Ava and Jack. When there was no mention of him after introductions were made, she'd assumed he wouldn't be there at all.

"Luke and Walker are tagging a couple of new calves," Ava said, following Violet's line of sight. "After we finish up your paperwork, Jack said he wrangled Walker into shopping with you for the stemware."

"No!" Violet blurted without even thinking. "I mean, I'm fine going on my own."

Squish.

She'd stepped in it. Like, *really* stepped in it.

Ava burst out laughing when she saw Violet lift her boot. "Welcome to Crossroads Ranch," she said. "Let's go get you back into those pretty suede booties you were wearing." She hooked her arm through Violet's. "I may have to borrow those. Now that we share shoes and all."

And because there was nothing to do but literally walk it off, Violet laughed, too, forgetting for the moment that she'd be spending the afternoon with the man she hadn't stopped thinking about since she'd kissed him without even knowing his name.

After signing her tax documents and employee contract back at the ranch, then slipping back into her tan suede booties, Violet felt both relieved and in control. She was going to have a steady paycheck. So she had to go shopping with Walker. She could do this.

"Okay!" Ava said, then held out a hand. "Welcome to the family!"

Violet shook her hand, her brows furrowing. "Family?" To her, family was simply her mother and father. She had grandparents in France whom she'd seen a handful of times growing up when they'd visited, but her grandfather's health kept them from traveling much now. She also had an aunt she'd never met. After her falling out with her sister, Maman had moved to the United States and had never gone back. It was just the three of them.

Ava nodded. "It's a job, sure," she said. "But when you work for a family business, you're automatically part of the family."

Violet smiled. "I guess that makes sense. My father owns a restaurant. I know his cooks and hostesses better than anyone else in my life, but I guess I never realized they were a family of sorts until now."

Ava tapped the home button on her phone and gasped. "Oh wow. Time flies in good company, but I have to run. Dress fitting." She beamed.

"You must be really excited."

Ava nodded. Her smile turned wistful. "I have been in love with Jack Everett since I was eighteen. Only took us eleven years to finally get it right."

Her smile and glow were infectious, and Violet couldn't help but join her. She was still smiling—and likely glowing—when Ava led her out of the kitchen and around the corner to the hallway that led back to the front door. Ava pulled the door open, and Violet walked smack into a wall of hard man chest.

Before she knew what she was doing, she inhaled deeply through her nose. She smelled the fresh scent of laundry detergent, the fainter hint of soap or body wash, and something that could only be described as man—a man she'd been this close to not once, not twice, but *three* times before—and it was a scent she'd never forget. Not that she wanted to.

Ava cleared her throat, snapping Violet out of her momentary stupor. God she hoped it had only been a moment.

"You're right on time," Ava said as Violet shuffled back a couple of steps.

"And *really* close to the door," Violet added, regaining composure.

"I was about to knock," Walker said dryly. "Jack said to pick you up at eleven thirty, and it's eleven thirty."

"And I'm gonna be late!" Ava held up her phone. "Gotta run! Violet, I'm so glad you're here. We'll catch up more tomorrow. Thanks for filling in, Walker!" And then, in a flurry of flailing limbs and long auburn waves, she was out the door, leaving Violet and Walker alone in the foyer of the Everett home.

He looked her up and down, his expression unreadable. So she decided to do the same to him. His blond hair was damp at his nape. She inhaled the familiar scent of soap and how it mixed so deliciously with his skin, confirming her suspicion that he'd just showered and making her mouth water at the same time. His beard was neatly groomed around those commanding lips. He wore a forest green henley and a pair of Levis that looked made to fit his body and his alone. The man himself looked like he stepped out of the pages of a fashion magazine, the title of which could only be *Rugged Hot Man She Wanted to Mount.*

Oh no.

"You don't have to do this," she said. "Chaperone me, I mean. Restaurant supply shopping is in my blood. Ava was in a rush, but I'm sure she gave you all the details of how many glasses they want broken down by type—red wine, white wine, champagne, and so forth. If you want to pass that on to me you can get back to tagging cattle or whatever else requires you to wear a cowboy hat and do cowboy-type things in the field."

He crossed his arms, expression impassive. "*Cowboy*-type things?"

She shrugged. "Isn't that what you do? I saw you and your brother with the calves doing the tagging thing. You probably have a horse or something, too."

"We have three."

Oh God. Now she was imagining him on a horse. In the hat. A T-shirt and jeans more like the ones he was wearing the day she met him—worn and dirty. Worked in. *Lived* in.

She swallowed. "Or your chair!" she practically shouted. "Maybe you want time to work on that? I'm just saying I got this stemware thing. I'm good. First day on the job, and I can handle it on my own."

Miles away from you and your clean, soapy, manly scent.

He nodded toward her booties, the ones that made her stand four inches taller than she was. "You dress for carrying boxes of breakable items like you dress for walking a mile with a two-tiered cake."

Her gaze dropped to her feet before meeting his eyes—goodness they were so blue—again.

She grimaced. "It's my first day on the job, and I wanted to look professional. You're the only one who met me for the interview, so I wanted to make a good impression. These are my good impression shoes." She pointed her toes. "You'd never guess they were a thrift store find. My whole wardrobe is." Heat rushed to her cheeks at the admission. Not because she thought he was judging her, but from the guilt of insinuating that she went without. She never resented her decision to leave school. But sometimes she wondered what it would be like if Maman's family knew they were struggling. Well—they would soon enough. "Anyway," she continued, "I didn't know about the stemware. *Or* the vineyard tour. Ava let me borrow a pair of her boots and I stepped right into *une tarte aux vaches*."

He raised a brow. "A what now?"

Violet blew out a breath. "A cow pie," she mumbled.

The corner of his mouth twitched. It would have been a perfect opportunity for him to call her *Teach*, but he didn't. Which was good because *Teach* was a nickname from the man who kissed her and played make-believe for a night. Coworkers didn't give each other nicknames, because coworkers were professional, which was exactly what she was going to be around Walker Everett from here on out, no matter how good he smelled or how much he belonged on the cover of her fictional magazine.

"You can't carry boxes of glass in those shoes."

He was right. With her booties—no matter how fabulous they were—she was in no shape to be lifting and hauling breakables. Her shoulders sagged. "No, I suppose I can't."

"And I'd advise against pushing a dolly's worth of boxes in those as well."

She adjusted her tote bag and squared her shoulders. "Advisory taken."

"And as much as I'd love to be doing 'cowboy-type things' instead of shopping, I'm going to go out on a limb here and say that you are quite in need of my services today, Ms. Chastain."

The ghost of a smile played at his lips, but he didn't seem to want to give her the satisfaction.

Violet rolled her eyes. "Can I at least drive?"

He motioned for the door. "Lead the way. I gotta save my energy for the heavy lifting I'll be doing in my sturdy boots."

She groaned and stalked toward the door, feeling him only inches behind her. When they got outside, she pulled her key fob from her tote and pressed the unlock button for her silver MINI Cooper—a hand-me-down of sorts from one of her father's early investors who'd barely driven the thing and then tired of it. He'd sold it to her dad for less than he could have purchased it from a dealer. It was before Maman started getting worse—before finances became an issue. And now it was her reminder of an easier time and that everything she was working for now was to somehow get her family back to that place.

Walker shook his head. "You're kidding, right? No way I'm going to fit in there, let alone several boxes of stemware."

She responded to his comment by opening the driver-side door, putting the key in the ignition, and lowering the vehicle's soft convertible top.

"Bet you'll fit now!" she called to where he stood, stubborn as a statue, outside the ranch house's door. "And I think you'll be pleasantly surprised with the trunk space."

Walker closed his eyes and gave another soft shake of his head, but it was a shake of acquiescence. He had no further argument. She'd actually won.

He confirmed her victory by running a hand through his damp hair and striding to the passenger door. He opened it, climbed in, and slammed it shut. Violet snorted as he sat knees to chest before finding the seat controls and sliding his chair as far back as it would go.

"Where to, boss?" She tied a scarf over her thick, dark hair, protecting her flat ironing work from the salty ocean air. It had only been a few weeks since her blowout—when Ramon had told her he preferred her hair straight, especially if she was working in his restaurant—and she wasn't going to let Maman's friend Lisa's work go to waste. Lisa was a stylist at the salon down the street from her father's restaurant. For the price of a good meal, she styled Violet's hair at no charge. She had a feeling Lisa would have done it even if no meal was involved, but that was how her family took care of their own. They kept everyone's bellies full even when bank accounts were tight.

He pulled his phone out of the pocket of his jeans—an awkward maneuver for a big man in a small space that he somehow made sexy simply by being him—and punched in the wholesaler's address.

She slipped on her oversized tortoiseshell sunglasses and pulled out onto the main road and off the Everett property.

"Shit," Walker hissed. "Left my aviators at my place when I showered. Turn around and head into town. It'll only take a second for me—"

"Got an extra pair in the glove box," Violet told him, a smile playing at her lips. "We have an appointment, and I hate showing up late."

He had to spread his legs to get the glove compartment open.

"You're shittin' me, right?" he said pulling out the heart-shaped frames.

Violet shrugged, then unsuccessfully suppressed a snort when the sun slashed right across his vision and he was forced to put the glasses on.

He shoved the glove box closed with a knee and crossed his arms over his chest, the thin cotton of the henley pulled taught over his lean yet defined biceps.

Then she noticed he hadn't yet put on his seat belt.

"Safety first, Mr. Everett," she said.

He mumbled something under his breath but then buckled up like he was supposed to.

With a self-satisfied grin, Violet connected her phone to the car's Bluetooth and put on her *Badass Chicks* playlist.

"Here we go!" she said as "Girl on Fire" by Alicia Keys filled the air between them, but Walker's shoulders and jaw were still tense. She laughed and gave his upper arm a playful push. "It's a beautiful day, Walker. Try to sit back and enjoy the ride."

He leaned his head against the seatback and let out a long breath as she breathed in the salty air, trying not to admit to herself how much more enjoyable *her* ride would be now that Walker Everett sat in the seat beside her.

CHAPTER SEVEN

Dorothy, Ava's contact at the glass distributor, was waiting for them when they arrived. Thankfully the ride had been less than a half hour, so Walker only had to suffer through Violet belting out Adele for mere minutes rather than the better part of two hours.

Maybe "suffer" wasn't the right word. It was now evident that Violet had the pipes to sing country and pop. But the sheer joy she seemed to get from it made something in his chest ache, and Walker Everett wasn't the kind of guy who ached for anyone or anything.

"You must be Violet and Walker," Dorothy said as they approached the building's entrance. "Ava said to keep an eye out for a pretty, dark-haired woman and a slightly younger version of Jack." She was a petite woman herself, probably a decade or so older than they were, with blond hair that hit below her shoulders and fell in waves atop a blue blouse that had a bow at the collar. "Nice specs, by the way," she said.

Violet giggled, and it took Walker a few seconds to realize that he was the punchline of the joke.

"Aw, hell," he said as he removed the heart-shaped sunglasses and shoved them in his back pocket.

The two women shared another laugh, and Walker grimaced—not because he wasn't confident enough to know he could pull off heart-shaped frames but because he wasn't all that fond of being laughed at, especially by the woman he'd been thinking about for days.

"Come on inside," Dorothy said. "I've pulled a selection for you to start with based on what Ava said the winery was looking for. I've even got us a little sampling set up so you can try the merchandise as it's intended to be used."

A sampling? What was she talking about? They were here to buy glasses and leave. End of story. No one said anything about *trying the merchandise.*

Dorothy led them into the building, which was basically a small warehouse. She took them down an aisle of tumblers and steins and through a back door that opened into an office—presumably hers—that boasted a table lined two rows deep with wineglasses in all different heights and sizes. Next to the line of stemware stood a bottle of red, a bottle of white, and a small silver bucket.

"We don't normally do this," Dorothy said, "but when Ava told me she was sending a sommelier, I thought you might enjoy it."

Shit.

"Oooh, this is going to be more fun than I expected!" Violet said as she bounced on the toes of her sexy-as-hell ankle boots that were basically the reason he was here staring at a table full of alcohol begging for him to drink it.

Damn it, Ava and Jenna and everyone who thinks I need to be around more people. Because this was what happened when he came out of hiding.

Walker barely moved past the threshold of the door.

"You really think it's a good idea to get all liquored up and then drive that sardine can back to the ranch?"

Violet waved him off. "You don't *drink* wine when you taste it, silly. You swirl it around in your mouth and spit it here." She walked to the table and held up the silver bucket.

He shook his head. "I don't taste it, and I don't spit it," he said evenly, but he could feel the threads of his control loosening by the second. It wasn't just being put in this position. He'd managed Violet's parents' party because he was able to focus all of his attention on her—on their one-night-only make-believe relationship. But this was different. If he stayed in this room, he'd be expected to sample or explain why he couldn't. Even if they were only employer/employee from here on out, Violet didn't know him as the mess he was a few months ago, and he sure as hell didn't plan on her finding out now.

Violet placed her hands on her hips. "You're going to be harvesting grapes to make *wine* soon. For the vineyard you own. And the tasting room I'm going to help run. I know wine might not be your favorite thing, but you can't sell the product if you don't know it, right?" She held up a goblet that looked to be made of a thick, sturdy glass and compared it with a stemless glass that had a slanted base. "Let me show you my skills while we decide to go with or without stems."

Dorothy was busying herself shuffling papers on the desk behind the table, likely trying to stay out of an increasingly uncomfortable situation. Though it didn't seem as if Violet was getting the message.

"I don't give a shit about stems or no stems," he said. "I'm here to carry boxes. You pick what you think works best, and I'll meet you up front."

Violet's mouth fell open, and he watched the sparkle in her brown eyes morph to something resembling hurt. It didn't matter. He needed out of this room, out of the building in general.

"But—" she finally managed.

He slapped the Crossroads business credit card on the table before she could protest any further. "See you up front." Then he stalked out the door, back through the warehouse and out to the parking lot. But instead of waiting at the car, he rounded the side of the building and slapped his palm hard against the brick.

"Shit!" He beat against the brick wall again. "Shit, shit, shit."

Ava's family had worked with this company for their own vineyard. Was this how they always conducted business—liquoring up their clients?

He shook out his hand and paced. Ava didn't have a cruel bone in her body. There was no way she would have sent him with Violet if she had any idea what he'd be walking into after not even three months of sobriety.

But it took several minutes of pacing for his breathing to slow, for logic to fully re-enter the situation.

This was his life now. This was the shit he'd have to deal with from here on out if he was going to make sobriety stick. The thing was, though, that it'd be so much easier to go back to who he was before—to the numbness that had gotten him from one day to the next for the past ten years.

Except he seemed to care what a certain high-heel-wearing, car-ride-singing, smart-as-hell knockout thought about him. That, as much as saying no to free drinks in Dorothy's office, was entirely new to him.

Eventually he made his way back to the MINI, using the trunk as a bench where he sat and waited for Violet to emerge from the building. He wore his heart-rimmed sunglasses with pride—and out of necessity because there wasn't a damn cloud in the sky—and tried to think of an excuse for his behavior that didn't involve him using the "A word"—alcoholic—just yet.

It was Dorothy who pushed through the door first. She motioned for Walker to come back inside.

"She picked some great stuff!" Dorothy called to him. "Got a dolly of boxes here with your name on 'em."

He dutifully retrieved the dolly as Dorothy and Violet said their good-byes. The two women hugged, and Walker heard snatches of conversation that mentioned a recipe and Paris and Dorothy coming to Santa Barbara for a visit.

Walker shook his head and laughed, not that he was surprised. Violet Chastain could charm the pants off anyone who crossed her path. He was speaking from experience.

He pushed the dolly out the propped-open door and headed to the car. Violet must have been close behind because the MINI's trunk popped open as he reached it. He peered inside.

"Huh," he said to himself. "That *is* some decent trunk space." All the boxes would actually fit, which meant he wouldn't be stuck holding a stack in his lap like Violet and the giant cake last weekend.

He fought the smile tugging at his lips, the one that might have him admitting to himself that he'd enjoyed pretending with Ms. Chastain a little more than he should have.

"Violet! Walker!" he heard from behind. "We forgot one box of champagne flutes. It's not that heavy if someone wants to come and grab them."

"I'm on it!" Violet called back to Dorothy as Walker squinted at the building. Violet was already halfway back to the door, and he was certain she was capable of taking care of the last remaining box, four-inch heels or no.

He shrugged and started gingerly loading his inventory into the empty trunk, fitting them in like fragile puzzle pieces. Well color him impressed. What her car lacked in legroom, it made up for in storage space.

He heard the crash of glass against pavement before he heard the scream. *Violet*'s scream.

She was only ten strides from the car, but he felt like he was moving through a thick swamp as his brain flashed from the present to when he was barely a teen—when Jack cried out for their father as he crashed down their home's wooden stairs, when the police and paramedics had burst through the front door and Walker was still too scared to leave his room, fearing he'd see his brother dead at the bottom of the steps.

"Walker! Hey—are you okay?" Violet's voice broke through the invasion of the past. "Because I could use a little help."

His vision cleared, and he realized he wasn't peering down at his dead brother. He was standing over Violet. Broken glass lay scattered in front of her, but it looked as if she'd fallen away from it.

"Are you okay?" he asked, his voice strained.

She rolled her eyes. "A bruised ego and anticipation of your *I told you so* for carrying a box in these shoes, but other than that, yes. I could use a hand, though." She reached out for him and then gasped as they both took in the same sight—a piece of glass embedded in her palm, blood trickling down her wrist and forearm. "Okay," she added, a slight tremor in her voice, "I might be a little less than okay."

"Oh no!" Dorothy came running up behind them. "What happened? Did the box break? Our packers are so good at making sure—"

"It was my heel," Violet said, now cradling her injured hand in the palm of the other. "It caught in a crack in the pavement. *I* dropped the box. And then, well, I dropped myself, too."

She forced a smile.

Walker was squatting next to her now. "Dorothy, are you folks good to clean all this up while I get Ms. Chastain to the ER?"

Dorothy nodded vigorously, shooing them toward the car. "Yes! Go! We've got things under control here."

With that Walker scooped Violet into his arms and carried her to the car. He set her down next to the vehicle, and she leaned against the passenger door.

"Before we get you all strapped in, I want to see if we can slow the bleeding, okay?"

She bit her lip and nodded.

"It doesn't look like the glass is in there too deep. If I can get it out—"

"Whoa, whoa, *whoa,* mister. You're—you're going to pull it out?" Her throat bobbed as she swallowed.

"I'm going to try," he told her. "I have a feeling you'll be a lot happier if I can. But if there's even the slightest bit of resistance, I'll leave it. I don't want to open the gash more. Getting it out, though, means I can wrap it up nice and tight—staunch the blood flow and probably make it hurt less."

She forced a smile. "I'm a big fan of less pain."

He cleared his throat. "Do you trust me?"

She nodded, though he guessed she didn't have much choice. Trusting him was pretty much her only option.

He untied the belt from her dress.

She gasped. "Wait, what are you—"

He raised a brow and tossed the belt over his shoulder.

"Tourniquet." Then he placed her hand in his palm. "Close your eyes. It's easier if you don't watch."

She squeezed her eyes shut. "For you or for me?"

He huffed out a small laugh. "Both of us, probably."

It was a clean cut, a little deeper than he'd let on, though she'd probably guessed that based on the amount of blood. But if the entry point had nothing jagged jutting off either side, it should come out easily enough.

As he reached for the shard, Violet started humming quietly enough not to distract him but hopefully, he guessed, enough to distract herself.

He pinched the glass between his fingers, and she sucked in a breath. It slid out with zero resistance, and he quickly wrapped the cotton belt around her palm until he'd used its entire length, tucking the end under where the makeshift bandage hit her knuckles.

"If I had a lollipop," he said softly, "I'd give it to you for being such a good patient."

Her eyes fluttered open, and she gaped at his handiwork, rudimentary as it was.

"You did it!" she whisper-shouted, grinning now, but he noted the sheen of moisture on her lashes. It had definitely hurt.

"How about we go and get you fixed up for real now, okay?"

She nodded, allowing him to help her into the car.

"And when you're all better, we're going to have a serious discussion about your shoes."

Violet snorted with laughter as he slammed her door, then rounded to the driver's side.

She handed him the keys after he adjusted the seat to fit his much taller build. But before she let them go, she squeezed his palm in hers.

"Thank you, Walker. That's twice now you've come to my rescue. I'm beginning to think you're a bit of a hero."

Heat spread from her hand to his, warming his entire being from the inside out.

He pulled away and started the car.

"I'm anything but, Ms. Chastain. You'll figure that out soon enough."

He headed out of the parking lot and onto the street, mentally kicking himself for talking to her like such a dick—distancing himself with the formality of her last name. She needed comfort, and all he could do was think of himself, of how he'd love to be whatever it was she thought she saw in him. But he knew that was impossible.

Walker Everett sure as hell wasn't any kind of hero, but when it came to Violet Chastain, pretending was what he did best. Maybe—just for today—he could be hers.

Luckily, midafternoon on a Wednesday was not a high traffic time at the ER, and Walker and Violet got right into an examining room.

She sat on the exam table, swinging her legs below her as she investigated her belt bandage.

"I guess this part of my dress is ruined," she said with a small laugh.

Walker was sitting in the chair against the wall, the one meant for the family member or loved one who was there for moral support. He'd spent plenty of time in hospitals as a kid when his mother was sick. But in later years, he was usually the one on the table himself. This was an odd vantage point for him.

The curtain flew open, and in walked a nurse—an older woman with short gray hair, a sturdy build, and a warm maternal smile. That was, until she saw him.

She looked at the chart, brows furrowed. "Walker Everett. Walker. Everett."

"That would be me," he said coolly.

"So you're *not* the patient?" she asked, her eyes meeting his.

Violet cleared her throat and waved her bandaged hand. "Um, no. I'm Violet? The name on the chart. *I'm* the patient." She turned to Walker. "Am I missing something here?"

He stared at the older woman long and hard until it finally clicked. Walker spoke before the nurse could.

"I, uh, broke my nose a couple months ago," he said. "Work injury. Nurse—" He squinted at her ID badge. "Nurse Sheila was on call when I came in to get it looked at."

He thought back to what he must have looked like when Jack brought him in after sleeping it off in a jail cell, his clothes full of blood and eyes so black and blue he was practically unrecognizable. He kept a picture on his phone as a reminder in case he sat down with the whiskey bottle one night and decided *not* to pour it back in. Speaking of his old friend, he was sure he smelled like he'd bathed in that bottle on that night a couple months ago, which he practically had. Walker knew about doctor/patient confidentiality and such but wasn't sure if nurses fell under that jurisdiction. He hoped to hell they did.

"You've healed nicely," Sheila said, scrutinizing his face. Then, seemingly satisfied, she turned her attention to Violet. "So tell me what you're in for today."

Walker let out a stealthy breath of relief.

Violet held up her hand. "I dropped some glass, *fell* on some glass, and cut my hand on some glass. Guess you could say it's a work injury, too." She winced when she glanced at Walker. "First day on the job. I really am the worst, aren't I?"

She forced a laugh, and Walker opened his mouth to say something to reassure her, but wasn't quite sure what the right words were. Jenna—Jenna would be perfect in a situation like this. She knew how to be someone's cheerleader even if they'd done something as silly as tripped over their own shoes—or fallen through a tavern window. But being the kind of person you depended on was out of Walker's realm of experience. Didn't stop him from wanting to figure out how to do it now, for Violet at least.

Sheila put down her clipboard and approached Violet, carefully taking the injured hand in her own. "Let's look at what we're dealing with here, okay? Then I'll get you cleaned up before the doc takes a look and decides whether or not you need sutures."

He started to back out of the room, but Violet worried her bottom lip between her teeth. "Walker, can you—I mean, I've never had stitches before. I know it's silly, but would you stay?"

He stopped and nodded, then slowly made his way to her side. Without really thinking, he took her good hand in his, and their fingers threaded together.

Sheila smiled, then busied herself with unwrapping the wound.

"Ooh, yeah," she said when the injury was visible. "This one's a beauty. Small but deep. A nice clean line, though. Dr. Chloe might even be able to do it with glue. Let me irrigate it and put some gauze on top to start, and we'll have you out of here in no time."

Violet nodded and squeezed his hand tighter. Despite what sounded like good news, all Walker heard was *Dr. Chloe*. She was the same ER doc who fixed up his nephew Owen when he and Jack were both hit by a car. She was also the same doctor who'd set his nose, which meant he was basically surrounded by women who knew the real him, at least enough so that they could let slip who that real him might have been—and possibly still be. He felt the facade he'd built with Violet threaten to crumble, so he simply stood there, gripping her uninjured hand as tight as she gripped his back, while Sheila went to work.

"Knock, knock," someone said from outside the curtain. "Can I come in?"

"All ready for you, Doc," Sheila called over her shoulder, and the curtain opened to reveal a pretty young woman, her straight dark hair pulled into a tight ponytail. The white coat and stethoscope around her neck were the dead giveaway for who she was.

"Hi, Violet. I'm Dr. Chloe."

Violet chuckled. "Don't doctors usually use their last names?"

The woman smiled and nodded. "I'm kind of the go-to for all the minors who come into the ER," she explained. "And they connect better with less formality. After a while I got used to introducing myself that way."

Violet let go of Walker's hand and reached out for an awkward left-handed shake.

"Nice to meet you, Dr. Chloe. I connect better with less formality, too."

The doctor then looked Walker up and down until her eyes widened with recognition.

"Walker Everett?" she said with unmasked incredulity. "You look like you're feeling a lot better these days."

His jaw tightened. "I am, thanks."

She stared at him for another few seconds. "Not too bad for my first nasal fracture," she said. Walker's eyes widened, and the doctor winked. "I'm kidding," she said.

"Been around longer than you think." She turned back to her patient. "Right, now, let's see that hand, Violet."

Nurse Sheila stepped back and made room for the doctor. Chloe lifted the gauze, dabbed the wound to clean away fresh blood, and then grinned.

"Sheila, can you prepare the surgical glue. This will be a quick fix."

Sheila's eyes brightened. "See? What'd I tell ya? If you're going to fall on some glass, do it however you did."

Violet laughed. "Maybe I should carry fragile items in spiked heels more often."

"No!" they all answered in unison, and Walker couldn't help laughing along with everyone else.

Fifteen minutes later Violet was patched up and signing her release papers.

"So, you can get the wound wet, but don't submerge it. The glue is strong, but too much water will eat away at it. And if you're right-handed," Dr. Chloe said, "I'd take it easy tonight and maybe for the next day. The wound will heal pretty quickly, in about a week, but you want to give the glue time to really set, and you don't want to agitate the cut while it's still so fresh. It's tough when the cut is in a place that gets used so often."

"Driving's not a big deal, right?" Violet asked. "I'm headed to Santa Barbara after this."

Dr. Chloe shook her head. "If you can avoid it, I would. Driving is such a subconscious activity that even if you tell yourself you won't use your right hand, the next thing you know you're white-knuckling the steering wheel, slamming on your horn, and shouting your favorite expletives at the jerk in the sports car because he cut you off and almost caused a pile-up." She blew out a breath. "Not that I'm speaking from experience."

Violet let out a nervous laugh. "O…kay. No driving. I guess I could find a place to stay in town tonight."

Walker cleared his throat. "Sheriff's girlfriend runs the B and B. She'll put you up for the night."

Violet shrugged. "Then I guess it's settled. I'm staying in Oak Bluff tonight."

In less than a day Walker had gone from figuring out how to avoid this woman, to holding her hand, to having her stay right next door to Lucinda's Antiques—and the apartment he rented above. He was in over his head, and yet he couldn't help the smile playing at his lips as they headed back out to Violet's tiny car.

"Your chariot awaits," he said, pulling open the passenger-side door.

She grabbed his hand and gave it a firm squeeze. "Thank you, Walker," was all she said.

He threw on the heart-shaped sunglasses and flashed her a rare grin.

"Anything for you, Teach," he said.

And he was beginning to think that might be the truth—that he would do anything for the woman who less than a week ago was a complete stranger.

Anything but admit who he really was.

CHAPTER EIGHT

I'm so happy to meet you!" Olivia Belle, the owner of the Oak Bluff Bed and Breakfast and girlfriend to the town's very own Sheriff Cash Hawkins greeted Violet and Walker in the foyer of the B and B. "Ava told me all about you, said she's so excited to have another woman on the Crossroads Vineyard team."

Violet smiled as Olivia started leading her and Walker up a narrow flight of stairs.

"Ooh, I just thought of something," Olivia said. "We're doing a wine tasting here Friday night. A couple of new vintages from Ava's family's vineyard. Maybe you'd like to join and show me the ropes? I mean, I'm a wine drinker but not a connoisseur. If it goes well, maybe we make it a regular thing? Business has been growing, so there's room in the budget..."

Violet's head was swimming and her hand throbbing. Right now all she wanted to do was collapse onto a bed and rest.

"Shoot," Olivia said. "I'm coming at ya too fast and too strong, aren't I? It's just that it's not every day you meet someone who fits in perfectly to your whole business plan, you know?" She winced. "And there I go again. I'll shut up now."

Violet laughed. She could use all the income she could get. But she needed to decompress after the disaster that was today. "That would actually be amazing," she said. "I could use the extra work. But is it okay if I hang in the room for a bit and get my bearings first? Then I'd love to talk more about it."

Olivia beamed. "Of course! And if you're really looking for some spare change, I've got connections. How are you with dogs?"

Walker rolled his eyes. "She's not walkin' the sheriff's dog, Olivia."

"Why not?" Violet shot back. "I love dogs." She'd never owned one, but how hard could it be?

Olivia raised a brow at Walker, then turned her attention back to Violet. "She's a great dog, and she usually rides along with Cash—the sheriff—but he's been talking about getting someone to take care of her when he's on duty for forty-eight hours or more at a stretch. I'll tell him you're interested." Then she opened the door in front of where they'd been standing to reveal rich hardwood floors, a small fireplace, soothing periwinkle blue walls, and a plush queen-size bed. In other words—complete and utter heaven.

Olivia's brown curls bounced against her shoulders as she clapped her hands together. "Do you like it? I've been doing a little bit of redecorating. No charge for the room tonight, by the way, and any night you stay and help with the wine stuff. Consider it part of your benefit package."

"I *love* this room," Violet said. "I doubt I'll be able to say no to a 'benefit package' like that."

Olivia grinned even wider. "I'll take that as an almost *yes*," she sing-songed. Then she squeezed Walker's shoulder. "You take good care of her." She winked at him and slipped out the door before Walker could say anything in protest.

Violet's cheeks heated. He'd already done so much for her, and she didn't mean only today. She was sure all he wanted was to get the hell back to his life—the one she seemed to keep interrupting.

"I'm fine. Really. You've taken care of me plenty already," she said, surveying the room and trying to sound breezy. "I'm sure you've got enough to do now that I've monopolized your whole day. *Again.*" She shrugged. "At least no surprise dinner party, right? Thank you, though, Walker. You were really great today. You could have *I told you so*'d me so hard, and I would have deserved it. Also . . . I'll pay for the glasses I broke."

Walker shook his head. "Dorothy texted while we were at the ER. She's replacing the glasses at no charge. I think she's worried you might take legal action or something since it happened on her property."

Violet plopped down on the foot of the bed and huffed out a laugh. "The only entity worthy of legal action are my shoes," she said, kicking a foot out in front of her.

"What is it with you and shoes, anyway?" Walker asked.

She shrugged. "I don't know. I guess it's my one thing I have just for me. A killer pair of shoes by a French designer—even if I have to scour every resale shop to find them—makes me feel like I have some semblance of control in my life. They make me feel like myself. It's silly." She sighed. "Doesn't matter. From here on out, I solemnly swear to dress my feet for the job."

Walker's brow furrowed. "You're not you without the shoes?"

She shook her head. "It's not like that. Or maybe it is. These are Louboutins, you know. Got them for twenty bucks!"

"Looboo *who*?" Walker asked, and Violet laughed.

"I've never said this out loud, so it's probably going to sound ridiculous, but my only connection to my French heritage are the shoes. I only speak French at home and only with Maman. But the shoes are with me all the time. And even if no one else knows, I do." She rolled her eyes. "See? It sounds ridiculous."

Walker shook his head. "I don't think that at all. Some of us need reminders of who we are—or who we used to be. It's not my place to judge what works for you. Until, of course, it causes you bodily harm. Then you get my two cents whether you want it or not."

He gave her a crooked grin, and her stomach did a flip-flop in return.

This man was getting to her in ways he shouldn't, making her want things from him she couldn't.

"You know what's way better than an identity crisis?" she asked, desperate to change the subject.

"What's that?"

Her eyes traveled into the open door of the bathroom. "That." She pointed toward the claw-foot tub. "I want to get out of these clothes and forget about real life for a while. Have you ever seen anything so gorgeous?"

Walker's gaze followed hers. He raised his brows. "Except the doc said not to submerge your hand in water. Think you can handle that?"

Violet pouted. "Right. Forgot about that part. But I mean, I can take a bath without getting one appendage too wet, right? As long as I don't do anything stupid like trip and fall face-first into the tub, thereby submerging *all* of me..." She grimaced. "I guess the day's track record doesn't speak volumes in favor of me not doing something like that, huh?" She stared longingly at the tub. "Some other time, I guess. Maybe if I do that wine tasting thing and stay the night again, the same room will be vacant. A girl can dream, right?"

She went to work unzipping her booties, which was easier said than done with one hand.

"Here," he said, kneeling at her feet. He wrapped a hand around her ankle, and lordy this man was a walking contradiction—hands rough and calloused yet his touch achingly gentle. He glanced up at her, his blue eyes meeting hers for one quiet moment. She skimmed her teeth over her bottom lip, and he dipped his head, removing one shoe and then the other, his hand cradling her ankle for several seconds even after the second booty had hit the floor. Maybe he wanted what he shouldn't, too. Would it be so bad if he did?

Violet swallowed as all her senses recalled the last time he'd had her ankle in his hand, how his fingers traveled the length of her leg and then slipped beneath her skirt.

She squirmed on the edge of the bed as heat coiled in her belly. This whole not being attracted to a man she worked with—or worked *for* in this case—was not going entirely as planned.

"Take it easy tonight," he said softly. "And while I'm *not* saying 'I told you so'"—he offered her a crooked grin—"I'm not gonna argue about that whole dressing your feet for the job promise, especially when you're on our little corner of the map."

She pressed her lips into a smile. "Noted."

He rested her heel on his thigh, then ran his palm up the back of her calf. His jaw tightened.

"Sorry," he said, glancing up at her. "I shouldn't have done that."

She shook her head. "Probably not. But what does it mean if I'm happy you did?"

"Means we got ourselves a situation," he said.

His eyes—those ridiculous, gorgeous blue eyes—were a steely, unreadable mask. The only hint she had that he was fighting as much of an inner battle as she was, was the fact that his hand hadn't moved.

"Right. A situation," she repeated. "Because I can't date someone I work for. Self-imposed rule seeing as how that worked out so well for me last time."

"And I can't date anyone right now. Another rule, I guess. Doesn't stop me from wanting—things."

His fingers kneaded her calf, and her mouth went dry.

"I hate that I'm such a rule follower," she said.

His mouth twitched into a grin, and hallelujah she was breaking through that veneer of his, even if they were treading a dangerous line.

"I've actually never been too good at rules," he said. "Broken a lot more than I've followed. That's for damn sure."

She nodded, then swallowed hard over the knot in her throat. Was that an invitation? Because it sure as hell felt like one. Maybe she wanted to break the rules, too. She placed her hand over his and slid it up her thigh, his fingers slipping under the hem of her skirt. They were rough on her skin, but they were warm. Strong. And she remembered too well what they were capable of.

"Looks like a pretty roomy tub. Maybe you could help me keep from getting my hand too wet." She couldn't say much for what was happening between her legs, though. It was more than physical with this stranger of a man. In the five days she'd known him, he'd been there for her in ways no other man had ever been, and she wanted more of that—craved it with every fiber of her being—while at the same time she knew getting involved with another employer was so not what she should be doing. Walker wasn't Ramon. He might not be a complete open book, but he wasn't hiding some secret family. What were the odds of him having a skeleton in his closet to match that? Besides, they weren't technically on the clock now.

His fingers twitched against her skin, and she sucked in a breath. But he slid her foot off his knee and stood. "I'll run the water and wait until you get in. Make sure there are no mishaps and all that. I should go then before either of us does something we'll regret."

And then he was gone, the water running, and her heart beating a rhythm she didn't quite recognize.

She flopped onto her back, silently chastising herself for pushing him too far. She'd asked him to bathe with her. Had she read the signals wrong? Rules or no rules, she swore he was flirting with her as much as she was with him.

She squeezed her eyes shut as logic pushed its way back into her thoughts.

Oh God. She'd just asked her *boss* to bathe with her.

"Nope, nope, nope, nope, nope," she chanted to herself.

"What was that?" his deep voice sounded from the open doorway of the bathroom. Her eyes opened wide, and she propped herself up on her elbows to see him standing there, her cowboy in shining armor, holding a luxurious white terry cloth robe over his forearm.

"For when you get out," he said matter-of-factly. "But—don't run off with it." He showed her the price tag hanging from the cuff of the sleeve. "Or you can kiss that complimentary stay good-bye."

What if she kissed *him* good-bye?

Violet! she silently yelled at herself. *Rules!*

He offered her the garment, and she stood and took it, dropping it on the foot of the bed.

"Can you…um…turn around a second?" she asked.

He answered by pivoting his body away from her.

She let out a breath and then unbuttoned her dress, removing it and her undergarments in a matter of seconds. Then she shrugged the robe over her shoulders, her eyes falling shut as she let out a soft sigh.

"Oh God. This feels amazing." She hummed with pleasure. "You can turn back around now."

Walker faced her again, his face once more unreadable. He was good at that, she realized—putting the mask back on.

"You need a minute or two alone with the robe before you hit the tub?"

She backhanded him softly on the shoulder, thankful for the joke to break the building tension. "It's an amazing robe. You should try one sometime."

"I'll add it to my bucket list." He nodded toward the bathroom. "I'll stay out here until you give me the all clear that you didn't take a dive or anything like that."

Her smile fell. She knew she was treading on thin ice already, but she couldn't keep the words from coming out of her mouth.

"So you're really leaving, huh?" Actually, she virtually applauded herself. What she'd wanted to say was, *Stay. Stay. Stay. Stay. God, please stay. Take off all your clothes, climb into that tub with me, and stay.* So by comparison, she'd done pretty damn well if she did say so herself.

He nodded once. "You know and I know that's the best course of action here."

"You're right," she said. "Of course you're right. Although, if you really want to get technical about it, I work for your brother. Jack's the one who hired me. And he did say something about being the managing partner of the whole Crossroads operation..."

Walker shook his head and laughed. "Of course he did."

"So we're just going to be friends. Colleagues and friends."

She held out a hand for him to shake. He stood there for a few seconds, then finally took her hand.

He let her hand go and took a step back.

"Any other place, at any other time, Teach, and I'd have broken every goddamn rule for you."

She shrugged the robe off and let it fall to the floor. His eyes widened as he took in her naked form, the only indication that she'd gotten to him at all. "I'd break 'em for you, too. Here's to better timing someday." Then she sauntered into the bathroom, turned off the running water, and lowered herself into the tub. A few seconds later she heard the door to room four snick shut.

She let her head fall back against the lip of the tub and let out a soft groan.

"Rules," she grumbled. "Stupid, stupid, rules."

Violet still had one good hand she was allowed to submerge in water. Thanks to Walker Everett, she needed it.

CHAPTER NINE

Walker stood in the hall for several long minutes while he and his erection had a silent argument. His brain tried to reason with his body offering logic like *She's on the rebound,* and *Employer/employee situations always get messy.* He even went so far as to bring his own sobriety into the fray with the reminder that *New relationships only add new stress to an already difficult recovery.* But all his dick had to say was *A beautiful naked woman asked you to bathe with her, and you said no. IDIOT.*

He was screwed either way. His body was simply hoping for the literal interpretation, but he wasn't allowing it.

He wasn't lying when he'd said he wanted her. He didn't remember ever feeling this sharply aware of his desire, nor could he recall said desire ever being this strong. It only took him another second to understand why.

He'd never been with a woman stone cold sober. Touching Violet like he did the other night—hell just taking off her damned shoe today—he'd never felt anything like it. He'd never *felt.* Not like this.

He'd had his regulars in the past ten years—an old high school girlfriend who texted him late at night for a house call every now and then; Becca, the girl who worked the checkout line at the local grocer. They dated, if you could even call it that. It was usually pizza, beer, and sex. Then there were the occasional tourists who found themselves at the tavern looking for some local fun, and Walker was always happy to provide it.

He hadn't been a dick—at least he hadn't meant to be. But the women who'd chosen to enter his orbit in the past understood what they were getting into, and if they didn't, they learned quick enough that Walker Everett wasn't anyone's project. No one was going to fix him if he didn't want to fix himself.

He wasn't always on a bender like the night everything quite literally came crashing down. But even the days he was sober, he was really only sober enough. There was always that fuzzy numbness that kept him from the one thing he'd avoided since he was fifteen—the ability to feel. He already knew he wanted Violet in the most primal, physical way. What the hell would it mean if he started wanting more? He was in no position to deal with that right now, nor would he put that burden on her. He'd have to keep his dick in his pants and his mind on something bigger—the decision on which he'd been teetering since he got the offer.

Living in the town where his mother passed away and his father turned into an unrecognizable stranger was hard enough. Living here sober was even harder. Working the vineyard with Violet Chastain nearby and wanting what he was in no position to want? It would be damn near impossible.

The goal was clear now. He had to get away so he could figure shit out without his past *or* present getting in the way.

He pulled his phone out of his pocket and fired off a quick text to Sam Callahan.

I'm in. Just need to make it to the wedding and then ready to get the hell out of here.

Sam's response came only seconds later.

Glad to have you on board. Details to come.

So it was settled. Walker was heading north to build a ranch. He would do what his brother asked of him—try to stay sober and get his life together. He just wasn't going to do it here.

On his way down the stairs, he heard some kind of commotion going on in the common room, which hopefully meant the foyer would be clear.

But he should have known better than to hope, especially with how swimmingly the day had gone so far.

"Well, well, well. Look who's taking care of our poor, injured, new employee."

Walker rolled his eyes at his middle brother, Luke, who stood at the base of the stairs with his arms crossed and a shit-eating grin on his face.

"What's with the clothes?" Walker asked his brother, nodding at Luke's plaid button-down and clean jeans. As far as Luke Everett's daily attire went, this was practically formalwear. "Got a wedding or something?"

Luke raised a brow. "Nice diversion, little brother. Lily and Olivia met with the Callahans today to talk about starting the restaurant addition. Lily decided since she was already here and Olivia had a giant kitchen full of food that she'd turn it into a dinner party."

Lily was the love of Luke's life *and* Luke's best friend's ex-wife. Yeah, that was a huge mess until it wasn't. She was also a chef who was opening her own restaurant in conjunction with Olivia's redesign of the B and B. Once that happened, business at the B and B was sure to double. Walker was handy enough in the kitchen, but Lily Green was a chef to be reckoned with.

"Jack and Ava are on their way," Luke continued. "They're waiting for Ava's parents to come hang with Owen. Texted you, but I'm not surprised you didn't respond. You know you're always welcome to be our"—Luke exaggerated having to count out all the couples—"seventh wheel," he said with a chuckle.

"I'm good," Walker said, brushing past him. He'd already done the check-in thing with Jenna this morning. The last thing he wanted was to end his day the same way, with the third degree on his life, his reclusiveness, or whatever from his brothers, the sheriff, *and* their significant others. Couldn't a man have a Wednesday night to himself to just be?

"You avoiding us because you want to prove you can go it alone, or are you avoiding us because you're drinking again?" Luke asked quietly, and Walker froze midstep, then pivoted to face his brother.

"You wanna grab the sheriff and give me a Breathalyzer? Happy to oblige," he said bitterly. Yet he couldn't blame his brother for suspecting. Walker didn't even trust himself to make this stick, but he was trying. When Jack had asked him to get sober, something shifted for Walker. He'd never be able to repay his oldest brother for the sacrifices he made to keep him and Luke safe from Jack Senior, and that was a burden Walker would carry for the rest of his days. The least he could do was try for him and hope that it would get easier, that one day he'd try for himself. That day hadn't yet come, though.

“I want to trust you, Walker. But you make it so hard when you shut everyone out.” Luke clapped his younger brother on the shoulder. “Just stay for dinner,” he said. “You’ve been avoiding us since you got home. I swear it’s only a meal and not any sort of inquisition. And whatever’s going on with Violet Chastain—”

“She’s none of your damned business,” Walker said, his voice low and controlled even though the further Luke pushed, the more he felt like this *was* an inquisition. The truth was, even though Walker had made sure that nothing further would happen between the two of them, he didn’t owe his brothers any sort of explanation.

“But she *is* my business,” Luke said. “Yours and Jack’s, too. She works for the family, and the two days she’s been affiliated with Crossroads Vineyard, she’s been with you for what looks like *more* than your average, day-to-day business dealings. While I know she’s a grown-up and can make her own decisions…”

He trailed off. Every muscle in Walker’s body tensed because he knew the part Luke didn’t want to say.

“I’m the drunk who couldn’t possibly have his shit together after only two months of being dry.”

“That’s not what I said.” Luke scrubbed a hand across his jaw. “Does she know?”

“Wasn’t exactly part of the interview,” Walker said.

“Shit,” Luke said under his breath. “Come have dinner,” he said. “Let Jack, me, and the sheriff see that you’re doing okay, and I’ll get off your back about this. I want to believe you’ve got the hang of sobriety. I really do. But you could have killed yourself that night at Nora’s. You don’t know what it was like for Jack to get that call from Cash—or for me to get the call from Jack. Jenna burst into tears when I told her, and then I had to talk her out of driving an hour to Oak Bluff in the middle of the night just so she could see you and know you were okay."

"Thank you," Walker said softly. "For not letting Jenna see me like that."

He hadn't even thought about what it must have been like for his brothers or his aunt to get that call. God, he'd been a selfish prick. He still was.

"Old habits die hard," he mumbled. His brother raised a questioning brow. "I'm doing the best I can," he said more clearly.

Luke nodded. "All I'm asking is for you to check in with us every now and then so I don't have to act like an overprotective parent."

Overprotective parent. Wasn't that a load of horseshit? The only way their father had tried to protect Walker after he and his brothers had already been removed from his custody was sending him a bottle of J.D. on his fifteenth birthday. Walker had downed the whole flask. Didn't matter that it made him sick only a couple hours later. The gift had done the trick. Like father, like son.

Walker scratched the back of his neck. "You know, you sound an awful lot like Jack lately."

Luke winced.

"What the hell's wrong with sounding like me?" Jack rounded the corner that separated the foyer from the kitchen. He popped some sort of flaky appetizer into his mouth.

"You're the oldest," Luke said, "and a father and a lawyer and basically the grown-up of the three of us. Saying I sound like you is as good as calling me Grandpa."

Jack swallowed. "Your girl sure as hell can cook, but *you're* an asshole."

Walker laughed at that, partly because he did miss this sort of interaction with his brothers but also because the attention was no longer on him.

"What are your dinner plans?" Jack asked.

Walker still hadn't given Luke a yes or a no, and he apparently didn't answer fast enough for his oldest brother.

"Looks like you're free. Come sit down." Jack led the other two brothers into the common room where a long wooden table was set for what looked like a feast. "Lily made a pot roast and these amazing pastry things with some kind of fancy cheese inside. No idea what they're called, but I think I already ate seven of them." He patted his stomach.

"It's called brie," Luke said. "Some fancy French cheese. But Jack's right. It's pretty damned delicious."

"I love brie." The woman's voice came from behind. All three men turned to find Violet Chastain standing in the open doorway of the kitchen. The ends of her hair were damp from the bath she'd taken alone. Walker's dick twitched at the reminder of the offer he'd rejected. She wasn't wearing her dress and her fancy shoes. Instead she wore a white, long-sleeved T-shirt that showed off her curves and a pair of hip-hugging jeans. On her feet? A pair of Chuck Taylors.

She smiled at the three men, giving Walker himself no more than a cursory glance. He supposed he deserved that. "Olivia realized I was here without a change of clothes. Ava contributed the shoes."

Walker's brows furrowed. "And she teleported these items to you?" Because hadn't he been in that room only fifteen or so minutes ago?

Violet raised her brows. "Looks like you don't know your Oak Bluff architecture very well. There's another stairwell that comes down to the kitchen. I was going to take a nap, but when Olivia mentioned food, I realized I hadn't eaten since breakfast. I'm so hungry I could eat a whole pot roast." She laughed. "I promise I won't, though."

Walker knew it was only a change of clothing, but seeing her like that—dressed down and relaxed—it was almost like she belonged in their little town. Oak Bluff looked real good on her, whereas when it came to him it didn't seem to fit anymore.

Luke stepped toward her, holding out his right hand. "Luke Everett," he said. "We haven't met yet."

She extended her bandaged palm. "Violet Chastain."

Luke hesitated.

"Oh, it's okay," she said. "It doesn't hurt. I'm all glued up and will be good as new by this time next week."

Luke shook her hand, but Walker could tell he was being careful.

"Nice to meet you, Violet. We're glad you're still on board to help prep for the wedding and winery launch after what happened today."

"You mean my silly accident?" Violet asked. "Because I'm just happy you haven't fired me yet." She gave him a nervous smile.

"No. I meant spending the day with Walker. That's enough to send any sane human being running for the hills." Luke laughed. "And fire you? Hell no. I'm guessing there aren't many sommeliers who'd put up with three ranchers who don't know a lick about wine."

Her cheeks flamed at the mention of Walker, but then she was laughing, too. "For someone who doesn't know about wine, you pronounced sommelier correctly. That's impressive."

Walker's jaw tightened…not because his brother was showing him up, but because he knew that comment was meant for him even though Violet continued to avoid his gaze.

"Well then maybe I'm not so clueless after all," Luke said with a self-satisfied grin. She was charming the hell out of him, not that Walker was surprised.

"Olivia invited me to dinner," Violet said. "But I didn't realize it was *everyone* down here. Feels kind of like the first day of middle school."

Luke looked her up and down appraisingly. "You're too tall to stuff in a locker."

Jack nudged Luke's shoulder with his own. "Maybe one of the athletic ones like I used for baseball. Had enough room for all my gear. What do you think?"

Walker rolled his eyes. "All right already," he said. "Enough hazing the new kid."

But he knew his brothers' teasing meant they liked Violet right off the bat. It also meant if he messed up with her, they'd likely kick *him* to the curb before they would her. All the more reason to stick to the rules, even if that wasn't his strong suit. The only problem? What was best and what he wanted were far from the same thing. That seemed to be a repeating pattern for him.

"Are you staying for dinner, too?" she asked, looking directly at Walker.

Two minutes ago he had one foot out the door. But he rationalized caving to his brothers by telling himself that he needed to figure out how to be around Violet and not want her. Plus the thought of her alone with his brothers, the sheriff, *and* their three female counterparts was enough for him to reconsider.

"It would be cruel of me to leave you alone with this bunch," he said. "Next thing you know Olivia will have you working here full-time, Lily will somehow convince you to be *her* sommelier or whatever the hell the word is, and Crossroads Vineyard will be shit out of luck."

He pronounced the *r* on sommelier on purpose. Last thing he needed was the whole lot of them knowing he was taking a liking not only to Violet but to her second language as well.

Jack slapped him on the back. "Well then, little brother. Looks like it's a family dinner after all."

There were no wineglasses on the dining table, only tumblers. Walker knew that was for him, that even before he'd said yes his brothers had counted on him staying, and wondered if anyone would say so. One of the reasons he'd been keeping his distance from his brothers was because it also meant steering clear of sobriety talk. Since Luke had already broken that seal, he crossed his fingers the subject wouldn't come up again tonight.

In the center of the table, along with the roast, a bowl of redskin mashed potatoes, and another of sautéed asparagus, there were two glass pitchers—one of fruit-infused water and one of iced tea.

"So this is your family, huh?" Violet asked quietly as Jack kissed Ava on the cheek and then started filling glasses while Lily put Luke to work cutting the roast. Olivia was doing something in the kitchen and Sheriff Cash Hawkins was playing backseat driver to Luke's carving of the meat.

"Against the grain, Everett. You have done this before, right?" Cash asked.

Luke elbowed the sheriff in the arm with his next carve, and Walker chuckled.

"Yep," he said as they stood in front of the long wooden table. "Family and then some."

"Sorry I'm late, y'all!" a woman called from outside the room. Walker would recognize that voice anywhere. "But traffic was a doozy. I knew I should have listened to Lucy and left earlier, but it looks like I haven't missed anything yet."

"Lucy predicts traffic now?" Luke asked with a teasing tone.

Jenna swatted him on the shoulder. "Hush, you. Lucy was right about you and Lily. She can be right about traffic, too."

But when she came into view, Jenna wasn't alone. Trailing behind her was a tall man with broad shoulders, his cheeks reddened either from a day in the sun or because he was here to tear Walker a new one for letting his daughter get hurt her first day on the job.

"Shit," Violet hissed under her breath.

"Did you invite him here?" Walker asked.

"No," she insisted. "I let them know not to expect me back in Santa Barbara tonight and that I was staying at the Oak Bluff Bed and Breakfast. I have no idea what he's doing here, and also—this is probably the worst time to tell you this—but I haven't exactly told my parents about our breakup yet."

Walker's teeth clenched as Jenna led Gabriel Chastain toward the bed-and-breakfast's dining room.

"Dad!" Violet said, running out to the foyer to cut him off at the pass. "What are you doing here?"

Jenna bounded into the room greeting everyone with hugs and kisses, diverting everyone's attention from Violet leaving the room. Well, if Violet was running interference, he'd better prep the team. And fast.

"Jenna," he whisper-shouted, and his aunt finally made her way to him.

"Aw. Is my nephew jealous I said hello to everyone else before him?"

He waved her off. "I need your help. And fast. You can give me all your *I told you so*'s later, but right now I need you to play along and make sure everyone else does, too."

She narrowed her eyes at him. "Walker Everett, what are you up to?"

He blew out a breath. "Violet's parents think we're dating." His aunt's eyes widened. "We're *not*. But for tonight I need everyone here to act like we are, and I'm putting you in charge of making sure everyone plays along."

He'd barely gotten the last word out before Violet and her father appeared in the dining room's open entry.

"Jenna…?" Walker said under his breath.

"I'm on it," she whispered. "But you owe me, and I always collect my debts."

He was sure she would, but right now he relied on her making her way around the room once more to subtly spread the word.

Violet smiled nervously at her onlookers—Walker's entire family and their friends.

"Hey, everyone. Um, so, this is my dad, Gabriel Chastain. He was a little concerned about my accident." She waved her bandaged hand. "And the fact that I wasn't able to make it home, so—overprotective guy that he is—he came to check on me."

Her tone was teasing, but Walker sensed the nerves beneath the surface.

"Good to see you, Gabe," Walker said as he held out a hand.

Violet's father shook it, his grip firm and his expression cautious. Walker could hear whispers floating about the room, and he hoped to hell it was Jenna doing her part.

"I meet you for the first time less than a week ago, and the next time my daughter sees you she's in the ER and isn't coming home for the night. We may need to rethink that whole first-name basis situation."

"Papa!" Violet scolded. "It was *my* shoe. It was *my* fault. *My* first day on the job that I royally screwed up."

A throat cleared, and Walker turned to see Jack rounding the edge of the long table.

"Mr. Chastain, I'm Jack Everett, the one responsible for hiring your daughter. I'm a father myself, so I understand your concern, but I can assure you that she's in good company in Oak Bluff with my brother and with the Crossroads family." He brandished that annoying lawyer smile Walker often wanted to wipe off his oldest brother's face, but for once he was happy it existed.

Gabriel Chastain's expression softened, but he wasn't smiling yet.

"Luke Everett," the middle brother said, waving his carving gear. "Normally I'd shake, but..."

"Sheriff Hawkins." Cash reached a hand across the table since he was only backseat carving.

"I'm Jenna!" Walker's aunt waved. "Aunt to the Everett clan. And this is Ava, Lily, and Olivia." She nodded toward each as she said their names. "Because goodness knows these boys need a few good women to keep them in line."

Finally Gabriel smiled, which wasn't surprising. It was damn near impossible not to when Jenna was around.

"Stay for dinner?" Olivia said, raising a brow at the spread before them. "We've got plenty."

Violet's father closed his eyes and inhaled. "Who's the chef?" he asked, searching the faces surrounding the table.

Lily Green—in a T-shirt that said I DON'T ALWAYS

BAKE . . . OH WAIT. YES I DO—raised her head proudly. "That would be me."

Gabriel Chastain grinned. "You did a coffee rub on that roast, yes? One of my favorites."

Lily beamed. "Yes! Your olfactory senses are well trained. I hear you're a chef, too."

"Ol-*what*?" Luke asked, and a ripple of laughter spread throughout the room, easing the tension once and for all.

Violet's father turned to face her. "I guess I overreacted."

She crossed her arms. "You know I don't live at home because I have to. It's for Ma—"

"I know," he said, sounding sheepish even with the low timbre of his voice.

"So if I make the decision not to come home, even after a very small, insignificant emergency situation, you can trust me, yes?"

He kissed her forehead. "Sometimes I wonder who the parent is, me or you."

The room was silent, and Walker felt like he was intruding on something he didn't deserve to be privy to. Violet wasn't really his anything, yet here she was, practically airing her family's dirty laundry in front of a room full of strangers, and she didn't seem to care. Walker envied that.

"How about that dinner invitation?" Jack asked, reiterating Olivia's offer, but Gabriel shook his head.

"Thank you," he said. "I have to get back to my own restaurant. But I'd love to come and check out your menu once you're up and running."

Lily bounced on her toes.

Violet gasped. "You drove ninety minutes to check on me and then turn around and leave?"

"Ninety-four," Walker said under his breath.

"Maman is having a very good night," Violet's father said to her. "She's working the hostess stand, doesn't even know I'm gone." He studied Violet's injured hand, flipping it over to see the bandaged palm. "I guess I'm trained to always think the worst. I'm sorry to have interrupted your evening." He directed the last part to the whole room.

Violet slid an arm around Walker's waist. "I'm in good hands, Papa. Promise."

Walker swallowed. All eyes were on him, everyone in the room knowing he and Violet were a lie—everyone but Gabriel Chastain. He knew he should say something, but he couldn't find the right words.

"Come back to Oak Bluff any time," Jack said. "We'd love to have you."

The older man nodded. "I'd love to get a tour of the vineyard, taste the grapes maybe, and get an idea of what your first vintage will yield. I'm always in the market for new local labels to add to my wine list."

Jack busted out the lawyerly grin once more, and the two men shook hands. "You got yourself a deal," he said.

Finally, Gabriel's eyes found Walker's. "My apologies for misjudging," he said, reaching for Walker's outstretched hand. "But now that she's going to be spending more time with you and working with you—still not sure how I feel about you two doing both—we ought to get to know each other a little better. Don't you think?"

"*I* think I'll walk you out, Papa," Violet said as she let go of Walker. "Last time I checked, I invited *you* to spend time with the men I dated and not the other way around." And as quick as their family dinner had turned into a charade, Gabriel Chastain was gone.

Seven pairs of eyes stared Walker down, but no one said

a word. So he decided he'd be the one to break the tension that was thick as molasses.

"I'm starved," he said. "Let's eat already."

He sat down, and slowly everyone followed suit—except for Cash and Luke, who were still cutting the meat. When Violet appeared in the doorway again, both Walker and Jack stood, but she waved them off and climbed into the seat next to Walker.

"You all are either the best damned folks to work for, or you're gonna fire me right now. Lord knows I wouldn't blame you. But I'd really like to get some of that roast first, if that's okay."

"Aw, Violet honey. We like you just fine, don't we?" Jenna didn't give Jack or Walker a chance to chime in. "But I want the story from you, nephew number three. You were awfully quiet throughout that whole exchange."

Walker painted on a smile. "Is that number three my birth order or my rank in who you like best?" he teased, but he knew he wasn't getting out of this.

She narrowed her gaze at him. "Please. Everyone knows Owen is my favorite."

"I got Walker and me into this situation," Violet said. "So it's only fitting I set the record straight." She waved at everyone around the table. "First, now that I know who you all are, hi. I'm Violet, and it looks like I go full throttle when I step in *une tarte aux vaches*."

"Oon-tarta-huh?" Luke said. "Can we go back to speaking English for the duration of the meal?"

Violet laughed. "Cow pie. Literally stepped in one earlier with Ava, then fell and broke the glasses. Now I'm asking you all to pretend like me and Walker are a thing. I do not know how you pulled that off, by the way, but bravo."

"You're welcome," Jenna said with a grin.

"So you and my brother are *not* dating," Jack said. It was a statement, not a question.

"We are *not*," Violet said. "But the other night when Walker drove me home, my mother just assumed, and she was so happy that neither of us had the heart to tell her she was wrong."

Luke pointed the carving knife at her from across the table. "Why not tell them the truth?"

"Why not point your knife somewhere else," Walker snapped.

Violet squeezed his shoulder. "It's okay. I owe you all the truth."

So she told them the whole story—minus the kiss the morning they met—right up until the part where she hadn't told her parents that she and Walker had broken up.

"You probably will fire me after this part," she continued, her gaze falling on Jack. "But if everything works out how I want it to, I'll be heading to France sometime this summer where my mother will hopefully receive experimental treatment that we were really hoping she could do here in the U.S. I swear this wasn't my plan when I applied for the job. I found out over the weekend that her local neurologist is unable to provide the treatment, and being a French citizen, she still has access to health care over there, and if this doctor in France is on the same time line that my mother's U.S. doctor would have been on—I'm rambling."

Something sank like a stone in the pit of Walker's stomach.

"You knew this all day and said nothing?" he asked.

She shook her head. "There's a lot of red tape to go through. Plus I have to convince my mother to agree to all this since it means burying the hatchet with the estranged sister she hasn't spoken to since before I was born, but that's beside the point. Nothing is set in stone, and this isn't how I wanted to tell you all—especially after my stellar first day on the job. But the truth is that I need the money. And you all seem like pretty fantastic people to work for. So if you'll keep me on for as long as I'm here, I'll help find a great replacement." She smiled nervously and looked at Olivia. "I can help with wine tastings until then, too." She turned her attention to Cash. "And I hear you have a dog who needs walking. Basically, anything I can put in the bank between now and then will be a huge help, and I know you all just met me and that I'm asking well beyond what I have the right to ask—"

"Winery job is yours for as long as you're here," Walker said. He stared his oldest brother down, hoping Jack knew that if he protested, Walker would fight him on it.

Jack said nothing, but there'd be words one way or another when the two were alone, and he figured it had nothing to do with Violet's temporary employment.

Olivia brushed a tear from under her eye. "Wow," she said. "Just—wow. You all love each other so much. I get so caught up in how much my parents can't stand each other that I sometimes forget how lucky I am that they're both still around. And healthy." She sniffled. "Friday night wine tastings are all yours for as long as you're here. Cash, tell her she can walk Dixie for you and that you'll pay her really well."

Cash cleared his throat. "Guess you'll be walking Dixie. And I'll pay you really well."

Ava laughed, but Jack's eyes were still fixed on Walker, his expression unyielding.

"But you two aren't really dating, right? Because that would be a conflict of more than one interest, little brother."

Walker's jaw tightened. He knew Jack cared little for the workplace conflict of interest.

"Nothing more than a show for the old man," Walker said coolly, then held his plate toward Luke and Cash. "Now let's eat."

After a tense silence when no one protested, Luke finally doled out the beef, then laughed when he saw how much he had left. "Lily always makes too much food. But it's so damn good it doesn't matter."

"Dibs on leftover meat," Cash said.

Jack chuckled, finally breaking his stoic mask. "Hawkins, when in the hell has there ever been leftover meat at a meal you've attended?"

Olivia rounded the table with a bucket of ice, filling everyone's tumblers. "Yeah, I have never seen that man leave a morsel of food behind." She set the ice on the table and approached the sheriff, pressing one palm to his chest and ruffling his dark hair with her other. "What can I say? My hardworking lawman's got an appetite."

Cash dipped his head and whispered something in Olivia's ear that made her blush.

Walker was surrounded by so much happiness it was almost off-putting, especially after everything that had already gone down. If it had been anyone other than his aunt, his brothers, or their friends, he would have taken one look at the scene before him and run for the hills. In fact, he'd intended to do exactly that after leaving a very naked Violet upstairs. But the whole evening had been—bearable. Maybe even a notch above that, possibly something resembling good.

He was ready for some space, though, but right now he was trapped with the woman he wanted desperately not to want amidst a room full of couples who were openly wanting one another with zero regard for his struggle.

Assholes.

"I should have said something about leaving," Violet said when the table chatter gave them the illusion of privacy. "I mean, I should have said something to you first."

Walker shook his head. "Look," he said. "About—"

"Rejecting me while I was naked and vulnerable?" she interrupted. Her tone was teasing, but Walker didn't miss the bite. It didn't matter that he'd made the right decision. He'd bruised her ego in the process. The alternative was admitting how much he hadn't wanted to leave. But if there was ever a wrong guy at the wrong time, he was that guy.

"I was out of line," she continued. "You made the tough decision for both of us—the right decision—and I shouldn't fault you for that. It was simply the adrenaline rush of the day, you know? I needed rescuing again. You did the rescuing. I found it sort of hot. But I'm over it. Ready to move on."

He flipped one of his forks over again and again on the cloth napkin. "Glad you can see it from my perspective," he lied. For him, wanting her had nothing to do with adrenaline, but he was getting good at this acting thing, masking the sting with an assuring smile. But it was more than a bruised ego he was hiding. The last time he'd seen her before dinner, she was wearing nothing but a robe pooled at her feet. Moving on for him would happen sometime after he forgot what she looked like naked. He figured that would take anywhere from one to five years.

He let out a quiet chuckle under his breath.

"Anyway, I guess this is payback," Violet added as she unfolded her napkin and set it on her lap.

"You mean this is the same as you dragging me to your parents' anniversary party and asking me to pretend to be your boyfriend? Because I don't see much dragging. Or pretending."

This got her to laugh. "No. I've definitely not been dragged here. Maybe stranded due to extreme clumsiness, but not dragged. Though my father did show up like I was a teenager who missed curfew, so I get a few points for humiliation in front of a roomful of strangers."

Walker raised a brow. "I suppose I'll give you that."

She leaned closer and whispered in his ear. "And the bath—though short-lived thanks to Olivia's knock on the door—was fantastic. Thanks for making sure I got in safely."

Along with not being able to forget what the woman next to him looked like with her robe on the floor, for the rest of the evening he'd be picturing Violet Chastain, naked and alone in the Oak Bluff Bed and Breakfast claw-foot tub, which meant another cold shower for him when he got home tonight.

The hustle and bustle of the room seemed to have died down. In fact, Walker heard nothing but his own blood pulsing between his ears as he noticed everyone's eyes on him and the newly invited guest.

"Is there a football game or something broadcasting on my forehead?" he asked.

Luke was spearing meat onto a serving fork and pointed said fork toward Walker. "Super Bowl was weeks ago, lil bro."

Right. When Walker was at the treatment facility. He hadn't even watched the game, because he hadn't known how to without, at the very least, a six-pack.

"Well, something seems to have piqued everyone's interest," he said, his jaw growing tight.

Ava gave Jack's shoulder a nudge with her elbow. "Stop messing with your little brother. Maybe if all three of you stopped taunting each other for a few minutes, Walker might come back the next time we do this."

Violet had her glass of strawberry and cucumber water to her lips and choked on her swallow.

Olivia, who'd seated herself on Violet's other side, patted her on the back.

"Oh no," she said. "I hope it's not on a piece of fruit. I thought I cut them large enough to—"

Violet held up a hand, asking everyone for a second.

"Little," she finally said through a small gasp. "She called you little, and after talking about the bath my mind just went—"

"Okay," Walker said, a little too loudly and definitely with too much enthusiasm. "I thought we were stuffing our faces with Lily's grub so we don't have to do all this—talkin'."

"Amen to that," Cash said. "I'm starved."

And with that, the attention that had been heaped on Walker and Violet was directed elsewhere. And once he'd wrapped his lips around a forkful of Lily Green's pot roast, Walker had gone from apprehension, to resignation, to complete and total ecstasy.

In his mouth.

"Christ, Lily," he said. "You need a restaurant or something."

Lily and Olivia laughed. "I'm so thrilled," Olivia said. "They're going to tear down the outside wall next week. It's why we're kind of under-booking the place for the next month. Getting as much done on the redesign as we can, especially before these two tie the knot."

She nodded her head toward where Jack and Ava, the bride- and groom-to-be, sat staring starry-eyed at one another simply from the mention of their upcoming nuptials.

"Y'all are so sweet I might cry," Jenna said with a palm pressed to her chest.

Walker fought the temptation to roll his eyes or react

negatively in any way. He begrudged Jack nothing and was happy as hell he and Ava had found happiness after so much heartache. But all the good surrounding him was a reminder of not only what he hadn't yet found but of what he'd missed choosing the bottle over his family.

His mouth grew parched, and his fingers twitched around the glass of iced tea he didn't remember pouring.

"You swear the construction will be done before the wedding?" Ava asked, snapping Walker back to the moment. "Because if my parents can't spend the night here, I'll be spending the night before our wedding with my mom and dad sleeping at the ranch, and that is *not* an option."

Jack shook his head. "Oh God, Olivia. Lil. No. Seriously. Not. An. Option."

The whole table laughed, even Violet. But there was something strained in her smile, and he wondered where that strain came from... if she could somehow sense what he was going through or if his odd version of a family reminded her of something about her own.

He'd had the whole happy nuclear family thing for a good long while, 'til just after he hit double digits. But it was hard to remember any of that now. When he looked back on his childhood, it started with his mother's death and his father's downward spiral. Everything else sort of seemed lost. He wanted to rebuild. He wanted to stay sober. But he'd never been afforded the distance from his pain to do so. That was why he had to get away. He'd wait until after the wedding. But then he'd take some time, figure himself out. He deserved that, didn't he?

Dinner went better than he ever could have expected. Violet fit into their little fold as if she'd always been a part of it. How was that even possible, that a woman who'd been a stranger only four short days ago felt like someone he'd always known?

"I think you've earned the rest of the week off," Jack told her as they all worked in the kitchen as a dish-washing and -drying assembly line. Though Violet got the job of simply stacking the items back on their shelves so she didn't have to use her injured hand too much.

"But I'm fine," she said. "See? I can put plates and glasses away without even dropping them."

Of course, as she said this, she fumbled with a dessert plate and almost sent it crashing to the floor. Almost.

Everyone looked at her, Walker included. He tried not to laugh.

"Fine," she said, rolling her eyes at herself. "Point taken."

"But we're still on for the wine tasting on Friday," Olivia piped in. "Oooh, I just thought of a great idea. Why don't you stay at the B and B until then? I mean, if you don't need to head back to Santa Barbara for anything. You could get to know our little town." She blushed and gazed wistfully at Cash. "I can call it that now, right?"

Cash finished rinsing a tumbler, handed it to Olivia to dry, and kissed her on the cheek.

"Ms. Belle, as far as I'm concerned, you *are* this town, because it wouldn't be home to me if you weren't in it."

All the women *Awwed,* and Walker was sure he saw Jenna swipe under her eye while Luke simply threw his hands in the air.

"What the hell are you doing, Sheriff? Jack, Walker, and I—we can't compete with a line like that. You know, I think I liked you better when you were surly all the time," Luke said.

Cash gritted his teeth. "I wasn't *surly,* Everett." He said this, of course, with a tone as surly as could be.

Olivia nudged him with her hip. "You did arrest me the day we met," she reminded him. "I love you, Sheriff, but you mighta been a little surly. It was sexy, no doubt about it, but I'm afraid Luke might be telling the truth." She bit her lip and grinned, turning back to dry more dishes.

Cash turned off the sink, dried his hands on a towel, and wrapped his arms around her from behind.

She yelped with laughter.

"Well then, I guess I'm damned glad you came speeding into my surly life," he said, burying his face in her neck.

"Who wants more coffee?" Olivia asked through a fit of giggles.

"Early appointment tomorrow morning," Jack said.

"And I have a sculpting class at eight. Shoot. Jack, can you get Owen to school before that appointment?" Ava asked.

Jack grinned. "Already in my calendar."

"And Ben and Sam are coming over tomorrow to work on the stable and barn for my property. Can't have Lucky living in a converted shed too long."

Violet's brows creased. "Who's Lucky?"

Lily beamed. "She's my pet cow. Been mine since she was born. Luke's starting a side business boarding horses and teaching kids to trick ride, which is what the small stable is for."

Jack continued his job as a lawyer while still helping maintain the ranch and vineyard. Ava had art school. Luke was going to take some of the Callahans' horse-boarding clients off their hands when they left to build their guest ranch up north in Meadow Valley. He was pretty much building a whole new business on his land, and Lily was putting in a restaurant at the bed-and-breakfast. Even Aunt Jenna had her small farm and the eggs she sold at the farmers market.

Each member of his family had something just for them. What was his thing? Building a piece of furniture here and there and selling it way under value of the blood and sweat he poured into it? Or was it being the misfit, the drunk, the one they'd always have to keep an eye on for fear he'd spiral again?

Walker truly didn't know, and that was the part that terrified him the most. If he was no longer the man he'd been for the past ten years, then who was he?

"Violet, will you stay the rest of the week?" Olivia asked again.

Violet pursed her lips as she seemed to work something out in her head, and Walker found himself waiting for her answer with an earnestness he didn't recognize.

Then she shrugged. "I mean…I don't see why I can't. I have to check on a couple of things back in Santa Barbara, but consider me in."

The kitchen was as good as new when they all piled out. Everyone said their good-byes, but Walker lingered, waiting for Cash and Olivia to disappear to her private room on the first floor. Then it was just him and Violet.

"That was really, really fun," she said, backing toward the front foyer stairway. "I had no idea what I was walking into this evening. Kinda scared the pants off me to be honest and made me appreciate even more what you did for me Saturday night—what you all did for me tonight. But your brothers, Jenna, the sheriff, Olivia, Ava, and Lily—they're wonderful, Walker."

He shrugged. "They're tolerable."

She laughed. "I know you care about them. You're not that good at hiding it. There's a big ole teddy bear hiding beneath that gruff exterior."

"Gruff, huh?" He took a step closer to her but kept his hands crossed over his chest.

She raised her brows. "Don't forget the part about the teddy bear. I'm envious of what you have with your brothers and your aunt. Even your friends. Our extended family is basically everyone who works at the restaurant. And they're great, but they're not really mine. Does that make sense?"

He nodded. If there was one thing he couldn't deny—even when he wanted to—it was the sort of claim he felt over his family. He guessed they felt something similar. But they were also each other's biggest reminders of the painful past that shaped them, just like this town. When you put it all together, it made for a volatile mixture, especially for Walker.

But *envious*? She wouldn't want what he had if she knew the whole story. She sure as hell wouldn't want him. If only she knew how hard he had to work at simple things like getting out of bed or attending family dinners without the booze. She wouldn't be so envious then.

He assured himself she only wanted the man he pretended to be, not the man he truly was. Still, he could offer up a small slice of honesty without rocking the boat too much. Couldn't he?

"Think you should know that as much as I love those sexy heels you wear with your skirts—when they aren't causing injury, of course—this is a pretty good look on you, too."

She gave him a pointed look. "And I think *you* should know that as much as I love that you find me attractive, it doesn't help me set aside this—this *want*."

He was still picturing her naked—her warm bronze skin, her brown nipples hard and peaked.

He stiffened inside his jeans. Yeah, he wasn't doing too well at setting his own want aside, either.

"You're right," he said. "That's probably my cue to leave."

She glanced up the stairs and then wrapped her hand around his wrist, heading instead for the door.

"Come on," she said. "Let's go."

His brows drew together. *He* was leaving. Not *they*.

"What? Where?" he asked.

"I spent my day shopping, in the emergency room, and then in this lovely but indoor B and B. It looks like a beautiful night. If I'm going to be working for your family, for the B and B, for the sheriff even, we should learn how to be around each other in a more friend-like manner. Don't you think?"

He huffed out a breath. "So we're going to be friends now?"

She nodded. "I don't have any rules about friends. Do you?"

He shook his head, waiting for his brain to form some sort of argument. But nothing came.

"Then show me Oak Bluff, friend." She slid her fingers through his and gave his hand a squeeze. "I want a tour from someone who was born and raised here, someone who can point out to me why this place is special enough that some people have never truly left."

CHAPTER TEN

Violet's new friend and employer led her to a storefront with a sign painted on the window that said BAKER'S BLUFF. If he hadn't already endeared himself to her at dinner with his wonderful family, he had now. A good friend always knew that the way to her heart was with food. "If you get here right before they open, at about five a.m., you can smell the bread baking. Nothing compares to their coffee, either. And the doughnuts—Jesus, the doughnuts."

Violet pressed her nose to the glass, remembering how she used to wander into her father's restaurant after school, entering through the kitchen door. She'd smell the same thing—fresh bread baking—but also savory sauces bubbling on the stove or the hint of sweetness in the air from whatever that evening's dessert specials would be. Every time she ate a molten chocolate cake—and there were many times because...molten chocolate cake—she felt like she was home. Food was an amazing trigger of sense memory. She guessed that was exactly what fresh pastries at this particular bakery were for Walker.

"Will you bring me here tomorrow morning?" she asked, then spun to look at him.

He was backlit by the streetlamp, his face cast in shadow, making him unreadable once more. So she stepped closer and peered up at him. His blue eyes were dark and brooding, but he pressed his lips into a grin, masking whatever memory had possibly been triggered.

"Best time to get here is right when they open, when everything's fresh. Means getting up at the crack of dawn. You sure you can handle it?"

She nodded, a smile spreading across her face. "I grew up in the restaurant business," she reminded him. "Daily produce and meat orders would have to arrive before lunchtime prep. Sometimes I'd help my father get everything packed in the cooler before I headed off to school. This is just to say that I am *so* your morning girl." Wait, that came out wrong. "I mean *a* morning girl—er…morning *person*." She couldn't stop the double entendres from spilling out of her mouth.

He scrubbed a hand across his beard and laughed. She liked the sound of it—the ease of being around him in this new light.

"Meet me here at five a.m. tomorrow. You won't be disappointed—morning *person*."

She laughed, too. Other than playing the part of responsible adult for both of them, Violet couldn't imagine anything this man could do to disappoint her, especially if it involved fresh homemade pastry and a cup of the town's best coffee.

Walker led her to the next building, which was a combination art and gift shop called Knicks and Knacks. He tapped softly on the glass toward the right of the picture window display.

"See that painting of the man playing catch with the boy, the dog in the background?"

It was hard to miss as it was one of only three pieces prominently displayed in the lighted window. She squinted at the artist's name on the corner of the canvas.

"Wow," she said. "Ava painted that? It's beautiful. That's Jack and their son?"

Walker nodded. "It's a long story, but Jack didn't know his son existed until Owen was nine. None of us did. Now they're getting married."

"Oh," Violet said. "Everyone at dinner seemed so happy. I kind of assumed it had always been that way."

He blew out a breath. "Not even close. Take a look in every window here, and you'll find a story. I live in the apartment above the antiques shop next to the B and B. Sheriff's mother, Lucinda, owns it. Before that, it was where Olivia's grandma grew up—and where she hid love letters from Olivia's grandfather while he was at war. It's why Olivia ended up in Oak Bluff in the first place."

Violet's hand flew to her heart. "This might be the most romantic little town on the map."

Walker shrugged. "No one's married yet. Anything can happen between now and Jack, Luke, or Cash putting a ring on it."

Violet scoffed. "That's a pretty bleak outlook."

He chuckled. "Darlin', I'm six feet four inches of bleak outlook, so I understand if you want to rethink this whole friend thing and keep it at employer/employee. Still no kissing, of course."

He raised his brows, and Violet backhanded him on the shoulder. "Well, what I lack in height I make up for in gobs of optimism, so I think we make the perfect pair—of friends, that is."

He laughed softly, then pulled her down the street, past the B and B so they were standing right in front of Lucinda's place.

She didn't care what he said. Oak Bluff on its own had charm enough to spare, but Violet was realizing it was likely generations of personal histories that kept everyone so connected to a place most couldn't find on a map. The only history she knew was her family's little apartment in Santa Barbara. Their restaurant. Maman's disease. But nothing that defined her like Oak Bluff defined its own people.

"What about you?" she asked hesitantly. He seemed willing enough to share about everyone else, but what was Walker Everett's story? What kept him tethered to this place that seemed to draw her in the moment she'd set foot onto the Crossroads property?

He shrugged.

"How about I show you the part that matters?"

He gave her hand—still resting in his like it was the most natural thing for them to do—a slight tug, and she let him lead her to where his truck was parked in front of the antiques shop he'd just told her about. He grabbed a couple of blankets from the cab, then led her off the town's main street and onto a sandy path toward the sound of waves lapping at the shore.

She breathed in the cool night air, the scent of it sprinkled with the salt of the sea. And there went her senses, triggering memories she wasn't expecting—her father packing food from the restaurant for them to eat at the beach. When she was little and multiple sclerosis not yet part of anyone's vocabulary, he and Maman would each hold one of her hands and swing her over the cool water lapping at the shore. She'd giggle and squeal when her toes hit the surf. If she closed her eyes, she could make herself believe she was there. Despite the miles and years between her beach and this one, she felt the undeniable comfort of being home.

Minutes later she was sitting atop a wool blanket on the sand, another one over her shoulders as she watched Walker build a small fire in a pit that looked like it had been dug in the sand years ago. She imagined all the things he did with his hands—working the ranch, the vineyard, building furniture. His quiet confidence drew her in further and puzzled her all at the same time.

He talked about Oak Bluff like it belonged to everyone else but him. When he was with his family at dinner tonight, he hung back and let the other conversations fill the room—like an outsider looking in. Yet when her father showed up without warning, he made sure the entire group played along with their pretend romance. So what was it about the ocean—a sight so common to the entire state of California—that made Oak Bluff his?

He sat down beside her, resting his elbows on his knees.

"So," he said. "France, huh? You want to tell me more about that? Or do I only get the abbreviated version my family got?"

Ah, yes, the elephant on the beach. She'd been waiting for this, but she wasn't getting into her issues when she was so close to learning something important about him.

"Oh no," she said. "You said you were showing me the part that matters. You tell me about this beach, and I'll tell you about France. Deal?"

"I don't believe I promised telling, but I guess if those are your terms I better adhere to 'em."

The glow of the fire let her see that he was grinning, but the smile faded as he leaned back on his elbows and stared out at the darkened waves.

“This was our mama’s favorite place,” he said. “She loved the ranch, but she loved the ocean more. Said she’d missed it her whole life growing up in Texas but didn’t know it ’til she came to California.”

Violet smiled. “Can’t argue with the truth. I can’t imagine living without a beach nearby.”

He was quiet for a beat but then continued. “She wanted to die here, but by the time she was in hospice, it was too risky to move her. So I came here on my own a few days before she passed, took a bunch of pictures on this crap digital camera, but it was the only thing I had.”

Violet’s voice caught in her throat. “So you brought the ocean to her.”

He nodded.

“Oh, Walker. I’m so sorry. Here I’ve been going on about my mom and what I’ve given up to try to help her, not even knowing that I was throwing in your face that I still had what you lost.”

She lowered herself onto her side and, friend or no, placed her cold palm on his cheek.

“How old were you?” she asked.

“Not quite eleven.”

Her eyes filled with tears for a woman she never knew and the little boy who wanted to give her one last gift before she died. “I’m sorry,” she said again. “I’m so sorry, Walker.”

“You know, sometimes I forget how much she loved this town. It’s good to be reminded of that.” He blinked, his eyes focusing on hers. “Your turn. Tell me more about France.”

His voice was strained. She wasn’t sure if he really cared about France or if he needed the diversion. Either way, she’d repay his honesty with some of her own.

She nodded. "There's this experimental stem cell treatment that can slow the effects of multiple sclerosis. In some people it might even reverse them—not completely, but enough to make life more livable, less painful. I read a recent study about it where a group of patients even went into remission. But it's expensive. And my mother's local physician doesn't offer the treatment. But a doctor in France does..." She trailed off.

"Okay," Walker said slowly. "That's pretty much what you said at dinner. Why the hesitation when you get to the France part?"

Violet pulled her phone from her pocket, opened her e-mail app, and showed him the unopened response from the French address.

"You're going to have to be a little more specific than that, Teach. All I see is an overcrowded inbox. Seriously. Who in the hell has over three hundred unopened messages?"

She waved him off. "I get a lot of spam. But this one"—she pointed to her aunt Ines's name—"this is my mom's sister. The one she hasn't spoken to in over thirty years. I've never even met her. After I found out about Maman's doctor saying no to the treatment, I e-mailed Aunt Ines behind my mother's back to ask for help. Her reply has been sitting here for two days, and I've been too damned scared to read it."

Walker tapped the screen, and Ines's e-mail opened.

Violet gasped.

"Hey," he said softly. "It's okay. Now you don't have to read it alone." He sat up and patted the spot between his legs. "Come on, Teach. You can do this."

Her heart raced as she maneuvered to a sitting position, scooting between his knees so her back rested against his chest.

She could do this.

"Breathe, Vi," he said in her ear, and she let out a nervous laugh, then followed his direction and sucked in a gulp of air.

And then she read the message aloud. It was in French of course, which meant Walker had no clue what she was saying. By the time she finished, however, she was shaking, and Walker was rubbing her shoulders, patient for whatever came next.

Like the truest, most caring friend she could have imagined.

"She wants to talk," Violet said finally, her voice trembling. "She already spoke to the doctor and has health insurance information and said she's thought about me and Maman every day for twenty-five years."

She was crying now, and she didn't know if it was because of her renewed hope for Maman or because from nothing more than an e-mail she felt an immediate connection with a woman she'd never met but whose same blood pumped through her veins.

Walker adjusted himself so he was facing her. She laughed and sobbed and swiped her arm under her running nose.

"I thought I was doing this all for my mother," she said. "But after spending the night with you and your family, I realize now how badly I want to go—for me. That's horrible, right? I mean, how selfish is that?"

Walker shook his head and tried to wipe away the tears, but they kept coming.

"You put school and your future on hold. And you committed to three different jobs tonight, none of which have anything to do with what you love—music. I'd say you earned the right to want a little something just for you. So why don't you let yourself off the hook, okay?"

Instinct took over, and she rose onto her knees and wrapped him into a hug. For a second he simply sat there, but then his strong arms were around her, steadying the rapid beat of her heart.

"You getting snot all over my shoulder?" he asked.

Violet laughed. "Probably. But that's what friends are for, right?"

"I was not aware of that part of our agreement, but I suppose I'll make the exception this one time."

They sat like that for a while longer, in the warmest, safest hug Violet had felt in a long time. Finally, she pulled away so she could look him in those deep blue eyes, and it all finally clicked into place.

"I think we can actually do this friend thing," she said.

He nodded once. "I think we can. And if it makes things easier for you and your folks—for them being okay with you spending so much time so far away—then I'm okay to keep on pretending when they're around. If that's what you need. I get with the whole France thing ahead of you that it's probably easier to let them think you're happy with work and—personal stuff."

She bit her bottom lip. "It's funny you say that. Because—well—despite my protests, my father wants to bring Maman to Oak Bluff for dinner. With us. Next week."

Walker's eyes widened. Then he cleared his throat. "Okay, then. My kitchen is small, but I know how to use it."

She beamed. "A man who can cook? Better be careful. Gabriel Chastain may very well fall in love with you. When we actually do break up, I think he might take it the worst." She laughed, but her heart felt ridiculously full. If their timing wasn't off, she'd be well on her way to falling for a guy like Walker Everett. Instead she'd settle for having him in her life however she could between now and whatever happened with France. She cupped his face in her hands, his beard tickling her palms. "Someday I'm gonna figure out how to repay you for being so wonderful to someone you barely know."

He shrugged. "How about you just keep on thinking I'm wonderful, and we'll call it even."

She held out her hand, and he shook it. "Deal," she said.

Then she bit back a grin as she looked forward to the next time one or both of her parents dropped by Oak Bluff and she and her new friend might have the opportunity to pretend again.

Somehow Walker had gone to bed *without* picturing Violet Chastain naked, without needing a cold shower, and without lamenting that she wasn't lying beside him. Instead he'd drifted off with a strange fulfillment he couldn't put his finger on. This morning, though, when his phone alarm went off at 4:50 a.m., he had the perfect finger to offer the early wake-up call—until he remembered he wasn't heading straight to the ranch.

He scrambled out of bed and threw on yesterday's jeans that were still pooled on the floor. He grabbed a clean T-shirt from a dresser drawer, went through his quick morning routine that included splashing water over his face and brushing his teeth, and then he was out the door and down the street.

He could see the front door of Baker's Bluff. It was propped open like it always was each morning. He was still a half block away when the scent of the air changed from crisp and salty to rich, warm, and aromatic.

He'd half assumed she would forget, but when he made it to the shop window, he could see Violet just inside the door.

"Mornin', Teach," he said as he strode up next to her. She was wearing last night's borrowed clothes, her thick, dark hair pulled into a ponytail. He liked this look on her—the one where she woke up in his town and rolled out of bed to see him.

"Shh," she said. She stood still as a statue, eyes closed. Then she inhaled through her nose.

Walker watched her with mild amusement. It had been a long time since he'd seen someone react to anything in Oak Bluff like she was now. In fact, he couldn't remember the last time he felt like that about his hometown.

"Mmm," she hummed, then opened her eyes. "If what I'm smelling is any indication of what I'll be tasting, I'm in small town foodie heaven."

He smiled. There was something about seeing things through her eyes that hit him in a way he wasn't expecting. He tried doing what she did, closing his eyes and breathing in the scent of the bakery, of the damp ocean air sneaking in through the open door, of the town he'd seen for so long as a prison. For a second his mind flashed to a memory of his mom walking out of Baker's Bluff with a box of doughnuts balanced on her forearms and a cup of coffee in each hand while Walker, his brothers, and their father waited on a bench outside. Always bigger than Walker was, Jack and Luke would usually get to the box before him, sometimes teasing him and holding him back while their parents laughed at the brotherly rivalry.

There was good here, once. He hadn't forgotten. But he still recalled what came after.

As soon as his eyes opened, he remembered standing at his mother's gravesite. He remembered his father knocking Jack down the stairs. And the bottle of whiskey good old

Dad sent Walker for his fifteenth birthday when they were living in Jenna's custody.

Like father, like son. But Walker was slowly crawling his way back to the surface, wasn't he? He'd made it through withdrawal he thought would kill him, through the dinner party with Violet's parents, and he'd narrowly escaped the wine tasting at the stemware wholesaler.

And hell if Violet calling him wonderful and trusting him enough to fall apart in his arms last night hadn't kept him from staring at that damned shot glass and bottle for the first time since he'd been home. She was saving him in ways he couldn't imagine even when the ghosts of Oak Bluff threatened to pull him back under.

"It's good, right?" Violet said, bringing him back to the moment. "Closing your eyes and tuning everything else out."

He cleared his throat. "Sure. Yeah." Then he grabbed her hand and pulled her the rest of the way into the shop.

"Come on. If we wait too long, everyone will wake up, and it doesn't count if we're not the first ones at the counter."

Violet clapped and bounced on her toes as she stared through the glass at uncut loaves of fresh bread, at cookies and turnovers, doughnuts and croissants.

"Pick anything you want, Teach. Breakfast is on me."

She turned to him, her smile softening as her deep brown eyes found his.

"Thank you, Walker," was all she said, but it felt like something more.

He'd never taken a woman to breakfast at sunrise, couldn't remember ever *wanting* to do such a thing. Yet here he was with a woman who'd answered an ad for a job and interrupted his life with those perfect, full lips. Now, somehow, she was something he wasn't sure he'd ever really had—a friend.

They sat outside the bakery on the same bench he used to sit on as a kid. She ate a chocolate croissant while he polished off his usual—a jelly doughnut—and they sipped their coffees and watched the sun come up over Oak Bluff Way. But he realized the sun wasn't the brightest spot in the town. *Violet Chastain* was. He'd finally put his finger on that indescribable feeling that had let him leave the whiskey bottle in the cabinet last night. *Connection.* She didn't know the real him, but maybe she'd never have to. With Violet around, he didn't feel the urge to numb himself to Oak Bluff's ghosts.

His phone vibrated in his pocket, and he pulled it out to find a text from his aunt.

Seeing if we're still on for this weekend at the market. Sylvie really wants to see the chair.

The chair. Shit. He had to finish the damned chair today, by tomorrow the latest, so the stain would be dry by Sunday.

He glanced to his right and saw Violet reading something on her phone as she raised her coffee cup to her lips. Damn those lips. He could be her friend and still admire an objectively sexy feature, right?

He shook his head. That kind of rationalization would do him *no* good sanding and staining a piece of furniture.

She looked at him with something that was a mix between a smile and a wince.

"So, Olivia texted. Sam and Ben—the contractors, I guess—want to come by this morning before heading over to Luke's, something about a permit and additional measurements they realized they need before starting the job. Anyway, the person who works the front desk called in sick, so Olivia asked if I could fill in answering phones for a few hours. Said she'd pay me for it." She shrugged. "I'm not really in a position to say no to extra income, especially when she's giving me the room for free."

Walker laughed. "Perfect timing, actually. I've got something I realized I need to take care of today as well."

His phone buzzed again. Still Jenna

By the way, I'm at the grocery store in Oak Bluff dropping off some eggs. Did I tell you they're stocking my inventory? Now you'll see Farm Fresh right on your local shelf. Hey, is that you and Violet across the street?

Walker squinted at the blond woman walking and texting as she crossed the street—with a live chicken following close behind.

"Here we go," he said under his breath.

"What's that?" Violet asked.

Before he could utter another word, Jenna was hurrying toward them, arms open wide and ready to hug the first willing—or *un*willing—victim.

"Hey there, nephew of mine."

Walker stood to greet her, deciding he'd get hugged and likely pecked on the toe of his boot by Lucy either way.

"Hey yourself," he said.

She threw her arms around him, and Lucy's beak went to town on his work boots as expected. Out of the corner of his eye, he saw Violet stand, too.

"Look at you two, up bright and early," Jenna said. "And here I thought I'd be the one sipping the first cup of coffee from the bakery today." She held Walker at arm's length, hands still on his shoulders. "I mean, I'm assuming you two just *met* for coffee, but feel free to correct me if I'm wrong."

Violet laughed and held up her right hand. "I swear on all the fresh chocolate croissants that we met so we could beat you to the punch. Just two friends enjoying coffee and a beautiful sunrise."

Jenna raised a brow, and Walker shook his foot hoping Lucy would lose interest in his boot. She didn't.

"Aw, come here, you," Jenna said, doling out hug number two to Violet.

She took a step back and crossed her arms, staring at the two of them. Actually, she was staring at their feet. That was when Walker realized there was no longer a chicken pecking at his toes. Instead she was pecking circles around both him and Violet.

Jenna cleared her throat, then shot an accusing look at Walker.

"What's happening?" Violet asked, her eyes nervously following Lucy. "Is it, like, an attack chicken?"

Jenna adjusted her purse on her shoulder, then grabbed Lucy midstride. The animal clucked her protestation as Jenna nonchalantly moved her to a nearby patch of grass where she refocused her nondomestic pet's interest on what looked like an early morning snack.

"She's not an attack chicken," Jenna said, turning back to Walker and Violet. "But she *is* psychic."

Walker groaned, and Violet snorted, then threw a hand over her mouth.

"You're—you're serious?" she asked, and Jenna nodded, unfazed.

"Lucy called it with Luke and Lily, and I'm seeing she has some *very* strong feelings about the two of you."

Except there was no *two of them* other than friendship from here on out. That chicken had no idea what she was talking about. She was merely sensing the initial attraction they'd both let simmer into something more professional and platonic.

Shit. Jenna damn near brainwashed him into thinking a chicken actually had an opinion about him and Violet. Or anyone for that matter.

"She's not psychic," Walker said.

"Hold up a second," Violet said. "I want to hear how she called it with Luke and Lily."

Jenna gave her nephew a self-satisfied smile, then turned her attention to Violet. "It's pretty simple. Lucy's really attuned to folks' hidden desires—even if they're ones folks don't even know they have. She lost her shit the first time she saw Luke and Lily together. Flapped her wings all crazy like she was gonna take flight or something. And look at the two of them now."

Lucy abandoned her patch of grass and darted for Violet's shoes. Violet yelped, but instead of pecking, the chicken nuzzled against her borrowed Chuck Taylors.

Walker threw his hands in the air. "You gotta be kidding me. I get nearly pecked to death, and Vi's her new nest?"

Jenna patted him on the cheek. "Don't take it personally. She just likes Violet better."

The two women burst into laughter, and Walker rolled his eyes.

"I got a chair to sand and stain," he said bitterly. "I'll leave you ladies to it." He kissed Jenna on the cheek and tossed his almost empty coffee cup into the trash as he began his stride toward Lucinda's antiques shop.

"Good-bye, Walker!" Violet called after him, still laughing.

"Bye, nephew!" Jenna added.

Then Lucy squawked.

"Not psychic!" he called back.

And then, only because they couldn't see his face, he grinned.

CHAPTER ELEVEN

The whole next week had been a whirlwind. After working the front desk at the B and B on Thursday, then walking Olivia and the guests through a delightful wine tasting on Friday, Violet had finally gone back to Santa Barbara for the weekend. Her hand injury barely an issue by Monday, she was back in Oak Bluff on wedding detail with Ava for Monday and Tuesday, but today she was on her own, stocking the finished shelves of the wine bar with the new stemware.

The place smelled like a new beginning—fresh paint with a hint of the outdoors hidden in what was left of the unfinished wood.

Her phone, which had been playing her aptly titled *Karaoke* playlist, was interrupted by an incoming call, which meant she had to stop belting Beyoncé's "If I Were a Boy" and catch her breath. It was Olivia.

"Hello?" she said before successfully doing the latter.

"Are you on a treadmill or something?"

Violet shook her head, then realized she was on the phone. "Nope. Just rockin' out while I work. As one does."

Olivia laughed. "Okay, *that* is something I definitely want to see, but right now I'm hoping you can help me with a cheese emergency."

Violet's brows furrowed. "A *cheese* emergency?" She'd grown up in the restaurant business and hadn't heard that one yet.

"So there's this cheese-monger Lily met at the farmers market who has—according to Lily's taste buds—the most mind-blowing aged Gouda you've ever tasted that would be perfect to pair with our cabernet for the next wine tasting on Friday. She's at the grocery store right now with a limited supply, but we are swamped and—"

"You want me to run over and pick it up? I was going to take Dixie for a walk soon, so I'm headed your way anyway."

She heard Olivia sigh. "You are a lifesaver! Thank you! See you soon!"

Violet shoved her phone in the back pocket of her jeans and brushed her hands together to shake off the dust from the unwashed glasses.

"Yeesh," she said aloud, remembering that she'd dressed exactly for the job today—unpacking boxes *alone* and walking the sheriff's dog. Also alone.

Her jeans were in good enough shape, but her white tank was slightly tinted with sawdust and maybe a little grime. She shrugged and adjusted her favorite black and white headscarf. She hadn't straightened her hair last night, and while she loved her hair's natural curl, her ringlets tended to fall over her eyes when she worked.

She looked down at her red-painted toenails and wiggled them in her flip-flops, wondering if Walker would be proud of her for dressing her feet for the job as much as she had the rest of her.

She'd only seen him once this week, and that was from a distance. She'd been entering the winery while he'd been working some sort of irrigation contraption on the vines. He'd waved. She'd waved—and noted that he was, again, shirtless—but that had been it. Which was fine because they were just friends. He was simply the type of friend who looked good with his shirt off. So what?

She shook her head at herself as she grabbed her purse off the top of the bar and headed out to her car. The short walk with Dixie would be fine, but it was too warm for the mile trek into town, especially in flip-flops. With her luck, she'd have some sort of footwear catastrophe again and likely wind up stranded on the side of the road with a broken ankle.

She found a spot right in front of the B and B, parked, and made her way across the street to the market.

Her skin prickled with goose bumps as the air-conditioning welcomed her inside. She scanned the small store's layout and spotted the deli and cheese section, making a beeline toward a woman situated behind a small canopied stand who looked to be packing up her display.

No. No. No. No. No.

"Tell me you have some of your legendary aged Gouda left," Violet said to the young woman behind the stand. She was taller than Violet, olive skinned, her dark hair cropped short against her angular face. Violet noticed her nametag said ANNA. "Please, *Anna*," she corrected. Violet liked the personal touch of calling someone by their name. Plus she figured she had a better chance of snagging what was left of the cheese if she was nice about it.

Anna gave her an apologetic smile. "I literally sold the last of it ten seconds ago. I'm sorry."

"But this is a cheese emergency," Violet said, repeating Olivia's words. "My friend really wanted that cheese for our wine tasting. It was supposed to be *the* cheese to go with the cabernet, and—"

Anna the cheese-monger pointed over Violet's shoulder. "Sold the last two wheels to that tall, strapping blond man over in produce."

Violet followed the other woman's gaze to where Walker Everett held a cantaloupe under his nose as he inhaled. His brows furrowed. They both stared at him for several seconds.

"Gorgeous," Anna said. "But he looks a little clueless."

Violet stifled a laugh as Walker shook the melon next to his ear, and she wondered what he hoped to hear.

"Thanks for the heads-up on the cheese," she told Anna, then slowly approached the produce section, not wanting to disturb Walker and his very serious cantaloupe examination.

She stood quietly behind him for a few seconds until his sixth sense kicked in.

He pivoted to face her, melon still in hand.

"You spying on me, Teach?" he asked with brows raised.

His skin looked mildly sunbaked, and his hair curled upward where it had grown over the top of his ears. And that beard—damn that sexy beard that made it so hard to tell if he was on the verge of a smile or frown.

She shook her head. "Okay, maybe a little," she admitted. "But you seemed so intent on understanding your fruit. I didn't want to break your concentration."

He palmed the melon against his hip like it was a basketball and he was figuring out his next shot, and reached toward her with his free hand.

Oh God. Was he going to kiss her? They were just friends. They'd decided. But what if he did? Would she let him, right here in front of the whole town?

She held her breath, but instead of his rough palm landing softly against her cheek, his thumb and forefinger pinched a rogue spiral of hair that had slipped out the top of her wrap.

"Curly," he said with realization.

She cleared her throat and nodded. "I usually flat-iron it. It's easier to deal with that way, especially at work. Or I keep it out of the way with this." She patted her head wrap and smiled nervously.

His brows creased, and he was studying her like he was looking at the melon, like she was some puzzle he was still trying to figure out.

She cleared her throat. "Also Ramon—you, um, remember Ramon—preferred my hair straight. So I got a blowout and—"

"He *what*?" Walker asked, his jaw tightening. "Are you telling me that asshole made you think there was any possible scenario where you weren't a goddamn knockout?"

"Walker, stop. You don't have to—"

But he didn't let her finish. "Will you wear it curly for our date?" he asked. "No. I take that back. Will you wear your hair however the hell you want for our date?"

She wanted to react to how ridiculously sweet he was being about the Ramon thing, to acknowledge tightness in her chest and the butterflies in her belly, but all she could focus on was one word. *Date*.

"Our *what*?" she blurted, almost choking on the second word.

He brandished the melon, then nodded to where his shopping cart sat next to the fruit stand. "Your parents?

Dinner at my place Saturday so they can get to know your fake boyfriend better?"

Violet threw her hand over her mouth. The night she'd walked her father out of the B and B following his impromptu visit, he'd made it clear he wasn't happy with the precarious situation she'd put herself in—dating the same man for whom she worked.

"We need the money," she'd insisted. And every minute she spent in Oak Bluff she realized *she* needed the escape.

"What about going back to school?" he'd asked with a sigh. "We can figure out a way to cover medical bills and you finishing your education. *We're* the parents," he'd reminded her. "You shouldn't have to take on this much responsibility at such a young age."

She hadn't known how to answer him, how to tell him that school had taken a backseat to getting Maman to Paris. To getting *herself* to Paris and figuring out the other half of who she was. So she'd steered the conversation back to Walker.

"What night works for you—to bring Maman back for dinner?"

His sous chef was trying her hand at running the kitchen, so he'd suggested this Saturday night. Three days from now. Walker not only hadn't forgotten, but he was planning to cook for all of them. Her throat tightened, and for a few seconds she stood there, mouth open, unable to speak.

"You all right there?" he asked, and Violet finally found her voice.

"We're really going through with this? I assumed I'd come up with some last-minute excuse, like Olivia needing me at the desk for the weekend rush or something."

Walker shrugged. "I've got burgers and Gouda. And Lily said I could do this fancy ham wrapped around melon for an appetizer."

Violet laughed. “Prosciutto?”

He pointed at her and grinned. “*That’s* it! You know, I’m pretty handy in the kitchen, but I’m going to let you in on a little secret.” He leaned in close, cupping his palm around her ear. His warm breath made her shiver. “Never bought a melon before in my life.”

She took a step back and smacked straight into what felt like a brick wall.

“Whoa, there. Sorry about that,” a deep male voice said.

Violet spun to face another equally tall and strapping man, but this one had short, dark hair where Walker’s was California sun-kissed and overgrown. The stranger was clean-shaven, so she could admire the square line of his jaw.

“Just thought I’d stop by and say hello, Everett. Haven’t seen you since—”

“Hey, Sam,” Walker interrupted, setting the melon back down with the others and shaking the other man’s hand. “It’s been a while, huh? This is Violet Chastain, Crossroads Vineyard’s new wine expert.”

Violet held out her hand. “I also do some work over at the Oak Bluff B and B. It’s nice to meet you.”

“Sam Callahan. I’m heading up the remodel on the B and B,” he said as he scrubbed a hand across his jaw. “Coworkers then, huh? I thought maybe—”

“Nope,” Walker said emphatically, cutting the man off again. “You thought wrong.”

Violet hoped she disguised her wince with a smile. It wasn’t that there was anything wrong with what Walker said. Whatever Sam was insinuating about the two of them, Walker was simply being honest—quickly and efficiently honest.

Sam gave her hand an extra squeeze before letting it go.

"Nice seeing you, Everett," he said. His eyes turned back to Violet. "And it was extra nice meeting you, Ms. Chastain. I'm guessing we'll be seeing a lot more of each other at the bed-and-breakfast." He smiled, gave Walker that male nod that could mean *hello, good-bye,* or anything in between, and walked away.

Violet was still watching him leave when Walker broke the silence.

"You're not going to need my services much past this weekend, I'm guessing."

She pivoted to face him, cheeks burning. "I wasn't—I mean, I didn't—"

He shook his head. "Doesn't matter what *you* did, Teach. He's already picking curtains or color swatches or whatever it is you do when planning a future with someone else."

He smiled ruefully, and ugh. Why did he have to call her *Teach*? Forget what she said about the personal touch of calling someone by their name. Nicknames were something else entirely. Was he flirting or simply being friendly?

She rolled her eyes. "I'm not picking anything out with anyone," she insisted. "I don't see why it matters, though, considering we're nothing more than friends."

"You're right," he said, his voice even. "Doesn't matter. What does matter is that you were about to show me how to pick the perfect cantaloupe—you know, so as to impress your parents with a fancy but no frills appetizer. Lily's words, by the way."

Violet grabbed a melon that was heavy in her hand. When she pressed her nose to the rind—its texture like raised netting against her skin—she breathed in deep and grinned. "So sweet," she said, then held it out toward Walker. "This is the one."

He reached for it, but she snatched it back.

"On one condition," she added.

He crossed his arms. "And what's that?"

She nodded toward his shopping basket. "I need one of those wheels of Gouda. You don't need both to make burgers for four."

He eyed her warily. "Yeah, but the woman selling the cheese said it's the best and that she won't have any more for at least a month. Figured I might want one for myself. Helping me pick a melon is hardly payment for the last of a dying breed."

Violet laughed. "Do you even know the difference between Gouda and the prepackaged processed crap you buy in the refrigerator section?"

"Sure do." He raised his brows. "Prepackaged crap is yellow."

He snatched the melon from her without incident, set it down in his cart, and tipped an invisible hat in her direction. "Many thanks, Teach. I'll see you Saturday."

"Wait!" she said, grabbing hold of his cart before he strode away. "I promised Olivia I'd get her that Gouda for Friday's wine tasting. You wouldn't want me disappointing my other boss, now, would you?"

He scratched the back of his neck and narrowed his gaze. "What's it worth to ya?"

"Please?" she asked, batting her lashes. *"S'il vous plait?"*

He chuckled but shook his head. "Oh no, you don't. I don't care how pretty those brown eyes are. You want a favor from me? Then I get to ask a favor of you."

She blew out a breath. "Fine. Name your price."

"Jack's meeting with a client, Ava's got her college class today, and Owen's at school. No one around to let the dog out."

Her shoulders sagged as her hope deflated. Flirting or not, she and Walker were having fun without it being awkward, weren't they? And here all he wanted was to assign her another errand like she was doing for Olivia and Cash.

"Sure," she said flatly. "I can do it right after I walk Dixie for the sheriff."

Walker's brows furrowed. "Nice of you to offer, Teach. But all this food shopping's worked up my appetite. Figured since I was heading over to let Scully out, I could raid Jack and Ava's fridge for lunch. Figured you might be hungry, too."

"Oh," Violet said. "I thought—"

"How about this?" he interrupted, then reached into his cart and handed her the coveted wheel of Gouda. "Run this over to Olivia, grab the sheriff's dog, and meet me in front of the antique shop in ten minutes. Dixie can hop in the back of the cab and come with us. Jack and Ava have a nice-size yard with a fence, and she and Scully get on great. They can have free rein while we fix ourselves something to eat."

Violet couldn't wipe the smile off her face if she tried.

"I think I'm going to like being friends with you, Walker Everett."

He winked. "I think you already do."

Twenty minutes later the sheriff's German shepherd, Dixie, was chasing Jack and Ava's chocolate Lab, Scully, through their spacious backyard while Walker rummaged through their fridge.

"So... this is the house you grew up in?"

He emerged from behind the refrigerator door with a jar of pickles in one hand, a stick of butter and a squeeze bottle of Dijon mustard in the other, and two deli bags hanging from his teeth.

"Oh my God. Do you need help?" she asked, but she was laughing. "Wait. First..." She held up her phone. "Say cheese!"

Instead his blue eyes shot daggers at her while she snapped the photo.

He spun toward the counter, dropping the bags and setting the pickles and butter down next to them.

"Thanks so much for the help," he said, but she could tell he was biting back a grin.

"Thanks so much for the photo op," she countered. "That might be my new wallpaper."

He grabbed a bag of sourdough bread from a basket and slid it her way along with a knife.

"If you actually do want to lend a hand. How about cutting us four pieces about a half-inch thick?"

She nodded. "I guess I can do that."

He went to work with his own knife, shaving a dill pickle into paper-thin slices. When she handed him the bread, he buttered the outside of each piece, then layered the inside with the mustard, cheddar cheese, turkey, and sliced dill.

She wrinkled her nose. "Pickles on a turkey sandwich?"

He huffed out a laugh. "You grew up in your dad's restaurant, and you're afraid of a little pickle? I'm disappointed."

Her brows drew together as he pulled a skillet from under the stove and fired up one of the burners.

"I'm not *afraid* of pickles. They're usually a side item is all. But I'm sure your weird sandwich will be delicious."

He raised his brows but said nothing, so she let him be. She knew her way around a kitchen well enough to find plates, glasses, and napkins, so she kept herself busy setting the table and filling their glasses with ice water. The kitchen looked out onto the backyard, and she could see the two dogs now resting in the shade. Beyond that lay part of the pasture, and farther out she could see the beginning of the vineyard. The view was nothing short of spectacular.

"This seems like a beautiful home," she said. "And the view. All that land."

"Mmm-hmm," was his only response as he turned toward the table, sizzling skillet in one hand and spatula in the other.

He slid one sandwich onto each plate, returned the skillet to the burner, and met her back at the table. With the spatula still in hand, he split each sandwich in two so that the cheese oozed onto the plates.

Violet's mouth watered.

"Feedin' time," he said, then dropped into his seat. He waited for her to sit before touching his food, but as soon as she joined him at the table, he tore into his sandwich like he hadn't eaten in a week.

Violet stared at the crisp, golden bread and the perimeter of burned cheese sticking out from the crust—her favorite.

Walker swallowed. "Thought you weren't scared of a few pickles," he teased.

He was right. She was the daughter of parents who'd taught her to love everything from escargot to spicy sardines. Certainly she could stomach pickles *on* her sandwich instead of beside it.

"You know what it is?" she said, lifting half her sandwich and pointing at him with it. "I love pickles. I do. But they have such a strong, powerful flavor, right? Like, if I'm at a restaurant, and they put the pickle too close to the sandwich so that it's touching, it's game over, man. The sandwich tastes like a pickle. So I'm simply wondering if putting the pickle *on* the sandwich and using heat to—you know—seal in the flavor is really the wisest choice."

Walker stared at her, said nothing, and took another bite.

Oh, screw it. She'd only had coffee and a banana for breakfast, and that was hours ago already. She sank her teeth into the crisp, buttered bread and tore off a hunk.

Her taste buds exploded with the tang of the pickle mixed with the heat of the mustard. The smoked turkey added an unexpected sweetness mixed with the sharp bite of the cheddar. Together, wrapped in the grilled sourdough, it was nothing short of perfection.

She moaned as her eyes fell shut, and even though she couldn't see him, she knew Walker was looking at her with a self-satisfied grin.

"*Mon Dieu*," she said. "If this is any indication of how you prepare a burger, my parents are going to be smitten."

"You're welcome," was all he said, and Violet realized that while Walker Everett was a man of few words—even fewer when he ate—he was also a man who could hold his own in the kitchen, and there was barely anything sexier than that.

"He's a good man," Walker finally said after he polished off his last bite. "Sam Callahan, I mean."

She took an extra few sips of her water so she wouldn't have to answer immediately.

"I wanted you to know," he added. "In case he asks you out."

Violet nodded as she amended her earlier assessment in her head. There was barely anything sexier than a man *friend* who could hold his own in the kitchen. Despite his making lunch for her today and what he was doing for her Saturday night, she had to stop looking for something that wasn't there and enjoy her time in Oak Bluff for what it was—a means to an end.

"Thanks for the heads-up," she said at last. "I'll keep that in mind."

CHAPTER TWELVE

Walker stood in the doorway with a platter of freshly grilled Gouda burgers and stared as he watched Violet move about his tiny kitchen, opening and closing cabinets until she found what she wanted. Having her in his personal space was both disconcerting and comforting all at once, and he couldn't figure out which part of that equation bothered him more.

"Oh, hey," she said, setting a stack of plates on the table and then grabbing the platter from him. "Sorry. I didn't see you standing there." She breathed in through her nose and hummed a satisfied sigh. "These look and smell delicious."

He cleared his throat. "Your dress is nice," he said, admiring the long, maroon garment that hugged her curves and flared slightly where it pooled over her simple, gold sandals.

She stuck her thumbs behind the spaghetti straps of the top and held them out like they were a pair of overalls or suspenders. "What? This old thing?" she teased. She blew a corkscrew curl out of her eyes.

He loved that she'd worn her hair curly tonight. She was beautiful no matter which way you sliced it, but tonight—despite their charade—she seemed so comfortable in her own skin. He envied that about her, about anyone who could simply *be.*

She looked him up and down, everything from his clean jeans to his green and white short-sleeve plaid button-down. "Thank you. You clean up pretty good yourself, though if we get too close we might look like a Christmas tree." She let out a nervous laugh. How close would they have to get tonight to look convincing as a couple?

He shrugged. "Guess we'll have to coordinate better next time." When they'd have to pretend again.

"I'll go grab my parents," she said, heading toward the other side of the apartment where a small balcony looked out onto Oak Bluff Way. Violet's mother and father each sipped a glass of the wine they'd brought as a gift to the host and hostess. Walker hoped his refusal was convincing but not rude, insisting that he never drank the night before he operated a circular saw, that he wouldn't want the remaining shelves of the winery to be compromised.

They'd all shared a good-natured laugh, but he was running out of excuses not to drink, and he wanted to hang on to the fantasy—that he wasn't an addict—for a while longer.

Thanks to the minuscule size of the place, Walker could hear Violet's mother through the opened sliding glass door.

"Prosciutto and melon," she said, holding up a cube of cantaloupe wrapped in the Italian ham and held together with a toothpick. "*Délicieux.*"

"That's all Walker," he heard Violet say. "He prepared the entire menu for tonight, which is why I'm here. Burgers are done. Go ahead," she added. "I'll get the dishes."

* * *

After a half-hour discussion over s'mores of how the Dutch pronounce "Gouda"—"It's *chow*-da," Violet's father insisted, pronouncing the *ch* like he was ready to hock a loogie—it was time to walk Mr. and Mrs. Chastain to their car.

Violet's father linked his arm with his wife, and Walker linked his hand with Violet's, her fingers snaking through his like it was the most natural thing in the world.

The four of them rounded the front of the antiques shop where Violet's father had parked.

"I guess I was wrong to worry about you working together and—well—you know," Gabriel Chastain said.

Walker let Violet's hand go to shake her father's. Then he slid his palm to the small of her back.

"Pa-*pa*," Violet scolded, but she was smiling.

"Thank you for dinner," Camille said, kissing her daughter on each cheek and then doing the same with Walker. "You are welcome in our home any time," she said. "On the weekends when Vee is home, Sunday dinners start at seven. Tell me you will come sometime."

He felt Violet's diaphragm contract as she sucked in a breath.

"I never say no to a home-cooked meal," he said.

"Then we will see you both soon," Camille added.

Gabriel opened her car door and helped her inside. The older woman was unable to mask the wince as she maneuvered into her seat.

He pulled Violet close, and she rested her head on his shoulder.

"Home next weekend, sweetheart?" Gabriel asked his daughter, his voice tight.

"Yeah," Violet said. "I'll head back after the wine tasting Friday night."

He kissed his daughter on the cheek and made his way to the driver's side of the car.

Walker stood there for several long seconds with Violet's body leaning up against his until the taillights of her parents' car were long out of view.

"I'll help you clean up," she said, the first to break the silence.

If he let her help, that meant the two of them alone in his apartment. But once she was there, the last thing he'd want to do is clean.

"I've got it under control," he said. "Probably easier for you to head back to the B and B."

She swallowed and nodded. "Probably." Then she threw her arms around him and pressed her warm lips to his cheek. "Thank you, Walker. For everything. I don't think I've ever had a friend like you."

He didn't know what to say to that, so he said nothing at all and simply hugged her back, savoring the feel of her body against his.

"Good night, Walker," she said, pulling away.

"Night, Teach."

And then she was gone.

It didn't take long to clean and dry the dishes, but by the time he finished, he was physically and emotionally spent.

He opened the cabinet above the fridge and stared at the shot glass and bottle. But he didn't pull it down, didn't pour that nightly shot only to see if he was strong enough to pour it back. He was already slightly drunk on the high of the evening, even if it had ended with the word "friend."

She'd been enough for him to pass the test.

She'd been enough to make him say no before the bottle was even open.

She'd let him play the part of the man he never thought he could be. Even if it was a game, she was saving him bit by bit, and that would have to be enough.

He strode toward his bedroom, replaying visions of her in that dress, her tight curls bouncing against her bare shoulders, and his jeans were suddenly tighter.

He chuckled. Maybe the game wasn't exactly *enough.*

He kicked off his shoes and padded into the bathroom, turning the shower to cold.

He'd get used to this part.

Eventually.

Violet sat on the twin bed she'd slept in since she was a kid with a packed suitcase beside her. Because of her "date" with Walker last weekend, she'd stayed in Oak Bluff for almost two full weeks. After Sunday dinner with her parents, she would be headed back to her free room at the B and B for another week of winery and wedding prep, German shepherd walking, and bed-and-breakfast reservation taking. She was grateful for her various sources of income, but she was starting to feel like two different versions of herself—the one in Oak Bluff who was getting used to her new jobs and setting her feelings for Walker aside, and the one in Santa Barbara who—when Walker wasn't around—spoke of him like he was the light of her life. There was also the Violet who was planning a trip to France unbeknownst to her parents, so it was probably more accurate to say she was living three lives at the moment. It was getting harder and harder to keep them all straight.

"Vee," her mother called from the kitchen. "Someone is at the door, and I am in the middle of preparing dinner. I think Papa is on the balcony. Answer it, *s'il vous plait*?"

Maman was having a good day, which meant she'd been

toiling away in the kitchen all afternoon—her favorite thing to do when she was able. Violet's father, though an amazing chef in his own right, enjoyed the days he didn't have to "bring the office home with him." This Sunday was one of those days.

Violet planned on washing and setting her curls tonight, but for now she had her hair wound into two buns on top of her head so that she looked a bit like Mickey Mouse. She threw open the front door, and her breath caught in her throat.

"Walker?"

Her eyes widened, and she backed away from the door without so much as inviting him in. Sure, her parents had offered him an invitation to drop by for Sunday dinner, but she didn't actually think he'd *drop* by without warning. She suddenly felt more exposed than she did the time she'd dropped her robe and let him see her naked.

"I probably should have called," he said. "But I didn't quite realize I was on my way here until I was pulling up your street. Friends are allowed to pay each other unexpected visits every now and then, aren't they?"

He stood there in a black and white plaid shirt, sleeves rolled to his elbows, and a pair of dusty but well-fitting jeans.

"Did I hear you say *Walker*, Vee? Invite him for dinner. There is plenty."

He raised his brows and stuck his head inside the doorway.

"I could eat," he said. "It *is* a ninety-minute drive here and back. I might be a little hungry." He furrowed his brows at the door's threshold. "You gonna invite me in?"

"Are you a vampire or something?" Violet asked. He narrowed his eyes, and she let out a nervous laugh. "I mean yes, come in. Show up without warning and have dinner while I'm dressed like I rolled out of bed just in time for class."

Walker raised a brow. "What class was that, and why the hell wasn't I in it?"

She rolled her eyes, feigning annoyance, but it didn't change that she sorta loved that he found her attractive no matter what. Even if they were no longer going to act on their attraction, it still made her wonder if what he was attracted *to* was more than the way she looked.

He stepped over the threshold and clear into her personal space.

They stood there staring at each other for what felt like an eternity.

"Don't be shy, Walker," she heard her father call over her shoulder.

Violet groaned and turned around, the humiliation of teen dating making an unexpected comeback. "Papa, really?" she said.

"Evening, Gabe," Walker said with a grin.

Violet's father waved her off, then rounded the corner into the kitchen.

She pivoted back to Walker, shaking her head as her cheeks filled with heat.

"I am really sorry about that."

Walker shrugged. "Maybe we shouldn't disappoint the man."

Violet's throat went dry. She'd resigned herself to nothing more than some suggestive hand-holding if her parents were around. But kissing wasn't out of the realm of possibility now, was it?

"Maybe we shouldn't," she said, but took a step over the line they'd already drawn.

Without another second of hesitation, he slid a hand around her waist, pulling her to him as he dipped his head, his lips brushing softly against hers. Her lips parted, and he teased her with one small flick of his tongue as his hand slid up her torso and his thumb brushed the side of her breast.

Because she'd spent the day in her pajamas, the girls were of course commando under her tank, which meant his small touch rocketed through her like a tidal wave.

She responded with something between a whimper and a sigh when he let his hand drop and he backed away.

"Sorry about that," he said softly, but a devilish grin played at his lips.

"Oh my God," she whisper-shouted. "You copped a feel!"

Her own smile belied any protestation. To be honest, she'd been thinking about kissing him—and other things—since their "date" last weekend.

Maman's cooking was beyond good, but the taste of this man on her tongue was simply beyond. And good lord the feel of his hands on her. How was she supposed to make it through dinner knowing exactly what those hands were capable of when they were alone? Good thing they weren't going to *be* alone any time soon. Plus, what those hands could do in private had nothing to do with their pretend relationship.

As if his driving ninety-four minutes to see her and greeting her with a bone-melting kiss wasn't enough, from behind his back he produced a small bouquet of irises. Violet gasped.

"You—you brought flowers?" she asked, incredulous. "Walker Everett, I never pegged you as a man who bought a girl flowers."

He whispered in her ear, his breath warm against her skin, "They're not actually for you."

She leaned back, her eyes narrowed. Then she glanced to where her mother was still happily working in the kitchen.

"What game are you playing at, mister?" she asked him.

An unannounced visit, flowers for Maman? Who was this man? He was playing his part far too well, which was going to make it all the more difficult when their little charade ended. For her parents, of course.

"Figure if I stay on Camille's good side, I'll get invited back. Think of all the places in this apartment I might be compelled to kiss my fake girlfriend. Hell, I might even be compelled to do it outside." He cleared his throat, and she knew his mention of outside triggered the same memory for him as it did for her. It would be a long time before she forgot the hood of his truck and those very capable hands doing very capable things.

"This isn't real, you know," she reminded him, and maybe herself, too. "We already agreed there are so many reasons why it can't be. *You* were the one who made the intelligent decision when I couldn't, remember?"

He nodded. "I do. But I wanted to test a theory."

"What's that?" she asked.

"That enjoying the perks of pretend maybe isn't the worst thing we could do."

She shook her head ruefully and hoped he didn't notice the heat creeping up her neck and to her cheeks. "No," she admitted. "I guess it's not." She turned her head toward the kitchen. "Maman, Walker brought you a gift."

A few seconds later Camille Chastain emerged from the kitchen. She still used her cane, but her steps seemed lighter today, less painful.

The woman's brown eyes brightened when she saw the flowers in Walker's hand.

"Oh! *De si belles fleurs*." She took them from him and breathed in their fragrance. Violet grabbed a vase from on top of the refrigerator and filled it with water. "Just beautiful," her mother said again in English. "What are you doing all the way down here on a Sunday evening?" she asked.

"Was visiting my aunt in Los Olivos," he said matter-of-factly. "Hope it's okay I took you up on your invitation without calling first. Figured if I was already halfway here I'd drive the rest of the way."

Violet placed the water-filled vase on the dining room table, and her mother deposited the irises into their new receptacle.

"Is this a regular thing?" Violet asked. "You visiting your aunt on Sundays?"

He gave her a playful smile. "It can be."

Violet bit back a grin of her own, but just barely.

Maybe Oak Bluff didn't have to be her only escape from reality. Walker brought some of that escape right to her door with a kiss that turned her knees to jelly and flowers for Maman.

After her mother's seafood gumbo and homemade mango sorbet, they played Scrabble, *le jeune contre l'ancien*—the young against the old—and Papa and Maman had wiped the floor with her and Walker, despite Walker's triple-word score for "pizza." No guy Violet had ever dated had ever fit in so seamlessly with her tiny little family. Not that she and Walker were actually dating.

Violet walked him out to his truck at the end of the night. Here they were, in the very same spot as the day they met. But he made no move to hoist her onto the hood of his vehicle, and she made no move to kiss him good night. Without her parents nearby, there was no need to perform.

"What are you thinking, Teach?" Walker asked. He stood with the car door handle gripped in his palm while she leaned against the side of the truck.

"I'm thinking that this was really nice, you coming

here for dinner." Kiss or no, simply being with him put her at ease.

He let go of the handle and shoved both hands into the front pocket of his jeans. "I guess that makes two of us. Because it was really nice hanging with you and your folks."

Violet crossed her arms, not sure what to do with her hands if they weren't splayed against his chest. "You're different here, you know—than you are in Oak Bluff."

She expected him to protest, but instead he nodded. "You're good around family. Me? Not so much. You hear anything more from that aunt of yours on another continent?"

His immediate change of subject was her cue not to dig any deeper into the Oak Bluff Walker versus Santa Barbara Walker situation. Plus, she'd been dying all night to tell him about Ines.

"We spoke on the phone late last night. She's wonderful, Walker. We talked about everything from games she and Maman used to play when they were kids to songs she writes and plays in local venues. She's a *musician*! Can you believe that? Here I thought I was such an oddball being the daughter of two chefs, but it all makes sense now. There's music in my blood, you know?" Her heart beat faster as the words spilled out of her mouth. "I know it sounds silly." She dipped her head, toeing a patch of gravel on the ground.

"Hey." Walker tapped her shoe with his boot, and she looked up. "There's nothing silly about feeling more like yourself. About connecting to someone you barely know. It's closer than a pair of shoes, right?"

She wondered if he meant just her and her aunt or if it was something more.

"Did she explain her disappearing act from your folks' life or vice versa?"

Violet shook her head. “She said it was Maman’s story to tell when she’s ready. She also said that she will do whatever she must to coordinate Maman’s treatment abroad but that she guessed I’d have a hell of a time getting her to agree to it.”

“You tell her yet?” he asked. “Your mother?”

Violet winced. “I’m sorta terrified, both of her reaction to going behind her back and to learning the story about what happened all those years ago. And don’t think I haven’t asked before. But she was always so good at brushing it off, saying the past was in the past. Somehow I think if she finds out Ines and I spoke, though, things will be different.”

He surprised her then by cupping her cheek in his hand. “Say the word on how I can help, and I will.”

Her throat tightened, and she placed a hand on his wrist. “Because we’re friends?”

He nodded. “Yeah, Teach. Because we’re friends.”

He dipped his head, and she held her breath, letting her eyes fall closed as he pressed a kiss to her forehead.

“I’ll see you tomorrow,” he said, pulling open the truck’s door. “Keep it up with the sensible shoes, okay?”

She laughed, then stepped back as he pulled the door shut and the truck’s engine roared to life.

Violet stood there for several minutes after he’d gone, lingering in the memory of his hand on her cheek and his lips on her skin, which was somehow more intimate than if he’d thrown her onto the hood of the truck like he had the first night they’d met.

She could do this—friends in Oak Bluff and pretending for the sake of her parents. At this point it seemed worse to fake the breakup than to keep up the lie, especially when she was practically living in Walker’s hometown. There was also her own selfish motivation—wanting to live in the bubble of having this amazing man in her life in whatever way she could. They were getting so good at make-believe that she could pretend there was no end in sight, even though there was.

CHAPTER THIRTEEN

Violet hummed to herself as she sat atop a bar stool while she tapped away at her laptop keyboard. For three Mondays their routine had been Violet working on something behind the scenes for the winery or Jack and Ava's wedding and Walker outside sizing and cutting shelves. But today it was 105 degrees outside with no shade, which meant no matter what Ava said about the mess, no way in hell was he doing out there what could just as easily be done in the air-conditioned tasting room. But in here it was much harder to keep the sawdust to the drop cloth under his small work station when all his eyes wanted to do was look up and across the bar at the beautiful woman who seemed able to maintain her focus much better than he could.

"Are you singing Mary Poppins?" he finally asked, and she froze in her chair, eyes wide as she looked at him.

"You can hear me all the way across the bar?"

Her hair was wound into a messy bun on top of her head with a pencil holding it in place, and damn she looked cute when she was caught in the act.

"Loud and clear, Teach."

She laughed. "Sometimes humming helps me concentrate. And who doesn't love 'Supercalifragilisticexpialidocious'?"

He brushed his hands off on his dust-covered jeans. "It'd probably be un-American not to."

"It'd be unhuman not to," she corrected.

He nodded toward her laptop. "Whatcha working on over there?"

She pulled the pencil from her hair, and the thick locks tumbled over her shoulder in messy spirals.

Shit. She'd gone from cute to sexy as hell in mere seconds.

Friends, asshole. Remember what's best for both of you. You'll get your damned kiss next Sunday and be happy with it.

"Wine pairings for the wedding menu. Ava's more than capable of doing it herself, but she's swamped with a course she's taking, Owen's baseball schedule, and—oh yeah—also planning a wedding. Your brothers are really lucky, you know? Ava and Lily are pretty amazing."

Ava and Lily were fine. He'd even admit they were great. But amazing was staring back at him from across the bar.

"You wanna break for lunch? I'm hungry as hell." More like distracted as hell, but food was at least a remedy for one immediate problem.

Violet tapped a couple of keys and then slammed her laptop shut.

"Sure," she said. "Where to? The B and B? I think Lily was making pulled chicken this week for the guests. Or we could do pizza at that little Italian place next to the market. We haven't been there yet. Or—"

"How about my place?" he interrupted as he rounded the bar so he was now standing next to her. "If you remember, I make one hell of a sandwich."

Her throat bobbed as she swallowed, and he somehow felt like he'd crossed a line. After all, Violet had only been to his place when they'd had parental supervision. But he really did have all the fixins for a great lunch. He also felt like avoiding the prying eyes of their small town today. Not that there was anything for anyone to see.

"Only if you have pickles," she finally said, and he let out a breath as she hopped off her stool. "And as long as I get to help prepare the meal. This is a working lunch, so you should put me to work."

He grinned. "You can help, Teach—if you ask me the right way."

Violet rolled her eyes, but he could tell she was biting back a smile of her own.

"Puis-je aider à préparer le déjeuner?" She batted her dark lashes, mocking him. *"S'il vous plait, monsieur?"*

Walker shrugged. "Only because I recognized a *please* in there, I'll let you slice the pickles."

Violet laughed, and they headed for the winery door just as Jack walked through it.

"Where are you two headed?" Walker's brother asked.

Walker pointed to the non-existent watch on his wrist. "Lunch," was all he said, but the word had enough bite to answer Jack's accusation.

"Violet, you mind if I borrow Mr. Sunshine for a second?"

"Not at all." She elbowed Walker in the side. "Meet you at the truck." Then she bounded out the door, leaving Walker and Jack alone.

Walker expected the riot act—about what, though, he wasn't sure.

"Come by the house for dinner tonight," Jack said.

Well, that was—unexpected.

"I'm busy," Walker said.

"Tomorrow, then," Jack countered.

Walker shrugged. "Pretty sure I'm busy then, too."

Jack ran a hand through his hair and let out a sigh. "What the hell's going on, Walker?"

Walker scanned the room, then pointed to his workstation. "Well, I'm cutting shelves, and Violet's working on some wedding assignment from Ava. You know...another day that ends in *y*."

"Cut the shit, Walker. I mean what the hell is going on with you avoiding your family? I mean what the hell is going on with you disappearing every Sunday night 'til well past midnight sometimes?"

Walker gritted his teeth. "Are you keeping tabs on me? Because last I checked, getting sober didn't mean I was under house arrest."

Jack tugged at the collar of his plaid button-up shirt. Walker noticed his brother was also wearing a pair of dark-wash jeans that looked like they'd just come off the shelf of some too-expensive mall store.

"You look like a lawyer pretending to be a rancher," Walker said. He regretted the words as soon as they came out of his mouth, but Jack was pushing his buttons, and this was the only way he knew how to push back.

"I'm a lawyer and a rancher," Jack said, unfazed. "And you're an asshole, but that's not the point. I'm not keeping tabs on you. Olivia runs her B and B movie night on Sundays. Common room faces the street. Sometimes she sees you pulling in."

Walker shook his head. "So the sheriff's *girlfriend* is spying on me. Even better."

"Olivia's a good woman," Jack said, and Walker could hear his brother's patience wearing thin. "She may not know you real well, but she cares about you. We all do. And maybe if we saw you a little more, we'd feel the need to show you how much we care a little less."

"Noted," Walker said with a nod. "We done here? Because Violet's waiting, and we're hungry." He brushed past his brother and almost made it out the door. Almost.

"You with her on Sundays?" Jack asked.

Walker stopped dead in his tracks.

"I know you haven't been at Nora's. I'm the first person she'd have called if she saw you walk through that door. Jenna says you've been stopping by but that you usually leave her place no later than six. So I figure you're either taking the scenic route home or you're playing house with someone who's going to up and leave eventually. I don't want to see anything set you back."

Jack paused, but Walker still didn't turn to face him.

"I don't come to dinner, big brother, because with you and Luke and everybody else in town, I'm Walker Everett, alcoholic who's still climbing his way out of a decade plus of hell. With her I don't have to be that guy." And with that Walker pushed through the door and out into the blazing sun.

He found Violet leaning on his bumper, her pale yellow T-shirt and cropped denim shorts doing nothing to save her from the heat. Beads of sweat sat along her hairline, and she fanned herself with what looked like a take-out menu from a pizza place outside of town.

"Your window was open, and I was roasting," she said. "So I took a chance on peeking under a sun visor, and *voila*! My own personal air conditioner."

Just seeing her sitting there—overheated but not complaining, blaming him, or judging the way he lived his life—lightened the weight of his and Jack's brotherly exchange.

"Everything all right in there?" she asked, nodding back toward the winery door.

"It's better now," he said, shooting her a grin. "C'mon. Time to eat."

Violet followed Walker around to the back of the antiques shop and up a staircase that ended at the small landing and door. Then he simply turned the handle and pushed the door open, ushering her inside.

"Wait," Violet said. "You don't even lock the door?"

He'd already been home when she'd come over the last time and had thought nothing of the unlocked door.

Walker winked. "That's Oak Bluff, Teach. Safest place on earth. At least in my very limited experience."

She laughed. "Right. Because no airports for you. Too many humans, and we know how much you hate those."

She slid past him and into the kitchen, which was exactly where they needed to be, but she kept on walking. The place looked different than before. She moved forward the two more steps it took to enter the living room and realized what it was. He'd cleaned the place up for her parents. But now the couch was covered with a tarp and piled with scraps of different types of wood. The room itself was more of a storage space for various pieces she assumed Walker had built—a step stool, a large mirror framed with a rich, dark wood, a knotted pine hope chest.

"Oh, Walker," she said, striding toward the chest and dropping to her knees. "This is absolutely beautiful. You're *really* good."

The wood floor creaked as he strode toward her.

"Been selling a couple pieces here and there at the farmers market where Jenna sets up shop on the weekends. Hoping to unload this one next weekend."

She ran her hand along the beveled edge of the lid, then

across the grain of the wood on the body of the chest, her finger tracing the shape of each individual knot.

"If I had my own place and disposable income, I'd buy it off you right now."

He crossed his arms and leaned against a patch of wall that was clear of one of his projects. "Why don't you just take it?" he asked matter-of-factly. "Hell, I can always make another."

Violet shot to her feet. "Don't you dare make another one, Walker Everett. This piece is one-of-a-kind." She poked him in the chest with her index finger, not understanding her sudden exasperation. "And don't you go offering your hard work out for free, either."

He wrapped a calloused hand around her wrist, firm yet gentle.

"You all right there, Teach?" he asked.

She stared at all the different shades of gold in his beard. "I'm fine," she lied. Two minutes inside his own personal space—the way it was when he wasn't putting on a show for Gabriel and Camille Chastain—and she was overwhelmed. This was supposed to be lunch. Sandwiches. Nothing more. She was gonna slice the pickles.

"Where are the pickles?" she asked.

He chuckled. "Fridge. Top shelf. Grown and pickled by none other than Jenna Owens. Even better than what we had at Jack and Ava's, though if you tell Jenna they had store-bought she'll flip her lid. Either that or she'll drive over to his place with a truckload so he doesn't run out again."

He released her wrist, and she immediately backed away and turned toward the kitchen.

"I take it back," he called after her. "The offer for the chest. I'd rather charge buckets of money for it than let it end up with the likes of you."

She flipped him off over her shoulder, and he laughed harder.

Good. Back to bantering like friends.

In between bites of bacon, lettuce, tomato, and avocado sandwiches—pickles on the *side* this time—Violet brought up her digital music library on her phone and proposed they play *Name the Song*.

"Whoever scores the best out of ten gets the last slice of bacon," she said.

Walker narrowed his eyes. "How dare you step between a man and his bacon, Teach. You're on."

They flipped a coin to see who would go first, and Walker won the toss, calling heads.

"Hand it over," he said, and Violet gave him her phone.

"Ten seconds per song?" she suggested, and Walker nodded his agreement.

He scrolled through her library for several seconds, then shook his head. "You know what? I'm not liking these odds. It's your list, so you're more likely to know the songs. I'm going to go to the music store app and find me a clip from there. But I do admire a woman who has the entire Tom Jones catalog."

"As you should," she said. "Now come on! Stump me. But remember that I *am* a music major."

Walker grinned. "Fine. Let's see if you majored in this." He pressed play on the song sample.

After only two notes, Violet slapped her hand on the table. "Aerosmith, 'Dream On'!"

Walker groaned. "I'm toast," he said. "And what's with the table slapping?"

Violet winced. "Sorry. It was my game show buzzer."

He chuckled and handed over the phone where she tried and failed to stump him with "Landslide" by Fleetwood Mac.

They went on like this for the next several minutes until they were neck and neck at question ten—Violet having incorrectly insisted that Fall Out Boy's "My Songs Know What You Did in the Dark" was titled "I'm on Fire."

"All you have to do is get this one little song right, and the bacon is all yours," she said, queuing up her final challenge.

Walker licked his lips. "Mmm. I can already taste it," he said. "And you should know that I do not share."

She grinned, enjoying his competitive side—one to rival her own—and then hit play.

"'Wannabe' by the Spice Girls!" he called out after three seconds, then followed up his correct guess with, "Shit. You used bacon to trap me into admitting I know the Spice Girls."

Violet burst into a fit of laughter. She couldn't remember the last time she laughed so hard or felt such ridiculous joy. Before Walker had a chance to react, she grabbed the prized piece of bacon and darted into the living room.

"Relinquish your trophy, and I won't tell anyone your dirty little secret!" she cried as she ducked for cover behind the couch.

"I thought I told you that nothing gets between me and my bacon," he said.

She peeked over the top of the couch to see him striding her way, then yelped when he skipped using the floor and leaped over the piece of furniture acting as her shield.

She tilted her head back and dangled the bacon over her lips. Right before she took a bite, though, Walker swooped in and tore the piece from her hand with his own savage bite, his lips colliding with hers as he did.

He chewed and swallowed while she sat there, frozen.

"Violet, I'm sorry," he said. "I didn't mean to—"

She threw her arms around his neck, her lips crushing against his. He didn't stop her—didn't even hesitate to kiss her back.

In a flurry of movement they stood, and Walker hoisted her onto his hips. She wrapped her legs around his waist, and he grabbed her ass for purchase.

"I have been wanting to get my hands on this *ass*et of yours for weeks," he said between heated kisses.

Her fingers tangled in his overgrown hair. "What are we doing?" she said.

"Lunch," he answered, his voice rough.

"Good enough for me," she said, and she turned off the part of her brain that wanted to ask more and decided to take what she wanted for once. Something only for her—even if that something was a man she'd say good-bye to before too long.

He walked her through his bedroom door and set her down so the backs of her legs were next to his bed. She pulled her T-shirt over her head, then her bra.

He nodded toward the lower half of her body. "How about we lose the shorts, whatever's underneath them, and the shoes."

She let out a nervous laugh, then remembered that Walker had already seen her completely naked thanks to her stunt that first night at the B and B.

She raised her brows, then kicked off her tennis shoes. Next she unbuttoned her shorts and shimmied out of them along with her underwear.

Walker drank her in with his ocean blue eyes. "You're beautiful, Teach," he said. "So damned beautiful in every possible way." He cupped her right breast in his hand, then dipped his head to kiss it, to swirl his tongue over her hardened peak.

She whimpered as his teeth nipped and his lips sucked.

For weeks she'd convinced herself that despite their short make-out sessions on the Sundays when Walker showed up for dinner, the friend thing was working out just fine. Yet now, with his lips and his hands on her like this, she wondered how she'd held it together for so long.

While he paid equal attention to her left breast, Violet worked open the button of his jeans and shoved her hand inside the waistband of his briefs.

Walker let loose a growl as she wrapped her hand around his thick shaft.

Seriously. How had they held off this long?

He pulled his shirt over his head, kicked off his boots, and stepped out of his jeans and socks. With one hand maintaining its firm grip, she got rid of his briefs with the other. Lunch had officially turned into dessert.

"Look at you," she said, stepping away so her eyes could take him in. "God, Walker. It, like, hurts to look at you."

He laughed, but the truth was he was beautiful in a way that made her ache—lean muscles from the physical work he did, a hint of sparkle as well as pain behind his bright blue eyes.

He found a condom easily in the drawer of his nightstand, and she rolled it over his thick, hard length like it was the most natural thing in the world, like she hadn't just met this man last month.

Wordlessly, he laid her down on the bed, and she let her legs fall apart, welcoming him.

He nudged at her opening and slid in easily, burying himself inside her and filling her so completely she thought her heart might burst.

She bucked against him.

"Patience, Teach," he said softly. "Lunch hour's not over

yet." Then he pressed his mouth to hers as they found a quiet rhythm that let both of them dial back the frenzy of movement and savor the moment.

He kissed her lips, her jaw, her neck, and savored the hardened peaks of her breasts.

"I think maybe we need to take more lunch breaks together," she said when he tilted his head up, his eyes meeting hers. "I mean friends—" she gasped as he slid out of her, the movement achingly slow, then sank back into her so deep she cried out.

He kissed her, tugged at her bottom lip with his teeth. "Sure," he said. "*Friendly* lunch breaks don't break any self-imposed rules."

He grabbed one of her ankles and threw it over his shoulder, then plunged inside her once more.

"*Dieu,* Walker," she said, then sucked in a sharp breath. "*Oh mon Dieu.*"

"Fuck," he ground out. "If I'd have known you'd turn all French when I got inside you, I'd have thrown the rules out the window long before now."

"*Plus fort!*" she cried, grabbing his perfect ass. *Harder.*

He slammed into her, either understanding her words or his body understanding her need.

"*Plus vite!*" she added. *Faster*. Then she gripped the backs of his thighs and coaxed him to pick up the speed.

"How do you say"—he asked between breaths—"I want to watch you?"

He slid a hand between them and swirled his thumb over her soaked center.

Her back arched, and she whimpered. "*Je... veux... te... regarder,*" she managed to say as he pulsed inside her, his thumb on her clit moving in the same rhythm.

"Well then, Teach, *je veux te regarder*."

He rolled onto his back so she was sitting on top of him, his hands on her hips as they slid slowly back and forth, each roll of her pelvis taking him deeper and sending her closer to the edge she wasn't quite ready to reach.

She dropped her head, her hair falling over her face, and lowered herself to kiss him. She nipped at his lip with her teeth, and he responded with a low growl, the sexiest sound she'd probably ever heard.

"Why is it so different with you?" he asked. But he didn't let her answer. He kissed her hard, and she rose onto her knees, sinking over him again and again, her body begging for release even though she never wanted this to end.

"Walker," she whimpered, and he moved in time with her, thrusting as she descended on him with fierce abandon, pumping harder and faster until her head fell back and she cried out, letting the climax wash over her in hard, crashing waves.

She collapsed onto his chest in a boneless heap of her former self.

He kissed the top of her head, then wrapped her in his arms.

Never had she felt so satiated, so cared for, so safe.

"Lunch tomorrow?" she asked, still trying to bring her breathing back to normal.

He chuckled but didn't say anything. And because she didn't want to break the spell, she burrowed into him, her body fitting against his like they were made to lay exactly like this.

But lunch tomorrow never came. Violet had to run two towns over to take care of a misprint on a batch of Crossroads Winery bottle labels unless the Everett family wanted their first pinot noir vintage to come from Cross*toads* Winery. She was gone most of the day.

On Wednesday Walker and Luke had to take Cleo, one

of their horses, to the equine vet for a bug bite that seemed to be giving her an allergic reaction.

Between dog-walking, grabbing a couple shifts at the B and B front desk, and leading a few pre-harvest vineyard tours to local restauranteurs, Saturday morning showed up out of nowhere, and she was headed back to Santa Barbara once more. One thing was for sure, though.

Violet would never have a better turkey, avocado, and bacon sandwich for as long as she lived.

CHAPTER FOURTEEN

Despite a week of missed connections, Walker showed up in Santa Barbara at six thirty Sunday evening, just in time for Papa's Asaro—a sweet potato–based dish Maman had introduced Gabe to years ago that was now one of the most popular menu items in his restaurant. Yet the African dishes Violet had grown up loving were starting to leave a bitter aftertaste. Her history—*Maman*'s history—was more than items on a French fusion restaurant menu. The closer she got to making Paris a reality, the more she began to feel like she was going home. Her parents would have to understand what this trip would mean not only for Maman but for Violet, too.

"Thank you for coming tonight," she said to Walker while they were eating, not realizing she'd needed him here until he showed up at the door.

Maman wasn't much in the mood for board games after coffee. The winces she'd tried to hide for Violet's sake were no use. Violet saw them anyway.

So, when the coffee was gone and Walker and Violet had cleaned the dishes, she headed for the door to accompany him to his truck.

"*Attendez*," Maman said. "Sorry. Wait, please," she added, translating her French to English for Walker's sake. Both he and Violet turned back toward the dining room.

Her father had snuck out earlier to help close the restaurant, so it was just the three of them.

Maman strode toward Walker, leaning more heavily on her cane than she had all weekend, and Violet knew she was in more pain than she was letting on. Was it her hip? Her foot? Both? Violet would ask after Walker left, but Maman would downplay as always.

When she was right before him, Maman set the cane against the wall and took Walker's bearded face into her palms. On instinct, he dipped his head so she wouldn't have to reach, and she kissed him softly on each cheek.

"Thank you," she said in her lilting accent.

Walker's brows drew together. "You're welcome. But I don't understand."

She patted him on the cheek and smiled. "I have not seen Vee smile like she does when you're around in months. Maybe it is years."

Violet's heart sank at her mother's words. It wasn't that she was wrong. It was that she had noticed, which meant Violet had done a shit job at hiding her worry, her stress. She'd made it a point to always paint on a smile when she was home, but she was different when Walker was here. She knew it, and Maman knew it, which meant those lines between fantasy and reality were blurring even more.

Walker nodded once. "My pleasure, ma'am."

She waved him off.

"You better start calling me Camille," she teased. "You make me feel *très âgé*."

Walker's expression grew puzzled again, and Violet laughed.

"Old," she translated for him. "You make her feel old."

"Go," her mother said, now shooing them out the door. "I know you like your private good-byes." She gave them both a knowing grin, and Violet hoped like hell that grin only meant that she knew about the lingering kisses against his truck and not what they'd done that first night they had met.

She smiled nervously, then threaded her fingers through Walker's and tugged him out the door and down the steps.

"Your mom doesn't..." he trailed off when they reached solid ground, and Violet knew he was thinking exactly what she was.

"Oh God, I hope not," she admitted. "But I feel like a teenager who got caught with her door closed while she had a boy in the room."

He raised a brow. "*Were* you a teenager who got caught with her door closed while she had a boy in the room?"

"Wouldn't you like to know?" she teased.

He shook his head. "It's bad enough I've *seen* that Ramon asshole. I don't want to know about anyone else who's had the privilege of touching you. I'd rather fool myself into thinking I'm the only one worthy of such an honor."

Violet snorted. "Honor. Very funny." Yet even though they were teasing each other, his words made her heart squeeze. Was he truly envious of the men she'd been with before him—or those who'd surely come after their little game ended?

Wordlessly, Walker lowered the tailgate, and they both sat in the bed of the pickup, their legs dangling over the bumper. Well, Violet's legs dangled. Walker's long legs ended with his feet planted firmly on the ground.

She traced lazy circles on his denim-covered thigh.

"You know," she said, "I'm beginning to think this might be getting too real." She cleared her throat. "For them, I mean."

She was sure he saw right through her. The truth was, no matter what label they put on it, what they'd been doing these past weeks had been more real than anything she'd had with any other men in her life.

"What about for you?" he asked.

She shrugged. "I'm not seeing anyone else. Not that I'd have time to. But I also don't want to see anyone else, Walker. That wasn't how this was supposed to go. I wasn't supposed to miss you when I left for Paris, and now I'm not sure how we say good-bye. All of those things are pretty damned real, don't you think?"

He was silent for several long moments before he spoke. "You want me to stop coming by?" he asked, his hand on the bare skin of her knee right under the hem of her skirt. Her breath caught in her throat, which seemed to give him encouragement to slide his hand higher.

She placed a palm over his, stopping him before she lost the ability to form words.

"I don't want to stop anything that we're doing," she said.

"You just stopped me from sliding my hand into your panties."

She smacked him playfully across the shoulder, and he laughed. God, she loved the sound of that laugh. It had been so hard to come by in the early days of knowing him. Now it seemed like he gave it to her freely, like she was the only one who got to witness it, and she sometimes wondered if that was true.

Her smile faltered when she focused on his initial response. He hadn't addressed the realness of their situation—whether he agreed or not. He'd only offered to stop making the drive to Santa Barbara, which—she realized now—was not exactly the reaction she'd hoped for.

"You know what I mean," she insisted. "Even if we blame our fake breakup on the very real distance between California and France, I'm worried about how disappointed they'll be when this is over...Maman especially."

But was she really talking about Maman anymore? Everything was set up in Paris, thanks to her aunt. But Violet was waiting until the last possible minute to tell her mother. She was no longer afraid of having done this behind her mother's back. What scared her the most was learning why Maman hadn't been back home for decades. Was it worth Violet missing out on half her family—half her heritage?

"Can I ask you something?" she said.

"Sure."

"I already told you I haven't been with anyone else. These past weeks that we've been *just friends*, have you been intimate with anyone else besides me?"

He chuckled. "Only myself whenever I think about you with that towel at your feet in the B and B after your accident."

She laughed. "And do you think you'll be intimate with anyone else before I leave?"

His smile faded. "No, Teach. I don't think I will."

It wasn't an admission of realness, but it was enough.

She lowered herself onto her back. It was dark, but a layer of clouds obscured the stars so that all she saw was a dim haze above.

Walker lay down beside her.

"Am I a terrible person for contacting my aunt behind Maman's back? For wanting to go to Paris for me as much as for her?"

"Hell no," he told her. He brushed a thumb under her eye, and she was surprised at the wetness against her skin. "I know a hell of a lot about guilt, Teach. If you let it eat at your insides and keep you from living your own life, it'll kill you if you're not careful."

And there it was, Walker Everett's own story slowly leaking from him as he let her past another small barrier. She didn't understand the guilt he carried or why he did, but she knew it was there, and somehow this brought them closer despite the reality of their days being numbered.

He didn't kiss her, didn't attempt to slide his hand underneath her skirt again. Instead they both lay there searching for stars they couldn't see and words they couldn't say until finally Walker had to make the drive back home to Oak Bluff.

Her parents were still in the kitchen straightening up when she made her way back inside. If she couldn't tell Walker how she really felt, it was about time she told them.

"Can I talk to you two for a minute?" she asked, her voice shaking.

"What is wrong?" Maman asked. "Did something happen with Walker?"

She shook her head. Maybe she was scared of how much she cared about him, but she wasn't scared of wanting something for herself anymore. Being with him—in whatever way they defined it—had given her a confidence she hadn't had before.

"I spoke with Ines. Your sister."

Her mother gripped the counter as her knees buckled, and Papa grabbed her elbow.

Violet gasped as her father led her mother to a dining room chair.

"Why would you—" he started. "Did she contact you?"

Violet shook her head. "There's a doctor in Paris who will do what Maman's doctor won't. She is still a citizen, which means there are options for health care over there, and Ines can help set up the treatment."

"You had no right!" her father shouted, and Violet shrank back. He'd never, in all her years, yelled at her like that, and Violet had the urge to run. But she stood firm, feet planted. There was no running from this anymore.

"I have *every* right," she said. "Maman is in pain, but she could get better. And I—I left school, Papa. You didn't ask me to give up my future, but I did. I put it on hold because I love you. I love Maman. And I would do anything for you both. But I need this, too. I need my family. I need to know where I come from other than Santa Barbara and Papa's heritage. You two know who you are, but I've missed out on *half* of my identity because of whatever happened in Paris before I was born!"

Her father stared at her, mouth agape, his eyes glassy with tears.

Maman reached out from where she sat and squeezed his hand. "She is right, Gabriel," she finally said. "We have been selfish. It is time she knows." Violet's mother finally met her eyes. "Sit, *cherie*. If you will forgive me, then I will go with you to Paris. I am the one who took half your life away. It is my responsibility to give it back."

So Violet sat at the other end of the table and listened to the part of her parents' love story she'd never heard—the one where Aunt Ines met and fell for her father first—and how he left her for Camille.

Maybe what she and Walker had wasn't so complicated after all. Maybe *real* wasn't easy like she'd always thought it had been for her parents. And maybe, just maybe, she was sick and tired of pretending.

CHAPTER FIFTEEN

Some days when Walker woke up, he forgot he was an addict. Other days it felt like his two months in rehab were yesterday. He could still feel the shakes. He remembered barely being able to make it to a toilet or a garbage can as his body convulsed and he heaved up whatever was left in his stomach, which was often nothing more than bile. He'd begged for just one drink, had even thrown a punch at his group leader for refusing him—a swing and a miss that got him sedated and strapped to a gurney while he was rehydrated with an IV.

It was his lowest point, at least the lowest he could remember. That was the reason he kept the picture on his phone of his messed-up face, pre–broken nose setting. Sometimes he needed to remind himself of what he'd forgotten. Even though he missed it, he hadn't poured a shot once this week. Despite their strained parting last Sunday night, he guessed Violet Chastain's presence in his life had a thing or two to do with that.

A fist pounded on the door, jolting him from his thoughts.

"What in the hell?" he mumbled, then strode toward the door. He threw it open, indignant at whoever had the balls to interrupt his morning, to find Sheriff Cash Hawkins in full uniform, aviators resting on the bridge of his nose.

"To what do I owe the pleasure, Sheriff?" he asked, not masking the bitterness in his tone.

Cash held out a legal-size manila envelope. "Messenger from the county courthouse dropped these off and I thought I'd bring them by. Your repayment terms for Nora's window."

Walker snatched the envelope out of the sheriff's hands and narrowed his eyes at the address on the front—*his* address.

"Don't see why home delivery is necessary when this is all stamped and ready to go. Seems a waste of good postage," Walker said.

Cash lowered his sunglasses and nodded at something over Walker's shoulder.

"You want to tell me what the hell that is?" he asked.

Walker turned, following the sheriff's gaze to the kitchen cabinet he'd apparently left open the night before. The one that held a bottle of whiskey and a shot glass.

"Damn it," he said under his breath. "It's not what it looks like, Sheriff." He turned to face Cash again. He thought about explaining that the bottle was his test. That he needed to have the temptation nearby to prove he could resist it. But it seemed like all he'd been doing since he got back was explaining. He wasn't drinking, and for the first time he realized he didn't have to prove that to anyone but himself. He and Oak Bluff might not be the right fit, but for the time being, this apartment was his home—even if he was renting it from the sheriff's mother. "Thanks for the delivery." He started closing the door, but Cash stuck his boot over the threshold before Walker could shut it all the way.

"You got a search warrant or something?" Walker asked coolly. "Because otherwise you're trespassing on private property." Cash opened his mouth to say something, but Walker cut him off. "My name's on the rental agreement, Sheriff. And Lucinda owns the place, not you. So unless you have some sort of legal cause to be stepping into my place uninvited, I think you'd better move your boot."

Cash's jaw tightened. "I'm not here as the sheriff, Everett. I'm here as a friend."

Walker let out a bitter laugh. "You arrested me, let me sleep in a cell, and now you're showin' up on my doorstep with the terms concerning the court's charges against me, questioning me about personal property. I'd say you've earned your title fair and square."

Cash removed his boot, his expression impassive, but he said nothing more. So Walker shut the door, then threw his fist at the wood frame. Not a swing and a miss, evidenced by a split knuckle.

He shook out his hand, then wrapped it with a kitchen towel before finally closing the damned cabinet.

Walker wasn't in one of those programs that gave you a sponsor, someone to do daily or weekly check-ins, to look over his shoulder and keep him from taking the drink he wanted every damned night. It didn't matter, though. Jenna showed up in his kitchen at the crack of dawn. Luke and Jack railroaded him into a family dinner he knew was all about making sure he hadn't yet messed up, and now there was Sheriff Hawkins. They were all waiting for him to fail, everyone except the one person who didn't know the truth.

Violet.

Walker pulled his phone from the back pocket of his jeans, opened the photo app, and stared long and hard at the picture from New Year's Eve—his face bloodied and his nose swollen, his eyes glazed over. He didn't recognize the man in the photo any more than he recognized the one in the mirror he saw each morning. All he knew was that he didn't trust himself any more than his brothers, his aunt, or the sheriff did. But he was the only one who could make this stick. He was the only one who could test himself night after night, alone with nothing but a bottle he wasn't ready to empty.

He unwrapped his hand and tossed the towel onto the counter, giving the image on his phone a final glance before closing the app and shoving the device back in his pocket.

He headed over to the ranch and went to the equipment shed to load the roller-crimper into his truck. He'd told his brothers he'd till the cover crop at the vineyard, but the large piece of equipment wasn't there. He scrolled through the recent texts on his phone and found the one he'd sent both his brothers last night.

Looks like rain tomorrow. Gonna grab the crimper and till the cover crop tomorrow before it hits.

Both had responded with the thumbs-up emoji, and it wasn't like his brothers to forget someone else offering to do some early morning work.

Something didn't add up.

He decided to walk to the vineyard, ready to give his brothers hell for stealing from him a morning of good, old-fashioned manual labor that would help him clear his head.

It was more than the sheriff interrupting his morning. He hadn't seen or spoken to Violet since he left her in Santa Barbara Sunday night. After admitting he wasn't sleeping with anyone else—and didn't plan to—he wasn't sure how to behave if he saw her, and he sure as hell wasn't sure what to say to make everything easy and fun like it had been for weeks. So he'd done the grown-up thing and avoided her, figuring if he didn't give himself the chance to say anything to her, he couldn't say the *wrong* thing to her. For all he knew, she was keeping her distance as well.

"You've got to be kidding me," he said when he finally got to the vineyard and saw not one but two other vehicles already parked on the side of the road—the roller-crimper in the bed of Jack's truck but no one doing a lick of tilling the crop. This morning kept getting better and better. He admitted to himself he had a lot of years of fucking up to answer for. He just hadn't counted on answering to everyone on the same damned day.

He scrubbed a hand across his jaw. This wasn't a case of his brothers forgetting he signed on for the job. It was an all-out ambush, and he was going to meet it head on.

He didn't have to go far. Jack and Luke were both leaning on the hood of Luke's truck drinking coffee, like they weren't even trying to hide what this was all about.

"Glad you still left me the work to do," he said to them both. "This gonna take long? Because I need to get up and down the rows before the rain hits." He tilted his head toward the cloud-covered sky that was quickly morphing from white to dark gray.

His brothers stopped talking to each other and turned their attention to him, not that he could read anything in their expressions, their eyes hidden behind sunglasses they didn't really need. But he could see Luke's brows raise as he took a long, slow sip from his coffee cup, obviously deferring to Jack.

"We need to talk," Jack said.

"I have a phone," Walker countered.

"Yeah, but you're shit at returning calls."

He couldn't argue there.

"You're only calling to invite me to dinner. I figured you understood that no response meant no, thank you."

"What happened to your hand?" Jack asked.

Walker shrugged. "Had a disagreement with a door."

Luke gave him a single nod. "Can't say I haven't been there before. You win?" The corner of his brother's mouth turned up.

Walker scratched the back of his neck. Enough with the games. "Either of you want to tell me what this is about, or do I need to keep spinnin' my wheels and asking questions? Because I got better shit to do than hang around with you assholes."

"Assholes, huh?" Luke said. "It's a shame you had to say that. We mighta gone easy on you if you'd been a little nicer, right, Jack?"

Jack shook his head, a hint of a smile slipping through his stoic expression. "Now when the hell has our little brother ever been *nice*?"

Before Walker had time to react, Luke stepped aside to reveal Jack shaking and then pointing what looked like a bottle of champagne at him, but he knew his brothers weren't dick enough to spray him full of alcohol when, despite his own doubts along with everyone else's, he'd made it—hell, how long had he made it?

"What the—" But his words were cut off with a point-blank spray of cold, fizzy liquid right at his face. And his torso. Pretty much up and down his entire body.

He tried to wipe his eyes, but his hands were as wet and sticky as the rest of him. So he blinked away the mess as best he could and spit out what got into his mouth.

Grape juice. Sparkling white grape juice.

"What. The hell. Are you doing?" He wasn't yelling. He

was too much in shock to yell. But seriously. He woke up this morning to get shit done at the vineyard, and this was the thanks he got?

Jack stuck the empty bottle under one arm and wiped his hands on his jeans. Luke handed Walker a towel they must have had at the ready because of course this was a premeditated act. Walker just couldn't figure out why.

"One hundred days," Jack said, and Walker could have sworn his oldest brother sounded choked up. This was saying a lot considering Jack was the rock. He was the one who held it together for all of them from the moment their mother's casket was lowered into the earth all the way until now.

"What the hell are you talking about?" he asked. Shit, he was soaked. The towel was worthless.

Luke grabbed the bottle from Jack and slapped it against Walker's torso.

"A hundred days sober, little bro." Luke winked. "Well, until now."

His brothers stood there, staring at him, until it sunk in.

Walker's eyes had always been on making it one more day. He hadn't thought there'd been enough *one-more-day*s to hit any sort of milestone yet. At the same time a part of him had been waiting for the other shoe to drop, for something to push him back over the edge. He'd flat out told Jack sobriety wouldn't work that morning in the jail cell, and despite what he'd apparently accomplished, he still didn't know who he was without the bottle.

But he'd been sober for a hundred days. And after their less-than-subtle chaperoning and what he thought was an inability to trust him to make it this far, he'd proved them wrong.

Maybe they'd believed in him all along.

After two months of inpatient treatment, all Walker thought he'd wanted was to fly solo and stay under the radar. But maybe having these two in his corner wasn't so bad after all.

"You assholes have been counting?" he asked, but the anger had already disappeared from his voice. He found a rogue dry corner of his shirt and wiped it across his face.

"Yeah," Jack said. "We're counting, and we're damned proud of you. But we're also your brothers, and we don't buy gifts and shit."

Walker shook his head, a devious grin spreading across his face.

"You know what? I wanna feel the love, Jack." He opened his arms wide. "Come give your brother a god-damned hug."

Jack held his hands up in surrender. "I have a meeting, Walker. I seriously do in, like, thirty minutes."

Walker shrugged. "And now I gotta shower before and after I do the damned cover crop. We all have to make sacrifices, big bro."

He barreled toward his brother, and because it was always two against one, Luke grabbed Jack from behind and pinned him in place until Walker smacked against him in a grape juice–dripping embrace.

"Assholes," Jack said. But he was laughing.

And then Walker realized he and his brothers were kind of, sort of, in a group hug, which was something they hadn't done since…ever. The situation had quickly changed from brotherly hazing to something a lot like affection, which—once again—was untread ground for all three of them.

Most likely coming to the same conclusion at the same time, the three men broke apart as quickly as they came together.

Walker tilted his head toward the sky and caught the clouds rolling in.

"Looks like the rain is coming quicker than we thought," Jack said.

The air was thick with humidity, but any warmth he'd felt at the sun first peeking through the clouds was gone. The temperature felt like it had already dropped ten degrees. Walker knew his window for getting the tilling done was a narrow one. So he pulled off his wet shirt and tossed it over the fence.

"No sense in going back to shower if the sky's gonna open up on me." Walker nodded toward both his brothers. "You're both still assholes—but thanks, I guess."

He didn't wait for them to respond, partly because he had to beat the rain and partly because he needed time to digest what had just taken place, what it meant that he'd made it this far and that the two people he thought had the least faith in him to succeed had placed their bets on him to come out the victor all along. So he lowered the roller-crimper off the truck and under the fence, hopped over it himself, then took to getting the soil's cover crop ready for the rain.

It was three hours later when he left the crimper under a tarp—courtesy of Luke—inside the fence. Since they'd stolen the piece of equipment from him in the first place, his brothers offered to pick it back up when one of them had the time. So Walker grabbed his shirt, now stiff with the drying juice, threw it over his shoulder, and began the walk back to the ranch.

Of course, that was exactly when the sky decided it had held out long enough.

A heavy, thick drop of water pelted him in the back of the neck. Then one on his shoulder. His forehead. Before he knew it, it was an all-out downpour, the grass growing slippery as soil turned to mud. He stepped quickly yet carefully, but it didn't matter. There was no such thing as careful when the path before him was nature's Slip 'N Slide. Soon he was flat on his back, the sticky spray of sparkling juice long washed away in the torrent, but he was far from clean.

He hadn't thought he'd make it a week let alone a hundred days. Maybe the guy he'd pretended to be for Violet really was *him.* Maybe what she saw in him was more than an act. Maybe he wasn't the busted-up mess in the photo anymore. But he'd been too chicken shit to admit why.

Violet. She saw in him what he never knew was there. But Jack and Luke saw it, too, now. It was about damned time Walker started seeing it himself.

He stood up laughing, his torso and jeans covered in mud, and somehow made it the rest of the way to his truck without falling again. The vehicle might have been a hundred years old, but it still pained him to think about the work it would take to clean the upholstery after today so that he'd be able to ride in it again. But he couldn't worry about that now. He needed to get the hell out of the rain and into a damned shower already.

He could barely see through his windshield as he rolled down Oak Bluff Way, but he saw enough to know that parking wouldn't be easy. It looked like every tourist and resident combined had rushed to the heart of town to escape the weather. The only spot he could find was two blocks past Lucinda's antiques shop—his current residence—and the Oak Bluff Bed and Breakfast.

Of course the downpour lasted the couple of minutes it took him to drive into town and park. Once he stepped out of the truck, it had already eased to a steady drizzle, making the car he'd parked behind easier to see. A silver MINI Cooper.

Looked like his and Violet's paths were finally going to cross. He blew out a breath, then shook his hair out like a wet dog trying to dry off its coat and strode down Oak Bluff's main drag in nothing but his mud-splattered jeans.

Shop doors opened and people emerged from their shelters to get on with their days as he made his way toward the antiques shop. Some of the locals simply waved and offered a chuckle along with "Good morning, Everett," while others stared at him like he was the Swamp Thing.

He guessed it wasn't that much of a shock. They'd seen him in much worse shape than this. The only difference was him being sober enough to notice their stares. A hundred days sober enough. They all probably thought he was still on a bender from the night before. Why the hell else would he be walking through town half-naked and covered in mud? He didn't give a shit what they knew or what they didn't. Because *he* knew.

Walker stopped midstep and pushed his hands through his drenched and muddied hair. A chill ran through his body, straight to his bones. He wasn't sure if he'd ever been soaked through like this before, and the rain must have made the temperature drop another five degrees. It didn't matter, though. None of it mattered.

A hundred days. Shit. He hadn't had enough faith in himself to think he'd last a hundred minutes. But here he fucking was.

"Walker?" a woman called, her voice tentative. But he knew that voice, even after days of not hearing it.

He turned and realized he was standing right in front of the B and B. Violet was approaching the edge of the property clad in a yellow raincoat and knee-high rain boots, with a dog leash in her hand, the other end connected to the collar of Oak Bluff's best-known German shepherd,

Dixie—the second of two very important females in the life of one Sheriff Cash Hawkins.

"You walking Dixie in the rain?" he asked.

She crossed her arms, leash still in hand. "That's how you greet a girl after not seeing her for four days?"

He took a step closer, not forgetting that he was wearing a hell of a lot less clothing than she was.

Her throat bobbed as she swallowed, and he didn't even try to hide the satisfaction in his smile.

"Hello, Violet," he said coolly. "You walking Dixie in the rain?"

She rolled her eyes. "I'm walking Dixie because I wanted to get out and stretch my legs during the dry spell before the rain hit again. Been holed up with Ava all week finalizing details for the wedding, helping her put together proposed vintage lists to sell to local restaurants, and I'm on desk duty the rest of the day at the B and B, which'll be teeming with patrons once the second wave of storms hits. Supposed to be a really wet day, so I figured I better get out while I can. Dixie wanted to tag along."

He looked her up and down, taking in her appearance.

"You're damned beautiful bundled up like that."

Her face was shadowed but he could still see her cheeks go pink.

"And you're half-naked and covered in mud," she said. "What the hell happened to you?"

He leaned down and whispered in her ear. "Everything, Teach." Then he pushed her hood down, cradled the back of her head in his palm, and kissed her right there in front of anyone who wanted to get a good look.

All his worry about how he and Violet were supposed to act when they saw each other again fell away. He didn't need to put a label on it or tell her it was real. All he needed was her lips on his. And from the way she kissed him back, it felt like this was exactly what she'd needed, too.

Dixie barked, and Walker released Violet and stepped back. Her eyes were wide, her fingertips searching for something on her freshly kissed lips.

Behind her on the front porch of the bed-and-breakfast stood Olivia Belle and Lily Green, mouths agape.

He tipped his nonexistent hat and grinned. "Mornin', ladies." His eyes found Violet's again. "And you have yourself a good walk, Ms. Chastain."

Dixie barked again, and Walker laughed.

Then he strode around Lucinda's Antiques, up the back steps, and into his apartment.

A hundred days.

This town and its ghosts might still have a grip on him, but maybe he wasn't so lost anymore.

He stood in the shower, palm braced against the tile, as steam filled the bathroom and the hot spray washed away the morning and maybe even much of the past year—at least the parts he remembered. He let the water beat down on him until it ran cool before he finally shut it off and wrapped a towel around his hips.

He wasn't sorry about the stunt he pulled with Violet. The second he saw her, he'd needed his mouth on hers. Based on the way her lips parted and her tongue tangled with his, he'd guessed the feeling was mutual. Eventually they'd have to address whatever it was they were avoiding, but for now he'd settle for the lingering taste of her.

He pulled the bathroom door open as an ear-splitting "SQUAWK!" sounded from down the hall, causing him to nail himself in the temple with the corner of the door.

"Christ," he hissed. "Damn it, Jenna!" he yelled louder,

making sure his aunt could hear him. Seemed like his apartment belonged to everyone but him. That was it. As soon as his aunt left—which was going to be very soon—he was heading to the hardware store to buy a new lock. This time he'd only make one key.

He stormed into the kitchen to find Jenna setting the table and her so-called psychic chicken pecking around the floor.

"Sorry!" She smiled at him nervously. "But Lucy hopped in the car with me without even asking. I wasn't planning on bringing her. But your brothers reminded me what day it was and told me you most likely got caught in the rain, so I brought you some homemade tomato soup so you don't catch your death."

He blew out a breath, his annoyance lessening. But he didn't want to give her the satisfaction of being right.

"It's spring in California. Even when it's cold, it's not *that* cold." He raised his brows. "And I thought that's what *chicken* soup was for."

Jenna gasped, then reached down to cup Lucy's—ears? Did chickens have ears? He thought maybe she didn't because otherwise wouldn't she know how goddamn loud she was?

"I really hope she didn't hear you say that."

He crossed his arms over his bare chest. "Jenna…You eat meat. *Chicken* meat."

She narrowed her eyes at him. "You better hush now, nephew. You know I'd never do such a thing with one of my own. Eggs only. And Lucy's just—sensitive."

He rolled his eyes. "Thanks for the soup. Suppose I better put on some clothes and eat it."

He *was* hungry. And his body was still hanging on to the chill of the drop in temperature outside mixed with the cold rain. It was probably why he hadn't wanted to get out of the shower until the last drop of hot water fell.

He padded back to his room and threw on a hooded sweatshirt and a pair of flannel pants. Then he joined his aunt at the small kitchen table, collapsing into the chair.

He sighed, then breathed in the savory aroma of the not–chicken soup. His mouth watered as he eyed the hunk of French bread on a plate in the middle of the table, and he didn't hesitate tearing a piece off, dipping it in the soup, and then shoveling it into his mouth like it was the first bite of food he'd had in months.

He groaned with pleasure. "Jesus this is good."

Jenna smiled. "If you play your cards right, I'll leave the rest for you in the fridge. I had a few too many tomatoes go ripe all at once, so I put 'em to good use."

He devoured the soup and almost all the bread until he realized he was very close to leaving nothing for his aunt.

He reached for the last chunk, then looked at her sipping soup from her spoon and froze midswipe.

"Take it," she said, waving him off with her other hand. "I hear you worked your ass off this morning after y'all had a little hundred-day celebration." She gave him a wink that admitted she knew and likely approved of the brotherly ambush he'd received this morning. Only because she was Jenna would he let it slide.

Walker had worked his ass off, covered in slow-drying grape juice. And then the rain decided to do its worst as soon as he was finally done. His muscles ached. Hell, his whole body ached. He hadn't felt it when he'd walked through the door, but now he was bone weary. Exhausted. It had been so long since he was even able to work like he had this morning.

"What else is on the agenda for the day?" Jenna asked.

He'd planned on working on a few pieces of furniture that were in various stages around the house. After Sylvie the jam lady had loved the chair, she'd asked for an end table. Word had traveled fast, and he'd all but set up a booth at the farmers market out of the bed of his truck, spending the past few Sundays socking money away for his trip up north before ending each evening with Violet and her family.

Violet. He'd been too caught up in the whole *get-his-ass-out-of-his-soaked-clothes* when he'd seen her—when he'd *kissed* her—but now it was registering. He hadn't simply wanted to kiss her. He'd missed her. To hell with the tenets of his recovery. He was who he was today because of who she saw in him, and he was falling for the amazing woman he'd been too scared to call anything other than friend.

His head was swimming. He couldn't focus on work or on how to define this thing between him and Violet. After putting his body through the ringer this morning, he needed to decompress before he could wrap his head around any of it.

"Darlin'," Jenna said, as if reading his mind, "you look like you could use a nap."

He laughed. "I'm a grown man. I don't *nap*." But it wasn't like he had anything he had to do, and Violet was tied up at the B and B for the time being. "But since you brought it up, I guess maybe an hour couldn't hurt."

He stacked the bread plate on top of his bowl, but Jenna shooed him away.

"Go," she said. "I made the mess. I'll clean up."

Lucy squawked her approval, and Walker narrowed his eyes at the animal.

"And I'll put her outside until I'm done," Jenna added.

He leaned over and kissed his aunt on the cheek. "Thank you. I probably don't say that enough to you."

He heard her breath catch, but she smiled.

"Happy one hundred days, Walker."

And with that he made his way back to his room where he practically face-planted into his pillow.

He heard the rain start up again outside. He assumed if Jack or Luke wasn't calling him to take care of the animals that they were doing their part to get them all indoors. Or maybe his ringer was off. He'd check later, but he'd left his phone on the side of the bathroom sink and he wasn't about to leave the sanctuary of his bed to find out.

He closed his eyes and thought of Violet, of how she'd kissed him the day they met and how he'd just kissed her in the rain. Maybe carpentry wasn't the only thing he wanted just for himself. Maybe he wanted Violet, too. But that would mean letting her know who he really was, and how would she look at him then? He wasn't sure he was ready to cross that bridge into reality just yet. So he drifted off to thoughts of a life where his mother didn't die, where his father never lost his way, and where there were no demons at the bottom of a flask.

Maybe if he thought hard enough, that life could be true.

CHAPTER SIXTEEN

Olivia wasn't exaggerating when she said the front desk went bananas when the weather took a turn. When it rained, it poured. Literally. And yesterday's storm had brought with it road-trippers who'd decided to call it a day and needed a place to sleep.

She'd only mistakenly double-booked a room twice, which surprised her. She'd figured it had more to do with how distracted she was after Walker—half-naked and covered in mud—kissed her right there with the whole town watching.

"What the hell was that?" Lily had asked when Violet returned from walking Dixie.

"Tell us *everything*," Olivia had added.

But the sky had opened up again and patrons had filed in one after the soaking other until the bed-and-breakfast was booked solid. It was already Friday afternoon, and Violet still hadn't had a chance to process Walker's kiss or to reconcile it with his completely opposite behavior since she'd seen him on Sunday night.

Without exactly saying the words, she'd initiated the whole *Where is this going?* discussion even though it—meaning their relationship—really had nowhere to go. She'd figured he needed some space to think, so she'd played the avoiding game just as well as he had. But…the kiss. He'd turned her knees straight to jelly and then sauntered away like it was the most normal thing to do—and then had gone straight back to acting like she didn't exist. Despite the expiration date on whatever their label was, he at least owed her an explanation for yesterday, right?

"Hey," Olivia said as Violet set out the white and red wineglasses along the table in the common room. "How's it going?"

Violet glanced up at her new friend and employer. "Tonight we have a Riesling, which is a sweet, floral white, and also a zinfandel, which is one of the sweeter reds. Sometimes I like to pair sweet with dry, but I'm in the mood for symmetry tonight. Does that sound weird?"

Olivia joined Violet, placing the tasting glasses along the other side of the table. She gave Violet a pointed look.

"You know that's not what I'm talking about," the other woman said.

Violet winced. "Yeah. I know."

"Not gonna lie. But that was one of the sexiest kisses I've ever seen." Olivia sighed. "I'm gonna have to talk to Cash about kissing me in the rain."

"Honestly," Violet said. "I'm not really sure *what* that was." She wasn't lying, even if her words were only half-true. It wasn't a shock for her to be kissing Walker in the general sense, but it was a shock to not hear from him all week and then receive such an unexpected greeting. She'd been the one to initiate the conversation about how real things were getting between them on Sunday night, and he'd been the one to leave without really letting her know how he felt. So she'd given him space.

What a difference a few days and a little rain made.

She laughed softly.

"Did I miss a joke?" Olivia asked.

Violet laughed again and then shook her head. "I was just remembering something funny." Like how Violet first introduced herself to Walker, much in the same unexpected way.

Olivia narrowed her eyes. "I can tell you're not quite ready to discuss"—she made air quotes—"the *Walker* incident. So I'm gonna steer this in another direction. I heard a rumor that you actually studied music in school and not any of this wine stuff."

Violet's eyes narrowed this time. "Did you really hear a rumor, or did Sheriff Hawkins run a background check on me to make sure you weren't hiring a convicted felon?"

Olivia held up her hands in surrender. "Okay. Guilty. I saw your transcript. You were a year away from graduating. Not that I don't love having you to help out around here, but did you quit school for your mom?"

Violet's eyes pricked with tears, and her cheeks grew hot.

"Oh, sweetie, I'm so sorry," Olivia said. "I didn't mean to upset you. I'm sticking my nose into all of your business, and we've only known each other a few weeks. I totally invaded your privacy. Please forget I asked."

Violet laughed. "No, it's okay. I don't mind talking about it. I'm just not used to a place like Oak Bluff—everyone knowing everyone else. Everyone knowing *about* everyone else."

Olivia sat down on the bench and gestured for Violet to sit across from her, so she did.

"I *know*," Olivia whispered. "I've been here only a few months and you'd think I lived here all my life the way people talk to me. *About* me. About me and the sheriff and whether or not I'm going to wear glass slippers to our wedding. Newsflash—he hasn't exactly proposed yet. But I did show up in town like Cinderella fleeing the ball, glass slippers and all, so the speculation isn't a shock. Also, I'm pretty much an open book. I guess people who want to be known get known." Olivia shrugged.

Violet nodded. She got that. And she was the type of woman who did want to be known. It was a matter of surrounding herself with the type of people who wanted in on that.

"Then there are those who've lived here their whole lives and are still an enigma," Olivia added with a raised brow.

She didn't name names, but she didn't have to. Violet knew she was talking about Walker again. But as much as she wanted to confide in a new friend, she didn't want to admit how much she wanted that kiss to mean. She needed words. An explanation in English, French, or any other language so long as she could plug it into Google Translate and figure out what it meant. But Olivia was right. Walker Everett was one hell of an enigma, and there was no guidebook or translation app that was going to help her with that.

"So, dropping out of school," Violet said, steering the conversation back to something she *could* explain. "I did it when things were getting really bad with my mom's MS. She couldn't work at the restaurant like she used to, and our insurance wasn't enough to cover a nurse to help out at home, so I quit to be hostess, table busser, and eventually a very underpaid sommelier for my father's restaurant—and an unqualified nurse for Maman on the days when she was in too much pain to be home alone." She shrugged. "It was really a no-brainer. I'll go back eventually."

Olivia reached across the table and squeezed Violet's hand. "I'm sorry about your mom. But it sounds like there might be some hope with this whole France situation that's gonna take you away from us soon?"

"Nothing can cure the disease," Violet said. "But the treatment could improve her quality of life. If I can help give that to her, then it's worth the sacrifice."

"Do you miss it? Having music as part of your professional life?"

How did you miss something you didn't quite have yet? She missed the internship hours she'd spent at her university's partner schools, working with kids from kindergarten all the way to middle school. But she'd never had a class of her own.

"I don't know," she admitted. "I mean, I have my playlists. I have ninety-four minutes in the car twice a week where I get to sing my heart out without annoying the hell out of other passengers."

She smiled at the memory of her first day with Walker, their drive to Santa Barbara where he had endured her singing, and how her stubbornness almost had her walking a mile with a two-tier cake in three-inch heels.

Olivia gasped. "I just thought of the most amazing thing!"

Violet laughed at the other woman's sudden exuberance. "Um . . . okay."

Olivia bounced on her bench and clapped. "I've got someone to work the desk until we close at ten. After the wine tasting, I'm taking you out for karaoke!"

Violet hesitated for maybe a fraction of a second before her eyes brightened and a smile took over her features. When was the last time she'd had any sort of girls' night?

She hadn't thought such a thing existed anymore. But tonight it would.

"Olivia Belle, you have yourself a deal."

It was after nine when Violet hopped into the passenger seat of Olivia's canary yellow Volkswagen Bug.

"Is this what you were driving when Sheriff Hawkins pulled you over?" Violet asked.

Olivia grinned. "Yep. And he didn't just pull me over. He arrested me. Handcuffs and everything."

Violet laughed. "Sounds like a great start to a relationship."

Olivia clicked her seat belt into place and put the car in drive. "It was pretty disastrous, that day the sheriff and I met. I mean, *I* was the disaster. Not Cash. My parents had a nasty divorce and have been living hatefully ever after for too many years to count. The biggest lesson they taught me was that I never wanted to end up like them. It *might* have messed with my ability to commit. Your parents seem pretty tight, though, yeah?"

Violet cleared her throat. "They are. But I don't think they have an origin story quite as romantic as yours." After getting the real story, she wondered how much she really knew about the people who raised her—about the relationship she'd always wanted to emulate. "Let's just say we might not be that different, you and me. I always thought my parents had this perfect, easy sort of love. So instead of being cautious, I dove headfirst into every relationship assuming if it was right—like they were right—that it would simply fall into place."

Olivia gave her a knowing grin. "You thought you knew the answer. I thought I could run to Oak Bluff and find the answer. But the truth is, I was never asking myself the right question."

Violet raised her brows and waited for her new friend to explain.

"It's not about what made it work for your parents or my grandparents or what made my mom and dad's relationship crash and burn. I was a runner. So the question for me was what would it take to get me to stay?"

"Cash," Violet said, assuming the answer was easy.

She shook her head. "I mean yes, Cash, of course. But it was because when I was with him I was home. I didn't want to run anymore because I was safe right where I was."

Why was Olivia telling her all of this? They barely knew each other. And *Violet* wasn't a runner. She knew exactly where home was. Other than her three years in college, home had been the same place for Violet's entire life.

Olivia turned on the radio as the chorus to Justin Timberlake's "Can't Stop the Feeling" came on, and she started dancing in her seat. "Okay, wine expert, show me your real skills!" She sang along with the song, loud and off key but with such ridiculous joy that it was contagious.

So that was that, the end of a conversation that was starting to make Violet squirm. She welcomed the distraction.

Olivia lowered the windows, and soon the two of them were belting out each song that followed so that the thirty-minute ride was filled with fresh air and loud music, with all of life's stresses tucked neatly away until tomorrow morning.

They pulled into the parking lot of a smallish rectangular building with a nondescript exterior except for the pink neon sign that read CENTER STAGE.

"How did you even know this place existed?" Violet asked.

They hopped out of the car, and Olivia pointed to a red Jeep Renegade parked a few spots away from them.

"That's Ava. She and Lily are inside keeping a couple of seats warm for us. Lily introduced me and Ava to this place a month ago. And because Cash, Luke, and Jack wouldn't be caught dead behind a microphone, we decided it would be our place whenever we needed some girl time. Figured tonight was one of those nights."

It so was.

The two women strode through the front door. Violet's steps felt lighter with each one she took. Inside, four-top tables took up the bulk of the floor space. She spun to find a large screen on the wall above the doors that displayed the words to the song that was currently playing, Bon Jovi's "Dead or Alive." To the left of the entrance was the bar, and straight ahead, at the far end of the one-room establishment, was a stage.

On that stage, putting his whole heart and soul into the song, was Luke Everett.

"Nooo," Olivia said softly under her breath. "I'm sorry, Violet. It really was supposed to be girls' night, but it looks like a cowboy or two are crashing."

Violet's heart sped up, and she scanned the crowded bar for one certain cowboy. She found two tables pushed together near the front of the room where Ava, Jack, Lily, and Sheriff Cash Hawkins currently sat. But Walker Everett was nowhere to be seen.

She blew out a breath. Was the kiss a fluke and he was avoiding her again? He'd seemed so sure of himself in the moment. She'd felt—something. But seeing everyone else here tonight except him had her doubting her instincts.

"If this is too weird," Olivia started. "I mean, I know

you don't want to talk about that smooch Walker planted on you yesterday..."

"It's not weird," Violet said, her voice sounding an octave higher than normal. To prove it she grabbed Olivia's hand and tugged her forward, meandering through the sea of tables until they reached their party. Lily was rapt watching Luke finish his song, but Ava, Cash, and Jack stood to greet them.

"I know!" Ava said over Luke's rendition of the popular eighties song. "We meant it to only be us, but Lily and Luke have barely seen each other all week since she's been overseeing the restaurant construction, and...well...he wasn't willing to give her up on the first night they both had free all week. So he tagged along—and brought Jack and Cash with him."

Cash grabbed Olivia around the waist and kissed her right there in the middle of the bar.

She laughed when he pulled away, her cheeks flushed. "I guess girls' night is everyone night!" she cried, no longer apologetic. Violet didn't blame her, nor did she begrudge Olivia or Lily or Ava a night with their men, even if it did make her the odd one out.

Violet settled in between Lily and Ava. There was an empty chair on Lily's left with a half-finished bottle of beer on the table, which she assumed was for Luke. Cash, Olivia, and Jack sat across from them. On Cash's left there was also an empty chair, but no drink. A completely vacant spot confirming that she was, without a doubt, a seventh wheel.

Luke finished his song to a roar of applause from the bar patrons. Even if his singing was awful—which it wasn't—Violet guessed the response would have been the same. There was no denying the Everett gene pool was filled to the brim with unquestionable good looks and charm. Throw in a pair of hip-slung Wranglers and some beat-up cowboy boots, and you had an undeniable fantasy of a man.

Not that Luke Everett had occupied any of Violet's fantasies this past week, but someone had.

Ava passed her the song booklet and a server came by and took drink orders for the newcomers. Olivia ordered a beer, and since Violet didn't feel like this was the type of place to order a merlot, she decided on beer, too.

"How about some tequila?" Luke said. "I'm feeling like this is a tequila kind of night."

Ava held up her hands. "I'm out. Jack and I are heading to my parents' after this to grab Owen."

Olivia joined in. "Same. Driving. One beer and I'm out."

Lily shrugged. "My day is wide open tomorrow, so count me in!"

Cash and Jack were in, too, which meant the sheriff was probably getting a ride home with Violet and Olivia. But that didn't leave much room for Lily and Luke. Oh well. Maybe Ava was dropping them somewhere on the way to her parents' house. Violet knew she had a ride home, and she guessed that was all that mattered. She could stand to let loose a little, too.

Looked like girls' night had turned into an all-out karaoke party.

Ava and Lily did a duet to "Don't Stop Believing," and after a shot of tequila, Olivia somehow dragged Cash up to sing "Don't Go Breaking My Heart." Except he didn't know the song, so Olivia had to keep pointing at the screen and showing him when his part came up, much to the amusement of the rest of the bar. They were definitely the comic relief of the evening.

By the time Violet picked a song and made her way onto

the stage, she was slightly buzzed—the good kind where everything made her smile and it felt like nothing could make this night anything short of spectacular. That feeling of being the seventh wheel was long gone, and she finally felt like herself in this group of people who were less strangers and somehow more than employers. Maybe Ava had truly meant it when she'd welcomed Violet to the Crossroads family.

She took her place behind the mic and readied herself for the music to start. She chose a song where she knew all the words, so she didn't need the screen. That was the excuse she gave herself when she told the DJ she'd be singing "Cowboy Take Me Away" by the Dixie Chicks. She liked the song and was good at it. It had nothing to do with any sort of unspoken thoughts or desires about an enigma of a man who'd managed to burrow his way under her skin after her brilliant idea to kiss a stranger.

Maybe their weeks together was all they'd have, but that didn't stop her wondering what he'd been thinking while—other than the kiss in the rain—they'd each kept their distance all week.

She finished the song to a standing ovation—at least from their two tables.

She laughed. "They're with me," she said, pointing to where Ava, Lily, and Olivia were whistling and catcalling. It wasn't until the spotlight dimmed and the screen went dark as the DJ readied for the next singer that she saw a familiar figure standing right inside the entrance, arms crossed over his broad chest as he leaned against the door. What was it about that cool, aloof lean that made him so sexy? Then she reminded herself that pretty much everything he did elicited that sort of reaction from her.

"Walker?" she said aloud, then added "Oh shit!" forgetting

she was still standing at the microphone, now apparently gripping it with white knuckles. Her voice reverberated above the din of the karaoke bar patrons as she peeled her fingers free and beelined for the stairs and then straight to the ladies' room—which turned out to be a one-person unisex bathroom. Even better.

She braced her hands on the edge of the sink and steadied her breath. Then she stared at herself in the mirror, giving herself a mental reminder that she was pretty damned amazing. She was juggling three jobs in Oak Bluff, coordinating her mom's treatment abroad—albeit behind her back—and just gave a kickass performance of "Cowboy Take Me Away." There was a chance the tequila and beer were talking here, but she'd only had one of each.

"You *are* amazing," she reassured herself aloud. "And if that stupid, gorgeous jerk of a cowboy doesn't get it, well then—his loss."

She washed her hands so the bathroom visit wasn't a total waste. Then she squared her shoulders, threw open the door…and walked straight into a hard, muscular chest. A man's chest. Walker Everett's man chest.

She yelped and took a step back. "Why do you keep doing that?"

"Doing what?" he asked, holding his hands up as if trying not to frighten her.

She slid out of the doorway and leaned against the wall of the little restroom alcove.

"Showing up when I don't expect you. We don't talk all week. And then you—you kiss me with no explanation, in *public* no less, and now here you are, right outside the door when I need a damned second to catch my breath. So tell me, Walker. What are you doing here *now*?"

His expression remained stoic as ever. "Picking up Luke and Lily. Since Ava and Jack are heading the rest of the way to Los Olivos, and Olivia can't fit everyone into that pocket-size car of hers, I told Luke I'd lend a hand."

Right. He was here for them, not her.

Violet narrowed her eyes at him. "Why weren't you with everyone tonight?" she asked.

"Working," he said.

It took her eyes several seconds to get used to the darkness of the hallway, but when they did she noticed his eyes were bloodshot, and his normally tanned cheeks were flushed. Despite her confusion at the past several days and what the hell was going on between her and this man, she rose onto her toes and cupped his face in her palms.

"You're burning up," she said.

"I'm fine," he answered back.

She rolled her eyes. He still wanted to push her away? Well, she certainly wasn't going to force her way in. "Okay, well, my ride is out there."

He shook his head. "Cash is going with Olivia, and I've got you, Luke, and Lily."

That feeling of the night soaring toward spectacular suddenly fizzled. She opened her mouth to protest, but what could she say? That she'd squeeze into Olivia's almost nonexistent backseat so she could be the third wheel to her and Cash when there was plenty of room in the cab of Walker's truck? She snapped her mouth shut and crossed her arms over her chest. It appeared they were at a conversational impasse.

"I should go pay for my drinks, then," she said, trying to come up with any means to vacate their little nook of the bar.

"Sure," he said. "I'll meet you all by the door."

She pushed off the wall, but Walker interrupted her attempted exit.

"Wait," he said, his voice quiet but insistent.

She blew out a breath. "For what?"

"For me to say what I need to say. The thing is, I'm real good at being a dick sometimes."

"Or asshole," she mumbled. "I was giving you space. At least, that's what I thought I was doing."

He let out a short laugh. "Or asshole. I'm an expert at asshole. You caught me off guard Sunday night. And then yesterday—I should have called after—"

"After you planted one on me so the whole town could see my knees turn to jelly?"

The corner of his mouth twitched. "I make you weak in the knees, huh?" he teased, but she shook her head.

"Sorry for the interruption. I believe you were in the middle of groveling for my forgiveness."

This got him to laugh. "I *might* have crashed yesterday afternoon and slept 'til morning."

"Because you're *sick*," she insisted.

He rolled his eyes. "I'm fine," he repeated, but she was far from convinced.

"You know, all you had to say after Sunday was that you needed some space. If that's what you need, I can give it to you."

He nodded. "In case you haven't noticed, I don't have much of a way with words."

She laughed. "Well, I appreciate the ones you give me. But right now I'm going to have to ask for your keys."

His brows drew together. "Why the hell do you want my keys?" He swayed slightly where he stood.

"That." She pointed at him. "You're sick and in no shape to drive."

"And you've been drinking. You've all been drinking."

Shit. He was right. Even if she'd only had the one shot and the one beer, it was enough that she'd felt buzzed onstage.

"Fine," she said. "But as soon as we get back, you need to take something to bring that fever down."

He offered her a single nod, and she decided not to push the matter any further—until they got home.

Home. Wasn't that an interesting word?

The ride back to Oak Bluff was interesting as well, to say the least, with a tipsy Luke and Lily in the back who couldn't stop sneaking kisses when they thought Violet and Walker weren't paying attention. But Walker didn't drive a luxury pickup with a spacious cab, which meant even if Violet and Walker weren't paying attention, they sorta were.

They pulled up in front of Luke's house thirty smooch-filled minutes later. Luke clapped his brother on the shoulder. "Thanks for the ride."

Lily popped her head into the front seat as well.

"Why don't you two come over for a late breakfast tomorrow? I can whip up an egg soufflé, and you can meet Lucky."

"Lucky the pet cow?" Violet laughed, and Lily nodded enthusiastically. "Thank you, but I'll have to take a rain check. I have to head back to Santa Barbara until Monday morning. I have some family stuff to take care of."

Lily wagged her finger at Violet. "I'm holding you to that rain check, then." She turned her head toward Walker. "Invitation still stands for you. You're welcome any time, you know."

Walker nodded his response, and Luke and Lily exited the truck.

They pulled back onto the road in silence. Despite her

understanding of Walker's behavior this week, the silence between them was still thick with tension.

"So," Violet said. "You ever do karaoke?"

He smiled. It was a small one, but a smile nonetheless. She'd take it.

"No. Luke's the one who likes to be the center of attention. I'll leave the karaoke to him."

She pivoted slightly in her seat as they turned onto Oak Bluff Way. "Okay, so if Luke is the attention seeker, who is Jack?"

"The hero," he said without hesitation. And something in the way he said it made her ache.

"And…you?" she asked.

He pulled into a spot on the street a block away from the B and B.

"The bad seed," he said. "The black sheep. The wreck. Take your pick."

"Sounds a little harsh," she said. "It doesn't seem like your brothers see it that way. Or anyone else for that matter. Everyone acts like they care a whole lot about you. Any chance you might be harder on yourself than everyone else is?"

He put the truck in park and pulled the key from the ignition.

"Anything's possible, Teach," was all he said before opening his door.

She did the same, hopping out onto the sidewalk where he met her to walk the rest of the way.

"So I still get to be *Teach* even though you need space?" she asked.

He glanced down at her and raised his brows. "It's what you want to be, right? A teacher? You'll be damned good at it once you get back to it."

Violet was grateful for the cover of darkness as she felt a rush of heat in her neck and cheeks.

"Yeah. It's what I want to be. Someday."

They stopped in front of the Oak Bluff Bed and Breakfast, and she fidgeted with the hem of her shirt.

"So you'll take something for the fever, right?" she asked.

"I'm *not* sick," he said. Then he sneezed. "Yeah, fine. I'll take something."

"So," she said, looking for that path they'd travel toward truly being friends this time, "a week ago this would have been the part where you kiss me good night. But you're sick, and maybe you still need space..." Didn't stop her from thinking about his lips on hers or that beard scratching her chin.

He exhaled a long breath. "No. I guess tonight we go our separate ways."

"We could hug, though," she blurted, not satisfied with *not* getting to touch him in some way, shape, or form before the night was over. "I am sort of a hugger."

She took a step toward him, and when he didn't back away, she slid her arms around his waist, pressed her cheek to his chest, and squeezed.

It took him a second, but then he wrapped his arms around her, too.

She breathed him in, taking in his scent because how could she not when they were this close?

"You're not a bad seed to me," she said. "In case you were wondering."

Then she pulled away and smiled at him.

"Good night, Walker. Thanks for the ride."

"Night, Teach."

He waited until she made her way up the walkway and

didn't turn from her until she pushed through the door to the bed-and-breakfast.

When she closed it behind her, she peeked through the beveled glass.

Walker lingered on the sidewalk in front of the B and B for the better part of a minute, his head tilted toward the starry sky. Then he shook it as if answering a question before he finally slipped out of her line of sight.

CHAPTER SEVENTEEN

Walker had been back in bed for the better part of an hour, his head throbbing and chest aching, when someone pounded on the door.

"Shit," he hissed. "What now?" Or better, *who* now? Because in the past two days he'd had check-ins from the sheriff, his aunt, and his two brothers with their congratulatory ambush. Everyone had just seen him sober at the karaoke bar as well, so that left him puzzled as hell and—though he'd only admit it to himself—feeling like complete and utter shit from whatever asshole bug had invaded his body.

It took everything in him to get himself upright again. He caught sight of himself in the bedroom mirror. He was almost unrecognizable. His thick sandy hair was flattened in places and stood on end in others. His eyes were bloodshot, and there was a thin sheen of sweat on his forehead. He wore a pair of gray sweats and stood slightly hunched, wearing his comforter like a cape as he clasped it over his shoulders.

He trudged to the door wondering how an hour could be the difference between feeling like crap and feeling like he'd been run over by a Zamboni.

Whoever was there pounded impatiently again.

"What the hell is your problem?" he yelled, throwing the door open to find Violet standing there about to knock again.

"Sorry!" she said, wincing. Then she reached a hand to his cheek. "I know you don't lock the door, but I didn't want to barge in. I knew it. You didn't take anything, and you're still burning up."

"Really?" he said, his voice hoarse and muffled with congestion. "I hadn't noticed."

She gripped him by the shoulders and spun him back the way he came without any resistance. "Back to bed, mister. I'm assuming you didn't take my advice because you thought you could sleep it off. But you can't. So tell me where you keep your thermometer, ibuprofen, decongestants. Basically, point me toward your medicine cabinet, and I'll get you whatever you need."

He shuffled toward the bedroom with her behind him.

"I don't have one," he said.

"A thermometer?"

He shook his head as he walked through the bedroom door, then turned slowly to face her.

"A medicine cabinet. I've only lived here a few months, and like I tried explaining, I *don't* get sick." He sneezed into a tissue he had hidden in his fist. "Didn't think I needed one."

She sighed and ran a hand through his crazy bedhead.

"Guess what, tough guy? You're pretty darn sick."

"I'm fine," he insisted, but knew he wasn't convincing anyone. "I *can* just sleep it off."

She laughed softly. “Yeah, you can. But you also need to push fluids and maybe take a little something to help you rest better. Stay here. I’ll be right back,” she said, then headed into the bathroom.

“Damn,” he said. “Guess I’ll have to cancel that midnight bull ride I was looking forward to.”

She popped her head out of the bathroom doorway and narrowed her eyes at him.

“Sarcasm? So you’re a snarky sick boy, huh?”

He collapsed onto his back and groaned, and he heard her rummaging under the sink where he kept a small stack of towels and washcloths. Then he heard her start the tap, and he half wondered if she was cleaning his bathroom now that she’d gotten a good look at it.

“This is my asshole brothers’ fault,” he mumbled as she sat beside him. “The sparkling grape juice and the damned rain.” He realized she might ask why his brothers sprayed him with grape juice and swore under his breath.

She laughed softly. “You don’t get sick like this from the rain.”

“That’s what I told Jenna, but here we are.”

Violet sat on the edge of the bed and shook her head, then laid a cool cloth on his forehead. “Whatever this is, it was brewing before you got caught in the rain.”

He closed his eyes and let out a long breath. “Shit, that feels good. Why didn’t I think of that?”

Probably because he wasn’t sick. He figured the more he said it, the more it would be true. Mind over matter and all.

Something else cold and wet hit his bare chest.

He hissed in a breath.

“Sorry!” she said. “I should have warned you that was coming.”

He shook his head. "Just surprised me. That one feels even better than the one on my head."

She pulled the comforter over him, and he opened his eyes.

"I know you're hot, but five minutes from now you'll probably have the chills. So you've got the cold cloths to cool you and the blanket to keep you warm. Try to get some sleep."

"You're leaving?" he asked, even though he knew it was irrational to want her to stay. He'd been a dick avoiding her all week and then pulling that stunt in front of the B and B. Now, after telling her he still needed space, he was one hell of a mess. He'd run from himself if he could.

He let out a bitter laugh. Wasn't that what he'd been doing for the past decade? Only his running always led to the bottom of a whiskey bottle. Now it felt like he had nowhere to go, so he was running from her—running as far out of town as he could.

His head throbbed. This thinking shit was starting to hurt.

She stroked the damp hair on his forehead, and damn her touch felt so good. "I'll be back. I'm running to the bed-and-breakfast to get you some of the basics. I'm sure Olivia has her own little over-the-counter pharmacy for the guests. I can't believe you have *nothing*."

He groaned. "I don't. Get. Sick," he insisted.

"Let it go. You're sick." Then she kissed him on top of the head and left him there to rest.

He fell in and out of sleep and also in and out of dreams while she was gone. In one dream he was eight, one of the last times he remembered being sick. It was before his mom had been diagnosed, so she was the one taking care of him. There was a flash of memory of him getting his throat swabbed at the doctor's office, then of his mom unwrapping one of those spaceship-looking popsicles for him to suck on because it had hurt so bad to swallow.

In what felt like seconds later, he woke in a cold sweat, gasping for breath, his hand to his cheek feeling the sting of Jack Senior backhanding him after he tried to pull an empty bottle from his passed-out father's grasp.

Shit. These weren't dreams. He was just too much of a mess to keep everything at bay, so instead it was all rising to the surface, every last bit of it from the first time his father split open Jack's lower lip to the last time he ever laid a hand on any of them—the time that left Jack broken and unconscious at the foot of the wooden stairs.

He heard the apartment door open and close again.

Hell. He didn't want Violet to see him like this, his body infected with who knows what and his mind poisoned with every damned memory he'd spent a decade trying to erase.

She rifled around in the kitchen—loud as hell as she did—but he couldn't fault her for it. She was there to help him, however noisy she was in doing so.

He squeezed his eyes shut, trying like hell to rebury what had already been unearthed.

The microwave beeped, and seconds later she strode into the room with a cutting board in her hands as a makeshift tray. She set it down on the nightstand, and he could see various pills in pairs along with a glass of water, orange juice, and a mug of something steaming.

"So," she said. "I've got two tablets of NyQuil if you want to sleep until Sunday, two Tylenol tablets, and two Advil—depending on your standard, over-the-counter pain reliever preference—and two daytime cold and flu capsules, which will probably be better for you to take in the morning once you're up and about. First we should take your temperature to see how bad things really are, though."

He swallowed hard. "Not really necessary. I'm ready to admit I have one."

She laughed. "Even when you're knocked down, Walker Everett, you're still pretty damn charming, you know? But I think the fever is pretty high. I want to make sure I shouldn't call a doctor or something."

"Fine," he relented.

Violet rolled her eyes but refrained from reprimanding him. "Open your mouth."

He held out his hand, beckoning for the thermometer.

"You're right," she said. "You're a grown man. I'm sorry. But depending on what it says when you wake up, you should probably see a doctor. I could call and make you an appointment."

He laughed. "Well, the last time I saw a doctor for a fever was when I was a kid, and I'm pretty sure my pediatrician, Dr. Peterson, retired and moved to Palm Springs."

She pursed her lips. "Fine. Let's just see what it says, and if necessary I'll stay the night…"

He raised a brow. She backhanded him softly on the shoulder.

"To make sure your fever doesn't spike any higher. If it's not any better in the morning, we'll find whatever doctor is open on a Saturday, even if we have to go to the ER. I'm not heading back to Santa Barbara without knowing you're okay. Okay?"

He groaned. "Okay, but no ER. It's a fever, not an emergency."

He rose up and balanced on the backs of his elbows, then grabbed the thermometer and stuck it under his tongue. It only took seconds for it to flash red and beep. He took it out of his mouth and looked at it.

"Is one-oh-three bad?" he asked.

She huffed out a laugh. "It's not great. Lucky for you, I've brought the pharmacy to your bedroom. Let me know what ails you most, and we'll pick the right combo of meds. And if you want to say to hell with all the chemicals and go the Chastain family natural route, I've got this."

She handed him the mug. He wrapped his hands around it and breathed in the steam rising from the rim. The warm ceramic felt good in his palms as a shiver ran through his body.

"My senses are a little off," he said. "What is it?" He pressed his lips to the rim and tilted the mug slowly to take a sip.

"Just some English tea, which is really great for the throat and pushing those fluids. And also a splash of whiskey."

With surprising force, especially with how weak he felt, he swore and threw the mug at the wall opposite her. Tea and whiskey sprayed across the sheet and comforter before the mug crashed into several pieces below the windowsill, the rest of the concoction spreading across the wood floor.

Violet screamed and jumped back from the bed.

"Shit!" he yelled. Then he held up his hands, trying to tell her he wouldn't hurt her, but she stood there, frozen, her hand over her mouth.

Christ, what the hell had he done? The look on her face was the same look he'd seen on his thirteen-year-old self in his fever dream after his father had hit him hard enough to rattle his teeth. Complete and utter horror.

Sober or not, this was who Walker was in Oak Bluff—a man still poisoned by his past. He'd thought he could hide it from her until their time ran out, but he was a damned fool. It'd only be a matter of time before something triggered him with his brothers, too. Or even Jenna. How long would they have to walk on eggshells for him? How long until he did irreparable damage to them like he'd just done to Violet.

Walker wasn't leaving Oak Bluff for himself. He was leaving for all of them.

He swung his legs over the side of the bed and planted his bare feet on the ground. He scrubbed a hand over his beard then looked her straight in the eye. "You should go."

Her hand fell to her side, and her mouth hung open. It took several seconds for her to formulate words. "Wait… what?"

"Go, Violet. Leave. Whatever the French word is for getting the hell out of my apartment."

Her breath caught in her throat. "I thought your sarcasm was cute before, but I take it back. You're a real asshole when you're sick. You scare the hell out of me like that, and I don't even get to ask why?"

He let out a bitter laugh. "Sick has nothing to do with it. This is me, Violet. The real me, and explanation or no, I'm not someone you want in your life, not for the short- or long-term." He picked up the two NyQuil tablets and held them in his palm. "I take the blue pill, go to sleep, then wake up and everything is like it used to be, right? Isn't that how it goes?"

She shook her head. "This isn't the fucking *Matrix*, Walker. You don't get to treat me like this, throw me out, and then erase what happened." She swiped at a tear under her eye—a tear *he'd* put there. "Who am I kidding, though, right? This is your bedroom, in your apartment, in *your* town. I'm just the outsider who never really belonged in your life. You're free to kick me out and do whatever the hell you want."

He couldn't do this with her. Not now. Probably not ever.

"Get out, Violet. I'm begging you. Get the hell out and don't look back. I should have given you this advice on the day we met. I never asked for you to kiss me to make your ex jealous, and I sure as hell didn't ask for your help tonight. So do yourself the biggest goddamn favor and pretend like we never met, and I'll get back to my life before you turned it upside down. *Now!*" She flinched, and her whole body trembled. Each word he spat at her tore him apart from the inside out, but he had to make her leave him. For good.

"Go to hell, Walker." Her voice shook, but she held her ground.

He lifted the glass of water in a gesture of cheers. "Already there, but appreciate the sentiment."

She swallowed hard, and he knew she was holding back the tears. Good. He didn't deserve them. He didn't deserve her.

"Fine," she said. "In that case, here's your final French lesson: *Va te faire foutre.* I'll even translate. Go fuck yourself."

Then she spun on her heel and stormed out of the bedroom, down the hall, through the kitchen, and out the back door. Only when she'd made it down the steps and around the front of the antiques shop did she stop, bracing a hand on the hood of his beat-up pickup truck. He knew because he watched her. He watched her breathe hard as she swiped her forearm under her eyes.

Then, she straightened as if she knew he was watching, her head held high as she sauntered back to the bed-and-breakfast and—likely—out of his life for good.

He stared down at the blue pills in his hand. He knew things couldn't go back to the way they used to be, but for tonight, at least, he could sleep, impervious to the memories and dreams that would still be there to haunt him when he woke.

CHAPTER EIGHTEEN

Violet's car was gone by the time he woke from his fever haze on Saturday. And because all he wanted to do was forget the way he treated her, he did the only thing he could when the bottle wasn't an option.

He worked.

The stable needed cleaning, and even though they had hired hands to help out with that sort of work, on the weekends it was only him, Luke, and Jack. So he took it upon himself to clean the stalls.

He tied the horses up outside, then started with the pitchfork, shoveling out any soiled bedding he found and loading it into a wheelbarrow. After that he swept the stalls, then killed the time waiting for the floor to dry by working out the horses one at a time.

It had been months since he'd rode and years since he'd done it sober. He'd forgotten how much he loved being in the saddle. But the arena wasn't cutting it. So he led Cleo, their oldest and most trustworthy horse, outside the fence and rode her through the field and up to the vineyard.

From the top of the hill he had a bird's-eye view of Oak Bluff—the small residential area, the main street, the ocean beyond. Everything seemed so small and insignificant when he had enough distance. It was when he was in the thick of it that things got to be too much.

He squinted hard at the park adjacent to the small elementary school on the outskirts of town. It looked like there was one person there either pitching or hitting. The bright blue baseball cap was almost certainly Dodgers, and if he didn't know any better, he'd say the *meeting* Jack claimed he had on a Saturday morning involved nothing more than a baseball glove and a basket of balls.

Walker decided to confirm his suspicions, tapping Cleo's flanks with his heels and directing her down the hill and toward the edge of town.

He tied the horse to the school's signpost. Then he pulled an apple from the saddlebag and gave her a treat.

He was full of sweat and dirt and about sixteen years of repression that was slowly seeping from every pore. He could use a little release.

"How's that meeting working out for you?" he yelled over the chain-link fence to his oldest brother.

Jack threw strike after strike over home plate, each ball hitting the backstop with a force that made Walker pity any catcher who used to play with his brother.

"I needed to think," Jack called back when he ran out of balls. Walker opened the trunk of Jack's SUV, which sat parked along the curb, knowing he'd find Owen's bat. It was too small for him, but it would do.

He swung the bat over his shoulder and strode through the dugout and onto the infield.

Jack went to work collecting the baseballs, setting himself up for another round.

"You wanna tell me what happened with Violet?" Jack asked. "Olivia said she was shook up about something last night. Said she wouldn't talk about it, but Olivia swore Violet was at your place after you left the karaoke bar."

Walker brushed the dust off of home plate and readied himself for his brother's first pitch.

"She was at my place," Walker admitted. "And no, I don't want to get into it."

Jack adjusted his Dodgers cap and wound up for the pitch.

Strike one.

A fastball right over the plate.

"Might be good to remind you I didn't have a full-ride baseball scholarship," Walker called to Jack.

Jack rolled his shoulders. "Might be good to remind you that I'm not taking it easy on you just because you're an amateur."

Walker took a couple practice swings before setting up again. "Noted." This time he anticipated the fastball and swung, tipping it over the right foul line.

"I'm a shit listener, but you want to tell *me* what's got your panties all twisted?"

Jack shook his head. "You don't talk. I don't talk."

Walker shrugged and toed the plate, setting himself up again. "Works for me."

His brother threw another strike. Then another. Soon they found a sort of rhythm.

Pitch. Hit (or sometimes only clip). Repeat.

The farther Walker's hits went, the harder and faster the pitch Jack would throw until finally Walker lobbed one over the right-field fence.

"Amateur my ass," Walker mumbled. It felt good to show up the superstar for once. So much so that he let his guard down, which was apparently a mistake.

Jack narrowed his eyes, wound up, and let fly a curveball that nailed Walker right in the hip.

Walker threw the bat and stormed toward his brother.

"What the hell is your problem, asshole?" he asked, giving Jack a good shove on the chest.

Jack shook off his glove and shoved his youngest brother right back.

"My problem? *My* problem? Just blowing off some steam, little brother. Nothing personal."

"It feels real personal," Walker countered.

"Where do you go when you're hiding out?" Jack asked.

Walker's brows drew together. "I'm around every damned day. Maybe I like to keep to myself at night or on the weekends, but what the hell does that have to do with you nailing me in the hip?"

Jack let out a bitter laugh. "I don't know. You almost kill yourself three months ago and now, even though I'm proud as hell you made it this far, you still seem a million miles away. How do I know you're okay when I don't see you for days at a stretch? After the storm the other day, I didn't even know you were in town until Luke said you were picking him up at the bar."

Walker scratched the back of his neck. "So if I'm off the grid for more than twenty-four hours I gotta be on a bender? Next time just bang on my door like the sheriff and accuse me point blank. Might actually work better than nailing me with an eighty-mile-an-hour curveball."

They were in each other's faces now.

"I didn't invite you on the field," Jack said. "You came at your own risk."

Walker poked a finger into his brother's chest. They had history that wasn't going to be erased by a pat on the back for a hundred days of sobriety. He got that now. There was over a decade of hell to set straight. Maybe this was the start. "You finally want to give me what I asked for?"

There was a lot that Walker forgot because of the drinking—black spots in his memory that would never return, and for some of that he was probably grateful. But he remembered what it was like when Jack came back home after ten years. He remembered the guilt of watching Jack Senior raise a hand to his oldest brother and not being able to do a damned thing to protect him. That kind of guilt never left. So one night after Jack came home last year, Walker asked his brother to hit him—begged him to unleash some of the pain he'd borne for him and Luke. But Jack wouldn't do it. Maybe now he would.

"Shit, Walker." Jack backed away. "I thought we were done with that. Me hitting you isn't going to solve anything."

All the fight seemed to leave his brother, and Jack bent over, bracing his hands on his thighs and breathing heavily.

"You know I haven't raised a hand to anyone since that asshole attacked Ava in high school. And even then it wasn't the right thing to do—not putting another guy in the hospital, anyway." Jack took another steadying breath. "I never wanted to be *him*—Jack Senior. And I don't think you did, either. He pushed you onto the path you've been on, but so help me if I'm not doing my damnedest to change your direction. But you gotta find a way to get past this need to punish yourself for something that wasn't your fault."

Walker paced his little patch of infield before facing his brother again.

"I almost drank last night," he finally said.

"What?" Jack asked.

"I said *almost*. I wasn't on a bender. I was sick."

Jack's brows drew together. "Sick? You don't get sick."

Walker crossed his arms. "That's what I said when Violet came over, but apparently the lack of alcohol killing off everything in its wake messed with my system or something."

Jack cracked a half smile. "Okay. So, not a bender. Tell me what happened."

Walker took off his sunglasses and pinched the bridge of his nose.

"Pitch me some strikes," he said. "*Only* strikes." It was a little league field. They could talk from pitcher's mound to home plate. Because standing here and talking was too intimate. He didn't know how to do this, but the bat and ball might distract him enough and give him that needed distance.

Jack adjusted his cap and nodded.

Walker was at the plate again a few seconds later, bat raised over his shoulder. Then he knocked his brother's strike clear into left field.

Jack wound up for the next pitch.

"There's a small bottle of whiskey in the cabinet above my fridge."

Walker had the good sense to duck as Jack's pitch went wild, nailing the chain-link backstop behind where Walker's head would have been if he'd been standing at full height.

Walker straightened and pointed at his brother with his nephew's bat. "I don't drink it. I just—test myself."

Jack lifted his Dodgers cap and swiped his forearm against his brow. He opened his mouth to say something, likely to chew Walker out, but Walker shook his head like he was shaking off the pitch his brother wanted to throw.

"You pitch. I talk. Or this ain't happening."

Walker could see his brother's jaw tighten all the way from home plate, but Jack kept his mouth shut.

"Anyway, by the time I got home last night, I was in bad shape," he called to his brother. "Fever and everything. Violet just sorta showed up after we got back from the bar and took care of things."

Jack pitched another strike. This time was a swing and a miss.

"She got me meds and made me tea."

"Shit," Jack said. He knew what was coming next.

Walker nodded. "Nice little shot of whiskey in the mug—her home remedy. And why would she think anything of it when I had my own damned bottle?"

"You didn't drink?" Jack asked, still not satisfied that Walker hadn't gone and chucked his hundred days out the window.

Walker let out a bitter laugh. "Threw the damned thing against the wall and scared the shit out of her before telling her to leave. And you know what? If I hadn't felt like I'd been run over by a truck and could have made it to the kitchen, I might have downed the whole bottle just to obliterate the sight of Violet looking at me like I was some monster—like she realized she was finally seeing the real me."

Jack threw another strike. Again, a swing and a miss. Because Walker couldn't see the ball anymore. Just Violet—her eyes brimming with angry tears after he was such an inexplicable ass.

"She didn't say anything," Jack said, winding up to pitch again. "But you gotta figure out a way to make this right, Walker. Not only for her but for yourself. You know, all this time I haven't been worried about whether or not getting involved with Violet was good for your sobriety. I've been worrying about how you'll handle it when she leaves. We're all gonna miss the hell out of her. So what does that mean for you?"

Walker straightened and dropped the bat to his side as Jack let the next pitch fly. It was right over the plate, maybe a little on the low side but a strike nonetheless. Unfortunately, Walker was now standing over the plate, too, and the ball hammered him straight in the gut.

He went down hard, landing flat on his back, the wind knocked clear from his lungs. He thought he heard his brother swear, but he was spending most of his energy both trying to catch his breath and trying not to vomit.

When he could finally see straight, he caught sight of Jack standing above him, his hand outstretched.

Walker reached for it, letting his brother pull him up.

"What the hell were you doing?" Jack asked.

Walker coughed. He pressed a palm to his torso and tried to straighten up. But it hurt too much at the moment to do so.

"I was thinking about how the hell to do what you said—to make things right with Violet. Can't you tell when a guy is pausing to think?" He pulled his shirt up to find a baseball-shaped welt forming on his skin right between his ribs.

Jack shook his head and laughed. "If that'd been a fastball, I'd have been calling nine-one-one."

Walker gritted his teeth. "Sure felt like a fastball."

Jack looked him up and down. "You sleep in the stable last night?" he asked, finally acknowledging Walker's less-than-stellar appearance.

"Cleaned it this morning," Walker said. "Then took Cleo for a ride and found you." He could almost stand straight now.

"How about you come by the ranch for a shower and lunch. And we can figure out how to fix this Violet Chastain situation."

But Walker already knew how to fix it. He had to leave her be and not get her tangled up in his mess any more than he already had.

"I could eat," he said. "But there's nothing needs doing about Violet. She's better off without me messing things up for her. She'll focus on work, and so will I. It won't be an issue."

Jack cleared his throat. "You've been selling those pieces you make at the market, huh?"

Walker nodded. He didn't think his brother paid much attention to his little side business.

"Been putting away some extra cash," he admitted.

"You want to tell me what for?" Jack asked.

Walker figured now was as good a time as any. "I'm leaving, too. Gonna take off for a while after the wedding," he said, finally putting some truth out there. "Sam and Ben are putting together a crew to help them build a ranch up north. Sam offered me a spot, and I took it."

Jack stared at him for a long moment. "I see," he finally said.

"That's how I'm gonna handle her leaving. It's how I'm going to handle all my goddamn ghosts. They're all here, Jack."

"So's your family," his brother said.

"And you'll be here when I get back. It's not forever," he said. "I know this means you won't be able to keep tabs on me twenty-four/seven, but shit, Jack. You got your distance. Now I need mine. I'm either gonna drink or I'm not, whether you're watching my back or I'm six hours away."

Jack gave his brother a slow nod. "I can't fault you for needing to put some distance between yourself and Oak Bluff. But if you don't answer my calls or texts, I will have

Cash call the local authorities and drag you out of bed just to make sure you're okay."

Walker laughed. "Seems like a waste of taxpayer money, doesn't it?"

Jack raised a brow. "If you don't want that on your conscience, you know what to do."

"Noted," Walker said.

"I'll clean up here and meet you back at the house." Jack clapped his brother on the back, and Walker choked out a breath.

"Hey," he said to Jack. "Injured man, here. Take it easy."

Jack laughed. "Not a chance, little brother. But I'll always be a phone call away when easy feels too far to reach. Don't forget that."

Then he walked away and started collecting the scattered baseballs.

Walker knew what his brother meant, and maybe now Jack understood that here in Oak Bluff, easy might always be beyond Walker's grasp. But the distance he needed wasn't from Jack or Luke or Jenna. He was starting to understand that now—after a fastball to the gut. He didn't need to let go of his family. Putting a few hundred miles between himself and this place, though—it was the only way he'd be able to let go of the past.

CHAPTER NINETEEN

After what she privately referred to as *the incident*, Violet got used to seeing Walker around town and treating him as nothing more than an acquaintance. After both of them admitted in their own frightened way that what they had was real, they'd taken a gigantic step backward and were now almost strangers. He hadn't offered her any more of an explanation about that night, and she certainly wasn't chasing him down for one. Their time was up, but she still had work to do before heading to Paris.

Last Tuesday, when she was at the bakery eating a chocolate croissant and reading up on the French doctor who would facilitate her mom's treatment, Walker ran in for his morning coffee. When she went to the market on Thursday night to pick out cheese and fruit to pair with Friday's wine tasting, there was Walker shopping for what looked like dinner for one. She'd smiled and said hi. He'd said hi back. And that was how it went—their foray into acquaintanceship, which she guessed was better than pretending the other didn't exist.

Who was she kidding? The whole situation was crap. It wasn't just that he hadn't apologized for that night he was sick. It was that she'd been falling for the man, and now the two of them couldn't even hold a conversation.

Today, after almost two weeks of short, minute-long encounters, they were stuck together staining shelves for the gift shop portion of the winery.

They worked outside in the hot, late-April sun.

Violet wore a black cotton tank and a pair of old jeans. Her thick dark hair was pulled into two French braids, which meant she couldn't hide behind her hair when she felt him looking at her—or when she wanted to look back.

Walker had a green bandanna tied around his forehead to catch the sweat, not that his T-shirt wasn't already damp. And hell if he wasn't sexy as ever like that—even if he was still an asshole.

"This probably isn't what you signed up for being a wine expert and all, was it?" he finally asked, surprising her by being the first one to break the silence.

Her back was to him as she stained a shelf atop his makeshift workbench.

"Right now, a paycheck is a paycheck, so I'm not complaining," she said.

"You going to the family dinner thing at Lily's tonight? I know you're not officially family, but Lily sort of considers everyone she knows as one of her own. I do remember you owing her a rain check," he said.

Her heart tugged at his line of questioning. It sounded almost like he *wanted* her to be at the dinner. And what if she was? Would they talk? Would things finally change between them?

And why was she overthinking a question as meaningless as him asking her what she was doing for dinner? They hadn't spoken in two weeks. He was making idle small talk. There was no way he truly cared what her answer was going to be.

She stopped staining midstroke and paused before turning to face him.

She smiled at him, but it felt forced. Because it was. There was nothing good about what she had to say.

"Are you okay?" he asked, setting his own brush down and looking at her like she was hurt or something.

"Yeah," she said, her voice coming out a higher pitch than normal. "Totally, yeah. I'm, um, not going to make it to Lily's tonight, though. Guess my rain check still stands."

His brows drew together. "So, she did invite you, and you said no?"

She nodded. "It was really sweet of her. Oak Bluff is starting to feel like a second home, you know? But I sort of already have plans." She held his gaze for a moment longer, then turned back to staining her shelf.

Walker, however, did not. He pushed the issue further.

"Other plans?" he asked. "Here in town?"

It was none of his business. She knew he knew that. Didn't stop him from asking or from waiting for her to respond.

She put her brush down and spun back in his direction, forcing herself to smile again.

"What are we now, Walker? Friends? I mean, we're being friendly enough to each other, and no one's throwing anyone out of his or her apartment, right?" she said, wishing she could swallow the words as soon as they left her mouth. "Anyway, friends can tell each other things without getting the other friend upset because this is how things are now that we're friends, right?"

He scratched at the back of his neck. "You just said *friend* four times in one sentence."

"Actually, it was two sentences. But duly noted."

Walker crossed his arms. "You can tell me whatever you want to tell me, Teach."

Her expression softened, and she let out a breath.

Teach. Why did he have to call her that when she wanted to stay angry at him, when she wanted the words she was about to say not to mean anything, but they already did to her.

"I have—a date."

It took a few seconds for her words to register. But then it was like she saw the thought bubble pop above his head.

A date. Pop.

"Walker?" she asked. "Everything okay?"

He was clenching his teeth, and his expression looked nowhere in the realm of *friendly*.

"I'm great," he said. "I'm great and you're going on a date." He let out a bitter laugh. "Look at that. I'm a goddamn poet."

"Walker—" she started, but he waved her off.

"It's all good," he said, his brush still in his hand. He turned back to his shelf, but this time she was the one not to turn back to hers. "I hope he treats you right, whoever it is. You deserve a hell of a lot better than—I mean, you deserve to be treated right, Violet. Period."

Despite the sincerity in his words, she watched as he dipped his brush in the can of stain and swept it back and forth across his shelf, his teeth clenched.

"It's Sam Callahan," she said, remembering Walker's reaction when she first met Sam at the market. "He and his brother Ben have been working on the remodel at the B and B all week, and we got to talking the other day. He asked if he could take me to dinner, and I said yes. You're okay with it, right? Because there's obviously nothing going on with us anymore. Unless there is something you want to talk about."

The thing was, though, that despite how cute Sam was and how easy he was to talk to, *he* was the one who felt more like a friend, and Walker still felt—confusing.

"Sam's a good man," he said.

"Yeah," she admitted. "He is. He told me he and his brother are heading up north soon. Anyway, it's just a date. Nothing serious."

Walker nodded. "Their family boarded horses when Sam and Ben were growing up. Parents split and their mom moved up that way with her new husband. Dad got hit with early signs of Alzheimer's, so they stayed around here, built up their own business, and took care of him."

"Oh," she said. "That's sad. And also kinda sweet that they took care of him. Is he—I mean, you said *took*."

"There's a real good facility near the land where they're building the ranch. Once they sell off the horses they'll get him settled there."

"I guess we all have our stories, huh?" Violet blew out a long breath. "Sounds like he's a real good guy. Thank you for telling me all that."

"You're welcome."

She took a step closer, then reached for his hand and gave it a soft squeeze.

She felt his muscles tense.

"Maybe one day you'll tell me your story," she said. "As easily as you told me his."

"Yeah. Maybe." Walker cleared his throat, and she let his hand go. She watched as he opened and closed his fist, wondering if he was trying to erase her touch as much as she was trying to remember his. Maybe she was letting him off too easily, not demanding an explanation for his frightening behavior. But she also knew that whatever the reason, it was eating at him. She could see it in the set of his jaw, in the tightness in his shoulders. He'd needed space, and she'd barged right back into his apartment. Maybe this would finally heal things between them, her giving him the distance he needed.

They turned away from each other then, back to their respective workbenches.

"You mind if I put on some music?" she called to him. "I always work better with music."

"Fine by me," he called back.

A few seconds later the opening of "Cowboy Take Me Away" blared from her phone, and she sang along to it like she did at the karaoke bar that night, telling herself that she was okay with the way things were between them now.

It was a good enough lie. The truth was that she still wanted to know every part of him, even if his story was a painful one.

But she deserved more than he was offering. She figured they'd gotten as far as they'd get.

So she stained her shelves and sang along to everything from country to pop to soulful R & B. Every now and then she snuck a glance over her shoulder just to look at him. And every now and then she caught him sneaking a glance right back.

Maybe he wouldn't be the cowboy to take her away from it all. But she could still wish he might have been.

When Walker was too restless to relax that night, he worked on every available project he had in the apartment—the rocking chair, an end table he'd been commissioned to make for the sheriff's mother and her new husband, a few more shelves he needed to sand before taking them to the winery to stain. But his concentration was shit. And he was too wired to sleep. He needed to get out of his confined space, needed air to clear his head. The next thing he knew, he was crossing from Lucinda's back lot into that of the Oak Bluff Bed and Breakfast until he'd made it clear to the other side. He'd barely been there two minutes before he heard the familiar authoritative cadence of Sheriff Cash Hawkins's voice.

"Sir, please step out where I can see you with your hands in the air."

A blindingly bright light shone on the cordoned off construction zone at the bed-and-breakfast's side lot. Walker stepped out and around the tarped-off hole in the B and B's kitchen wall—hands raised—where he'd been inspecting the Callahan's demo work as well as the start of their building out the walls.

"Just me, Sheriff," he said, having recognized Cash's voice.

A dog barked.

"Can you make sure Dixie isn't gonna chew an arm off or something if I step any closer?"

Cash lowered the floodlight and clicked it off. Then he dropped to a squat to give his German shepherd a scratch behind the ears.

"It's okay, girl. It's only Walker being an idiot." The sheriff stood to face him again. "Jesus, Everett. What the hell are you doing snooping around at ten thirty at night? Olivia was grabbing us a bottle of wine and saw a shadow through the tarp. She swore she was about to be robbed or worse. She was already nervous living with a busted open wall, but now you've gone and scared her half to death, which means instead of being inside on my night off with my girl, I'm out here wondering why in the hell you're snooping around a construction site you're not working on."

Walker looked Cash up and down, realizing the sheriff was wearing a B and B robe over a pair of sweatpants.

"Nice outfit, Sheriff."

"Careful, Everett. I can still arrest you."

The two men and Dixie made their way onto the sidewalk and then the lit porch of the B and B's entrance.

"Couldn't sleep," Walker said. "So I thought I'd come check out the progress. Didn't mean to scare anyone. Olivia the only one on duty tonight?"

Cash crossed his arms. "Tell me this isn't about a girl."

The B and B's front door flew open to reveal Olivia Belle—also in a fluffy white robe.

"Did you find the attacker or robber or whoever it was? Did you have to call for backup? What is Walker Everett doing here?"

Cash nodded in Walker's direction. "Here you go, darlin'. Your ruthless attacker. Says he couldn't sleep so he wanted to see how the Callahans were doing with the restaurant addition."

Olivia narrowed her gaze, looking Walker up and down as she noticeably took in his attire, a solid black button-down with the sleeves rolled to his elbows and his cleanest looking pair of jeans. "Why are you dressed so nice to rob me?"

Walker rolled his eyes. "I'm not here to rob or attack anyone. I've been working with Sam and Ben on the winery. Wanted to stop by and see how they were doing over here."

Olivia tapped her index finger on her pursed lips as she seemed to puzzle something out. Then her eyes widened.

"You were checking up on Violet!" she gasped, and turned her focus to Cash. "See? I told you there was still something going on there. She said they were just friends now, but I didn't buy it. Not after that kiss two weeks ago." She shook her head. "You don't think I forgot about that kiss, do you? I had a front row seat! Plus I've noticed a lingering tension with you two like I did when Lily and Luke claimed they wanted nothing to do with each other. I have a knack for these things, you know."

Cash groaned. "And apparently it's rubbing off on me. Look, Everett. I don't like getting involved in anyone's business, especially when it comes to—to matters of the heart. But like it or not, I've got a personal stake in the matter. You and your brothers are as close as it comes to having brothers of my own."

Walker huffed out a bitter laugh. "That why you arrested me and locked me up New Year's Eve or why you came banging on my door telling me you don't trust me to stay sober? Hell of a way to treat family."

"Hey," Olivia interrupted. "He arrested me, too. Cash just has a very strict code of ethics. He shows his love by following the rules."

"Of the law." Cash's jaw tightened. "You both *broke* the law. In *my* town. It was more than your own safety you put at risk. It was everyone else's, too. Whether it's driving fast or drinking so much you can't feel the pain of a busted-up nose, your behavior—both of you—put this town at risk. And damn it, Everett. You had a bottle of Jack in your cupboard after three months of sobriety, and you want to give me hell for not trusting you? Now here you are snooping around private property after hours—turning your nose up at the law once again. Tell me why I shouldn't arrest you for trespassing right now."

Olivia smacked Cash lightly across his shoulder. "Oh come on, babe. You're not really gonna—"

Walker interrupted her, holding out his hands, wrists pressed together. "Have at it, Sheriff. That's what you really think, isn't it? That I'm a danger to myself and society?"

"Christ, Everett. I know you think much doesn't happen in this town, but I've seen a car wrapped so badly around a light post we could barely identify the passengers. And I saw what you looked like sprawled on the pavement over a blanket of glass, your face so bloodied I thought I'd be calling your brothers outta bed to identify your body. So excuse me if I'm not celebrating. A few months is nothing compared to ten years of addiction."

Olivia gasped. "Oh, Cash..."

"It's a hell of a start!" Walker shot back. "Tell me why everyone's still waiting for me to fall off the wagon—you, Jack, Luke. It's not enough I went into this willingly. It's not enough I've kept my head down and stayed off the radar. So tell me the answer, Sheriff. When's it gonna be enough?"

But the truth was, Cash Hawkins wasn't the person Walker was trying to convince. He didn't blame anyone for not trusting him after such a short time when he didn't trust himself. Didn't mean it was easy to hear that Cash thought the same thing he did.

The sheriff opened his mouth to answer, but before he could, Walker felt cool metal around his wrist as he heard the handcuff click into place. He glanced down to see the second cuff clasping just below the sleeve of Cash's white robe.

Both men yanked their wrists, but it was a futile effort. They looked up to see Olivia dangling the key in between them.

"You boys need to settle this and move on. Thought you might need a little motivation."

"Olivia..." Cash said carefully, but she shook her head.

"You're free when you figure out a way to kiss and make up—or whatever you two need to do to settle an argument."

Cash shrugged. "My right hand's still free." He balled it into a fist.

Walker's jaw tightened. "I'll take you with my left. It's not a problem."

Then Cash made a quick move that Walker realized too late was an attempt to grab the key from Olivia, and he socked the sheriff in the gut.

Olivia yelped as Cash doubled over, and Walker watched the key fly from her hand and into the darkened bushes.

Walker was too focused on the key to catch the sheriff sweeping his leg out and knocking Walker to the ground—which subsequently yanked Cash to the ground as well. The two men rolled off the porch and into the cold, damp grass as a silver SUV rolled up in front of the property.

Walker and Cash were both on their backs. Each scrambled to get to their feet, which only caused them to stumble over each other again so that when Sam Callahan rounded the front of the vehicle to open the passenger door for Violet, the two men were on all fours, having scuffled all the way to the edge of the property, Cash yanking at Walker's wrist as the sheriff retied his robe.

The first thing Walker saw from his vantage point was a black, strappy sandal with a long, spiky heel. *Damn Violet and those shoes of hers.* His vision of Violet's sexy leg was obscured by Sam Callahan dropping to a squat so he was eye level with the other two men.

"Sheriff," he said with a nod. "Everett. Interesting night?"

Slowly, both men pushed to their knees and then to their feet. Cash's white robe was streaked with green grass stains, and the top couple buttons on Walker's shirt had been ripped off, leaving it half open and his chest exposed.

Once on his feet, he could see Violet fully—a simple, short-sleeve black dress to go with the not-so-simple shoes, her hair in thick dark spirals over her shoulders. Her lips shone with a clear gloss, and her cheeks held the slightest hint of pink.

She was ridiculously gorgeous as always, even as she stared at him with her arms crossed and brows raised in stark accusation.

"Good evening, gentlemen. Thanks for the welcome."

Olivia sprung up from where she'd been hidden in the bushes. "Found it!" She ran toward the four others standing on the edge of the lawn. "I found the key!"

Cash held out his free hand as Olivia dropped it into his palm with a nervous smile.

"I thought I was doing the two of you a favor," she said. "I can see now that I didn't think long enough before acting on the idea. Lesson learned," she said with a laugh.

"I should probably go so you all can deal with whatever it is you're dealing with," Sam said. Then Walker watched as he kissed Violet on the cheek—and as she wrapped her arms around him and gave him a parting hug.

"Thank you," she said as they released each other. "I had a really nice time."

Sam smiled the sort of broad, heroic grin of a man accustomed to saving the damsel rather than being the one to actually put her in distress.

Walker's chest tightened.

"I meant what I said," he told her. "The offer still stands."

Violet smiled. "I'll think about it. Thanks again, Sam."

The sheriff unlocked the cuffs and dropped them back into the robe pocket from which Olivia had apparently swiped them.

"Good night—everyone," Sam said before hopping back in the vehicle and heading off down the street.

For several long seconds it felt like a standoff between Walker and Cash while the two women looked on.

"You assaulted an officer," Cash said to him coolly.

"Oh my God," Violet said.

"It's not what it looks like," Olivia interrupted. "It was my fault."

"You raised your fist," Walker countered. "I thought I was playing defense. I didn't know you were going for the key."

Cash grunted something under his breath. "I suppose that is a feasible explanation for your unlawful behavior this time around." He held out a hand.

Walker hesitated, but then he grabbed it. The two men shook.

"We're done for tonight, Everett," the sheriff said. "But not for good."

Olivia grabbed the sheriff's hand and tugged him toward the door.

"Night, Walker," she said. "I hope you found what you were looking for tonight."

The two of them—Olivia in robe only and Cash in his stained one along with his sweatpants, strode hand in hand up the sidewalk, back to the porch, and through the front door, leaving just Violet and Walker at the edge of the property.

"Do I even want to ask why Olivia cuffed you to the sheriff in the first place?" Violet said.

"Probably not," Walker replied.

She nodded slowly. "Fine. That's not the question I'll ask, but I do have one."

He raised his brows. "Out with it, then."

"Why are you at the B and B? Cash was off duty tonight, but Olivia had the desk until ten. They were supposed to be doing a late-night date once she was off the clock, too. But I don't remember you being part of their plans."

Walker scrubbed a hand over his beard. "I was checking out Sam and Ben's work on the construction. I wanted to see..."

He trailed off. He was tired of lying to her. He could at least be truthful about tonight.

"That's not actually true," he said.

"Oh?" was all she said in response.

"I came here to see if you were back yet, and when I figured it was too early for you to be home from a *good* date—and why wouldn't it be with Sam? I decided to hide out behind the demo area for a bit so I could see whether or not you really liked him. If you kissed him good night, I'd guess that you did, and I'd have gone home and dealt with it."

She stared at him like he had a third eye, and he didn't blame her.

"I didn't kiss him good night," she said flatly.

He nodded. "Is that because you had an audience or because he wasn't the man you wanted to kiss tonight?"

She narrowed her eyes at him. "All these weeks I've known you, you've been this ridiculous puzzle I've tried to figure out. Unsuccessfully, I might add. And now you're admitting to trying to spy on my date to figure out what you could have just asked me."

He ran a hand through his hair and pulled from it a leaf and a few blades of grass.

"You're right," he said. "Maybe it's time I let you ask me."

"Ask you what?" she said hesitantly.

He shrugged. "Anything you want, I guess."

"And you'll answer? No matter what the question is."

He nodded. "I figure I owe you that much."

She fidgeted with the small purse slung across her torso. "Were you jealous I was out with another guy tonight?"

Wow. Looked like she wasn't pulling any punches.

"Yes," he said coolly. "Out-of-my-mind jealous."

"Even though you threw me out of your apartment weeks ago and still haven't told me why?"

"Yes."

"Do you want more from me than friendship, Walker?"

He glanced down the street in the direction Sam had driven.

"Sam Callahan is a good man," he said.

She blew out an exasperated-sounding breath. "That's a cop-out answer. If there was no duty or bro code or whatever excuse you've been using to push me away, would you still want to be with me?"

He stared into her questioning brown eyes. "Yes."

She groaned. "You are infuriating. Do you know that?"

He knew. "Been called worse."

"Not that you get to ask any of the questions here, but so we're clear, Sam and I are just going to be friends. Turns out there's a guy I'm hung up on who's keeping me from being able to move on. So until I get him out of my system..." She trailed off.

Walker bit back a grin. "You did a damned good job of hiding it."

She shook her head. "Not from him. Or Olivia. Or Cash even. Before I left tonight, Olivia asked me if I was really sure I wanted to go through with the date since there was still so much tension between you and me. Apparently the one time I try not to wear my emotions on my sleeve, they just leak right out of me when everyone seems to be watching."

He took a step toward her, but she backed away.

"Why?" she asked, throwing her hands in the air. "Why do you think that I can't handle whatever is going on with you? Why do you think I'm capable of dealing with all of the other shit going on in my life but that I'm not strong enough to handle yours?"

He held out his hand for her, but she hesitated.

"You're the strongest person I know, Teach. I'm the one who's been weak."

Her eyes softened, but he knew it wasn't going to be that easy. He needed to let her all the way in. He didn't expect her to forgive him, but he at least wanted her to understand before she left. He wanted her to know once and for all how he felt about her, but he wanted her to trust him, too. To trust that it had always been real even if he hid the biggest part of himself from her.

"Come with me," he said. "I'll show you."

She turned toward the antiques shop, staring up at the apartment above and then spun back to face him.

"I know," he said. "I scared the hell out of you last time you were there. And I think, maybe, you know why. But it's the one thing you're afraid to ask—and the one thing I still don't know if I can say aloud. If I don't say it, then maybe it won't be true. And maybe you won't look at me like everyone else in this town has at one point or another."

He dropped his hand, and they stood there, gazes locked on one another, an impasse of sorts.

"I get it," he said. "Too little too late and all that."

He started toward the apartment, and she didn't stop him.

He'd pushed her too far, and he didn't blame her for not wanting to let him back in now. He'd pushed everyone away who wanted to be there for him—his brothers, his aunt, even Cash, who, when he wasn't arresting Walker, was the closest thing he had to a tried-and-true friend—because he thought recovery was something he had to do alone. He thought he could do the same with Violet, keep her at arm's length and not ever truly let her in. So why did it feel like someone punched a hole clear through his chest?

He strode up the back steps and into Lucinda's apartment. He opened the cabinet where he'd hidden the opened bottle of whiskey rather than pouring it out, set it on the table along with his shot glass, then sat down and stared at his two old friends.

The sheriff was right. A few months was nothing compared to almost half a lifetime. He didn't know how to be anyone other than an alcoholic. It would be so much easier to just be who everyone else expected—to play his role in the story that always ended with him messing shit up.

He'd been the asshole of all assholes when he was drinking, but there was no excuse for the way he'd treated Violet when she'd made an innocent mistake with that damned mug of tea. Now that he was ready to tell her the truth, it was too late. Walking away was the smartest thing for her to do.

He held the shot glass in his hand, flipped it over a couple of times, then set it back down.

Not tonight. Even if she couldn't give him another chance, he wouldn't fail her because of it.

Instead he headed back to his room, stripped out of his clothes, and collapsed onto his bed. He was so damned tired of it all. How the hell would he make it through the end of the summer before he could pick up and leave?

It took a good twenty-five minutes of lying there, wishing for sleep to come. When it did, it was like a tidal wave of drowsiness he couldn't fight if he tried. He welcomed it, telling himself when he woke up everything would be different. He fucked up with Violet, but he was done pushing everyone else away. No more self-imposed exile. His family wanted to be there for him, so maybe it was high time he let them.

His room was pitch-black when something clattered loudly in the kitchen. It took his eyes several seconds to adjust as he fumbled for the phone on his nightstand but instead sent it crashing to the ground.

"Shit," he mumbled, which seemed like the only word he knew these days.

His eyes finally registered the time. It was half past midnight.

He stood, rolled his neck along his shoulders, remembering his ridiculous battle with the sheriff on the B and B's front lawn, when he realized he'd been so preoccupied with Violet's date that he hadn't eaten since lunch.

Food. He needed food.

A dish clanked against the sink in the kitchen, and he rolled his eyes. How was his aunt always showing up when he needed to eat? He had to draw the line at past midnight.

"Seriously, Jenna?" he called down the hall. "Showing up at the crack of dawn is one thing, but the middle of the—"

He stopped short at the kitchen entryway where he found not his aunt but Violet rinsing the few dishes he'd left in the sink.

He blinked twice, making sure he wasn't running another fever and maybe hallucinating.

Nope. It was her.

She wore a black tank, a pair of red-and-black-checked flannel pants, and a pair of tan fuzzy boots. Maybe they were slippers. He wasn't sure. Walker was pretty clueless when it came to women's fashion. All he knew was that

Violet Chastain could make a garbage bag look good simply because she was Violet.

His first instinct was to kiss her, which was always the first thing he wanted to do when he saw her. But she hadn't snuck into his apartment and tiptoed into his room, telling him she'd give him another chance. She was—cleaning. So as much as he'd started to hope the moment he saw her, he hung back, not wanting to spook her into running out the door again.

She turned off the tap and braced her hands on the edge of the counter.

He cleared his throat. "I thought we came to an agreement earlier," he said. It was more like she had agreed he wasn't worth the fight anymore, and he hadn't fought for her. In his head he could hear all the right words—The *I'm sorry* and *I should tell you the truth* and *You deserve better, but it's hard for me to admit why.* Everything was there, behind a stubborn, stupid, jackass mouth that, when opened, only ever uttered the wrong thing or thought of the right thing when it was far too late.

She finally pivoted to face him, and her brows raised as she caught sight of his almost naked form. But she just as quickly seemed to regain her composure.

"You drank iced tea at my parents' anniversary party," she said.

He crossed his arms over his chest. "I did."

"You got so angry when Dorothy wanted us to sample the stemware before we bought it, and I shrugged it off. Then at Lily and Olivia's dinner party after I hurt my hand—at a bed-and-breakfast that does wine tastings with a table full of brothers who own an up-and-coming winery—not one goblet or flute was set out on the table."

His chest tightened. So it was going to happen like

this—her figuring out his lies and then turning her back on him for good. He wasn't sure he could handle it.

Jack had it all wrong. It wasn't just her leaving that would break him. It was her thinking the worst of him before she did. But he wouldn't stop her. She'd come here to confirm what he'd wanted to tell her in his own careful way. He owed it to both of them to see it through now, even if it would be his undoing.

"You've got a good eye," he finally said.

"Every Sunday dinner with my parents, you always said no to a glass of wine because of the long drive back to Oak Bluff, and no one ever thought twice about it."

He shrugged. "You saw what you wanted to see, and I let you."

"And that night after the karaoke bar, when you scared the shit out of me and behaved like a complete asshole, it was because..." She swiped a finger under her eye, then blew out a shaky breath as she stared at the items he'd left on the kitchen table—the bottle of whiskey and the shot glass.

Even though she was correct, she didn't want to say it, to accuse him if there was a chance she was wrong. And he wouldn't make her.

"Because you served liquor to an alcoholic," he said flatly.

She nodded. "I helped Olivia with all those wine tastings. When I saw her inventory, that some of it was from Ava Ellis's family vineyard, it should have hit me, you know? She and Cash were drinking a bottle of it tonight, and it took you admitting you still wanted to be with me for it to all fall into place. Why hadn't Olivia broken out a bottle for a dinner party Ava attended? It was for *you*. You—you have a hard time even being around it."

It wasn't a question. She just—knew.

"It's getting easier every day," he said.

"How long have you been sober?"

He let out a bitter laugh. "If I make it through today? One hundred and sixteen days."

"Oh my God." Her hand flew to her mouth much like it did when he'd slammed the cup of tea against the wall.

"Don't," he said. It was like he could see the wheels turning in her head. "Don't apologize to me after what I did. I don't deserve it, and I sure as hell don't deserve your sympathy. I did this. I fucked up. Hell, I've been fucking up for a lot of years. Just because I'm sober now doesn't mean I'm all of a sudden getting it right." He realized she'd taken advantage of his unlocked door. "Guess you decided not to knock this time, huh?"

She shook her head. "I still think a person ought to lock their door when they're not in the house and when they turn in for the night. You're liable to get random women walking in off the street to do your dishes." She laughed softly. "I was in bed, trying like hell to talk myself out of coming here because maybe this is too much. Maybe it is too hard." She shrugged. "But it's *you.*" She nodded toward the items on the table. "Did you—did you drink?"

He shook his head. "I thought about it. I think about it every night. But no. I didn't." He picked up the bottle and unscrewed the cap, and breathed in the sweet aroma that still smelled like home to him.

"I'm not ready to pour it out," he said. "Not until I'm doing it for the right reason."

"And what reason is that?" she asked.

He ran a hand through his disheveled hair. "I thought if I did it for you right now that it would be some sort of grand gesture, but I can't stay sober for you, Violet."

She stared at him, her eyes coating with a sheen of tears.

"If I'm sober for you or my brothers or Jenna, then what does that mean when none of you are around? If I'm not doing it for me, then I'll drink the first chance I get when I know I won't be caught. It's why as soon as Jack and Ava tie the knot, I'm getting the hell out of town."

Her eyes widened. "Where?"

"Up north with Sam and Ben to build the ranch. Figure that'll give me the time and distance I need to see if I can really do this."

She worried her lip between her teeth, and it made him want to kiss her like he always did, but he had no right to do such a thing.

There was nothing more than a couple inches between them, but it might have been an entire canyon for how far away she still felt.

"How long will you be gone?" she asked.

He shrugged. "I don't know. Right now I'm considering the ride up to Meadow Valley a one-way ticket. How about you and France?"

She huffed out a laugh. "Same. We sure are a pair, huh? There's one thing I don't understand. Why didn't you tell me, Walker? Did you think it was something you could hide for however long this thing between us lasted? I mean—I've all but infiltrated your hometown where I'm guessing I was the only one in the dark. If that night hadn't happened, there's a good chance the issue might have come up before summer."

She had a point.

"I've never been good at thinking past today. And once it was out there that I was leaving—that whatever this was was only temporary, I didn't think I'd have to. I thought I could be someone else with you—with someone who didn't know."

She rubbed her bare arms with the palms of her hands. "When you said you were getting out of a long relationship and weren't ready to date..."

He laughed softly. "Yeah, whiskey and I had a ten-year thing going. Guess I wasn't ready to rebound."

She nodded. "Speaking of rebound, I finally told my parents about France."

His brows furrowed. "I don't follow."

She hopped up onto the counter, her legs dangling as she fidgeted with the hem of her tank. "Well, it turns out when my dad was studying abroad in Paris during college, he didn't immediately meet and fall in love with my mother. He met my aunt first."

Walker hissed in a breath between his teeth. "Shit. That is heavy."

"My father really, truly cared for her, but it was through Ines that he met Maman. He didn't cheat. He didn't even express his interest in Maman until after he'd ended things with Ines, but she didn't take it well. She told my mother she never wanted to speak to her again." Violet buried her face in her hands and shook her head. "She has nothing but regret for the things she said to my parents, and Maman still blames herself for breaking her sister's heart. They both let their stubborn pride keep them from reconciling all these years. I don't think my parents realize what not knowing my family has done to me. Maybe they didn't mean to, but the truth is, they all robbed me of such a huge part of my roots." She hesitated. "Which is why I'm not sure when I'm coming back. It's more than being there for my mom's treatment. I think I need to be with my family for a while. You know?"

He cleared his throat. "When do you leave?"

She winced, like she already knew how much the answer

would gut him. "The beginning of May. Things happened quicker than I expected."

His chest tightened. "That's not even a week. You—you won't even make it to the wedding?"

She shook her head. "I'll be enrolling in university there after Maman finishes treatment, but it's thanks to you," she said. "You made me read that first e-mail from my aunt. You convinced me that it was okay to want this for me *and* for Maman. You made me brave, Walker, and no matter what happened before or what might happen in the future, I will always be grateful for that."

He strode toward her and placed his hands on her knees. "Please," he said. "Don't let the last time we kissed be the last time we kissed."

She cupped his face in her hands, and he leaned into her touch. God he'd missed her.

"You know my whole story now," she said. "First I need yours."

"Fair enough," he said. He held out his hand, and she took it, hopping off the counter and following him to the couch. He sat in the corner, legs stretched the length of the cushions so that she had no choice but to climb between them, and she did so willingly. She leaned her back against his chest, then took each of his hands and wrapped them around her midsection. He held her like a life preserver, and that's exactly what she was. She'd saved him time and again without him even realizing it. But it wasn't enough. To be the man she needed, he had to be strong enough to save himself, which meant facing the past that left him broken and bleeding on a bed of glass 116 days ago.

So he ripped off the Band-Aid, the words tearing from his lips in a torrential downpour of his past.

He told her about his mother—Jenna's sister Clare—whose face he fought to remember these days. How cancer took her when he was barely eleven and how grief took his father and never let him go. He told her how Jack Senior turned to the bottle and became a monster instead of a father. How his older brother Jack took the brunt of the abuse in order to protect Luke and Walker, even though it almost killed him. And how for Walker's fifteenth birthday, even when the brothers had been removed from their father's custody and sent to live with their aunt, their father had sent him the gift—a bottle of whiskey—that would set him on the path that would eventually land him in a jail cell with a busted-up face and his last chance at getting things right.

Violet was still beneath his arms, and he couldn't tell if she was breathing let alone what the hell she might be thinking.

"Shit," he said after letting out a long breath. "This is the point in the story where I say that I could use a fucking drink right about now." Except he didn't want one. Somehow putting it all out there took away its power.

She backhanded him on the thigh, a sign—at least—that she'd heard him.

"What?" he said. "The situation needed lightening up. Too soon?"

"Yes," she said, crawling to her knees and turning to face him, but she was smiling. "So what do we do now?"

"I think I earned my kiss."

She answered him by snaking her hands around his neck and pulling his lips to hers. He tasted the mint of her toothpaste and the salt of her tears. He tasted the regret of what he'd put her through and the gratitude that even when he fucked up, he'd still given her the courage to want for herself.

"I'm in love with you, Teach," he said.

She squeezed him tight, burying her head in the crook of his neck.

"You know, Olivia told me the only way to find the answers I was looking for was to start asking the right questions. So tonight, when I decided to come back over here, I asked myself why, after everything, I couldn't move on with a great guy like Sam."

"What'd you come up with?" he asked hesitantly.

"That I'm in love with you, too. That whether it's Oak Bluff, Santa Barbara, or Paris, *you're* home to me. And maybe that means someday geography will be on our side again. But until then, I just want to be here." She pressed her palm to his heart, and he kissed the top of her head.

"Always, Teach," he whispered. "Always."

And then they fell asleep, lulled by the rhythm of each other's breaths.

CHAPTER TWENTY

You sure about this?" Walker asked.

"Yes," she said. "This is how I want to spend my last night in Oak Bluff. With *you.*"

They'd spent several nights in his apartment, but much of the past week Violet had been back in Santa Barbara packing.

Tonight, though, was for room four, with the bath running and Walker Everett a willing participant in her bath-time fantasy.

She stood in the white terry cloth robe that was the most comfortable thing she'd ever worn, then giggled at Walker wearing its matching counterpart.

"I look ridiculous, I know. So how about you get me *out* of the robe and into—well, into *you.*"

She shrugged. Who was she to argue? She untied her robe and let it fall to the floor.

"Jesus," he whispered.

Her belly tightened.

She stepped over the pile of terry cloth and strode the

two feet to where he stood. She untied his robe as well, and a second later he was as naked as she was.

"Wow," she said aloud, having lost her inner monologue. She stared at his taut, muscled torso. At the dusting of dark blond hair that covered his chest and the trail of it that led from his belly button to his long, hard length.

She pressed one hand against his torso and raised the other toward his face. She brushed a finger down the bridge of what she considered his perfect nose, despite the fact that it wasn't exactly straight. Only now she understood the reason why.

"Did it hurt?"

"Yes," he whispered, then dipped his head toward hers. She kissed the bridge of his nose. "Not as much as saying good-bye to you will, though."

He cradled her face in his hands, then kissed her so softly her chest ached.

"You promised no sad stuff," she whispered. "Not when there's a bath to be had."

She gripped the base of his shaft and stroked him from root to tip.

He growled. "You don't play fair, Teach."

"Good thing you love me," she said.

"Good thing I do."

She released him and turned toward the bathroom door.

"Wait," he said, his voice rough. "I need a second to take you in. How do you say *beautiful* in French?"

"*Belle*," she said. "Or *jolie*."

"How do you say, 'You are beautiful'?"

She crossed her arms over her torso, impatient with her admirer.

"Walker, can't we just—"

He raised a brow. "Patience, Teach."

She groaned. "It's different depending on if you're referring to a man or a woman. If I were saying it to you"—she pressed a palm to his chest—"I would say that *Tu es très beau.* Maybe even *Tu es* trop *beau.*"

Her thumb swept back and forth over the dusting of hair on his chest.

"What's the difference?"

She kissed his neck, and he hummed in what she hoped was pleasure.

"*Tu es très beau* means you are very beautiful. *Tu es trop beau* means you are *too* beautiful."

He laughed, then hooked a finger under her chin so her eyes met his. They were a storm of blue and gray, of heat and desire.

"You think I'm *too* beautiful?"

She rolled her eyes. "Come on, Walker. You have seen a mirror once or twice in your life, right? I'm not even sure I cared whether or not I was making Ramon jealous that morning. I think on some level, when I saw you, I *had* to kiss you."

He tucked her curls behind her ear. "You sure as hell were a woman on a mission."

"Yeah. I'm kind of a steamroller. Not my best quality."

He shook his head. "You know what you want, and you don't let anything get in your way. No way you should apologize for that. You're just lucky it was me there that day and not one of my brothers. They're both taken—and not as good-looking."

She laughed. "I see you let my compliment go straight to your ego."

He shrugged. "I don't see any reason to argue with the truth. But you're still skirting the issue. How do I tell *you* you're too beautiful?"

Heat flooded her cheeks, but she didn't falter, her gaze staying fixed on his. "*Tu es trop belle.*"

He dipped his head to kiss the side of her jaw. "*Tu es trop belle.*" He then paid equal attention to the other side. "*Tu es trop belle.*" Next came her shoulders, then the slope of each breast, and with every kiss he repeated the words like a mantra—*tu es* trop *belle*—until she wondered if he'd forgotten all other words entirely.

His lips swept across her dark, hardened peak, and she cried out softly at how sensitive she was to his touch.

Without warning, he lifted her into his arms and backed toward the bathroom. He lowered her gingerly into the tub, then turned off the water.

She noted the condom packet on the edge of the sink, and her belly did a flip-flop.

This time it was her turn to pause and take him in, the man she loved.

Holy hell. Walker Everett was *trop, trop beau*. That sun-kissed sandy hair, the beard. His torso was tanned, which made Violet imagine him outside in the vineyard, the pasture, or in his makeshift workshop behind the winery. Wherever it was he was shirtless and working hard. With his hands.

She giggled and buried her face in her palms.

"Not quite the reaction I was hoping for," Walker said unamused.

She peeked between her fingers.

"No. It's not that. It's—" She blew out a breath. "I'm letting my imagination get the best of me. I need to stop fantasizing and simply be in the here and now."

He lowered himself into the tub and slicked his hair back with a splash of water.

Both of them sat with their knees bent, neither one yet

daring to stretch their legs the length of the tub and into the other's space.

"I'm just going to do the math, here," he said. "The first time you saw me, you *had* to kiss me. I'm too beautiful. And now you're fantasizing about me. I don't know, Ms. Chastain. How are you ever going to let me leave this room?"

She splashed him, and he retaliated by grabbing her ankles and sliding her toward him. Then he slid the rest of the way to meet her. She yelped with laughter, then realized how close they were.

He reached for the condom, but she shook her head.

"I'm—on the pill," she said. "Since this is the last time we'll do this in—I don't know—what if we're together without anything between us?"

He let the condom fall back on the counter, then wrapped her legs around his hips. "Nothing between us," he said. "I kind of like that idea."

"I kind of do, too," she said.

So he kissed her—sweetly at first. His fingers kneaded her hips, then traveled up her back. Despite the warm water, she had goose bumps. Her belly coiled and her heart squeezed. How was it possible that a couple months ago she hadn't even known this man?

He pulled her to him.

"I love the feel of you against me," he said before kissing her. Then his hand went to her breast where he gave her a soft pinch.

She gasped.

His palm trailed farther down until it stopped at her pelvis. Once again she forgot to breathe as anticipation burned at the tip of every single one of her nerves.

She squirmed against him.

"Patience," he sing-songed in his deep voice.

His thumb found her aching center and traced small circles around it.

She whimpered. She'd never last like this. He was driving her out of her mind, and the only cure for it was him. Inside her. *Now.*

She gripped him at the base of the shaft, rose onto her knees, and sank over him with ease.

"Jesus, Violet." His voice was hoarse as he gripped the sides of the tub. "Like a fucking glove," he ground out.

She wrapped her arms around his neck and kissed him. "You know that steamroller part of my personality?"

He laughed. "You just took what you wanted. Didn't you?"

"Mmm-hmm. Patience is not one of my strong points." She squeezed her legs around him, taking him deeper than she thought he could go. She sucked in a trembling breath.

He pulsed inside her.

There was absolutely nothing left between them—no lies or half-truths, no fear or anger or regret. Just Walker and Violet. Together like they were meant to be, even if it was for one last time.

"Tell me again about how much you love me," he said.

She laughed, squeezing her legs around him tight. "I love you, Walker Everett. And I'll be back for you one day." But then her laughter quickly turned to tears.

"Hey," he said softly, kissing her with more gentleness than he should be capable of considering their current situation. "I thought the rule was no sad stuff."

She let out something between a laugh and a sob. "To hell with the rules," she said.

He kissed her again. "Yeah. To hell with them." He tucked her wet hair behind her ears. "Tell me how to say it in French."

She nodded, forcing a smile. "*Je t'aime*, Walker."

"*Je t'aime*, Violet."

* * *

The ride to the airport was a solemn one with Walker and Violet in the back of her father's car, Papa and Maman in the front. Papa would be out the end of the week when Maman started treatment, but he wanted to give her and Violet a few days alone with family to reconnect. They'd worked it out that he'd stay for a week, go home for three, and keep up the pattern until Maman was well enough to come back home.

But Violet and Walker? They didn't have a plan. He was committed to the construction of the ranch up in Meadow Valley, and she was committed to a full semester schedule. It would be at least six months before they'd see each other again, *if* they'd even want to by then.

She'd want to. She was sure of it.

As if he could sense the fears running through her head, Walker threaded his fingers through hers and squeezed.

"We'll figure it out," he said. And because she had to trust that they would, she nodded. The alternative was admitting that this good-bye was *the* good-bye, and she wasn't ready to do that.

When they pulled into the departure lane of the terminal, Violet's breath caught in her throat. First she saw the balloons, then Olivia wildly waving both hands in the air. Lily was jumping up and down trying to get their attention, and Ava simply waved. Behind them stood Cash, Luke, and Jack.

She laughed. "I can see why you hate airports," she said, remembering his thoughts on the matter that first day they met. "They let just about anyone hang out around here."

He kissed her palm before letting her go.

"How did they even know what car we'd be in?" she asked. "Did you put them up to this?"

He grinned. "I guess your good-bye dinner the other

night wasn't enough. They wanted to give the newest member of the Crossroads family a proper send-off. Who was I to argue?"

Her blood-related family was about to stretch across international date lines, but Violet knew that if she came back, she'd have a whole other sort of family waiting for her.

Walker took her as far as he could go, which was barely past baggage check-in, before they had to say those dreaded words.

"Remember what you said that day after the ER, about me being some sort of hero who kept rescuing you?" he asked.

She nodded. "You saved me from my own bruised ego, from disappointing my parents, and from being afraid to want something for myself. I think that qualifies you as a hero."

"Maybe," he said, wrapping his arms around her. "But here's the thing. I'd barely been out of rehab at your parents' party, and I'm not gonna lie. I was so sure that everyone was betting against me that it would have been really easy to prove them right."

She pressed her palms to his chest. "What made you change your mind?"

"This beautiful woman who saw me as someone else. She made me want to be that someone else, even when I didn't think I could. But I have to see if I can do it without her. I have to see if I'm worth it, whether you think I am or not."

She slid her hands up and snaked them around his neck. "Oh, Walker. I hope you figure out how wonderful you are because I've always known."

"You make me want to be a better man, Vi. I'm gonna figure out how to do that, and then I'm coming after you, no matter where you are."

"You better." Her throat tightened. "You know, it wasn't only that first day that I *had* to kiss you. That I couldn't *not* kiss you. It's every time, Walker. Every single time I see you, it's impossible to think about anything else until I plant one on you, or you plant one on me."

He laughed. She'd really miss that sound, especially when she was the one to elicit it from him.

"Then kiss me already, Teach. What the hell are you waiting for?"

She kissed him then like she had when she didn't even know his name. She kissed him for coming to her rescue time and again and for finally letting her come to his. She kissed him because she couldn't *not* and because she never wanted to stop. Though eating and breathing would eventually get in the way—but she'd worry about those issues later. Right now, she was wrapped in the arms of the man she loved, and she was going to savor every last second she had with him.

"I love you," she finally whispered against him when she knew it was time to get in line for security. "And this is way harder than I ever thought it would be."

"I know," he said, his voice tight. "So let's skip the hard part. I won't say it if you won't."

"Okay," she agreed. Because she knew the power of words, whatever language they were in. If you said something out loud, then it had to be true.

She was moving to France.

Walker was driving seven hours up North.

She loved him and his Oak Bluff family.

He loved her right back.

All of these things were true. But good-bye? She wouldn't say it. Not today.

"Vee," she heard her mother say. "It is time to go."

She lowered herself from her toes and unclasped her hands from around his neck.

"Love you, Teach. Go take care of your mom and follow that dream."

She nodded, swallowing back the tears. She wouldn't make this harder for him.

"Love you, cowboy. Go take care of you. I'll call you when I get there."

He winked at her. "Don't tell Jack or Luke, but for you I'll actually answer."

She kissed him one more time and then followed Maman to the TSA line. When she turned back to steal one last look, Walker was gone.

CHAPTER TWENTY-ONE

This is disgusting," Walker said. "I'm glad I can't drink this stuff."

"It's tradition!" Ava cried through peals of laughter.

"It's so gross," his nephew Owen added. "But so awesome, too!"

Jack stood across from Walker in a tux, his pants rolled up to his knees and his feet buried in a barrel of grapes—the same as Luke, Walker, Jack's son Owen, and Ava in her juice-spattered wedding gown on Jack's other side. Jenna stomped around in the barrel next to Walker, hooting and laughing as Lucy the psychic chicken squawked about the grass.

"We tried!" Lily and Olivia said in unison as each held a handful of Ava's dress in an attempt to keep it from the stomping bucket.

But here was the thing about stomping around in a bucket of grapes. Juice splattered. Any idiot should know that, and Walker prided himself on being any idiot.

"Don't worry," Cash said with his phone pointed at the

group. "I'm getting it all on video so we can remind everyone where the first Crossroads vintage began."

Grapes squished between Walker's toes, and he swore he could have been stepping on a bucket full of eyeballs. Based on how much the splattered juice looked like blood, he double-checked to make sure he wasn't bleeding.

"Come on, little brother," Luke said. "Make like you're enjoying this unless you want Jack and me to make sure you are."

Oh, hell no. Not today. Walker was almost twenty-six years old. The brotherly hazing had to be done by now, didn't it? And even though he was happy for them, if he wanted to pout about watching Jack and Ava profess their love for each other when the woman he loved was thousands of miles away, then so be it.

Camille had started treatment, which meant Violet spent more time at the hospital each day—which meant finding times when they were both awake to talk was harder and harder. They'd gone from talking twice a day, to once, to every few days. Now it had been more than a week since they last spoke. Walker guessed she'd found more than family in Paris. Each day he was surer that she'd likely moved on. His family needed to face it. He scrubbed a hand across his whiskerless jaw. He might clean up good, but he was still a grumpy stick-in-the-mud with Violet gone.

"Don't," Walker warned. "Whatever you're thinking, just don't. Have some respect for the sanctity of marriage." Or something to that effect. He hoped he sounded convincing.

But the first handful of grape guts didn't come from Luke or even Jack.

He wiped the goop from the side of his face and narrowed his gaze at his new sister-in-law.

"Didn't think you had it in you, Ellis," he said coolly.

She gave him a taunting nod. "It's Everett now—little brother."

"That's it," he said. And by the time he'd stooped to scoop up a handful of smashed grapes, it was an all-out wedding-party grape war.

Guests backed out of the danger zone but stayed close enough to snap photos. Lily and Olivia said to hell with Ava's dress—as it was very much ruined at this point—and joined in the fray. Jack, Owen, and Luke were already covered in it when they all locked eyes on Walker, who hadn't even thrown his first handful.

He hopped out of his bucket and ran, but the two men, the boy, and now somehow the sheriff were all on his tail. How the hell were they all running so fast on bare feet when he was slipping and sliding at every turn?

Walker took one of those turns too sharp, and his feet lost purchase all together, sending him sailing through the air and onto his back, effectively knocking the wind straight from his lungs.

His assailants gave him a short reprieve to catch his breath, but as soon as he could breathe regularly again, they were on him like a cow pie on an unsuspecting boot. Soon they were nothing more than a rolling ball of tuxedoes and grape juice, and all he could hear was a mixture of laughter, hoots and hollers, and the artificial clicking sound of smartphone cameras.

"Okay!" he called out. "Are we done yet? Because the party hasn't even started, and I don't think the new Mrs. Everett is going to let us set foot in the winery like this."

Jack and Luke rolled off him. Owen had already fallen out of the grape brawl and was now lying on his back, laughing. Jack and Luke showed their age a little more, breathing hard with an occasional chuckle.

"He's right, you know," Ava said, standing over them. Then she held up her hands in surrender. "I know. I know. I started it, and I don't regret a thing. But how about we all head back to the ranch for a quick change before we get this party started? There are plenty of hors d'oeuvres and drinks to keep everyone busy until we get back."

They all agreed and followed Ava on her trek across the pasture and back toward the ranch.

What a sight they must have been had anyone been looking on from the house. But there was no one there. No ghosts, he realized, waiting to drag him back under. Once he'd let the memories come to the surface in his kitchen with Violet, he hadn't felt like he was being eaten alive from the inside out. Their power over him lessened until he realized he was the one in control, not his past.

"Shit," he said under his breath. *He'd* been the goddamn keeper of his demons this whole time. Not Oak Bluff. He didn't need to leave to stay sober. He needed to let go, and it looked like he'd done that without even knowing.

As they trudged up the front porch steps, their feet sticking to the wood, it all hit him like a ton of bricks.

"I'm not going to Meadow Valley," Walker said, and Jack and Luke both stopped short of the door. Ava and Owen headed inside, giving the three men some time alone.

"What are you talking about?" Jack asked. "You're heading out in the morning, aren't you?"

On a whim, Walker had applied for a passport a couple weeks ago, thinking if Violet had needed him in Paris, he could be ready at a moment's notice. Granted he'd never been on a plane before, and his hatred of airports and crowds and most people in general hadn't changed. But, see, there was this woman he loved. And he'd launch himself straight to the moon if it meant seeing her again.

Sam and Ben might want to kick his ass for backing out at the last minute, but he didn't care. Not when he realized it wasn't distance he needed. It was *her*.

"Yes," Walker said. "I mean, I guess that depends on flights."

Luke shook his head. "Whoa, whoa, whoa. Hold up a second. You're flying now? Didn't you just get the truck tuned up for the long car ride? Jack, I think the grape fumes are getting to him or something. He's talking bullshit again. Gotta say, I didn't miss it. I like when the things he says make sense."

Jack was smiling, and Walker realized they were both messing with him.

"You're going to get your girl, aren't you?" Jack asked.

Walker nodded.

"You coming back?" Luke added.

This time Walker shrugged. "I think so, either when she kicks me to the curb or when she's ready to come back herself. It also depends on you two—because I want to be a part of the ranch, the vineyard, all of it. It is a family business, after all. I just know right now I need to go."

Luke laughed. "God what I wouldn't give to see *you* walking around Paris. You've never even been on a plane, have you?"

Walker swallowed. He'd ridden his share of horses, even been thrown from one or two. He'd been in a handful of bar fights and had fallen through a picture window and nearly killed himself. Yet he was scared to hop on a large machine and fly across the country and maybe an ocean or two.

Or maybe he was afraid he'd get there and Violet would have already moved on. There was only one way to find out.

"So, how the hell do I buy a plane ticket?" he asked.

* * *

Walker wasn't sure with the time difference if it was two days later or three. All he knew was that he hadn't slept in over twenty-four hours and he was in a country where he couldn't say much more than *I love you, You're too beautiful,* and *Go fuck yourself.*

He didn't think any of those would go over too well with a taxi driver.

He threw the small duffel over his shoulder and stepped through the arrivals door and into the Paris sun.

It was a little cooler than California's sun, but other than that it felt the same.

He found the taxi line and hopped in the next available car.

"*Où voudrais-tu aller?*" the man in the driver's seat asked. Walker hoped that meant the guy was asking for a destination.

"Saint-Louis Hospital?" he said, the answer coming out like a question.

"Ah, *Americain*, yes? You want *hôpital de Saint-Louis*?"

Where Walker had pronounced the name of the hospital like the city in Missouri, the taxi driver said it in what he assumed was the correct way. Walker anticipated much of this in days, maybe weeks, to come.

The ride was excruciating, mainly because of the traffic. Walker still hated traffic. It was nearly an hour before they pulled up in front of the hospital's main entrance.

Walker handed the man his credit card and trusted that he swiped the right amount since he'd never dealt in Euros. Then he practically sprinted into the building.

"Camille Chastain?" he said, and the woman behind the desk smiled politely at him before typing something on a keyboard and then checking her computer screen.

"Fourth floor," she said in accented English, and he was suddenly grateful for his terrible pronunciation of the French language. "Room 412."

"Thank you!" he called out as he ran toward the elevators. "I mean *gracias*. No! *Merci*. It's *merci*. I knew that."

He didn't care what an idiot he sounded like because he was minutes—maybe seconds—away from seeing her.

When the elevator doors opened, he took off down the first available hallway, realizing too late that he'd gone the wrong direction.

Patience, he reminded himself. Because he'd never been one to rush. Until now.

He finally found room 412 and approached it with caution, but the door was closed.

"The doctor's with her right now, so I was heading downstairs for a snack."

Violet's voice came from behind him. It was tinged with a slight accent, and he realized that must have been the first English she'd spoken since their last phone call.

He spun slowly to face her, preparing himself for all possible reactions. What he wasn't expecting was for her to launch herself at him as soon as their eyes met, but he caught her in his arms just the same.

"Sorry," she said, taking a step back. "Steamroller, remember?"

He laughed, then wrapped a hand around her wrist, tugging her closer once more.

"I'm not letting you get farther than arm's reach from me again," he said.

She gasped, her hands cupping his cheeks. "Where's your beard? Who is this strange man claiming to be Walker Everett? Explain yourself."

But she was grinning, exploring his face with her fingers.

"Figured I'd try something new for the wedding," he said. "Being that I'm a new man and all. Also Ava begged me to do it for pictures. Don't tell her, but I'm kinda scared to say no to her."

Violet laughed. "God, you're so beautiful it hurts, you know that?"

He wrapped a finger around one of the curls he'd missed so much. "Nah. *Tu es trop belle*."

Tears pooled in her brown eyes even as she smiled.

"But what about Meadow Valley?" she said, realizing where he was supposed to be. "The ranch and the job and does Sam want to kill you for bailing? I bet he wants to kill you for bailing."

She was talking a mile a minute, and though he couldn't quite keep up, he understood. He was taking her in, processing the moment, realizing that he was an idiot for thinking she'd react any other way than she'd done. Because this was the woman who loved him, who refused to say good-bye.

He grinned. She was a little thinner, probably from the stress of prepping for her mother's procedure and getting ready for school, but other than that, this was the happiest she'd ever looked, and he liked to think he had something to do with that.

"Sam wasn't happy when I told him," he said. "But then again, he knows you, so he understood."

"How long are you here?" she asked hesitantly.

He kissed her then, answering her in a language that wasn't English or French but something all their own.

"It was one hell of a hard road to finally get home," he said. "I'm not going anywhere for a while." He paused. "Actually I gotta be back at the ranch in a month. Now that I'm not heading up to Meadow Valley to work on Sam's ranch, Jack and Luke are counting on me to take the lead on ours. Can't leave my brothers for too long. But I hope you'll come back—eventually."

Her breathing hitched, and she nodded. "I am. I mean, I will. Eventually. But welcome home for now, Walker Everett. Paris has no idea what it's in for."

"It sure as hell does not," he said with a grin. "Maybe I should have given some warning."

He kissed her again, savoring the moment and realizing there'd be plenty more to come.

"They've got ranches here, right? Horses and cattle and all that?"

She laughed, her lips parting into a smile against his.

"They do, but don't you worry. I'm not done with Oak Bluff yet. I've got me a whole new family back there I can't wait to see again." She grabbed his hand. "But there are a lot of people here I'd like you to meet." She laughed, the sound giddy, and it made him feel as light as air. "There's so much lost time to make up, and I can't believe you're here for part of it."

He believed her that she'd make it back to his little corner of the map someday soon, but Violet had it figured out early on. It didn't matter where they were as long as the miles didn't stretch between them. From here on out Walker knew he was home as long as she was there.

EPILOGUE

The following summer

The next player put on his batting helmet and stepped up to the plate. On the pitcher's mound, Owen Everett readjusted his cap and toed the dirt.

"What did I miss?" Luke asked, jogging to meet Walker where he stood behind the chain-link fence backstop. "The breakfast rush at the restaurant was insane, but Lily would have had my ass if I'd left without her."

Walker looked over his brother's shoulder to the small parking lot beyond the opposing team's dugout. Lily, Olivia, and Sheriff Cash Hawkins were striding away from Cash's police-issue Tahoe and straight in their direction.

"Sheriff use the siren?" Walker asked.

Luke laughed. "Hell yes, he did. None of us were going to miss Owen pitch a no-hitter."

Ava and Jack approached from the concession stand, and Walker swore his oldest brother was carrying a bouquet of corn dogs. Ava already had one of her own in her right hand while she rested the left on her very pregnant belly.

Before anyone could say anything else, Walker heard the distinct sound of a baseball smacking the leather of the catcher's glove followed by the umpire's unmistakable, "Strike two!"

The whole group erupted into applause and hollers, much to the dismay of the opposing team. Walker couldn't blame them. His eleven-year-old nephew was single-handedly wiping the floor with their team.

He raised his can of La Croix—he blamed Violet for his new drink of choice—and whooped even louder. "That's my nephew!" he yelled.

Jack handed him a corn dog and then backhanded him on the shoulder.

"You're gonna break his concentration if you don't dial it back," his brother warned. "Where is that girl of yours, by the way? She's supposed to make sure you behave at these things."

Walker tilted his head back to where Violet's MINI was parked. "Phone interview for that music teacher position at Owen's old elementary school."

Thanks to a couple of brothers who'd seemed to have a bit of a soft spot when it came to matters of the heart, he'd managed to finagle *two* months in Paris when he'd finally figured out it was Violet he needed more than anything else, but she'd stayed on longer, finishing up her last year of school while Maman recuperated and they both reconnected with family.

"Oak Bluff is home now, though," she'd told Walker when he'd had to head back. "I know who I am whether it's in Paris, Santa Barbara, or anywhere else in the world. I think you taught me that before I even left."

"When?" he'd asked, twirling one of her curls around his index finger.

"When you told me you wanted me to do my hair however I wanted for our pretend date with my parents. *Not* that I needed your permission." She'd raised her brows, and he'd smiled. "As much as I'd spent my life searching for something I thought was missing, I never felt lost around you. I just felt like—me."

Jack shook his head and laughed, bringing Walker back to the present. "How the hell do I have a kid going into middle school?"

Ava bumped her hip against Jack's. "And a new one arriving pretty much any day now."

Owen wound up for pitch number three, and it was as if the batter never saw it leave his nephew's hand.

"Strike three!"

"Holy shit," Ava whisper-shouted. "Second out, bottom of the ninth. He's gonna do it!"

The batting coach pulled what would likely be his final player to the side of the dugout for a short one-on-one, and Jack groaned. "Owen's never struck this kid out before." He took an angry bite out of his corn dog, and Walker couldn't help but laugh.

He surveyed the scene before him—Jack and Ava married with a new baby on the way; Luke and Lily engaged and getting hitched right before Christmas; Cash and Olivia finally realizing they don't have to live where they work and building a new home on a nice piece of property on the outskirts of town.

And then there she was, striding toward him with a smile that lit up his whole damn world—a world that, less than two years ago, he swore would eventually crash down around him. It almost had. Yet somehow he'd made it here. He'd made it back to the place he'd left. And every day he was here—with Violet—Oak Bluff became less and less a reminder of what he'd lost as it transformed to a place where so much had been found.

"Aunt Ines's plane got in on time, but we're going to have one more thing to celebrate other than Maman's one year of remission." She bounced on her toes. "I got the job," she said, loud enough that he could hear but not so loud as to break the concentration everyone seemed to be investing in Owen's next three pitches.

Walker slipped his fingers through hers and gave her hand a gentle squeeze. They'd celebrate as soon as they all got through this inning.

"I'm here! I'm here! I'm here!" Jenna whisper-shouted as she ran up the parking lot curb and joined the fray. "I should have skipped the market today, but I have so many regular customers on Sundays. Did I miss it?"

"Last batter," Luke said. "At least we hope."

"Strike one!" the ump yelled as Owen's opponent tipped the ball over the left foul line.

No one in the Everett clan made a sound.

Owen lifted his cap and swiped his forearm across his sweat-dampened strawberry blond hair. Then it was time for pitch number two.

This time the ball sailed straight over the plate faster than Walker had ever seen Owen throw a ball before.

"Strike two!"

Walker could feel all of them collectively holding their breath. He was a part of this—a part of them, a realization that still shocked the hell out of him when he stopped to think about it.

He pulled Violet's hand to his lips and kissed it. "If he pulls this off," he said softly, "I say you stop shacking up with me in that tiny apartment and we get a real place in Oak Bluff. Together."

Now that Luke was running his riding school and Jack and Ava were expanding the family, he'd come home to officially take over the day-to-day management of the ranch so Jack could focus on the winery. Weekends, though, he still spent at the market, selling his homemade furniture not because he needed extra pocket change to run outta town but because he liked doing it—liked spending time with his aunt and that goddamn psychic chicken of hers.

Her eyes widened. "What if he doesn't?"

Walker shrugged. "Then I don't know where to put your knotted pine hope chest."

She sucked in a sharp breath. "You never sold it? You kept it for me?"

He nodded, and then the whole field went silent.

Walker caught Owen giving his dad a subtle look and Jack giving his son an equally subtle nod.

"You son of a bitch," Walker said. "You taught an eleven-year-old how to throw your fastball."

Jack grinned. "This kid's so much better than I ever was. I don't think I was the one doing the teaching."

Owen let the ball fly. The batter swung straight across home plate, right where the ball had already zoomed past.

Holy shit.

"Yes!" Jack yelled. "That is *my* son, ladies and gentlemen!" And then he and Ava were running out onto the field with the rest of the players' families as Owen's teammates lifted him above their shoulders.

Walker drew Violet into his arms. "New job? No hitter? Looks like we got ourselves plenty of celebrating to do tonight."

He scooped her into his arms, and she yelped with laughter.

"Congratulations, Owen!" he called over his shoulder, then piloted the woman he loved to her tiny little car.

"What are you doing?" Violet asked through peals of laughter.

He lowered her to her feet and then kissed her like it was the first day they'd met—like he couldn't *not* kiss her.

"I'm going to gas up this machine, throw on those heart-shaped glasses, and find us a new home today. What can I say? I'm a man of my word."

"*Walker*," she tried to protest, but he shook his head.

"*Emménagé avec moi*," he said. His French was still elementary at best, but he was learning more each day. For her. "Move in with me, Teach."

She bit her lip and nodded, her eyes pooling with tears.

"I love you," he said.

"I love you, too." She gasped. "And think of all the games we can play driving around town. The license plate game. Punch Buggy. I Spy. Wait! Even better. Carpool karaoke. I'm mentally making a playlist of songs that go with house hunting—like U2! 'I Still Haven't Found What I'm Looking For'!"

Walker rolled his eyes but grinned from ear to ear as he opened her door and she collapsed into her seat, still making road trip plans.

He'd move in with this woman he loved more than he could imagine, and he'd make her a million hope chests if that was what made her happy.

But he absolutely, without a doubt, drew the line at karaoke.

Delaney Harper thought she'd seen the last of Meadow Valley Ranch after a nasty divorce left her broke. But when she learns that her ex sold their property, she heads back to her past to claim her share of the land... even if it means pushing out the dreamy cowboy who's taken up residence there.

See the next page for a preview of

MY ONE AND ONLY COWBOY

Delaney slammed the key into the ignition and peeled out of the ranch property in a matter of seconds, her heart thudding against her chest, her eyes burning with the threat of tears.

Her lawyer—a.k.a. her cousin Debra—said she couldn't promise anything without seeing the forged deed. What was she thinking waltzing onto someone else's property and expecting he'd just hand it over? And what kind of town closed down on a Friday when the holiday wasn't until Monday?

Meadow Valley.

She'd loved the small town when she and Wade were newlyweds—and when she'd almost gotten the shelter up and running. Now, though, when she needed the town to behave for her, it left her in the dust.

A stop sign loomed ahead, so she pressed her foot to the break. Something popped, and she yelped as the car lurched. Then instinct took over, and she steered the vehicle into the grass before it came to a complete halt, smoke pouring up from the hood.

"No, no, no, no, no!" she growled at her traitor of a vehicle.

She sat there for several long minutes, half hoping that whatever happened to her car would right itself if she just waited it out. When that didn't seem to be working, she pulled out her phone and Googled the number for the town's auto repair shop, Meadow Valley Motors. It rang four times before the voicemail picked up.

"Welcome to Meadow Valley Motors. Just like the rest of the town, we're closing shop until after the holiday. Leave a message, and we'll return your call by the end of the day on Tuesday."

She tossed the phone onto the passenger seat and groaned, whacking her head against her seat back.

"Tuesday? I'm stuck like this until Tuesday? Why is everything closed already?" Her voice rose both in volume and in pitch.

She looked down at her phone and saw the seconds still ticking by on the timer.

Great, she hadn't ended the call, which meant her building tantrum was recorded for posterity. She vigorously pressed her index finger again and again over the red icon on the screen, just in case the first try didn't take.

She was supposed to breeze into town, get a copy of Wade's forged deed, and get the ball rolling on reclaiming her land.

A hand rapped against the driver's-side window, and Delaney yelped for the second time in ten minutes. She looked out to see Sam Callahan standing on the road next to her, his arms crossed and a cowboy hat casting a shadow over his eyes.

He towered over the vehicle like a movie villain ready to take down his rival.

She tried to open the window so she could talk to him from the relative safety of the car but realized that a car that wouldn't move was also a car whose windows wouldn't open. It was also growing hotter by the second. For all intents and purposes, Delaney was sitting inside a slowly heating oven, which meant she had no choice but to open the door and get out.

She stood, brushing nonexistent dust off her jeans, then mirrored Sam Callahan's stance, arms crossed and everything.

"Ms. Harper," he said with a nod.

"Mr. Callahan," she said coolly, nodding back. "How'd you know I was here?"

He glanced back toward the guest ranch, which was easily visible from the road.

"Heard your car give up on you. Hell, everyone did. You spooked the horses. It's lucky my brother was done giving his lesson or we mighta had an emergency on our hands."

Delaney threw her hands in the air. "Does this not look like an emergency? Not that it matters because Meadow Valley is not dealing with any emergencies until sometime by the end of the day on Tuesday. *Tuesday*!"

Sam cleared his throat. "Sheriff and deputies are on call all weekend. So's the fire department. All our firefighters are trained paramedics. You got an emergency that needs policing or immediate medical attention?"

She squinted into the sun, trying to gauge his shuttered expression. But it looked like he was biting back a grin.

"I suppose you think this is funny? The big bad landowner comes back to claim what's hers and gets stranded on the side of the road."

He scratched the back of his neck. "It's not *un*funny."

She gritted her teeth and fought the urge to scream.

"Look," he said, "I got a towing hitch and trailer I can put on the back of my truck. I can take you and your car to the inn—I'm assuming you have a reservation—and someone from the shop will come grab it on Tuesday."

Delaney winced. "Reservation?"

Sam nodded. "Festival in town this weekend. Lots of family reunions. Inn fills up real fast. We got a bit of their overflow, but most festival goers like to stay in town. We're off the beaten path."

She glanced back at the car, then at Sam again. "It cools off at night, right? I can just recline the seat and—"

"You're kidding, right?" he interrupted. "You're not actually considering sleeping in your car."

She shrugged. "Look, I wasn't planning on being in town overnight. So, no, I didn't make any sort of reservation. Not like I can really afford it anyway, so if you don't mind, the car will suit me just fine."

Sam rolled his eyes. "Will you just get in the truck?"

"Where are you taking me?" She didn't like being at this guy's mercy. She didn't like being at anyone's mercy. All she wanted was to stand on her own two feet, and Wade had taken that away from her. Now here was this big bad cowboy who'd built his business on *her* land thinking he could swoop in and save the day.

"I've got an empty room in the guest cabin," he said. "You can stay there until Tuesday when you can either get this thing fixed or put it to rest for good."

She opened her mouth to protest, but he cut her off.

"No charge, of course. Especially if that land is half yours like you say it is."

She narrowed her eyes. "It *is.*"

He shrugged. "Well then, looks like I have a few days to convince you to let me buy you out. Seeing as how you're in financial straits, it seems to be a win-win for both of us."

Delaney jutted out her chin. "Thank you, but I don't take handouts. I'll stay at the ranch, but you'll let me earn my keep. And my financial *straits* are none of your business. Once my land is returned to me, I'll get back on my feet. So there will be no need to convince me of anything. I'm sure your little business can survive on half the land."

She grabbed her phone, purse, and keys from the car and sauntered off toward his truck. Only when she was sure he couldn't see her face anymore did she blow out a long, shaky breath.

She could do this. This place used to be her home turf, and with any luck, it would be again. It wasn't like she was looking to steal Sam's business from him. She was just looking to get hers back.

She yanked on the handle of the car door and hopped inside the silver Ford truck. It was still running, and the air-conditioning poured out from the vents in heavenly gusts. She couldn't help the small moan that escaped her lips or the smile that spread across her face. Growing up in the desert, she was no stranger to the heat. But she'd always hated it. She'd begged her parents year after year to take her and her sisters somewhere cold for a family vacation. But it was always the same excuse.

"If we shut down the motel, we shut down our income, and you know we can't afford to do that," her father had said. So vacations were relegated to an overnight stay at the Bellagio when they could scrape together enough money—a quick trip to the Grand Canyon or the Hoover Dam when they couldn't. Wade had promised her a honeymoon in Colorado as soon as they had enough money. But she learned early on that *enough* meant poker funds or Wade's next no-fail business venture that always failed, and soon enough equaled in debt. So here she was, twenty-nine years old, and she'd still never seen snow.

"You all right there?" Sam asked, sliding into the driver's seat.

She pointed toward his door. "Close it. You're letting all the beautiful cold air out."

He chuckled. "And you expect me to believe you were going to spend the night in your car? I doubt you'd have lasted five minutes let alone four nights out there. No air, no plumbing, no change of clothes?"

She crossed her arms. "Just because I like cool air doesn't mean I can't rough it when necessary."

He threw his hat in the back seat of the cab, put on a pair of aviators, and set the truck into gear, pulling onto the road and around her stranded vehicle.

"Wait!" she cried. "What about towing my car?"

He shook his head. "I said I *had* the gear. Not that it was hitched and ready to go. Plus, it's hot as hell right now. Figure I'll wait until dusk and then come back." He cleared his throat, but it sounded very much like a stifled laugh. "I don't think you have to worry about anyone stealing it."

She blew out a breath. He had her there. Mildred—or Millie for short—was the affectionate name she'd given the red Honda Civic when she'd bought it used eleven years ago. She saved every cent she'd earned working nights and weekends all throughout high school and while she'd commuted to Pima Medical Institute, where she earned her associate's degree as a veterinary technician. Millie was the one thing she truly owned, and now she was just a heap of metal on the side of the road, left to bake in the blistering sun.

"Fair enough," she finally said. "But I don't want to leave her—I mean it—too long."

The corner of his mouth twitched. "That old beater has a name, doesn't it? Or should I say *she*?"

"It might," she admitted.

He nodded and then gave his dashboard an affectionate pat. "Steely Dan here hasn't let me down yet." He paused, and when she didn't say anything, he added, "Your car's in good hands—at the ranch and when the shop opens up next week."

Her shoulders relaxed. She and Sam were in opposition when it came to the piece of land they both wanted, but she guessed that didn't mean they were enemies.

He pulled back up the main drive of the guest ranch but passed the cabin where they'd first met, rolling to a stop in front of a stable instead.

"Come on," he said, pulling the key from the ignition. He grabbed his Cattleman out of the back seat and set it on his head.

Her brows furrowed. "Where are we going?"

He took off his sunglasses. Finally, after all this time of playing it straight, he grinned, and holy hell was he that good looking when they'd met? His chocolate brown eyes darkened with mischief, and his teeth—straight and white—had the tiniest little gap between the front two. She liked perfect little imperfections like that. They gave a person character. It was what drew her to Wade—his crooked smile and asymmetrical nose. She should have seen the red flag when he'd told her his nose had been broken one too many times to be properly set. She'd eventually seen first-hand what a broken nose looked like when Wade couldn't pay one of his "associates" back for the money he'd lost.

The line of Sam's nose was nice and straight. That alone told her he wasn't the type of guy other men messed with.

"Time for you to earn your keep," he said.

All the tension that had left her body on the short ride over came back as he led her into the stable and straight to a wall where a large pair of dirty overalls hung on a hook. He pulled them down and tossed them to her. She coughed as she caught them, a puff of dust invading her air space.

"Huh," he mused. "We should probably wash those sometime this month."

Delaney's eyes widened. *This month*?

"Horses are out in the arena right now, so it's the best time to muck out the stalls. Pitchfork is hanging against the side of the first stall. Gloves and wheelbarrow are over there." He pointed over her shoulder. "Make sure you really scrape under the shavings to get rid of anything that's wet. I'll let one of our stable boys take care of the wheelbarrow and add fresh bedding after the stalls are dry. I'll even send someone over with a thermos full of ice water. I hear mucking is thirsty work."

She stared at him for several long seconds, but he said nothing. He was serious.

Forget what she'd thought about his eyes or his teeth or that stupid straight nose. She knew what he was doing. He was going to try to break her spirit—to make her give up before the real fight even started. Well, he messed with the wrong woman. When she did her clinical at a Vegas petting zoo, she did everything from grooming llamas to catheterizing a goat with a urinary obstruction. Hell, she grew up taking care of the family's two dogs and three cats. This was nothing. A horse stall was nothing more than a giant litter box. A giant, foul-smelling, filled with larger-than-cat-sized waste litter box.

She dropped her bag on the ground, raised her brows, and wriggled into the overalls. She pulled out the gloves that hung from the bib pocket and put those on, too.

"Anything else, Mr. Callahan?"

He shrugged and was gentleman enough to hand her the pitchfork. It took everything in her not to growl at him in response. Instead she smiled pleasantly.

"Thank you for your generous hospitality."

He winked. "You're welcome. Happy mucking." He sauntered out the stable door. When Delaney heard the roar of his truck's engine and was sure he was out of earshot, she gritted her teeth and finally let loose a guttural sound that would have raised a cat's haunches or sent a pit bull to cower in a corner.

Pitchfork in hand, she pushed open the first stall door and winced at the mess inside.

What Sam Callahan didn't realize was that her spirit had already been broken by one man too many. He didn't have that kind of power over her. She'd muck his stall and take whatever else he threw at her, but she wasn't backing down. She'd come for what was hers, and she wasn't going anywhere until she got it back.

ABOUT THE AUTHOR

A librarian for teens by day and a romance writer by night, A.J. Pine can't seem to escape the world of fiction, and she wouldn't have it any other way. When she finds that twenty-fifth hour in the day, she might indulge in a tiny bit of TV when she nourishes her undying love of vampires, superheroes, and a certain high-functioning sociopath detective. She hails from the far-off galaxy of the Chicago suburbs.

You can learn more at:
AJPine.com
Twitter @AJ_Pine
Facebook.com/AJPineAuthor

ROCKY MOUNTAIN COWBOY

SARA RICHARDSON

To Jenna LaFleur

CHAPTER ONE

In a small town like Topaz Falls, Colorado, the grocery store was the last place you'd want to go if you didn't want to be noticed. But when your diet consisted mainly of Honey Nut Cheerios and you'd run out of milk, you had no choice but to show up at Frank's Market in full disguise.

Jaden Alexander pulled his blue Colorado-flag stocking cap farther down his forehead so that it met the top of his Oakleys. Not that the sunglasses were inconspicuous. They were a custom design, made exclusively for him when the company had courted him for sponsorship six years ago after he'd made his Olympic debut. No one else would know that, though. To other people, he hoped he looked like just another ski bum who moonlighted as a bartender or waiter during the off-season. With any luck, no one in town would realize that J.J. Alexander—dubbed the Snowboarding Cowboy by the media—had come home.

The door still chimed when he walked in, the same way it had when he'd done the weekly grocery run for his grandma twelve years ago. In fact, it looked like Frank hadn't changed much of anything. The same depressing fluorescent lights still hummed overhead, casting bright spots onto the dirty linoleum tiles. He passed by the three checkout stations, where two bored cashiers stood hunched behind their registers, fingers pecking away on their phones.

One of them looked familiar enough that a shot of panic hit Jaden in the chest. But the woman didn't even look up as he slipped into the nearest aisle, so maybe he was just being paranoid. Death threats on Twitter would do that to a guy. Ever since the accident, going out in public wasn't exactly his favorite thing to do. He'd been ambushed by photographers, reporters, and fans who'd written him off, and he was not in the mood to deal with any public showdowns tonight.

"J.J. Alexander? That you?"

Anyone else and he would've shaken his head and kept right on walking, but he knew the voice behind him. He'd never get away with walking on past without a word. He turned around, and right there at the end of the aisle stood Levi, Lance, and Lucas Cortez. Back in high school, Jaden had bummed around with Levi until Cash Greer passed away. After that, Levi had gone to Oklahoma to train as a bull rider, and Jaden had finally been accepted to train with the U.S. ski and snowboard team.

"Holy shit, man." Levi sauntered over the way a bull rider would—all swagger. "I didn't know you were back in town."

"Hey, Levi." Jaden forced his jaw to loosen and nodded at each of the brothers in turn. "Lucas. Lance." Now, those three had changed in twelve years. They'd all cleaned up. Still cowboys in their ragged jeans and boots, but each of the brothers was clean-shaven and more groomed than he'd ever seen him. Wasn't a coincidence that they all had rings on their left fingers now too. Jaden slipped his sunglasses onto his forehead, grateful the store seemed empty, so they shouldn't attract too much attention.

"Actually, I'm not back." His voice had changed since the accident. These days he had to fight for a conversational tenor instead of slipping into defensive mode. "Not permanently anyway. I'm only here to consult on the new terrain park at the resort." The Wilder family had been looking to expand their ski hill outside of Topaz Falls for a few years now. He'd never been a fan of the Wilder family—no one in town was—but the job had offered him an opportunity to lie low for a while.

"Heard that's gonna be quite the addition up there," Levi said. "I also heard your grandma sold the ranch a few years back. You got a place to stay?"

"I rented a place on the mountain." He didn't acknowledge that bit about his grandma. Hated to think of her stuck in that facility in Denver. He hadn't had a choice, though, once the dementia started. She'd taken care of him—raised him—seeing as how his dad had been a loser and his mom a free spirit who'd rather live the gypsy lifestyle than hang out with her kid.

Four years ago, the roles reversed, and he was the one taking care of Grams. Back then he couldn't do much for her. He was too busy splitting his time between Park City and Alaska, chasing the snow so he could stay in shape. After she'd started wandering off, he'd moved her into the best facility in Denver and dropped in a couple of times a month to visit, even though she no longer knew him.

"Sorry to interrupt, but I need backup." Lance moseyed over. As the eldest Cortez brother, he was serious and stern. He used to scare the shit out of Jaden when they were kids, but from the looks of things, he'd mellowed out. "Jessa didn't tell me there were a thousand different kinds of tampons. I have no clue what to get. Any ideas?"

Uhhh... Jaden looked around, realizing for the first time they were in *that* aisle. The one he never set foot in. On purpose anyway.

"There's regular, super, super-plus..." Lucas shook his head as he examined the products stacked on the shelves. "I thought we were buying tampons, not gasoline."

The brothers laughed, and even with the anxiety squirming around his heart, Jaden cracked a smile. "So this is what happens when you get hitched, huh?" Oh how things had changed. Used to be, on a Friday night, he and Levi would drive up to the hot springs on the Cortezes' property, share a few beers, have a bonfire, and get to at least second base with whatever girl looked good that night. Now these three spent their Friday nights shopping for woman-stuff.

Levi glared at his eldest brother like he wanted to string him up by his toenails. "We were out for a beer when Lance's wife called with an"—he raised his hands for air quotes—"emergency."

"She was in tears," Lance said defensively. "And quit bullshitting us. If Cass had called, you'd be doing the same thing right now."

That seemed to shut Levi up.

Lucas looked at his brothers with humor in his eyes. "Naomi loves me too much to put me through that."

"Yeah?" Levi shot Jaden a sly grin. "That why she sent you to the store for hemorrhoid cream after Char was born?"

And that was Jaden's cue. There were some things you couldn't unhear, and he definitely didn't want to know anything about having babies and hemorrhoids. "Well, it was good to see you guys. Maybe I'll see you around."

He made a move to slip past and leave them all behind, but Levi walked with him. "Hold up. How're things going?"

The familiar anxiety slipped those cold fingers around Jaden's heart and squeezed. He'd been conditioned. Anytime someone looked at him like that—used that overly sympathetic tone of voice—he wanted to turn and bolt before they could bring up the accident. "Things are fine," he lied. Things had fallen apart after that race. In his life and in his head. Three months later, he still didn't know how to put it all back together.

"I saw the crash on TV."

Yeah, Levi along with the rest of the world. If they hadn't witnessed it during live coverage of the race, they'd seen it in the extensive news analysis afterward.

"You all healed up?"

Did it matter? "Pretty much. I've got a few pins in my arm, but who doesn't?" The joke fell flat, and the anxiety squeezed harder, shrinking his heart in its suffocating grasp.

"Haven't heard much about the other guy in a few months." Questions lurked in Levi's tone and in his eyes. Jaden could see them surfacing.

Had he done it on purpose? Had Jaden intentionally taken out his biggest competition on that last turn when it looked like he wasn't going to win the gold? Everyone had already made up their own answers, so why did it matter what he said?

Breathe. Keep breathing. Never thought he'd have to remind himself to do things like that. "Beckett is still in a rehab facility." Scarred and broken. Still trying to relearn how to walk…

"Damn. Sorry to hear it."

Jaden already knew sorry wasn't enough. Not for Kipp Beckett, not for the reporters, not for the officials. Not for fans of the sport. Not even for himself.

"For what it's worth, I didn't think you did it on purpose." Levi was trying to be supportive, but the fact that he said it at all meant he'd thought about the possibility. Same as everyone else.

"I didn't," Jaden said simply. "I wouldn't." In the replays, it might've looked like he'd lunged into Beckett—who'd been his rival in the snowboard-cross event since they'd both started out—but the truth was that he'd caught an edge and it had thrown off his balance. He couldn't recover. He couldn't stop the momentum that pitched him into Beckett, that sent them both careening through the barriers, cartwheeling and spinning until the world went silent. When the snow had settled, Jaden had gotten up, and Kipp Beckett hadn't. His body lay twisted at an angle, and he was unconscious, maybe dead.

Shock had numbed Jaden to the fact that his arm was badly fractured. He'd fallen to his knees next to Beckett before officials had raced in and forced him away. The papers and news shows and magazines all said Jaden was sneering as the medics tended to him. He wasn't. He was crying.

"I would've taken the silver." If no one else believed him, maybe Levi would. "I didn't care that much." He didn't value the gold more than someone's life. Did he? God, the news reports had made him question himself.

Levi gave him a nod. "Looked to me like you caught an edge. Could've happened to anyone." He clapped him on the shoulder. "Hey, why don't you stop over for a beer sometime? I just finished building my new house. Need to break it in."

"Sure." Jaden said it like he did that all the time—stopped by a friend's house for a beer. But it had been months.

Months since he'd had a real conversation with another human being. Months since someone had actually smiled at him. When he wasn't working on the mountains, his days consisted of sitting silently on the back deck with his chocolate Lab, Bella, sprawled at his feet while he tried to figure out how everything had collapsed.

"What about tonight?" Levi shot a look toward his brothers. "Since my evening got interrupted and I'm now free."

"I've gotta head back up the mountain tonight." They were discussing the possibility of lighting the terrain park for night boarding. "But I'd definitely like to hang sometime. Let me know what else works." Levi was the first person who'd actually heard him when he said he didn't mean for any of it to happen.

Maybe he had one ally in a world full of enemies.

* * *

Up until this very moment, Kate Livingston thought the worst thing about camping was the bugs. No, wait. Actually, the mosquitos in Colorado weren't nearly as bad as she had anticipated. So far she'd seen only one medium-sized spider, which wasn't even hairy like some of them in L.A. So, before this moment, maybe she would've said the worst thing about camping was the dirt. Yes, definitely the dirt. She could feel it sticking to her skin, grainy and disgusting as she lay swaddled like a baby in the brand-new sleeping bag that still smelled like synthetic fluff.

Another flash of light split the sky above her flimsy nylon tent. Which had cost about $450, by the way. And now the damn thing was sagging underneath the weight of a rain puddle that had collected right over her head. *Waterproof my ass.*

She squirmed to unearth her arms from the sleeping bag and typed in a note on her phone. *Extreme Outdoors Lightweight Backpacker Tent—Sucks.* Unsatisfied, she underlined, highlighted, and changed the word *sucks* to all caps.

When she'd landed the position as a senior editor for *Adrenaline Junkie* magazine, she had envisioned herself sitting in a corner office overlooking the hustle and bustle of Beverly Hills while she sipped frothy lattes and approved spreads and attended photo shoots with male models who cost upward of a thousand dollars for one hour of work.

But there had been some budget cuts recently, Gregor, her managing editor, had explained on her first day. They weren't working with as many freelancers, and the editor who was supposed to do a gear-test backpacking trip on the Colorado Trail for the fall issue had suddenly quit, so…

Here she was, on an all-expenses-paid trip through hell.

The ceiling of the tent drooped even lower, inching toward her nose. A drop of rainwater plunked onto her right eyebrow right as a crack of earsplitting thunder shook the ground.

Now she knew. She knew that the worst thing about camping was not bugs or dirt but a thunderstorm in the mountains. In fact, she would probably die tonight. Either from getting skewered by a lightning bolt or from a heart attack, whichever came first.

"I went to Northwestern journalism school," she lamented over the pattering rain. After she'd walked out of there with her master's degree, she'd assumed she could have her pick of jobs. But nope. Anyone could call themselves a journalist these days. It didn't matter if they had interned at the *Chicago Tribune* or if they knew AP style or even how to use a fucking comma. If they had fifty thousand followers on their blog, they were in.

Let's just say respectable jobs in the world of journalism weren't exactly knocking down her door. So when the opportunity at *Adrenaline Junkie* had come up, she'd done more than jump on it. She'd immersed herself in it. So what if she'd never actually camped? It wasn't her fault her father was a yuppie attorney and her mother a neurologist. They didn't believe in camping. But she could read all about it on the Internet.

Who cared that the one time she'd felt a surge of adrenaline in the great outdoors had come when she'd lost her Gucci sunglasses in a rogue wave on the beach? She'd never swam that fast in her life. It was a job—a senior-level job—and she could finally move out of her parents' basement and away from her role as the butt of every family joke. Both her older sister and her younger brother had become doctors too. Just to make her look bad.

If only they could see her now.

Bringing the phone to her lips, she turned on the voice recorder. "Day one. The Extreme Outdoors Lightweight Backpacker Tent appears to be made out of toilet paper." She wondered if she'd get away with making that an official quote in her four-page spread. "I've worn a rain poncho that repels water better than this piece of—"

A scratching sound near her feet cut her off. The walls of the tent trembled. Yes, that was definitely a scratching sound. A claw of some kind? "Mary mother of God." The whisper fired up her throat. She wasn't sure if it was the start of a prayer or a curse. She'd have to wait and see, depending on how things turned out.

Scrunching down farther into her sleeping bag, Kate held her breath and listened. There was a huffing sound. An animal sound. A bear? Yes, this definitely called for a prayer. "Oh, God, please don't let it eat me." She squirmed to the corner of the tent where she'd stashed her overstuffed backpack. Yes, she'd read all about how she was supposed to empty the food from her backpack and hang it from a tree in a bear-proof container, but she hadn't actually had the time to find a bear-proof container before she left L.A. Surely bears didn't like freeze-dried macaroni and cheese...did they?

Quickly and silently, Kate dug through the gear until she located her copy of *The Idiot Guru's Guide to Hiking and Camping*. The binding was still crisp. She'd meant to open it on the plane, but she'd forgotten that she'd downloaded *Sweet Home Alabama* on her phone, and God she loved that movie. And Reese. She'd waved to Reese once, across the street on Rodeo Drive, and she'd actually waved back! Well, she might've waved back or she might've been pushing her hair out of her eyes. It had been kind of hard to tell.

But anyway. The bear...

Using her phone as a flashlight, Kate flipped through the pages in search of a chapter about bears while a dark shadow made its way slowly around the tent. "Come on, come on." Hadn't the Idiot Guru thought to inform other idiots what to do if they encountered a bear?

The shadow paused and swiped at the nylon wall.

"Oh God, sweet Jesus." Kate ducked all the way into the sleeping bag, taking the book with her. If nothing else, maybe she could use it as a weapon to defend herself. It was thick enough to do some serious damage. Yet somehow there was no chapter on what to do when a bear was stalking you from outside your tent.

Okay. Think. When she'd first gotten this assignment, she'd read something on the Internet about animal encounters. Was she supposed to play dead? Make loud noises? She fired up the satellite phone again—waiting for what felt like five years for the Internet to load—and searched *bear encounter*.

Big. Mistake. Apparently, bears did eat people. There were pictures to prove it. Adrenaline spurted through her in painful pulses. How could anyone *like* this feeling? Adrenaline junkie? More like adrenaline-phobic. It made her toes curl in and her skin itch. Alternating between hot and cold, Kate crossed her legs so she wouldn't pee in her only pair of long underwear. Lordy, she had to go so bad...

A whimper resonated somewhere nearby. *Hold on a second.* She hadn't whimpered, had she? No. She was pretty sure her voice wouldn't work right now. Did bears whimper? She wouldn't know because the Idiot Guru had left out that critical chapter...

The creature outside her tent whimpered again, softly and sweetly. Kate peeked her head out of the sleeping bag. The shadow was gone, but the whimpering continued.

Holding the sleeping bag around her like a feeble bubble of protection, she squirmed over to the zippered flap that the company had touted as an airflow vent and inched it open until she could see. The rain had slowed some, but it still sprinkled her nose as she peered outside. The shadowy figure of an animal lay a few feet from the tent, still whimpering weakly. But it appeared to be much smaller than she'd originally thought. Way too small to be a bear. It looked more like... a dog.

"Oh no. Poor thing." Kate fought with the sleeping bag until it finally released her. She unzipped the tent's main flap. After slipping on her boots, she slogged through the mud and knelt next to the dog. It was a Lab. A chocolate Lab just like the ones she'd seen playing fetch on Venice Beach. "Are you lost?" she crooned, testing the dog's temperament with a pat on the head. The dog licked her hand and then eased up to a sitting position so it could lick her face.

"You're a sweetheart, aren't you?" She ran her hand over the dog's rain-slicked fur. The poor love shook hard, staring at her with wide, fearful eyes. "I'll bet you don't like the storm, do you?" she asked. "Well that makes two of us. Come on." She coaxed the dog into the tent. "You can wait out the storm with me." And...seeing as how she couldn't stay out here harboring a fugitive dog... "First thing tomorrow morning, we can head into the nearest town so we can find your owner."

Then she'd find herself a nice hot shower, a real meal that didn't require boiling water on a camp stove, and a plush queen-sized bed where she could finally fall into a dry, peaceful sleep.

CHAPTER TWO

Bella!" Jaden jogged down the hall of his rented ski chalet, hoping to God that his dog was simply hiding under the massive king-sized bed in the master suite.

He tore into the room, flicked on the lights, and hit the floor next to the bed. His heart plummeted. *Damn it.* He should've brought her up the mountain with him tonight. Or at least locked the doggie door so she couldn't get out. If he would've known a storm was coming, he would have. And he would've kept her right by his side. Though it'd been only a month since he'd gotten her from a rescue in Denver, he'd already learned that lightning and thunder sent her over the edge.

Back in the hallway, he stopped at the closet to grab his raincoat and pull on a headlamp and his hiking boots. As soon as he'd heard the first clap of thunder, he'd told the crew he had to get home, but he wasn't fast enough. It had taken him a good hour to navigate the ATV down the steep slopes in the rain, and Bella could cover a lot of ground in an hour, especially if she was running scared.

Jaden slipped out the French doors and onto the back deck. The rain was drizzle now, but thunder still rumbled in the distance. He cupped his hands around his mouth and yelled for the dog again. The echo of his voice sounded hollow and lonely—small in the woods that stretched out on all sides of him. Hundreds of thousands of acres of pine and spruce and clumps of aspen trees. There were jagged cliffs, rivers brimming with snowmelt, and predators—mountain lions and bears. And his poor dog started shaking at the sight of a rabbit crouched in the grass.

Panic drove him down the steps, and he jogged into the woods, whistling and yelling her name. He hadn't counted on getting attached to a dog. Lately it'd been hard enough to take care of himself. He hadn't slept a full night since the accident. Hadn't felt much like eating, either. The lingering depression brought on by the knowledge that he'd ruined someone's life.

But the last time he'd gone to visit Gram, he'd driven by one of those fancy local pet stores. They were doing an adoption event outside. As soon as he'd seen Bella hiding in the corner of the pen, he knew she'd be coming home with him. They had the same struggle. Anxiety. He'd recognized it right away. According to the worker, Bella had been rescued from a farm where they'd found over thirty emaciated dogs that had been abused and neglected. And that was it. Over. Done. No decision to be made. He knew she needed him as much as he needed her.

"Bella!" The wind made his shouts sound so futile, but he had to do something. It killed him to think of her out there in the overwhelming darkness, terrified and cold and running blind. He knew how lonely it was. That's what he'd been doing since the accident—navigating an endless darkness. The dog had been the first light he'd seen in a while. She'd taken the edge off the silence that had consumed his life.

After the dust had settled, friends had stopped calling. Fans had stopped seeking him out. His grandma had started talking to him like he was a stranger. And there were times he felt like he had no one in the world.

But then Bella would come and lie at his feet. She would trot by his side while he wandered the trails in search of freedom from the burden that always seemed to weigh him down. Every morning, she would whine at him from the side of the bed, coaxing him back to life because she needed him.

She needed him to feed her and play ball with her. She needed him to protect her and to show her that there was good in the world. That not everyone would kick her or lock her in a cold, dingy basement or use a chain to strangle her when she peed on the floor out of fright. She still wore the marks of violence on the fur around her neck. It had taken a few weeks for her to trust him, for her not to cower in front of him when he'd call to her. It had taken her a few weeks to realize he wasn't going to hurt her or leave her. And now she was alone again. He'd fucked up.

"I'm sorry!" he yelled. Maybe the wind would carry the sound of his voice right to her. "Come on, Bella, I'm sorry!" Mud slurped at his boots as he tromped straight up the side of the mountain. "I won't leave you out here." It didn't matter if it took all night. He'd rescue her the same way she'd rescued him.

* * *

Amazing how sunshine could make everything look so different. In the radiance of a bright morning, even the piece-of-shit tent looked pretty.

Above Kate's head, the blue nylon seemed to glow with a happy optimism. She turned on the phone's voice recorder and brought it to her lips. "Day two: waking up in the Extreme Outdoors Lightweight Backpacker Tent doesn't suck. It's actually a very pretty color." Maybe she wouldn't write up the tent as the worst creation since tiny backpacks hit the purse market. (Seriously, how could Kate Spade have jumped on that bandwagon?) She was feeling generous this morning. Almost giddy.

The dog licked her cheek. At some point during the night, Jane Doe—as Kate had come to call her after discovering the dog was a lady when she'd taken her outside to pee at four o'clock in the morning—had snuggled right up against her in the sleeping bag. Now they lay side by side, spooning like a happy couple. "You saved me, Jane," Kate murmured to the dog. "You know that?" Today, there would be no bugs or dirt, and she'd get her first real meal since the cab had dropped her off at the trailhead... Wait. Had that only been yesterday? Huh. It seemed like eons ago.

In the sleeping bag, Kate could feel the dog's tail wagging against her leg. "I know, I know. I'm ready too." She glanced at the time on her phone. Seven o'clock in the morning wasn't too early to get up and at 'em when you were in the backcountry. Right? With any luck, she could be sitting in a cute little coffee shop in town by eight o'clock with her new best friend Jane Doe curled up at her feet.

On that note... She shimmied out of the sleeping bag and pulled on shorts and a tank top, which she had to rip the price tags off of since she'd had to purchase all new clothes for the trip. Once she was dressed, she dug out a stale bagel from her backpack and gagged down half before holding the other half out to Jane.

The dog sniffed warily before taking a hesitant bite.

"I know. They're much better toasted and served with flavored cream cheese." Strawberry. Or maybe with just a touch of honey. Kate's mouth watered. "Don't worry, girl. We'll find some real food in town." There had to be a deli or a diner nearby.

Speaking of town... She rifled through her things until she located her topographical map. Not that she had any clue how to read the lines that supposedly told you how steep the terrain was. "But I do know how to find the closest town." She pointed out the small black dot to the dog. "Topaz Falls, Colorado. Sounds like the kind of place that might have a really nice spa, don't you think?"

Jane panted happily.

"All we have to do is head down the trail to where it meets up with the highway; then we'll be home free." Easy enough. She folded up the map, stuffed it back into her pack, and then shoved her feet into the brand-new hiking boots that had given her blisters yesterday. She stood gingerly, stiff from a night on the thin foam pad, which was supposed to be the best on the market. (More false advertising.)

Jane whined as Kate unzipped the tent. Then the dog bounded outside like she couldn't wait to get started. Kate couldn't either. Over her shoulder, she eyed the nylon structure that had taken her the better part of three hours to set up. (The packaging had boasted a twenty-minute setup—what a scam.) Would it hurt to leave it behind? She'd tried it out for one night. And she'd also gotten to try out the camp stove and the sleeping bag and the foam pad and the collapsible lantern. Did one really truly need to spend seven days on the trail with those things to get a good read on the gear? She'd drawn her conclusions in one night—it all sucked.

"Come on, Jane." Kate slipped on her backpack and set off down the trail, not looking back at the tent. She'd tell Gregor it hadn't survived the storm. That she'd spent the rest of the week building her own shelters out of sticks and logs and leaves. Maybe he'd give her a promotion.

Hiking with a dog was actually fun. Jane would run ahead with her nose to the ground, and then find a stick and bring it to Kate with her tail wagging. She'd toss the stick, and the dog would take off, leaping and running as though this were the best day of her life.

The feeling was contagious. Having company made Kate slow down and actually enjoy the scenery. Yesterday, she hiked the few miles to her campsite with her head down, faltering under the weight of her thirty-pound backpack, cursing the day Gregor had been born. But today she noticed things. Like the way the sun glinted off the new green aspen leaves. And how when she passed a certain kind of pine tree—she didn't know which—the scent of butterscotch would trail in the air.

The mountains were much prettier than she'd given them credit for yesterday. Purple and yellow and white wildflowers dotted grassy meadows that flourished under the shelter of the trees. It was peacefully quiet but not silent. Birds trilled and somewhere water shushed and a pleasant breeze sighed through the thick branches. So basically, if it wasn't for the dirt and the bugs and the thunderstorms, the mountains would be perfect.

They reached the trailhead much faster than she'd thought they would. But then again, she'd never been good at judging distances on a map. The trail broke through the trees and into an open space flanked by the dirt parking lot where the cab had dropped her off yesterday. A few cars sat in the lot but not a soul was around. "Okay."

Kate swung her backpack to the ground and found the map again.

Jane trotted over and plopped down panting like her lungs were on fire.

"Just have to figure out which way to go," Kate said reassuringly. Which way had she come from in the cab again? When she'd first looked at the map, she'd assumed they had to go west, but now she wasn't so sure. She stared at those little lines, but they all seemed to blur together. Her head felt a little funny. "Water," she gasped. She'd forgotten. Gregor had reminded her that she had to stay hydrated in the high altitude of Colorado. Letting the map fall to the ground, she uncapped her water bottle and guzzled half of what was left.

"Hi there."

Kate turned toward the pleasant, somewhat shy voice of a woman.

"I noticed you were studying a map. Is there anything I can help you with?"

The woman walked over, and she looked like she knew what she was doing. Her hiking boots and lightweight pants were worn and dusty, as though she headed out on the trail every day. She wore a wide-brimmed straw hat, and her golden auburn hair hung in two braids down her shoulders. The kindness in her eyes instantly put Kate at ease. Jane, too, judging from the way the dog stood and started to wag her tail.

Kate picked up the map, realized she'd been holding it upside down, and turned it around. "I'm trying to figure out how to get to Topaz Falls from here."

Even when the woman frowned, she looked friendly. "That's a good ten miles down the highway." She seemed to assess Kate's attire. "It'd be a long walk. I'd be happy to give you a ride if you want."

Kate pulled her sunglasses down her nose. “Seriously?” She didn’t mean to gawk at the woman, but Kate had once stood on the shoulder of the 405 in L.A. with a blown-out tire and cars had whizzed past like she was a statue. No one had even stopped, let alone offered her a ride.

“Sure.” The woman shrugged like it was nothing. “We do that kind of thing all the time around here. We get tons of long-term hikers coming through. A lot of them hitchhike into town.”

Kate sized the woman up. Normally she’d never get into a car with someone she didn’t know, especially in L.A., but there was no way a psychopath could smile like this woman.

“I’m Everly Brooks.”

Everly—what an angelic name. “Kate Livingston.” She held out her hand for a professional introduction, even though she really wanted to hug the woman’s graceful neck. Maybe even give her a kiss of gratitude on the cheek. “I work for *Adrenaline Junkie* magazine and was out doing a gear-test run.” Was that what the real adrenaline junkies called it? No matter. “This sweet dog wandered into my camp last night during the storm. So I thought I would head into town to find her owner.”

“Oh...” Everly’s pretty eyes grew even bigger. “Then you’re in luck. My friend Jessa owns an animal shelter just outside of town. I’m sure she’d be happy to help.”

“Perfect.” Things could not be more perfect right now. Kate could take Jane to the shelter so she could be reunited with her family—a good deed for someone else. Then she could find a place to stay and get a head start on writing her gear-test article from the comfort of a hotel—a good deed for herself. Gregor would never know that she hadn’t spent a week out on the trail.

"I'm parked over this way." Everly led her to an old-fashioned Ford pickup truck that was spotted with rust. Kate climbed in, and Jane jumped into her lap as though she knew she was going home.

It took a few tries to get the old clunker started, but soon enough they were on their way, and Kate relaxed against the seat. "Thanks again for going to all of this trouble." Nothing like this had ever happened to her. A complete stranger going out of their way to help…

"It's no problem," Everly said. The truck puttered down a two-lane road bordered by thick, earthy-scented forest on both sides. "So you must do a ton of backpacking with your job, huh?"

Kate startled. "Oh. Yeah. Sure. You know…" She hoped Everly knew because she sure as hell didn't.

"Where's your favorite place to go?"

"Hmmm." She drummed her fingers against her thigh, pretending to mentally compare the many incredible places she'd backpacked. "I guess I would have to say Banff." That was somewhere in Canada. Someone had raved about it at the office last week. Surely it had a lot of trails and scenery.

"Oh my God, I love Banff." Everly's head tipped as though she were picturing it. "Did you do the Consolation Lakes Trail near Moraine Lake?"

"Of course," Kate said, and then quickly added, "It's beautiful."

"I know," her new friend agreed. "It's one of the most beautiful places I've ever been."

"So what do you do?" Kate asked before Everly could get another question in. She'd pretty much run out of ideas for any additional discussion on spectacular backpacking destinations.

"I run a small organic farm and operate a farm-to-table café that barely breaks even." Everly laughed as though embarrassed. "Doesn't sound so great, but I love it."

"Actually it sounds amazing." Kate could picture it. A cute little farmhouse against a mountain backdrop. It sure beat her tiny apartment that looked out on an alley back in Burbank. There were probably animals and wildflowers and the same beautiful aspen trees she'd seen in the forest. "I'd love to see it."

"Sure. After we take the dog to Jessa's, we can swing by my place on our way back to the trail."

Kate shifted Jane so she could see the woman's face. "The trail?"

"Yeah." Eyes on the road, Everly turned the truck off onto a dirt driveway and drove underneath a framed wooden sign that said CORTEZ RANCH. "I figured you'd want to get back to your trip after you get the dog settled."

"Right. The trip." The lonely, miserable, dirty camping trip. There was one problem with that scenario. Kate no longer had a tent. And she seriously doubted her ability to ever find that thing again. "Actually, I might stick around town for a few days," she said thoughtfully, as though the idea had just occurred to her. "Restock on supplies and stuff." Enjoy a few meals, maybe a massage or a day of pampering to recondition her skin. "Do you know of any good places to stay on short notice?"

"Sure." Everly drove them past a couple of rustically elegant houses with wide stained logs held together by heavy steel brackets and accents of stone. The kind you'd see featured in *Adrenaline Junkie* as the perfect adventure ranch destination.

"The Hidden Gem Inn is the best accommodation in town." Her new friend parked outside of what looked to be a refurbished barn. The modest sign above the double doors announced it as the HELPING PAWS ANIMAL SHELTER.

"Jessa's sister-in-law Naomi and her husband opened the inn almost two years ago," Everly went on. "It's a beautiful bed-and-breakfast right in town. Best food outside of the café." She smiled humbly. "And gorgeous. It's a historic home, built during the silver rush, but it's been all redone inside."

Kate could almost feel the warmth of a luxurious shower. The softness of a brand-new mattress. Geez, she was practically tearing up. "It sounds like exactly the kind of place I'm looking for."

CHAPTER THREE

Ditching the tent on the trail was hands down the best decision she had ever made. Kate sipped her high-priced cabernet sauvignon and popped a dark chocolate truffle into her mouth.

Who knew that a small town like Topaz Falls would have one of the best wine bars she'd ever had the pleasure of experiencing? The Chocolate Therapist was something out of a fantasy—all streamlined and modern and classy without crossing the line into pretentious. After meeting with Jessa Cortez and discovering that no one had contacted her about a lost dog, Kate had offered to keep Jane with her—a fostering situation, if you will—while Jessa checked around. It wasn't only that she wanted an excuse to stay off the trail. She happened to love Jane Doe, too, so it was a win-win.

Once that had been settled, Everly had driven Kate and Jane Doe straight over to the Hidden Gem, where Naomi had upgraded her into their best suite at no charge. Then Naomi and her husband, Lucas, even offered her an extra car they currently weren't using, just in case she needed it while she stayed in town to help locate Jane's owner.

It didn't matter what she needed; Kate's new bestie Everly would say, "I have a friend for that."

After Kate had enjoyed an extended time-out in the marble-tiled steam shower of her new suite, Everly had insisted they walk Jane Doe to Main Street so she could show Kate around and they could have an afternoon treat. Her new friend had brought her straight to the Chocolate Therapist, where the owner, Darla Michaels, had hooked them up with the best wine and chocolate pairing that could possibly exist in this world.

"I can't remember the last time I felt this happy." Kate took another sip of wine. She and Everly were sitting outside at a bright orange bistro table—with Jane Doe contentedly curled up underneath. The patio looked out on a downtown area where quaint shops with striped awnings lined the cobblestone sidewalks. Baskets of bright-colored annuals hung from the wrought-iron streetlamps, and the mountains hovered in the background like a beautiful barricade constructed to keep reality out. It was something straight out of a storybook fairy tale, safe and fictional and untouchable. "I might never leave Topaz Falls," Kate told Everly, popping another truffle into her mouth.

Everly laughed. "Watch out. That's exactly what happened to me. I showed up here thinking I might stay a few months, and over two years later, I can't seem to leave."

"I can see why." It wasn't only the mountains and the whimsical small-town charm. It was also the people, all connected, all watching out for each other—and even for the strangers who found themselves in their midst. "I can't thank you enough for—"

"What the hell are you doing with my dog?"

The angry male voice came from behind. Kate turned at the same time Jane Doe shot to her feet, whining and yipping.

A man stalked toward them, his chiseled features locked into a punishing scowl. He dodged people on the sidewalk, looking as out of place as Oscar the Grouch at Disney World.

The dog immediately hurdled the fence and made a beeline for him, ending the dramatic scene with a leap directly into his midsection.

"Bella." The man caught her and knelt, setting her paws on the ground as he wrapped his arms around her. "Jesus, pup. Where have you been? I looked for you all night."

Kate glanced at Everly and mouthed, "Do you know that guy?"

Everly shook her head with a pained expression. Yeah, he didn't seem like a very personable man, but that had never stopped Kate before. She pushed back from the table and stood, calmly letting herself out of the patio's gate before ambling over to where the joyous reunion was still taking place.

"Ahem." She cleared her throat.

The man looked up at her, and immediately the soft relief on his face tightened into anger. Even with the tension that pulled his cheeks taut, there was something vaguely familiar about his features. Though he wore a stocking cap and sunglasses, she could swear she'd seen his square jaw and that exquisite mouth before…

"Why the hell was my dog sitting under your table?" he demanded, standing upright. He was half a foot taller than her, easy, and had broad, fit shoulders, she couldn't help but notice through his T-shirt.

"How about you thank me for rescuing your dog from the woods during the storm last night?" Kate asked cheerfully.

No one would ruin this perfect afternoon for her. "She wandered into my camp."

"Your camp?" He flicked his glasses off and swept an irritatingly skeptical look from her head to her toes. "*You* were camping?"

Okay, sure. She would be the first to admit she didn't exactly look the part right now. On the way to the Hidden Gem, Everly had driven past a boutique and Kate had seen this lovely sundress in the window. What could she say? It was love at first sight. The soft pink dress had layer upon layer of delicate, embroidered lace with eyelet trim at the neckline. You couldn't find things like that in L.A. It was both modern and sentimental at the same time. And, since she would be staying in town for a few days, she couldn't resist a few purchases. "Yes, I was camping." Her smile dimmed at the smug look on his face. "In fact, I was on a seven-day backpacking trip," she informed him, glaring right into the man's eyes. They were steely and blue. Whoa. Unmistakable eyes. Famous eyes…

Well, what do you know? J.J. Alexander—disgraced Olympic snowboarder—was walking the streets of Topaz Falls. She knew she'd recognized him!

Kate kept her expression in check. He obviously did not want to be identified, given the hat and the sunglasses, which he'd quickly slipped back on.

"So, what? You were going to keep my dog forever?" he asked, backing down a bit.

"Of course not." She gave him the dutiful smile of a Good Samaritan. "I hiked all the way down the mountain and brought her to the Helping Paws Animal Shelter first thing this morning." And look where that had led her. Right to Jaden freaking Alexander. He'd hidden from the media ever since a reporter tried to accuse him of assault right after the accident. The accusations turned out to be bogus, but after that, J.J. had disappeared. No stories, no interviews, nothing. And now here he was, standing in front of her like some ruggedly wrapped gift from God. If she could score an interview with J.J. Alexander, she'd never have to go on another backpacking trip again.

"I'm Kate Livingston, by the way." She stuck out her hand, but the man simply stared at it.

He hesitated, obviously not wanting to share his name.

"Your dog is such a sweetheart," she went on to compensate for his silence. He couldn't walk away. Not yet. Not until she figured out an excuse to spend more time with him. "Bella is it? I was calling her Jane Doe. Anyway, she slept in my sleeping bag all night. Curled right up next to me and kept me warm. Didn't you, girl?" She knelt and scrubbed behind Bella's ears.

The dog gave her a loving, slobbery lick across the lips.

Laughing, Kate stood back up and wiped her mouth. "We definitely bonded."

"I can see that." J.J. didn't seem to appreciate it much either, judging from his frosty tone. "Well, thanks for bringing her back." He turned. "Come on, Bella."

"Wait." Kate flailed to catch up with him.

The man stopped and eyed her like he was considering making a run for it.

Humiliation torched her cheeks, but she muscled through it. Typically she didn't chase men down the street, but this was an emergency. "Why'd she run away?"

J.J. seemed to debate whether he was obligated to answer the question. Finally he sighed. "She hates storms. And I'm working long days at the resort. Sometimes nights too. I didn't know there'd be a storm, so I didn't lock her dog door."

Long days at the resort, huh? "Poor thing." Kate petted the dog again, seeing the perfect opening into J.J. Alexander's world. Thankfully, the dog ate up the attention, wagging her tail and whining for more. "When we were hiking this morning, she never let me out of her sight. She seems to get lonely easily."

"Yeah." J.J. watched her interact with Bella. "She's a rescue. Doesn't like being alone."

Kate turned up the wattage on her sunny expression as if an idea had suddenly lit up inside her. "Well, I love your dog, and it just so happens that I'll be in town for a few days, so maybe I could help."

"I thought you were backpacking." J.J. obviously didn't want to take the bait, which meant she'd have to use another angle. Something other than *her* love for the dog.

"My tent was damaged in the storm, which means I'll have to finish out my vacation in town." She nearly gagged on the word *vacation*. Maui was a vacation. Hell, she'd even consider Miami to be a decent vacation. Camping was so not a vacation. "I'd love to watch Bella while you work. Like a doggie day-care thing. I can pick her up in the mornings and spend the day with her so you don't have to worry about her running off."

"That's okay." The man still stared at Kate like she was a lunatic. "She's fine."

"It would be better for her than sitting around a lonely house all day," Kate prompted. If the earlier reunion was any indication, this man loved his dog. So all she had to do was convince him it would be best for Bella. "I'll take her on hikes, and we can play fetch. She can play with my new friend Naomi's dog at the Hidden Gem. Oh, and I bet she'd love swimming in the river at the park."

His torn expression revealed that, yes, Bella did indeed love to swim. What Lab didn't?

"So you'd pick her up in the morning and drop her off after I got home?"

"Yes. I'd love to spend more time with her while I'm in town," she assured him. "You don't even have to pay me." Getting to know J.J. Alexander, aka the Snowboarding Cowboy, would be all the compensation she needed.

* * *

There had to be a catch. Why would some hotter-than-sin woman offer to watch his dog while he worked? For free?

Jaden eyed Kate Livingston from behind the anonymity of his dark sunglasses. She sure didn't look like she belonged anywhere near a backcountry trail. Her silky black hair had that perfect beach-wave thing going on, which he suspected she'd paid good money for. And her skin...it was rosy and flawless. Not lined from the sun like his. Her eyes were the most striking feature about her, though, so dark they were almost black and narrowed slightly in the corners like she had some exotic mix of genes.

His body's swift reaction to her raised his defenses. He'd met women like Kate. All sunny and rosy and completely fake. He'd even had a good time with a few of them, but those days were long behind him.

To get his eyes off the temptation in front of him, Jaden glanced at Bella. His dog had attached herself to Kate's side as though trying to convince him to close the deal. He could see the plea in those sorrowful eyes. *Aw hell.* He was such a sucker. Bella would love having the company. He'd worked almost eighty hours this week, and his poor dog had been on her own.

What would it hurt? The woman—Kate?—hadn't seemed to realize who he was. Bella liked her. And he liked the fact that he wouldn't have to worry about the dog running off again, which would mean he wouldn't have to spend another night tromping all over the mountain searching for her.

Last night had been hell. He hadn't slept at all. He'd hiked until dawn, yelling and whistling and searching until he'd had to go up to work. As soon as the crew had quit for the day, he'd gone home to print some of those lost dog posters he'd seen plastered to lampposts when he was growing up. Which now he wouldn't need.

"So what do you think?" Kate persisted. Yeah. Persistent. That was the only way to describe her. She looked like a woman who had no trouble getting what she wanted.

"I guess it would work."

"Great! Oh, that's so great." A smile made her eyes sparkle. Something about her seemed so young. She was happy; that's what it was. Happy all the way down deep, like Gram used to say.

"We can start tomorrow," Kate said as she hugged the dog again. "We'll have so much fun, Bella! We'll play all day! I'll pick her up at eight. Okay? Make sure to send along everything she'll need for the day. Food, her leash, any toys she'd like to bring, treats."

"Uh..." Jaden blinked at her. Damn Kate had a lot of energy. It felt like she'd boarded a speed-of-light train and he was hanging on the back. "Sure. Okay. That's fine."

"I'll need your address. And I didn't catch your name."

"Jay," he blurted. "My name is Jay." He quickly rattled the address for his rental so he could get the hell out of there.

"Very nice to meet you, Jay." Kate leaned over and gave Bella a kiss on the top of the head. "I'll see you both tomorrow." With a twinkling wave, she sashayed back to her table, where one of her friends was waiting.

"What the hell just happened there?" Jaden asked Bella on the way back to his Jeep. "Did you have to crawl into *her* sleeping bag?" Out of all the sleeping bags in the backcountry, his dog had somehow found the one that held a tempting, aggravating, overly cheerful Disney princess.

"Couldn't you have found some transient guy?" he muttered as he helped Bella jump into the passenger's seat. "That would be a lot less complicated." Something told him he wouldn't be able to keep himself in check forever when Kate Livingston was around. And he'd eventually want to do more than look, seeing as how it'd been a damn long time since he'd had the opportunity. The first sight of her in the strappy little dress had him rubbernecking in a bad way. Not that he'd admit it to anyone else, but that was the only reason he'd seen Bella. He'd noticed Kate first.

Jaden started the Jeep and drove away from Main Street, his eyes sticky with fatigue. All he wanted to do was go home and eat his bowl of Honey Nut Cheerios and then fall into bed. Maybe he'd actually sleep tonight. For once he felt tired enough. But unfortunately, he couldn't go home. Not yet.

"We've got big plans tonight," he announced, trying to muster some enthusiasm.

Bella stuck her head out the window, her lips flapping as she sniffed the air.

"Levi was an old friend of mine. Back in high school. He invited us over for a beer, if you can believe that." Bella probably couldn't, seeing as how they hadn't visited anyone's house since he'd adopted her.

He turned off the highway and onto the familiar dirt road where he used to race bikes with Levi. The Cortez Ranch had gotten a major upgrade since he'd been gone. Originally, there'd been only one house on the property.

Now there were four that he could see. Two were newer, one right across from the corrals and one farther up the hill tucked into a stand of aspen trees. That would be Levi's house. He'd described it over the phone but hadn't done it justice.

It wasn't obnoxiously large like the house Jaden had rented near the resort, but it was impressive all the same. Hand-hewn logs stacked one on top of another, stone siding coming halfway up the structure, and a copper roof that must've set him back a good hundred thousand.

Jaden parked the Jeep and let Bella out, taking his time on the stamped concrete stairs that led up the front porch. Stupid that he was nervous. Levi had been pretty mellow at the store, but still…his team had turned on him. When he was winning competitions, they'd become like his family, but after the accident, they'd quit calling, quit inviting him out, quit acknowledging they ever knew him. As his ex-girlfriend and fellow USA team member had reminded him, it wasn't personal. They simply couldn't afford the bad publicity.

His teammates hadn't been nearly as bad as the random strangers, though. The people who had verbally attacked him on social media…and on the streets. It had all made him withdraw from everyone, everything. Social anxiety, they called it. He'd finally looked it up on the Internet.

Bella whined and scratched at the front door, coaxing him onward as usual.

"Yeah, yeah, yeah. I'm going." If it weren't for the dog, he'd probably never get off the couch.

Levi's front door was as grand as the house—stained wood with an inlayed frosted window. He knocked, half hoping his friend wouldn't be around. Maybe he'd forgotten or maybe something had come up—

The door swung open, and Levi greeted him with a hearty handshake. “Glad you could make it.”

Jaden kept his grip firm. “Me too.”

Bella jumped up on Levi. “Happy to see you too, pooch.” He stepped aside. “Come on in.”

Jaden walked into an open-concept living room with high arched ceilings, dark plank floors, and a stone fireplace that took up one whole wall. Even being brand-new and so extravagant, the place still had the cozy touches that made it a home—clusters of pictures and books strewn on the coffee table and some of Levi’s bull-riding memorabilia on the walls.

“Let me grab you a beer,” Levi said, heading for the kitchen on the other side of the room.

“Sounds great.” Jaden wandered closer to the fireplace to get a better look at the framed photographs arranged on the mantel.

An image of a blond woman in a wedding dress—Cassidy, he presumed—stood out from the others. She was dancing barefoot in a grassy meadow, laughing, looking past the camera, presumably at her new husband. “That’s a great shot.” Not posed or unnatural, but spontaneous and full of emotion.

Levi handed him an IPA and studied the picture with a tender expression. “That’s my wife.” He said it like it still surprised him. “Cass. Remember her? Cash’s little sister.”

He vaguely remembered, but Cash had made sure that none of his idiot friends had come within a twenty-foot radius of her, so Jaden hadn’t known her well.

“She’s a nurse in Denver. Working today.” He grinned. “Still have no idea how I got her to marry me.”

“You lucked out, I guess.” That was a joke. Judging from the other wedding pictures, Cassidy looked as happy and in love as Levi. Something told him luck didn't have much to do with it.

The doorbell rang, sending Bella into one of her happy-barking fits. For being so anxious, she sure seemed to like meeting new people.

"Hope you don't mind," Levi said over the noise. "I invited some other friends."

Tension laced up his spine, pulling his back tight. "Nope. Don't mind at all." It was crazy how casual he could force his voice to sound even when that feeling of dread crawled up his throat.

He hung out by the fireplace while Levi opened the door, and Bella greeted the two new visitors with a nose to their crotches.

"Bella, off," he commanded.

She obeyed but whined until they both gave her some attention.

"This is Mateo Torres and Ty Forrester," Levi said, waving Jaden over. "We trained together forever, and now we run a mentoring program when we're not on the road."

"Nice to meet you." He shook each of their hands briskly. Gram would've been proud of him remembering his manners, even when his throat seemed to shrink.

"J.J. grew up on a ranch a few miles from here," Levi told his friends. "We used to raise enough hell that his granny thought about sending him to boarding school."

"Not true." Gram never would've sent him away. "She couldn't get rid of me." He forced a grin. Maybe after enough pretending, it would eventually start to feel real again. "There would've been no one to do the work on the ranch." But Gram had loved him too. The way a mother was supposed to. He'd never doubted that.

"I bet you've got some awesome stories," Mateo said.

"I'm always looking for new material that I can use to humiliate Levi."

Jaden took a sip of his beer and nodded. "I can help you out with that."

"I've got plenty on you." Levi directed the words to Mateo as he went to get more beers from the fridge. He handed them out while the three men compared who had the worst dirt on who.

Jaden stayed out of the conversation. If they'd watched the news in the last three months, they all had dirt on him, and he didn't want to talk about the accident.

Eventually, the pissing match ended, and Levi led them all out to the back deck. Bella followed behind and then trotted down the grass. It seemed his friend had chosen the prettiest spot on the property for his house, right up against the mountain, hidden in a stand of aspen trees. Evening sunlight filtered through the leaves, making everything seem calm.

"House looks good," Mateo said, examining the stone fire pit before flicking a switch to turn it on.

"Yeah. Real fancy, Cortez." Ty kicked back in one of the reclining chairs. "Let me know if you want a roommate."

"Yeah, Cass would love that." Levi pulled two more chairs over and gestured for Jaden to sit.

He had to admit…it wasn't half bad sitting there on the deck with these guys, watching the sun start to sink behind the peaks. It was easier than he'd thought. No questions about the accident. No judgment in their eyes.

"I'm thinking about buying some land so I can build," Mateo said. "Got my eye on a piece of property right on the edge of town. What about you?" He glanced at Jaden. "You sticking around Topaz Falls or you got something else in mind?"

"I'm still deciding." Originally, he'd planned to take off as soon as they'd finished up the project at the resort. He owned a condo in Utah and a cabin in Alaska, but he didn't have a home anywhere. "I guess I wouldn't mind sticking around." The statement surprised him as much as it seemed to surprise Levi.

"That'd be great," his friend said. "Just like old times."

Jaden couldn't resist. "Only now you have a wife who wouldn't take too kindly to you going up to the hot springs to drink beer and skinny-dip with Chrissy…what was her last name again?"

They all laughed.

"Cass would kick your ass," Ty said.

"True statement," Levi agreed. He turned to Jaden. "But seriously, you'd love it here. Small town. Great community. Old friends. You'd be welcome."

Welcome. That one word sparked hope. Maybe Jaden didn't have to live in hiding forever. Maybe he could come back to the place he'd always thought of as home.

CHAPTER FOUR

So this is where a professional athlete went to hide.

Kate climbed out of her borrowed Subaru and walked up the driveway of what could only be described as an ultra-sleek modern take on a ski chalet. The squared structure had been built right into the side of the mountain, constructed mostly of stained concrete and floor-to-ceiling windows, which must've been made from some special type of glass because you couldn't see anything inside.

Standing in front of the heavy glass door, she suddenly felt an agonizing attack of insecurity. Since Jaden had judged her attire yesterday, she'd dressed more carefully for the part she was about to play. Immediately after their encounter, Kate had asked Everly to take her shopping so she could pick out a couple more earthy outfits. Today she wore fitted hiking capri pants with a bright pink moisture-wicking tank top. She'd pulled up her thick, wild hair, taking an extra half hour to make sure the bun looked genuinely carefree and messy. Which it wasn't, of course.

There must've been two hundred bobby pins holding it in place. But she'd hidden them carefully. Outdoorsy chicks wouldn't spend an hour on their hair. They wouldn't have changed clothes four times either.

It wasn't that she was nervous to see J.J. Alexander, necessarily. Though the man did have a certain presence that made it difficult to look away. It was more the fact that she had a very limited amount of time to convince him to do an exclusive with her. He didn't seem especially open to interviews at the moment.

But this was it. Her chance for a big story. The story that could make her career. She'd show his personal side. She'd take off his mask for the entire world and dig deeper and deeper until she captured his every emotion, the true heart of who Jaden Alexander was.

"Jay," she reminded herself in a whisper. She had to call him Jay. It didn't bode well that he hadn't even given her his real name, but he would open up. People loved talking to her. She made sure of it. Once, in journalism school, she'd gotten a three-hundred-fifty-pound college lineman to cry during an interview when she'd asked him about his favorite childhood pet.

That in mind, she patted her messy bun into place and rang the doorbell.

Squinting, she watched for a shadow to emerge from behind the glass door, but nothing happened. Tapping her foot, she rang it again. The distant sound of barking could be heard somewhere inside. Within a few minutes, Bella was bouncing and lunging against the door. Where was J.J.? *Jay,* she quickly corrected. Had he changed his mind about their arrangement?

Right when she was about to turn around and stalk back to the car in defeat, the door opened. Bella hurtled outside, yipping and whining and covering Kate's bare arms with kisses.

When Kate looked up, she nearly fell over, and it wasn't from Bella's weight against her legs either. J.J.—Jay, God, that was going to mess her up—looked a lot different than he had in his stocking cap and sunglasses. His light brown hair was mussed into spikes, and he still had the sleepy eyes of a little boy. Except he was shirtless. And there wasn't anything boyish about his bulletproof pecs and tight abs. Either he did five hundred sit-ups every day or the man had some crazy good genes. Or maybe he had a distant relation to the mythological gods...

"Sorry I didn't answer right away." Drowsiness lowered his voice into a sexy tenor. "I guess I overslept."

"It's no problem." She hiked her gaze up to his eyes. How long had she been staring at his shirtless torso? And more importantly, had he noticed? "I oversleep all the time," she babbled. "It seems like I'm always the last one rolling into work."

His head tilted as he studied her. "What do you do?"

Oops. She had to be careful with questions like that. Lucky for her, he still seemed a bit groggy. "Boring stuff. Really boring." She'd already made herself a vow that she would tell the truth as much as possible. "I edit stuff. Unimportant stuff that no one reads." At least, that could describe her first few weeks at her new job. But once she wrote this story, things would change.

She swept past him and walked into the house before he could fire off more questions. "Wow. This place is amazing. Seriously impressive." A little cold for her taste with the gleaming white walls, uniform leather furniture, and the glossy, seemingly unused kitchen.

"It's the only place I could find on short notice."

Kate made the mistake of turning around to smile at him. He still hadn't put on a shirt, the jerk. "So what did you say you're doing at the resort again?" she asked, running her hand along the white marble countertop in the kitchen.

"Actually, I didn't say." His voice was no longer deep and sleepy. Now it was just dull.

She waited out the awkward silence until he gave in with a sigh.

"I'm on a crew that's helping build the new terrain park."

"Sounds fascinating." She kept her gaze even with his. *Don't. Look. Down.* Or she'd get all weak-kneed and woozy at the sight of his hot body again. She couldn't afford to let Jay make her weak-kneed and woozy. "So you must be into snowboarding, then."

His eyes dodged hers. "I guess."

Wonderful. He was very informative. Getting him to open up and agree to an interview wasn't going to be easy. Good thing she had a whole week. She would have to get creative about making excuses to spend time with him. He didn't seem overly thrilled with the fact that she currently stood in his kitchen. *Well get used to it, buddy.*

Kate turned and started opening the grayish glass cabinets.

"What're you doing?" Jaden walked over and closed one. "Why are you going through my stuff?"

"I'm looking for the dog food," she told him, opening another cabinet. Which was completely empty. "Remember? I'll have Bella all day. I'm sure she'll get hungry. Or did you already feed her?"

After he shook his head, she opened yet another cabinet. Wow. The man had about six boxes of Honey Nut Cheerios stacked above the sink. And he was looking at her like she was crazy? "When's the last time you ate a real meal?"

"I eat." He stiffly marched past her and disappeared into a pantry for a minute. When he came back, he had a dog dish and a bag of food. "She eats twice a day. Once in the morning and once in the afternoon." He shoved the stuff into Kate's hands. "Think you need anything else?" He clearly wanted her to go, and that was probably best since he refused to put on a shirt and she couldn't stop ogling his body.

"Nope. I think this is it. We're good. Right, Bella?" With a bright smile, she turned and headed for the door. "I'll have her home at five o'clock sharp."

Jay followed behind her. "If I'm not here, you can just let her into the house through the garage. The code is one-two-three-four."

She laughed, caught between amusement and a nervous giggle. "Wow. It's like Fort Knox."

He shrugged, tensing those broad shoulders. "Don't have much to worry about way up here."

That was true. Well...the normal person didn't have to worry about much, but J.J. Alexander had just given her the code to his house. Which meant he'd basically handed her an all-access pass into his life.

* * *

Was it just him or were the days getting longer? Jaden shouldered his backpack and started the hike back to the ATV he'd left at the base of the mountain. Eight o'clock. Damn. Late again. Good thing he had someone to watch Bella. Even if the woman happened to be overly chipper and obnoxiously nosy at eight o'clock in the morning. At least all that energy should be good for wearing out his dog. Hopefully Bella had gone to sleep after Kate dropped her off.

"Hey, J.J., hold up." Blake Wilder came sprinting down the hill, and Jaden swallowed a groan. The man had never been his favorite person, but he had to admit—begrudgingly—Blake obviously knew what he was doing. Since the man had taken over resort operations four years ago, they'd almost doubled in size.

Jaden strapped his backpack to the ATV and waited.

"Looks like things are coming together ahead of schedule," Blake said as he approached. "I called out the inspectors for the end of this week. Think we can make it?"

"With the hours we've been putting in? Definitely." A few more twelve-hour days and they'd wrap up this project. The thought didn't thrill him as much as it seemed to thrill Blake.

"You got any idea what you'll do next?"

That question had haunted him for the last few days. "Haven't thought about it much." What options did he have except to go hide somewhere else? Last week, that would've been his first response, but Levi's optimism the other night had made him think twice about picking up and leaving again.

"I'm going to level with you here, Alexander." Blake only seemed to be able to remember people's last names. "I want a bigger focus on snowboarding around here. That's the direction we need to go. And I think you're the guy to get us there."

Jaden couldn't remember the last time he'd laughed, but he was this close. "I'm not exactly well loved in the snowboarding community anymore," he reminded him.

"But you still have a name. You still have the knowledge and experience I need." That was the other thing about Blake Wilder. When he looked at people, he saw only how they could meet his needs. "I could create a position for you here. Manager for the terrain park. I need someone out here every day during the winter season."

"You're offering me a full-time job?" Was this a joke?

"You're the perfect candidate," Blake insisted. "You'd be responsible for daily risk assessments, inspections, and the maintenance and testing of all the features."

Which meant he'd have to get on a board again. Anxiety skittered through him, headed straight for his heart, and dug in its claws. That's where it always hit him, deep in the chest, poking and taunting and squeezing until the palpitations started. He couldn't even think about getting on a board again.

"The salary wouldn't be what you're used to making. But you'd get full benefits. And there'd be bonuses if you were willing to do some public events to help with publicity."

Public events? Hadn't Blake seen what a train wreck his life had become? Jaden would show up for the public event, and there'd be hecklers and media and the same shit storm he'd been trying to escape. He climbed onto the ATV, ready to start the engine and get the hell out of there. "Thanks for the offer, but I don't think it'll work out." He'd never strap his boots onto a board again.

"Think about it." Blake backed away. "Offer stands for a while. But I'd need a commitment by the end of the project. If it's not you, I'll have to find someone else."

He wanted to tell him he didn't need to think about it. He'd never be able to do it, even if he wanted to. Instead, he gave the man a nod, put on his helmet, and then drove down the mountain.

By the time he made it to his street, the sky was nearly dark, but he could make out a faint outline of a car parked next to the curb in front of his house. Had the media found him somehow? Instinctively, he slowed, but as he got closer he realized it was only a small SUV that looked suspiciously similar to the one Kate had been driving.

What the hell was she doing at his house at eight thirty?

He parked the ATV in front of the garage and cruised through the front door, looking around the empty rooms.

"Hello?" Not even Bella ran to greet him.

Just when he was about to go out front and search Kate's car, he noticed the French doors to the back deck had been left cracked open. He jogged over and slipped outside.

"Oh, good. You're finally back." Kate stood at the grill wearing a white apron and wielding a huge set of stainless steel tongs. "Perfect timing."

Jaden looked around once more to make sure he was in the right house. Yep. It seemed to be his rental. His deck. His grill that she was leaning over. What was he missing here? "What're you doing?"

"Making you dinner," she said as though this were a normal everyday occurrence. "Filet mignon with grilled asparagus." She flipped the sizzling hunks of meat. "Oh! And mashed potatoes with bacon and garlic."

Uh…"Why?" That was the only word he could seem to manage from the fog of shock. He couldn't deny that Kate Livingston was gorgeous. Even more captivating under the soft glow of the globe lights strung overhead. Captivating in a way that triggered his anxiety. For the last couple of months, he'd done his best to feel nothing. It was easier. But she stirred something. A craving that ached all the way through him.

"What do you mean why?" She seemed to laugh so easily. "Okay. I admit it. This is a pity dinner."

"A pity dinner." He couldn't seem to do much more than repeat her.

"All you have in that lavish kitchen of yours are six boxes of Honey Nut Cheerios." She shrugged and turned back to the grill. "I feel sorry for you. How long has it been since you've had steak and potatoes?"

"Eight years." He hadn't eaten potatoes for eight years. They had too much starch, and he'd had to keep his body fit.

She spun and gaped at him, those standout eyes wide with a look of genuine shock. "Eight. Years?"

"I've had steak. Just not potatoes." But he'd loved mashed potatoes growing up. That might've been his favorite food. Gram used to dump in butter and real cream and fresh herbs from the garden…

"God, really?" she repeated. "Where have you been? In prison?"

"No." But actually, these last three months had felt like exile. Not that he could tell her that.

"Well, I hope you're hungry." Kate walked over to the patio table, which had already been set with dishes and silverware. "Because we have a ton of food. And Darla insisted on sending me home with some wine and truffles." She uncorked a fancy bottle and poured the red wine into two glasses.

Jaden stood right where he was. He had no clue what to make of Kate Livingston. She seemed friendly and innocent. Or maybe that was just the dimples in her smile. Maybe she only *looked* friendly and innocent. Maybe she'd go all *Fatal Attraction* on him any minute. "Why are you here?" he asked again, and this time he wasn't being polite. "Why are you in my house making me dinner?"

Kate set down her wineglass, her shoulders slumping from confidence to surrender. She seemed to think a minute and then turned and walked toward him as though giving up. She stopped a foot away, her mouth no longer smiling. "I'm lonely. Okay?" Her chipper voice had mellowed. "Things in my life aren't awesome right now. I'm not exactly in a place I want to be. And after I saw your house this morning, I figured maybe you were lonely too."

Now, that he could understand.

"Okay, then," Jaden said, taking his place at the table. "Let's eat."

CHAPTER FIVE

Well, what do you know? All those things her mom said about the truth being the best policy were actually legit.

Kate pushed her plate away. As soon as she'd admitted to Jaden that she happened to be lonely, too, everything changed. He still wasn't a Chatty Cathy by any means, but during their dinner, she'd managed to make small talk, and he'd answered all of her questions about the new terrain park in impressive detail.

Unfortunately, he didn't seem interested in talking about anything else, and all the effort she was making to carry the conversation while doing her best to ignore his smoldering good looks was starting to wear on her.

Kate checked him out again. Was it possible that Jay had gotten even hotter as they sat there across from each other? Or was that the wine talking?

"Thanks for dinner." Jay tossed his napkin onto his empty plate. There was something magnetic about his eyes when he wasn't so sullen. They were focused and open. Good listening eyes.

Kate looked away. "I'm glad you liked it." It'd been a while since she'd cooked for someone who actually appreciated it. The last guy she'd dated would head straight for the television and turn on the latest football game after they ate, leaving her to do the dishes. But she wasn't *dating* J.J. Alexander. Ha. That would be...ridiculous. She wasn't here to get lost in his magic eyes or sigh with rapture when he smiled, which was so rare that the shock of it made her heart twirl every time.

She was here to get a damn story.

"You seem cold." Jay eyed the goose bumps on her arms.

Cold. Right. Sure. That's what it was...

"Want me to turn on the fire?"

She looked past him to the dark outline of the mountainous horizon. When the sun had slipped behind the peaks, the temperature had dropped about twenty degrees, but she hadn't noticed until he'd said something. A fire already burned low in her belly. "Uh. Sure. Yeah. A fire would be great."

Jaden bent and opened a small door on the side of the table, and as if by magic, flames illuminated the decorative rock piled in the center of the table.

In any other situation, it would've been intimate and romantic, with the stars glistening overhead, the shushing of the wind in the pine trees. But this was an interview. So instead of settling back into her chair and enjoying the peaceful night more than she should, she leaned forward and folded her hands on the table, ignoring the way the fire made Jaden's face glow. "So, Jay..." She smiled, summoning her impeccable small-talk skills. "What do you do when you're not working on terrain parks?"

"In the past, I've competed." His eyes hardened again, as though petitioning her to leave it at that.

Only she couldn't. "You don't compete anymore?" She

figured he'd come back eventually, like all those other professional athletes who were mandated to take a short time-out after a scandal but then eventually came back and made their victorious reappearance.

"No. I can't compete anymore."

He can't? That's not what all of the news reports had said. It sounded like his injury had been relatively minor, all things considered. "Why not?"

"I crashed." His face remained perfectly still. There wasn't even a twitch in his jaw. "Got injured."

It seemed she wasn't the only one who exceled at telling the partial truth. What could she expect, though? He didn't know her, didn't trust her. She'd have to earn that over time.

"So what about you?" The fact that Jaden was actually asking her a question obviously meant he wanted to change the subject. "Do you like being an editor?"

"No." Huh. Had she ever admitted that out loud to anyone else? "I mean, after graduate school, I always saw myself doing something different," she corrected. "Something more important."

His eyes softened again as he gazed across the fire at her. "Like what?"

She didn't even have to think. "Writing stories that change the world." That had been the reason she'd pursued journalism in the first place. She could've become a doctor like her brother and sister, but she loved words. She saw power in words. "I wanted to be another Gloria Steinem. A journalist. A political activist."

"So why aren't you?"

Easy for him to say. He probably still had millions of dollars squirreled away somewhere. But she hadn't wanted to fulfill her parents' prophecies that she'd have to live in their posh Beverly Hills basement in order to survive. "I had to find a job." It was more than that, though. It was the rejection. She'd written a couple of pieces, figuring if she couldn't get hired at any of the prestigious publications, she could work her way there by freelancing.

So she'd written a profile about a girl she'd met on the Metro. After seeing her for a few days in a row, Kate struck up a conversation with the young teen and learned that she'd recently joined a gang. Once she got to know her, Kate had written an article detailing the plight of young women in poverty and why more and more are turning to gangs in order to survive.

All total, she'd amassed forty-three rejection emails from various publications, telling her that either no one wanted to read about girls in gangs, or the article wasn't exactly what they were looking for at the moment, or she had a bland writing style. Kate sighed. "According to the rejection letters, I'm not good enough."

Jaden shrugged. "Then you make yourself good enough."

"I don't know how." She'd done everything. She'd aced journalism school. She'd gotten in touch with all of the contacts she'd built over the years. No one wanted her.

"Well, you shouldn't give up."

He'd given up, though. "Why can't you go back to competing, then? Athletes overcome injuries all the time."

"It's more complicated than that," Jaden said, staring into the fire. "And anyway, we're not talking about me. We're talking about you, Kate." He raised his eyes to hers.

She actually shivered when he said her name. At some point, she'd lost control of the conversation, and worse, of her heart. It beat hard and hot and fast. *Shit.* She couldn't do this. Couldn't fall for him. "I should do the dishes." Clumsily, she gathered up their silverware and plates and slipped into the house with Bella following at her heels. Easing out a breath, she carted everything to the kitchen sink.

Unfortunately, Jaden did not head straight for the television set to turn on whatever sports match would be playing in May. Nope. He came right into the kitchen and stood behind her. "I can do the dishes."

"That's okay," she sang as she turned on the faucet. "I've got it." She'd intended to use the few minutes of rinsing and washing to regroup, but it was obvious that she wouldn't be able to recover. She could feel him standing behind her, feel her body being drawn to his…

"Sorry if I said something that made you uncomfortable." Jay reached around her and turned off the faucet.

"Oh no, not at all." She didn't know what to do with the wet plate in her hands. It wasn't anything he'd said. It was the way he'd started to look at her. The way he was looking at her now. Like he saw much more than she'd ever intended for him to see.

"I didn't mean to overstep." He inched closer, his gaze settling on her mouth. "But I think, if you want something, you should go after it."

"Mmm-hmmm." Kate carefully set the plate back in the sink before she dropped it. This was happening. Even with the warning lights of panic flashing behind her eyes, her body was moving closer to him.

Jaden's hand reached for her, fingers gentle against her cheek as he turned her face to his. The touch melted into her, softening her hesitations right along with her knees. Jay looked at her for a moment, and all she saw was a man. Not J.J. Alexander, or a snowboarding champion, or a die-hard athlete who'd taken out his competition.

He was a man as caught up in the currents of seduction as she was.

This is a terrible idea. The thought flitted through her mind but found no place to land before Jay's lips came for hers and everything fell silent. The power of him overtook her senses. In the darkness of her closed eyes, she saw sparks of red. She smelled a subtle hint of aftershave—scents of rosemary's spiciness.

A sound come from his throat, an utterance of want, need, hunger.

She answered with a moan when the stubble of his jaw scraped against her cheek as his lips fused with hers.

And the taste of his tongue...It was wine and notes of chocolate, ecstasy in the hotness of her mouth. A helpless sigh brought her body against his, and he held her close in those strong arms as though he wanted to keep her right there. "This is even better than dinner," he breathed, lips grazing her cheek before teasing their way down her neck.

"Better than dessert too." Her whisper got lost in another moan. His lips left a burning mark on every spot they kissed—between her jaw and her ear, the base of her throat, the very center of her collarbone.

"Even better than dessert," he agreed, his voice low and gruff. He raised his face to hers, and that rare smile hiked up one corner of his seductive mouth before he kissed her again, deeper this time, leaving no question that he was taking his own advice and going after what he wanted.

She wanted it, too, so much she was lost in it—the rush of passion and emotion he brought rising to the surface. She could kiss this man forever. Every morning and every night. Every time he offered her the gift of his smile. Except...the word clawed its way through the exhilaration of a first kiss, a potential new love.

Except.

He had no idea who she really was, what she was really

supposed to be doing here. The thought rushed in as cold as the mountain air outside, forcing her to break away from him.

Holding her fingers to her lips, she stepped out of his reach, struggling in vain to catch her breath. “I have to go.”

“Go?” Jay looked as dazed as she’d been ten seconds ago.

“Yes.” She rushed past him before he could touch her again. She couldn’t think when he touched her. “I’m late.”

“For what?” he asked, following behind her.

“For…book club.” She hastily packed up the cloth market bags Naomi had loaned her. There were other things too—the apron she’d taken off outside, the corkscrew for the wine. But she would have to get those later. “Everly and her friends invited me,” she said. “It’s at Darla’s place. I totally lost track of time. I’m so sorry.” Before she could make it to the front door, Jay slipped in front of it, blocking her escape.

“I’m the one who’s sorry. I think I misread something.”

“No. You didn’t.” He definitely hadn’t misread her attraction to him. “This just…caught me off guard.” She’d made him dinner to get him to talk to her. Instead she’d ended up seducing herself.

“Yeah, it was pretty unexpected.” He seemed to search her eyes. “But I don’t mind being surprised once in a while. Do you?”

“No. I don’t mind being surprised.” Not normally. She loved surprises. But she liked them better when they came without a dagger of guilt stabbed right into her chest.

“Good.” He stepped aside and even opened the door for her. “Thanks for making me dinner, Kate. It’s been a long time since anyone’s done something like that for me.”

The words twisted the knife. “You’re welcome,” she murmured before she slipped out into the night.

“See you tomorrow morning?” he called behind her.

No. She should say no and walk away from this right now. But what would that look like? Her going back to search for her tent and resume her week on the trail? She'd already told Gregor about the detour, and he'd told her to get an interview with J.J. Besides, maybe it would help Jaden too. From what she'd seen in the short time she'd spent with him, he had some unresolved issues surrounding the accident. Maybe talking about them would help.

With that in mind, she forced herself to turn around and even dredged up a smile. "See you tomorrow."

CHAPTER SIX

Kate drove straight to the Chocolate Therapist. Yes, indeed, she needed some serious therapy.

Once again, she'd mostly told the truth. She happened to know her new friends were having their book club meeting tonight, and book club meetings were a great place to talk, right? To get advice on what to do when the subject of what could be the biggest, career-defining story of your entire career ambushes your plans for an interview with a sexy kiss that could've easily led to more. So. Much. More.

With a screech of tires, Kate swerved to the curb in front of Darla's wine bar and hit the brakes, scrambling to get out of the car. The effect of Jay's very capable lips had yet to wear off. Her hands hadn't trembled like this since she'd once mistaken her Uber driver for Zac Efron. He was a dead ringer.

The restaurant sat empty and dark except for a glow coming from a back hallway.

Kate rapped her fist against the glass. This was a disaster. Jay had gone from being distant and unreadable to kissing her in the span of one dinner. And that kiss . . . it was unforgettable. She couldn't pretend like it didn't happen. The memory of his smile, his lips—softer than she'd imagined they would be—had already burrowed into the section of her heart where her favorite moments lived on forever.

After another hearty knock, Darla finally came jogging out from the back room. The woman happened to be knockout gorgeous. A few years older than Kate maybe, with jet-black hair streaked with red and cut into a stylish pixie. Her skin had that youthful glow women paid good money to achieve, but Kate had a feeling Darla didn't care that much. Her clothes were stylish but subtle, too, as demonstrated by the chic tunic she wore over black leggings and fabulous leather boots. Where did she find those in Topaz Falls anyway?

Kate shook her head. She could not get distracted by a pair of boots right now.

On her way to the door, Darla waved as though they'd known each other for years instead of two days and quickly unlatched the lock. "So glad you could make it!" She waved Kate inside. "Naomi said you couldn't come because you had other plans."

"I did." And they'd been thwarted by a shunned snowboarder who apparently was not the monster everyone wanted him to be. "But my dinner got a little out of hand and I need some advice."

"Then you're definitely in the right place." Darla linked their arms together as they walked down the back hallway. "You don't know how happy I am to see you." She leaned closer. "We were supposed to discuss *Mind-Blowing Intimacy* tonight. Can you believe it?" They paused outside an open door. "Things have really gone downhill around here since Jessa and Naomi both married."

"We can hear you," Jessa called from inside the room.

"It might be good for you to discuss a book on healthy relationships," Naomi added as Kate and Darla walked in.

The coziness of the space instantly put Kate at ease. It was set up like a living room that could've been featured in an HGTV episode. Jessa and Naomi sat on a sagging old Victorian couch while Everly occupied one of two overstuffed chairs on the other side of a rectangular coffee table that looked like it had been made from an old door. The pops of color in the bright paintings on the walls and the polka-dotted pillows had as much personality as the women in the room.

"I'm not interested in a relationship that lasts more than twenty-four hours," Darla informed Kate with a wicked smile. "I'm all for simple, uncomplicated sex."

"Hear, hear," Everly agreed.

"Does that exist?" Kate couldn't help but ask. Because in her world, even a simple kiss came with complications.

"No. It does not," Jessa insisted. "In chapter eight of *Mind-Blowing Intimacy*, it says, and I quote, 'Every act of sexual intimacy leaves its mark on the human soul. Sex does more than bring two bodies together. It also unites their hearts and spirits and intellects, bringing the two into one.' "

"Good Lord," Darla muttered. "She's got the whole damn book memorized."

"It's a very insightful book," Jessa shot back. "Even Lance thinks so. We read it together. He really enjoyed it."

"Ha!" Darla led Kate to the open chair and then wedged herself between Jessa and Naomi on the couch. "I don't think it was the reading he enjoyed. How many times did you and Lance have mind-blowing sex after reading a chapter in *Mind-Blowing Intimacy*? Hmmm?"

Jessa's face turned red. Kate didn't know a woman could blush that much. "That's not the point."

"Lance is no idiot," Everly commented, helping herself to a cookie from a platter that sat on the coffee table. "A chapter in some boring book is a small price to pay for good sex."

"What do you think?" Jessa directed the question to Kate like she'd decided to give up on Darla and Everly. "In your experience, are sex and intimacy mutually exclusive?"

Kate considered the question. Not that she had a ton of experience with either. In fact, her most recent kiss would rank right up there with the most intimate experiences of her life, and she'd only met the man yesterday. How sad was that? "It's probably different for everyone. I'm sure when you're married to the person you love the most in the world, sex feels a lot more intimate." She smiled at Darla to show she meant no offense. "Some people don't want that, but I wouldn't mind having it someday."

"Oh, speaking of sex...how was your dinner?" Naomi asked with an interested smirk.

"Dinner? Who'd you have dinner with?" Everly demanded.

"She made dinner for J.J. Alexander tonight," Naomi informed the room. An echo of girlish excitement went around.

"I heard he was back in town," Darla murmured. "Or at least back near town. Working at the resort. How the hell did you score dinner with him?"

"It's a long story." And it didn't show Kate in the best light. "I'm watching Bella for him while he's working on the mountain."

"Smart move," Jessa said with admiration. "The way to every man's heart is through his dog."

"So did you two enjoy more than dinner?" Darla scooted to the edge of the couch as if the suspense were killing her.

"No." A sweltering blush contradicted her. *Yes, yes, yes.* "Well, kind of. He kissed me."

More cheering ensued, but she muted it with a shake of her head. "It's not good."

"The kiss wasn't good?" Everly asked.

"The kiss was good." So tender and meaningful. Something told her J.J. didn't kiss just anyone. She let her head fall back to the cushion with a sigh. "But I was only having dinner with him so I could get an interview. Except he doesn't know that yet. I was too afraid to tell him I worked for *Adrenaline Junkie*. I wanted to get to know him first. So I wouldn't scare him off…"

"Sounds to me like you got to know him." Darla elbowed Jessa and Naomi with an amused smile.

"So what's he like?" Everly reached over and handed Kate a cookie.

She ate the chocolate chip goodness, still trying to process the last two hours of her life. "He's…different than I thought." She wasn't expecting a snowboarder to have so much depth. Sure that was a stereotype, but in her experience, stereotypes existed for a reason. "And he's definitely a different person than the media made him out to be." Kinder. More thoughtful.

"The media made him look like a bona fide asshole," Darla said.

"Only he's not." Kate was pretty sure her eyes had gotten all dreamy and pathetic but it couldn't be helped. "He's actually a really good person." A little surly maybe, but he'd been through a lot.

"Oh boy," Naomi muttered. "I've seen that look before."

"She's smitten," Jessa confirmed.

Smitten? Despite her current predicament, Kate laughed. She definitely wasn't in L.A. anymore. "I like him," she admitted. "But I also have to get this story."

Her four new friends traded around perplexed glances.

"All right," Darla finally said. "Here's what you should do. Spend more time with him so he'll know you're not a threat."

"But don't wait too long to tell him the truth," Everly added. "And when you do tell him, make sure he knows you have his best interests in mind. That you want to help him repair his image in the media."

"That sounds like a good plan." She had a whole week here, so she could spend a couple more days with Bella. Maybe hang out with J.J. too—on the condition that there was no more kissing until he knew the truth.

* * *

"What do you think, Bella?"

Jaden rearranged the orange gerbera daisies in a vase he'd found stashed in the pantry. The flowers reminded him of Kate. Bright and cheerful, but delicate too. They definitely made a statement on the patio table, much like her. She'd left an impression on him last night with that dinner, and now he intended to do the same by making her breakfast.

The dog took a curious lap around the table, her neck stretching and nose sniffing at the very edge.

"Sorry, pooch. The bacon's for the humans." Jaden pushed the platter of meat and pancakes farther to the center so they'd stay out of reach. After spending so much of her life hungry, Bella had a tendency to get wild about food. "But I promise you all of the leftovers if you behave."

Could he behave? That was the real question. Last night's kiss had stoked something he hadn't experienced in months. Emotion. It'd shocked him to feel something when Kate had looked at him all unsure and shy from across the fire. The flames had made her face lovely and soft. Then, when he'd gotten so close to her in the kitchen, desire had surged hot and fast, triggering him to act before he could think it through.

Sometimes it was good not to think. He hadn't thought about Kipp or the accident the whole evening. It'd been nice to focus on someone else's problems for a change.

After that, though, he couldn't stay away from her. Kissing her had roughed him up on the inside, chipping away at layers of detachment he'd built until his heart felt raw and exposed and alive again. This morning, he'd woken with a craving for more. Which is why he'd hauled his ass out of bed early enough to make a grocery run so he could surprise her the way she'd surprised him.

The doorbell rang at 7:59. Right on schedule. Bella went crazy, leaping and scratching at the door as though she somehow already knew her new best friend was there to play. "Easy, girl." He gently nudged her out of the way and opened the door.

Kate didn't look as cheerful this morning, but she didn't have to smile to hold his attention. The fireworks between them last night had already changed the way he saw her. She wasn't just an attractive woman anymore. She was downright arousing, especially in a blue hiking skirt that hit midthigh and her white tank top. She'd left her black hair down, wavy and soft around her tanned shoulders. Jaden couldn't look away. Yeah, he was at full attention. "Morning," he finally managed.

"Hi." Her indifferent tone and focus on Bella instead of

him dismissed his greeting. "Are you ready for a fun day, Bella? Come on, girl. Let's go."

The dog started for the door.

"Sit, Bella," Jaden commanded in his *I mean business* voice. She did, but she definitely whined about it. "You can't go yet," he said to Kate. "I made you breakfast."

The woman glared at him the same way she had last night when he'd told her it had been eight years since he'd eaten mashed potatoes. "Is it Honey Nut Cheerios?"

Oh yeah, he'd surprised her. "It's pancakes, actually. And bacon. Fruit." That used to be Gram's special Sunday morning breakfast on the ranch. He hadn't made it since she'd moved into assisted living, but what could he say? This was a special occasion. "Isn't that what normal people have for breakfast?"

Her lips tightened as though she was trying a little too hard to look annoyed. If you asked him, she looked spooked. "I wasn't aware you were normal."

He wasn't. Or at least he hadn't felt normal until she'd pressed her body against his last night. "Have breakfast with me, and I'll show you how normal I am." She was the one who'd made him feel normal, who'd given him the chance to be someone other than J.J. Alexander, the Snowboarding Cowboy.

Kate glanced back at her car. "I don't think I can stay. I have a lot planned for Bella today, so we should probably get going."

"You have a lot planned for my dog?" he asked, making sure his skepticism didn't go over her head. "Like what?"

"Well...you know..." How could he know when she didn't even seem to know? "I'm bringing her to the inn to meet Bogart," Kate said, looking satisfied with herself. "That's Naomi's dog. He's really sweet."

Jaden resisted the urge to smile. "Do you have reservations to meet Bogart?"

"Um...not exactly, but I don't know Naomi's schedule." Kate's cheeks were pinker than they had been when he'd first opened the door. That was good, right? She didn't seem to be hesitating because she couldn't stand him. She just seemed to get nervous around him.

He opened the door wider. "All the food is made. Table is set." He'd even picked out flowers.

"Okay. Fine." She stalked past him and followed Bella to the kitchen. "I'll have breakfast with you."

"Perfect. Everything's out on the deck." Jaden led the way and carefully gauged her reaction as she stepped through the door.

Kate's dark eyes widened when she saw the flowers on the table, but she didn't mention them.

They each took the same seat they'd sat in last night. The ambiance was different, though. Bright and warm and relaxed. Actually, scratch that. Kate's bare shoulders looked tense.

"Nothing like starting the day off with a good breakfast." Jaden took the liberty of serving her pancakes and syrup, along with a helping of fruit and a few slices of bacon before he filled his own plate. She didn't answer, but silence with Kate didn't press into him like it did with some people. It was...easy.

Bella wriggle-crawled her way underneath the very center of the table as though she couldn't decide who would be most likely to drop her a crumb.

Kate took a bite of the food and chewed slowly. "Wow." Her face perked up. "These pancakes are incredible."

"Mmm-hmmm." He tried one too. They were light and airy, exactly the way he remembered. "It's my grandma's recipe. She always whipped the egg whites forever. Then she would carefully fold them into the batter."

"They're so fluffy." Kate seemed fascinated, inspecting them as she cut another bite.

"So this breakfast isn't as painful as you thought." He'd intended the words to make a point, and Kate seemed to take it in stride.

"No. It's not painful at all." The first hints of a smile relaxed her face. "The food isn't half bad. Way better than Honey Nut Cheerios. I'm glad I stayed."

Jaden set down his fork and held her gaze. "Only for the food?" Because he wasn't enjoying the pancakes as much as he was enjoying sitting across from her, sharing breakfast with someone.

"Not only because of the food," she murmured with an unsure glance. "But...my life is a little complicated right now."

Join the club. He seemed to have secured a lifelong membership. "So is mine. That's why it's nice to have something uncomplicated. Dinner. Breakfast." He needed that. Something normal. Another presence in his world. Conversation. He hadn't realized how much he needed it until last night. For some reason, he found it so easy to be honest with Kate. "I like you. Spending time with you is...simple. And nothing in my life has been simple for a long time."

"I like you too." Kate's smile grew, finally resembling that quirk of her lips she'd shown off when he'd kissed her last night.

"So let's not complicate it," he suggested. "Let's have dinner while you're in town. And breakfast. Maybe lunch once in a while. Whatever works."

"That sounds perfect." She poured herself a glass of orange juice. "So what's complicating your life right now?"

A familiar tension crowded his gut. "Let's make a pact not to talk about our complications."

Kate tilted her head as she studied him. "What are we going to talk about, then?"

"Um..." Talking had never been one of his talents. "Our families?" That would be a short conversation on his part. "Funny stories from when we were growing up?" He had plenty of those. "But why don't we start with our most embarrassing moments?" That should be good for a laugh, keep things light.

Kate dropped her head, suddenly extremely interested in her food again. "Um...no thank you."

"Ohhh...you must have a good one."

"I hardly know you." She hastily helped herself to more pancakes, drowning them in syrup. "Why would I tell you my most embarrassing moments?"

"I think you're being dramatic," he teased. "I bet your most embarrassing moment isn't even embarrassing." She'd probably gotten toilet paper stuck to her shoe or something lame like that.

"Oh, it went way past embarrassing," she assured him. "It was humiliating."

"Now I have to know." Jaden refilled his mug of coffee from the pitcher he'd brought out. Though for once he didn't feel like he needed it. He'd slept better last night than he had in months. "I swear I won't tell anyone else."

"Fine." She left a dramatic pause. "My sophomore year of high school, I asked a boy to homecoming."

"That doesn't sound so bad."

Kate narrowed her eyes. "My friends convinced me I should decorate his car. So I skipped our last class and spent an hour covering his beloved Mustang in flowers and streamers and balloons and cute little signs."

"Uh-oh." He had a feeling he knew where this was going.

"Yeah." She crossed her arms and leaned back. "So when the bell rang, the entire school walked out to the parking lot and there I was, sitting on the hood of Tommy's car with a rose in my mouth and this huge, obnoxious, glittery sign asking him to go to the dance with me."

A laugh was brewing. He could feel it starting way down deep. Jaden held his breath so it wouldn't come out.

"When the guy came out and saw me," she continued, "he was horrified. He kept yelling about his car. How could I touch his damn car?"

"Ouch." *Don't laugh. Whatever you do, don't laugh.* It was hard, though, considering she told the story in a way that made him picture every detail.

"He said no, by the way. He said he wouldn't even go to Taco Bell with me."

That did it. Jaden could no longer hold back. But at least she laughed too. "See? I told you it was humiliating. Now you have to make me feel better about myself and tell me yours."

"Right. A promise is a promise." Even though his didn't even compare to the scene she'd just detailed for him. "My most embarrassing moment was in high school too." Wasn't everyone's? "I was in English class screwing around, being loud and obnoxious, and the teacher made me get up to apologize to the whole class."

"I have a hard time seeing you as loud and obnoxious."

"Oh, trust me." Before a couple of months ago, he'd been a lot more outgoing. He'd always preferred to think of it as extroverted and friendly rather than obnoxious. "Anyway, in front of the whole class, Miss Tolbert said, 'You come up to the front of the room right now and tell the class you're sexy. I mean sorry!'" He mimicked the old woman's voice for effect.

Kate did not look amused. "That's it? You're telling me that the most embarrassing moment of your life has to do with you being hot?"

Yeah, he had a feeling she wouldn't be impressed. "Miss Tolbert was a hundred years old. And that's all anyone could talk about for weeks. You should've heard the rumors that went around about us."

"I'm sorry." She shook her head, her sleek black hair swooshing around her shoulders. "That doesn't count as an embarrassing moment."

"Why not?"

"Because it probably made you a legend in your school," she grumbled. "It sounds to me like that was Miss Tolbert's most embarrassing moment, not yours."

Jaden laughed. "I never thought of it that way." But the woman had a point. "If it makes you feel better, I would've gone to homecoming with you."

"Right." She made a show of rolling her eyes. "Sure."

"Why don't you believe me?" Seriously. He would've killed to go to homecoming with someone as intriguing as Kate Livingston.

"You were this big-time snowboarder jock, and I was a newspaper nerd." She huffed. "I highly doubt you would've gone to homecoming with me."

"Maybe I would've surprised you," he said, eyeing her lips. The same way he'd surprised her last night...

"You've definitely accomplished that, Jay." Kate stared into his eyes with a slow smile. "I think it's fair to say I've never been more surprised by someone in my life."

CHAPTER SEVEN

Today's the day, Bella." Kate uttered a heart-cleansing sigh and gazed at the dog, who sat with her ears perked in rapt attention in the passenger seat of the borrowed Subaru. They'd been sitting in Jay's driveway for ten minutes, but Kate hadn't been able to get out and face the man.

"I have to tell him." Time was running out. Over the last week, Gregor had called and texted roughly twenty times, asking how the story was going, checking in to see if she'd finished a draft yet. She'd been putting him off, telling him that Jay had been extra busy so she hadn't collected all the facts yet. Which hadn't been a complete lie. Jay had been extra busy this week. She'd simply neglected to tell Gregor that Jay had been busy with her.

Since he'd made her breakfast that morning, they'd settled into something of a routine. She would arrive at the house around eight to pick up Bella, and Jay would make her breakfast before she and the dog went about their day. At five, she'd bring Bella back to the house and either pick up dinner on the way or cook something on the grill. They'd sit out on the back deck under the stars, wrapped in blankets while the fire flickered between them, and entertain each other with stories late into the night. He hadn't told her anything about the accident yet, but that was okay because there was so much more to him.

He'd told her about being raised by his grandma, who took over the ranch when her husband died in his early forties, about how she was a better shot than any of the men in the county, about how he hadn't heard from his dad since his sixth birthday, and how his mom moved around the country in an old Airstream trailer, sometimes sending him postcards from wherever she happened to be living at the moment.

Kate had told Jaden things too. She'd told him about the time she'd done an undercover investigation on the recycling efforts at her middle school. It turned out they weren't recycling at all. At the end of the day, everything from the recycling bin got dumped into the garbage, and she'd exposed their deception in the center spread of their extracurricular newspaper.

She'd told him about how, when she'd declared writing as her major in college, her parents, along with her brother and sister, had staged an intervention dinner where they took turns telling her all of the reasons she would fail to find a career. Then she'd told him how her family had been all too happy to reiterate those reasons, along with a hearty round of *I told you so*, when she couldn't find a job.

Those were the real Kate Livingston stories. The ones that hid behind the happy smile. The ones that made her who she was. She couldn't remember the last time she'd shared them with anyone else.

By day three, breakfast had turned into one big flirt fest, with Jaden teasing her and touching her a lot, placing his hand on the small of her back or brushing her hair over her shoulder when she pretended to be offended by one of his jokes. Dinner had turned into rushing through the food part to get to the make-out portion of the evening, where they'd lie entwined on the couch, kissing with an intensity that seemed to grow stronger every day.

"God, how am I going to tell him?" It would ruin the alternate reality they'd created together. With him, she suspected, escaping from horrible memories about the accident, and her finally allowed to simply be Kate. Not a screwup in her family's eyes or an outdoorsy badass in her colleagues' eyes. It had been strange at first, being herself, but she'd started to love the feeling.

Bella yawned with a squeak and curled up in the seat as if she figured they'd be there awhile. Oh, how Kate wished they could be, that she could put this off a little bit long—

The front door of the house opened, and Jay stepped out, looking like an enticing cross between a cowboy and a mountain man in his boots, jeans, and a threadbare gray T-shirt. Even from this distance, his smile summoned hers as he slowly walked to the car.

"Hi," Kate called through the open window. It sounded more like a dreamy sigh than a greeting. Heart thudding in her throat, she scrambled to let Bella out before climbing out of the car herself.

"Didn't realize you were already here." Jaden knelt to pet Bella, who was whining and pawing at his legs like she hadn't seen him for a month.

Kate tried to keep her smile intact. "Just pulled up a minute ago." Now that was a lie.

"Perfect." The man stood, and she couldn't believe how different he looked than he had the first day she'd met him. His face had relaxed, and his lips loosened into a smile whenever he saw her. Even his posture seemed stronger, taller, and less reserved.

"I want to take you somewhere." Jaden eased an arm around her waist and brushed a kiss along her temple. "I've got dinner packed," he whispered in her ear.

Even with regret and guilt swelling through her, she couldn't resist leaning into his touch, savoring it. Once he found out about her story assignment, he might never touch her again. "Maybe we should eat here. So we can talk." She couldn't tell him the truth in public. The setting for this conversation had to be perfect. They had to be alone.

"We can talk where I'm taking you." Jaden released her and strode up the driveway. "It's kind of a hike, so we'll take the Jeep." He punched in the garage code. Then he walked back to her and took her hand, guiding her to the passenger side and opening the door for her.

He did things like that all the time. Small gestures like moving aside to let her go first through a doorway or always leaving the last bite of dessert for her. In the evenings, he'd walk over and slip her sweatshirt on her shoulders when he could tell she'd gotten cold. Kate closed her eyes as Jaden let Bella into the backseat and then strode to the driver's side and climbed in.

How was she going to do this? She'd rehearsed the words a hundred times. Before she'd pull up to his house every morning, she would say them again. But then he would greet her and kiss her and he was so happy that she didn't want to ruin it. She didn't want it to end.

"You okay?" he asked, backing the Jeep down the driveway.

"Fine," she murmured, close to tears. "Just a little headache." Heartache.

"Here." He reached back into a small cooler and pulled

out an ice-cold water bottle. "Water usually helps. It's easy to get dehydrated at this altitude."

"Thanks." Her throat felt raw. She opened the water bottle and took a long sip. She had no idea where they were going, only that it was up. Up the street, then up past the resort, and then up higher still on some lonely dirt road that cut through the wide spaces between trees that Kate assumed were ski runs. Patches of snow still dotted the mountainside, but there was grass too—new and green. Luckily, they didn't need to talk. With the Jeep so open on top, wind whistled between them, which meant Kate didn't have to force the words that churned in her stomach. He wouldn't have heard them anyway.

While the Jeep bumped along, Jaden brought his hand over to rest on her thigh. "Feeling better?"

Nodding, Kate closed her eyes and breathed in the cooling air. She loved the feel of his hand on her, warming her, reassuring her.

After one more switchback, he parked the Jeep, and she raised her head. They were above the trees. There was more snow up here, but she hardly cared about the temperature. The view to her right consumed her. It was endless. A blue-hazed vista of snowcapped peaks hovering above a watercolor of reddish cliffs and green, tree-studded mountainsides that came together in long, lush valleys. There were little round lakes so far off in the distance that they looked like puddles. "This is incredible," she breathed.

"One of the reasons I loved boarding so much." Jaden gave her thigh a squeeze and then got out of the Jeep. "That view never gets old."

He let Bella out and started to rummage through things in the back of the Jeep before meeting her on the passenger side. "It's colder up here," he said, helping her put on a fleece jacket. It smelled like him—like male spice. The same scent that always filled her senses when they were kissing.

Taking her hand, Jaden led her a few steps away from the Jeep, where a large snowfield still smothered the grass. The view once again stretched out in front of them, a painting she wanted to jump into.

"This is the snowfield where I started out," Jaden said. "My buddies and I would hike up here, out of bounds, and we'd board as long as we could. All the way through June some years."

She threaded her fingers through his, holding on to his hand tighter. "You never got caught?"

"Nah. They didn't keep a close eye on things around here during the summer months." He couldn't seem to look away from the snow. "Even as a kid, I loved it. Being out here made me feel so free."

"I bet you miss it," Kate said quietly. She could see it in the sad slump of his shoulders, hear it in the shaky tenor of his voice.

"I almost killed someone." He paused and swallowed hard like the words had the power to strangle him. "A few months ago. At the Olympics." Jaden faced her as though he wanted her to see the pain on his face. "I was trying to take the lead, and I lost control. Plowed right into my rival and took him out."

Kate looked up into his eyes, and she couldn't lie to him anymore. "I know."

"You do?" He dropped her hand and stepped back. The sudden uncertainty in his glare cut off the rest of her words. She couldn't tell him about the article. Not yet. "I kind of put it together. Jay—J.J. You're a snowboarder. You've been in an accident..." He had to realize that she would've heard about it. Everyone had heard about it.

"You never said anything." His expression was guarded, the same way it had been when she'd met him on the street.

Kate eased closer to him, looking intently into his eyes so he would remember she wasn't a threat. "You didn't bring it up, so I figured you didn't want to talk about it."

"I haven't." The rigidity in his shoulders seemed to give way. "Not with anyone. The days after were so intense. With the media, and surgery to reset my arm." He turned back to the snowfield with a blank stare. "Then they told me Kipp had a spinal cord injury. That he wouldn't walk again. And I couldn't function. I couldn't sleep or eat. I had nightmares constantly. Everyone was saying I'd done it on purpose..."

"Of course you didn't do it on purpose." She turned him back to her. God, he was so tormented by it. She couldn't stand seeing him that way, so lost. "Tragedies just happen sometimes. You didn't cause it. You didn't bring it on him or yourself." She took his cheeks in her hands and guided his face to hers. "You are a good person, Jaden Alexander. You didn't deserve this. You didn't deserve to be crucified in the media." But she could change things. She could tell his side of the story. "You need to stop hiding and let people see who you really are. I can help. I can write—"

"First I need to get back on my board," he interrupted, gazing at the snowfield again. "That's why I brought you here. I can't do it alone."

Kate studied him. That was his total focus. Getting back on the board. And yes, he did need that. So talking about the article could wait. "How can I help?" she asked. "You want me to cheer you on? Take a video so you can remember this moment?"

"No." For the first time, he looked amused. "I want you to board with me."

"I'm sorry, what?" This time Kate was the one who backed away. "As in *snow*board with you?" As in strap a piece of wood or whatever the hell it was made out of to her feet and go racing down a freezing cold snowfield?

Jaden's smile answered the question. That was exactly what he wanted her to do. Which proved he was crazy. The man was nuttier than a five-pound fruitcake. "I can't snowboard," she informed him. "I don't even *have* a snowboard." So there.

"I grabbed one from the rental shop, along with some boots that I think should fit you fine."

Damn his thoughtfulness. "I've never been snowboarding." She eased a few more feet of distance between them. "This might come as a shock, but I'm actually not outdoorsy. At all."

"I know." He approached her, taking her forearms in his hands, and dear Lord his touch wrecked her.

"You do?" she almost whispered. Here she thought she'd played her part of the outdoorsy chick pretty damn well over the last week.

"I kind of put it together." One corner of his delicious mouth lifted higher than the other. "That's one reason you were so eager to help out with Bella, right? Because you didn't want to go back out on the trail to finish your mysterious trek?"

"I hate camping," she confessed. "I hate the bugs and the dirt and peeing in the woods. Oh, and I hate the stupid tents that suck at being waterproof."

Jaden laughed. "I figured." He pulled her close, locking his hands at the small of her back. "But I don't think you'll hate snowboarding."

"I guess we'll find out." For him, she'd give it a try. She'd do pretty much anything to make him happy, to hear him laugh again. Even if it involved adrenaline.

* * *

"I don't know about this." Kate reached for Jaden's arm and peered down at the snow that stretched out below them.

"I don't know about this either," he admitted. What had appeared to be a pristine, sparkling field of snow suddenly looked a lot more like an icy death trap. Now he knew what could happen. He knew he had no control out here. Life could change in seconds if he made one wrong move or caught an edge.

But he also knew that things could be restored, that there could be healing, if he found the courage to seek it out. Kate had reminded him of that. She'd proven there could be light at the end of his tunnel of despair, but you had to work for it. So here he was, slowly inching toward that light, sweating and sick to his stomach.

He'd purposely chosen this spot because it wasn't as steep as some of the other areas he used to frequent, which meant it should be an easy place for Kate to learn. But he couldn't seem to move his legs. Might as well be honest with her. "I'm not sure I can do this." Stay standing. Glide over the snow the way he used to without a thought. Even just the feel of the frozen ground beneath him was enough to trigger the memories of kneeling at Kipp's side, seeing him unresponsive…

Grunting in her cute, soft way, Kate inched her snowboard toward him until she was close enough to squeeze his hands. "You can. Let's do it together." A brave willingness came out in her smile, which meant he couldn't wimp out now. He'd told her everything, and she still looked at him the same way. The ugliness of his story didn't shock her, or overwhelm her, or even make her question his integrity. He'd never been given a greater gift.

"Okay." Jaden locked his weak knees and then held her steady with an arm around her waist. It was awkward with both of them on their boards, inverted sideways on the mountain, but she would need his help.

"First, you want to find your balance." He assumed the position so she could see—weight centered, knees soft.

She emulated his posture. "Like this?"

Taking her hips in his hands, he set her back slightly. "Perfect. How does it feel?"

"Awkward." Her body wobbled. "I don't like having my feet strapped into something."

"You'll get the feel for it." And he would do his best to keep her upright. Maybe that would distract him from the sudden surge in his blood pressure. "Make sure to keep your center of gravity low, then put more weight onto your downhill leg." He let go of her and showed her what he meant, sliding down only a foot so he could catch her or break her fall if he had to.

"Whoa..." Kate eased her weight onto the downhill leg, arms flailing. Somehow, she caught herself and balanced, inching the board down to where he stood.

"You're a natural." He couldn't resist touching her, taking her hands and seeing the color rise to her face.

She looked up at him from under those long eyelashes. "I don't know about that, but this isn't as terrible as I thought it'd be."

"It's not as terrible as I thought it would be either." She kept his mind off the fears. "I meant getting back on a board isn't as terrible," he clarified. "Not being here with you." He eyed her mouth, trying to decide how hard it would be to kiss her when they were both standing on snowboards. "I like being here with you."

She smiled softly at him, still holding on to his hands.

"Thank you for letting me be here. For trusting me." The last words wobbled out, full of emotion.

Screw keeping our balance. He leaned over and kissed her, securing one hand on her forearm to keep her upright and stroking her cheek with the other.

When he pulled back, Kate seemed to be breathing harder, though they hadn't actually gone anywhere.

"So we have to go all the way down to the end?" She moved her gaze down the slope.

It was either that or ditch the boards and hike back to the top. "If you're up for it."

"I guess," she muttered, but she also smiled.

"We'll take it slow." He released her and eased into the board again, sliding it slowly down the hill in a path she could follow.

Kate started out behind him, but her balance was off.

"Low center of gravity," he called.

"I don't know how!" She started to panic, body lurching, her arms flailing, the board going vertical. She picked up speed, coming straight for him.

Uh-oh...

Just before she plowed into him, he opened his arms, catching her against his chest. The momentum knocked them both backward, and Kate landed on top of him.

Bella barked and ran circles around them, as though she wanted in on the game.

Jaden grinned at Kate. "At least I broke your fall."

"Oh my God, you should've seen your face." She shook with laughter, which made him laugh too. It felt good to laugh. Felt good to be out here on the mountain, lying in the snow, feeling this woman against him. There was nothing quite like feeling Kate against him.

When they would lie on the couch after dinner in the

evenings, their legs tangled as they kissed and touched and murmured about how enjoyable it all was, he felt normal and whole. Part of something again. The last time she'd pulled away and said she'd better get going, it almost killed him, but he hadn't wanted to push her. He needed her to want him as much as he wanted her.

Did she? Did that growing hunger gnaw at her the way it did him?

He closed his arms around her. "Will you stay with me tonight? I don't want you to leave."

She propped her chin up on her fist. "That depends... how comfortable is your bed?" She was teasing him again. And damn he loved it.

"The bed is okay. But you should see the tub in the master bathroom."

"Big enough for two?"

"I'd hope so. It takes up half the bathroom." When he first saw it, he'd thought it was a ridiculous waste of space, but now he could see the benefits of having a huge tub.

"Perfect." Kate moved her face closer to his, her eyes full of everything he needed in his life—humor and fun and depth too. She seemed to see so much in him. The good. What he thought had been lost.

"I'd love to stay," she murmured. "I'll need a good hot soak after this little adventure."

"In that case, let's cut this run short and hike back up." He snuck his hand into her fleece coat and felt his way up her chest.

She rolled her eyes in mock annoyance, but her heart beat faster under his palm. "We just got here."

"Snowboarding is overrated." Especially compared to sex.

She wriggled away and maneuvered to a sitting position. "We can head back soon. But first I want to see you ride all the way down there." She pointed to where the snow tapered off into wet, soggy grass. "You need to finish this run, Jaden."

He loved the sound of his real name on her lips. "What about you?"

"I'll watch. That's how I learn best anyway." She took his face in her hands and pressed her lips to his, brushing them softly, waking him once again. "Go. Alone. Do what you came here to do." She obviously understood how much he needed this, to rediscover peace out here.

He reluctantly stood, surprised to find the dread was gone. There was nothing but anticipation. Starting out slowly, he eased his weight onto his downhill foot, cutting across the mountain before leaning into a turn. Slushy snow sprayed all the way up to his face, cold and familiar. He let himself pick up speed, taking the turns quicker, carving a wavy line into the snow. Wind sailed across his face, stinging his nose the way it always did when he really cut loose and flew.

"Woohoo!" Kate cheered behind him, clapping and whistling. He crouched lower, using the momentum and speed to cut and jump, feeling lighter than he had in three dark months.

CHAPTER EIGHT

They didn't even make it inside the house before Jaden started to kiss her. He moved swiftly around the Jeep and opened her door, taking her hand.

The captivated, aroused look on his face heated Kate all the way to her core.

Seeing him on that mountain—facing whatever demons had chased him through the last few months—had done something to her. She no longer cared about the article. Or Gregor. Or her stupid job as a senior editor. She wanted Jaden. All of him.

Bella scooted out of the Jeep after Kate, barking as though she didn't understand what was happening.

Jaden seemed to ignore the dog. His eyes were intense on Kate's, speaking all sorts of hot, scandalous things without saying a word. He pinned her against the side of the Jeep, kissing her lips, sweeping his tongue through her mouth. Then he pulled back, stealing a glance at her, smiling that private, sexy smile.

Bella wedged herself between their legs and whined.

"It's okay, pup." He reassured her with a quick scratch behind the ears before Kate directed his gaze back to hers by threading her fingers into his hair and holding his face in place so they could take the kiss deeper. So much deeper. His lips were fused to hers with a heat that set her skin ablaze and made her body burn for him. "Inside," she managed to gasp. "Take me inside."

He hoisted her into his arms, and she wrapped her legs tightly around his waist as he carried her through the garage door. Kate was so busy kissing him that she caught only a glimpse of poor Bella tagging along behind them.

Jaden brought her through the kitchen and then the living room, all the way to the master bedroom, kissing her mouth with a recklessness she happily matched.

He paused near the bed. "We forgot all about the dinner I packed."

"Later," Kate gasped. "We can have dinner in bed."

"I love that idea." He carried her across the room and set her feet on the floor just inside the bathroom.

He hadn't been exaggerating. The bathtub in the master suite was enormous. A freestanding rectangle that was tucked into a marble-tiled alcove in front of a large picture window that looked out on the mountain. It was straight out of a fantasy—gleaming white porcelain with a crystal chandelier dangling overhead.

"Holy mother," Kate murmured, staring at the beauty over Jaden's shoulder.

He held her close. "Are you using me for my bathtub?"

"Yes," she said with fabricated certainty. Then she worked her hands up his chest underneath his T-shirt and leaned into him, running her tongue along his neck until she'd reached his ear. "Is that a problem?"

"Nope." He jumped into action, plugging the drain and

turning on the water, holding his hand under the faucet to test the temperature.

The running water seemed to spook the dog. Bella scampered out of the bathroom and plopped herself on a cushy pillow next to the king-sized bed. Obviously the dog was not a fan of baths.

Jaden left the water running and came at Kate again, lifting her back into his arms. “It feels so good to hold you,” he whispered against her shoulder. He carried her to the king-sized bed and set her on the very edge, standing close enough that she could raise his T-shirt and kiss his tight abs.

His breath hitched each time she pressed her lips to his skin. As she tasted him, his hands smoothed down her hair. He stepped back and took her right foot in his hands, removing the boot, and then her sock, watching her eyes the whole time. He did the same with her other foot, caressing her toes with his thumb until she lay back on the bed, moaning like she was already halfway to an orgasm. “Wow. You’re amazing.”

“Are you using me for my massage skills?” he asked, running a single finger down the length of her foot.

“Yes,” she whispered. She loved the way he touched her. His hands were so strong, knowing and perceiving, taking their cues from the sounds she made, the movements of her body.

Jaden grinned. “Use away.” He inched closer and caught the waist of her yoga pants in his fingers, tugging them down her hips, efficiently taking her lace underwear with them. Moving even closer to the mattress, he edged his body in between her legs and leaned over to unzip the coat she was still wearing. He worked slowly, watching her face between long gazes down her body like he didn’t want to miss one detail.

Gently, he pulled one of her arms out of the coat and then the other, shoving her jacket aside before securing his hands to her waist under her T-shirt. "You're so beautiful, Kate. Such a good person." The words were almost solemn, as though he didn't think he deserved this, deserved her. But he didn't know.

She cupped her hands on his shoulders, bringing him down to lie over her. "You're a good person too. Strong and thoughtful and funny." So profound in his thoughts, tender in his touch. "I've made mistakes." The biggest one lately not telling him everything the first day she'd met him.

"Mistakes can be forgiven." He slid his hands higher up her rib cage, pulling off her shirt and letting it pool behind her.

"I hope so." She drew in a long, sustaining breath as his finger traced the very edge of her lace bra.

One of his hands eased under her back and popped the clasp, and then he shifted onto his side next to her and pulled the garment away. His gaze swept over her, dark and greedy. Jaden kicked off his own boots, pushed off the bed, and pulled her up to stand with him, pressing her body to his as he maneuvered back to the bathroom. He broke away only long enough to shut off the water, and then he had her back in his arms.

Kate took over, peeling his shirt up and over his head, letting it fall to the floor next to them. She kissed his neck, his chest, sliding her tongue seductively over his skin while she unbuttoned his jeans and pushed them down, taking his boxers with them. "Actually, maybe I'm using you for your body." She stood back to admire him—all that hard, angled muscle tensed into perfection.

"Like I said…use away."

"Oh, I plan to." Keeping him in anticipation, she stepped

into the tub and slowly lowered her body to the water. Resting her head against the side, she closed her eyes. "Ohhhhh."

"That good, huh?" Jaden climbed in and settled his back against the opposite side to face her.

"I can think of something better." She shifted to her knees, opening her legs to straddle his hips.

His chest expanded with a long breath. "You've changed so much for me." He gazed steadily into her eyes. "It's been so long since I've felt anything..."

"What do you feel now?" She ground her hips into his, moving over his erection, feeling it slide against her, slick and hard.

"You." He held her tighter against him. "I feel you. Everywhere. In my head. In my heart. In my arms." He kissed her so torturously slow, as though he wanted to make it last as long as possible. But there was too much passion surging through her, too much want nudging her closer to the edge.

She stilled her body, and Jaden sat up straighter, bringing his mouth to her breasts, nipping and kissing his way from one to the other. Her head fell back, the ache for him driving deeper into her.

He traced his lips up her chest and back to her mouth while his hands caressed her back. He paused and looked into her eyes. "What are you thinking?"

"How much I want this," she murmured. "How much I want you." It had all happened fast but he'd let her see everything, his pain, his heart. Way more than any other man had ever allowed her to see.

Kate stood on weakened legs and stepped out of the tub. Within seconds, Jaden stood with her, kissing her as he slowly eased her backward toward the bathroom vanity. He lifted her and set her backside on the marble countertop and then opened a drawer and found a condom. She leaned over and kissed his shoulder while he put it on. "I need you inside of me," she whispered, tugging on his hips and arching her back to bring him in deep.

Jaden wrapped his arms around her as their bodies came together, moving in a rhythm that loosened her feeble grip on control. He angled his hips on each thrust to graze that magic spot, again and again until she was gasping and throbbing and too close to pull back. Bracing her hands against the countertop, she pushed up to meet his thrusts, welcoming the explosion of sensations as it burst forth inside of her, moaning his name so he knew he could let go too.

"God, Kate, you're amazing," he uttered between jagged breaths. Jaden held her tighter, rocking his body, reigniting her climax until he trembled with release.

He hunched over her, his forehead resting on her shoulder.

"Wow," she murmured into his hair.

He raised his head and kissed her softly, still out of breath. "Wow."

"I'm exhausted." She could hardly hold herself up anymore.

Jaden straightened and took care of the condom before wrapping a towel around his waist. Then he came back and lifted her into his arms and carried her to the bed.

They both fell to the soft mattress, lying side by side. His fingers stroked her bare arm. "I wasn't just saying that earlier. You really have changed things for me."

Kate entwined her fingers with his and brought his knuckles to her lips.

"You're the first person who's bothered to see me," he went on. "No one else cared what happened. Everyone wanted a fallen champion, a villain, so that's what they turned me into."

Kate propped herself up on her elbow and looked at him for a long, beautiful moment. "I see who you really are." And she would make sure everyone else saw it too.

* * *

Waking up had never been Jaden's favorite thing, but it had been especially brutal since February. Most mornings he would've much rather kept his eyes closed than face the world, but not when he had Kate in his bed. Since the sun had come up, he hadn't been able to stop looking at her.

He still held her in his arms, her body curved against his, their legs tangled together. Kate was asleep, her face still somehow just as stunning as it was when she smiled at him.

At some point during the night, Bella had snuck onto the bed and curled up at their feet as though she couldn't stand to be left out.

A lazy contentment weighted Jaden's body. He wanted this. Waking up with someone every morning. Feeling the silkiness of her hair over his arm, feeling her breathe so peacefully against him.

In so many ways, Kate was still a mystery. All he really knew about her was that she lived in L.A. and worked as an editor. But she didn't seem to love it there. He wouldn't either, not with the constant crowds and the paparazzi everywhere. Maybe she'd be open to moving. For the first time since the accident, he could see settling down, sharing his life with someone. And he wanted it to be here in the mountains. At least if he took the job at the resort, he'd have stability, a beautiful place to live where the community had seemed to accept him back. He would have something to offer her.

Kate stirred and stretched her arms. Her eyes opened,

and that gorgeous smile of hers bloomed when she looked at him.

"Morning, beautiful."

"Morning." She wriggled closer and wrapped herself into him.

He couldn't resist playing with her long, soft hair as she laid her head back down and closed her eyes.

"Not a morning person?" he asked innocently.

"Normally I am, but we didn't exactly get much sleep last night." She kept her eyes closed, still smiling.

"Sorry." He wasn't. Not at all.

"I'm not sorry." She peered up at him as though her eyelids were too heavy. "It was the best night I've had in a long time."

"Me too." This whole week had been some of the best moments of his life.

"What time is it?" Kate asked through a yawn.

Unfortunately, he'd been keeping an eye on the clock. He almost lied, but she could easily see for herself. "Nine."

"Nine?" She shot up to a sitting position. "Aren't you late for work?"

He sat up, too, leaning over to kiss her neck. "Yep."

"Then you should go." The words didn't have much conviction.

"Don't want to." He pulled the comforter away from her chest and admired her full breasts. "I'd rather stay in bed with you all day."

Kate lay back down and turned on her side to face him. "Aren't they doing inspections?"

"Mmm-hmmm." He couldn't seem to pry his gaze away from her body.

"Then you need to be there, mister." She pushed at him playfully. "Go. Right now. They won't be able to sign off on everything if you're not there."

Yeah, yeah, yeah. Blake had already sent him three panicked texts. Jaden scooted off the bed. "What about you?"

"Bella and I will be fine. Won't we, sweetie?" Kate reached down and petted the dog's head.

"You'll be here when I get home?"

"Yes. I have some work to do today too," she said cryptically. "But I will most definitely be here when you get home."

"As long as you promise." He pulled on clothes and his boots but couldn't resist going back to the bed where Kate still lay watching him. Her black hair was mussed and gorgeous, her eyes still sleepy and innocent.

"I'll see you later." He kissed her, and she held on to him a little longer.

"Hurry home," she murmured. "I'll make a special dinner."

"Can't wait." He forced himself to leave then, before he started taking off the clothes he'd just put on.

The drive up the mountain didn't ease the ache that had tortured him since he'd left Kate in his bed. When he made it up to the site, Blake jogged over, looking more relieved than pissed.

"Glad you're finally here," he said.

"Sorry. Got a little hung up this morning." Could've gotten more hung up if it hadn't been for his damn responsibilities.

"The inspector is taking some pictures." Blake pointed to a man who was currently sizing up the towrope. "I hope it passes."

"It'll pass." Jaden had no doubt. Every detail had been well thought out and executed perfectly. He'd made sure. That was the only thing he'd had to focus on for the last month. And now that the project was ending, he knew what he wanted to do next. "By the way, I'll take the job," he said to Blake.

The man nodded as though he wasn't surprised. "This have anything to do with the woman you borrowed the snowboard for?"

"Yeah." But it was more than that. "I want to be part of a community again too." He wanted to start over in the same place he'd started out.

CHAPTER NINE

Kate hadn't been this nervous since that fateful day when she'd asked Tommy to homecoming. She finished setting the table and stood back to admire the simplicity.

After the embarrassing car decorating debacle, she'd learned that sometimes subtlety was best, so no balloons or flowers or cheesy *Please forgive me!* signs on the table tonight. No humiliating rejection either. It would be different. She and Jaden may not have known each other long, but he seemed to get her. He would understand why she'd kept certain things from him. And once he read the article she'd written, everything would be okay.

"Right, Bella?" she asked, kneeling to give the dog some love.

Gregor had texted her early that morning to tell her he needed a draft of the article by noon or there'd be serious consequences. "Not that I care about the consequences," she explained to Bella. Writing the article had become something bigger. She'd spent the whole morning pouring her heart into her keyboard, and the words had flowed. She'd likely get fired for writing a personal exposé on what an incredible person Jaden Alexander turned out to be instead of capturing what everyone expected, but it would be worth it.

Sure, Jaden would be surprised, but she could explain everything over dinner. It was a simple meal—lasagna and a hearty Italian salad. She liked to think of this as half an apology dinner, half a makeup dinner. Or at least she hoped they would make up after they had the inevitable conversation she'd been avoiding for a week.

"He'll forgive me," she murmured.

Bella licked her cheek in agreement.

"He'll understand just like you do." Once Jaden read her words, he would see how much she cared about him.

"Hey, gorgeous."

Kate straightened and spun to the French doors. "Hi." The sight of Jaden standing there in his jeans and boots sent a wave of heat crashing through her. "You're home early." She thought she had another half hour to prepare for this.

"We finished up ahead of schedule." He took a step toward her but was blocked by Bella, who wanted his attention first. "The inspector was impressed," he said, giving his dog a pat on the head.

"Well good. That's great." God, she already sounded guilty, and she hadn't told him anything yet.

"I may have gone twenty over the speed limit all the way back here too." He wrapped her in his arms and lowered his mouth to hers. Nope. Uh-uh. She couldn't get distracted now. She had yesterday, but enough was enough. Gently, she pushed him away. "Why don't you sit down? I'll go see if the lasagna is ready."

Without giving him a chance to respond, she hurried to the kitchen, opened the oven, and peeked under the tin foil. The cheese had bubbled to perfection. *Okay. Whew.* She was really going to do this. Kate patted her pocket where she'd stashed the printout of the article. After a quick explanation of the situation, she'd hand him that right away. Before he could even ask questions. The article would make everything okay.

When she finally carted the lasagna outside, Jaden was throwing the ball for Bella.

"Dinner's ready," she called, setting the casserole on the trivet she'd put out earlier.

"Looks good." He jogged over. "But not as good as you." His gaze slowly trailed down her body. "Maybe we should eat later..."

No, no. They had to do this now. Kate scolded him with a little smirk as she sat down. "We don't want it to get cold."

"Right." Disappointment tugged at his mouth, but he sat too. "So what'd you do today—" His phone buzzed. "Sorry." He dug it out of his back pocket. "Guess I'll turn it off. I've been getting calls from weird numbers all afternoon."

Kate paused in the middle of cutting him a generous slice of lasagna. "Calls?" Her heart glitched. Coincidence. It had to be a coincidence, right? She'd sent Gregor the article at noon, just for his opinion, but it wouldn't go to print for a few more weeks...

"Now I got a text." Jaden was squinting at his phone. "'What's your response to the *Adrenaline Junkie* article?'" he read. He looked up at Kate. "I had no idea *Adrenaline Junkie* was doing an article."

Oh no. No, no, no. Kate couldn't seem to move. Her body had frozen to the chair. Instead of beating, her heart was zapping in her chest. "Oh God."

"I know." Jaden rolled his eyes. "They've left me alone for a long time. Why are they all of a sudden interested again?"

Tears flooded her vision as she stared at him wide-eyed.

"I'm sorry. Jaden, I'm so sorry." Regret burned through her, thawing the shock, letting her move. She got out her phone and went to *Adrenaline Junkie*'s website. Sure enough, her article had been posted on the blog, and it already had 14,253 shares on social media.

When she looked up, he was staring at her. "Why?" His voice hollowed as though he was afraid to know. "Why are you sorry?"

"I wanted to help." She dug the folded papers out of her pocket. "To tell your side of the story."

"Wait." His eyes narrowed into that distrustful glare she recognized from before. Before he knew her. Before he'd kissed her. Before they'd made love. "You sent them an article about me?"

"No." *Don't cry.* She couldn't let herself cry. "I work for them. I'm a senior editor there."

"What the fuck?" He pushed away from the table and stood. His eyes had hardened like he didn't want her to see the pain behind his anger.

Kate stood too. "I printed out the article so you could read it. I was going to show you tonight. I had no idea they'd post it today. It wasn't supposed to go to print for a couple of weeks." As if that made any of this better.

Hand trembling, she handed him the papers, but he ripped them into pieces and tossed them into the wind. "I can't believe this. You played me. You never told me you worked for *Adrenaline Junkie*."

"I was afraid to." She eased a few steps closer to him, but he backed away. "I knew you wouldn't even talk to me if I told you where I worked."

Jaden shook his head. Closed his eyes. When he opened them, the anger had been replaced with indifference. "Go. Get out."

"Wait. No." He hadn't even read the article yet...

"You got what you wanted out of me." His jaw went rigid. "Now you can go."

"I'm not like that." He knew her. He knew the real Kate Livingston almost better than anyone else. "I don't use sex to get stories." She inhaled, calming the desperation in her voice. "I really feel something for you, Jaden. And I think you feel something for me too."

"I don't." His tone was as dull as his eyes. "I feel nothing for you."

The apathy in his gaze tempted her to look away, but she refused to give in. "Nothing? Really? Because you said all that stuff. About me changing things for you...about wanting to trust someone again."

"And you proved I can't trust anyone."

No. She'd proved that he could get back on his board. That he could come out of hiding. That he could feel something again. He just needed to remember that connection they'd built. "I'm sorry I didn't tell you about *Adrenaline Junkie*. I should have. But spending time with you wasn't only about the story for me."

He studied her for a minute, as though trying to judge her sincerity. "Why did you offer to watch my dog?" he finally asked. "Did you know who I was when we met on the street that day?"

Before she even answered, she knew she would lose him. But she couldn't lie. "Yes."

"And you saw an opportunity to use my trauma to your advantage."

"No," she whispered. "I didn't know..." How deeply he'd been wounded by all of it. How it haunted him so much. "I never meant to hurt you. I only wanted to help. If you would just read the article—"

"You're the fakest person I've ever met." Anger simmered beneath the words. "You're worse than the reporters who ambushed me on the streets." Jaden turned and strode down the deck stairs, heading for a trail worn into the tall grass at the edge of the forest. "Bella, come." The dog looked at Kate and whined.

"Come, Bella," he commanded again.

Head down, the dog trotted across the yard to follow him.

Kate wanted to follow him, to force him to read what she'd written about him. She'd put her heart into that article. But it was too late. She'd lost him.

Before Jaden disappeared into the trees, he glanced at her over his shoulder once more. "You need to be gone when we get back."

* * *

If Kate had learned one thing about the women of Topaz Falls, it was that they were always prepared.

When she pulled up at Everly's adorable café on the outskirts of town, Jessa, Naomi, Darla, and Everly were all there to greet her. They ushered her into the old converted farmhouse where they'd already claimed a booth, and they were armed with enough comfort food to feed a whole cast of brokenhearted rejects from *The Bachelor*.

"We've got chocolate and scones and muffins and wine and brick-oven pizza," Darla announced.

"We wanted to cover all our bases," Jessa added, patting the open seat next to her.

"Thanks." Kate slumped into the booth, unable to look any of them in the eyes. She'd given them the gist of what had happened with Jaden via text so she wouldn't have to relay the story in person.

"It's a great article," Everly said, pushing a plate across the table. "Very heartfelt."

"Has he read it?" Naomi asked quietly. Her baby girl was sleeping contentedly in a wrap secured around her shoulders, and she obviously didn't want to wake her.

"No. I printed it out for him but he ripped it up." Kate winced at the sting the memory brought.

"Well that's dramatic." Darla popped a truffle into her mouth.

"I'm sure he'll calm down when he reads it," Jessa offered.

"I don't know." His eyes had been cold and dull. Not full of feeling like they were when he'd looked at her before. "He has every right to hate me." Though she hadn't exactly meant to, she'd tricked him. He was right. She'd seen an opportunity, and she'd selfishly pursued it, never considering how it might hurt him. Or her. "I should've told him a long time ago." Like her new friends had recommended. They could all be sitting there saying *I told you so*.

"It seems like people are really connecting with the article, though." Everly glanced at her phone. "Up to 24,953 shares already. It's going viral."

Yeah, she'd heard. On her way over, she'd called Gregor to have a few words with the man about posting something before she'd approved it, but he'd been too busy counting hits on their website to care much.

"So what are you going to do now?" Jessa asked, cutting a slice of pizza into petite bites. "Head back to L.A.?"

"I don't have much to go back to. I quit my job." She hadn't planned to, but when she was talking to Gregor, Jaden's words had echoed back in her head. *You're the fakest person I've ever met.* He was right. She didn't want to be a fake anymore. Even if it meant she had to slink home with her tail between her legs and move back into her parents' basement for a while.

"In that case, you can stay in Topaz Falls." Naomi's excitement woke the baby. She quickly stood to sway Charlotte back to sleep.

"Yes!" Everly, Jessa, and Darla whispered in unison.

"Stay?" She had a feeling there weren't a ton of jobs for unemployed writers in a small town like Topaz Falls. "But I have to work."

Darla's face brightened. "I've been thinking about hiring a manager so I can have a little more freedom to pursue my hobbies."

Everly grinned. "She means so she can have more time to date."

Darla ignored the snickers. "You'd be perfect management material," she said to Kate. "You're friendly, a good communicator, detail oriented..."

"Not to mention gorgeous," Jessa added. "That'll be good for business."

Kate looked from face to face with another round of tears brewing. "It sounds incredible." She had never fit anywhere. Not really. Not in her scholarly, overachieving family, not in her job. And here were these women she'd met only a week ago making a place for her.

"We're not fully booked until July." With Charlotte back to sleep, Naomi slid into the booth across from Kate again. "So you can stay at the inn for another month until you find your own place."

"And if you need more time, I've got an extra bedroom," Everly chimed in.

"Wow." A job, a place to live. But more importantly than either of those things, it came with the most generous, lively, compassionate friends she'd ever met. "Okay. I'd love to stay."

Excited squeals woke the baby again. Naomi stood and

swayed while Darla poured everyone a celebratory round of prosecco.

"Cheers!" Jessa held up her glass, and they all clinked away.

"I can't believe I'm moving to Colorado." Maybe Jaden would stay too. Maybe after time, he would give her another chance to prove to him that he could trust her with his heart.

"And you won't have any problem building a freelance writing career now," Jessa pointed out. "Not after the article goes viral."

That was true. With all of the exposure the article was getting in the mainstream media, she'd have a more recognizable name. "But that's not why I did it."

"Of course not." Everly reached over and squeezed her hand. "But maybe now you can focus on the kinds of things you've always wanted to write. You'd be great at profile pieces. Diving past the surface to really capture someone's heart."

Gratitude welled up in Kate's eyes once more. "Maybe I'll start with a profile on the extraordinary women of Topaz Falls."

CHAPTER TEN

Secluded Mountain Cabin on 30 acres! Exceptional privacy! Hidden driveway!

Jaden clicked on the real estate listing that promised the escape he needed. *Perfect.* The place was in No Man's Land, Canada, which sounded like paradise right now, considering it had been almost three days since that article had gone viral and the influx of calls and texts from reporters all over the world hadn't even started to slow down. Some paparazzi idiots had even camped out at the end of the street just waiting for him to leave.

At the moment, moving out of the country looked like a pretty damn good option. Except Canada might not be far enough away. Maybe Siberia…

Bella slunk into the office with the same forlorn posture she'd moped around in since Kate had left three nights ago. Didn't matter that Jaden had taken the dog on two hikes a day via their secret trail out back, or that he'd thrown the ball for her, or even that he'd given her extra treats. She still gave him those sad, pathetic eyes every time he looked at her.

"Come here," he said through a sigh. The dog trotted over. Was it just him or did she look more guilty than sad this time?

Bella came and sat at his feet, and sure enough, she had something in her mouth.

"Drop it," he commanded.

The dog complied all too happily. Didn't take him long to figure out why. It was a hair tie. Kate's hair tie. The one Jaden had tugged on to free her soft, long hair when she'd spent the night with him, when it felt like nothing could damage the connection they'd built.

Except for lies. Those could pretty much destroy anything.

The ache that had taken up residence in his gut sharpened. "You've got to get over her, Bella." Yeah, sure. He was telling Bella. Not himself for the thousandth time. "I know it's hard being here." Seeing as how this is where the three of them had played house for the better part of a week. "But we'll move on."

He scrubbed his hand behind the dog's ears until she leaned into him with a purr-like growl. "I'm looking for a place to go right now. We can start over." Again. He was getting pretty damn good at it. "Then it won't be so hard to forget." And yet he already knew how that logic worked. He hadn't seemed to forget either one of his parents, even though they'd pretty much abandoned him the day he was born.

Jaden turned back to the computer screen. What choice did he have, though? When he and Kate were messing around about her using him for his bathtub and massage skills, he had no idea how much truth hid inside those jokes. While he'd been thinking about a future with her, she'd been carefully taking notes on his story so she could expose him to the masses. How could he have been so stupid?

A sound outside the window forced him to leave that question unanswered.

Bella's ears perked.

Awesome. Just what he needed. The paparazzi sneaking around his backyard. Jaden shut his laptop and crept along the office wall, staying just behind the curtain. He almost laughed when he peered out and saw Levi Cortez tromping across the back deck like some kind of criminal.

The dog saw, too, judging from the mad swing of her tail. Bella scratched at the window, barking and whining at the prospect of company.

"Easy, girl." Jaden nudged her out to the living room, where they met Levi at the French doors. "What're you doing here?" he asked as he let him in. He had a feeling he already knew.

Levi sauntered past him in his cowboy's gait. "Haven't heard from you for a while. Figured I'd check in. And I saw the photographers outside, so I came around back." The man sat on the leather couch in the living room and leaned back like he had all day. Bella followed him, nosing his hand as though she'd been starved for attention the past three days.

Jaden stood where he was. "You could've called."

"I have called. You haven't answered."

Yeah, he hadn't even looked at his phone in a good twelve hours. After getting a text that had asked if he planned to marry Kate Livingston, he'd thrown the damn thing in a drawer. But Levi wasn't here to simply check up on him. And Jaden had had enough bullshit for one week. "Why are you really here?" He positioned himself in the chair across from the couch so they were facing off.

Levi grinned. "You haven't had the pleasure of meeting my sisters-in-law, Naomi and Jessa. But they're about as obstinate as a bull that's lost his balls. And they happen to like Kate. So here I am."

Jaden shook his head to stop Levi right there. "You're wasting your time," he informed his friend. "I can't stay here now. I've already found a place in Canada. You have no idea what it's like to have to hide in your house."

"So quit hiding. Who cares if they take pictures or write more stories?" Levi leaned forward, resting his elbows on his knees, still casual but also more determined. He obviously still had that stubborn streak. Typical bull rider.

"According to Jessa and Naomi, Kate's pretty broken up about everything."

"She's good at pretending." Jaden knew that for a fact. He'd replayed every scene of their tryst in his head. Every kiss. Every story she'd shared. Not once had he suspected she'd turn on him. That was the worst part. After everything he'd been through, he'd become an expert at sniffing out ulterior motives, and she'd completely snowed him.

"I get why you're pissed off," Levi said. "But it seems to me you used her too."

The anger that had only started to recede churned again, growing bigger, stronger. "How do you figure?"

The edge in Jaden's voice didn't seem to faze Levi. He simply shrugged. "When we talked on the phone last week, you told me you didn't think about the accident when Kate was around. So you used her as a distraction. Or did you screw her that night for *her* benefit?" The obvious sarcasm confirmed Levi already knew the answer. It also confirmed that word about him and Kate had gotten around Topaz Falls faster than Jaden could've dreamed.

"I guess that's it, then. We were using each other." That wasn't how it felt, though. He hadn't intentionally used her. It wasn't about the sex for him. It was that he thought she'd made the effort to see him. The real him. The one no one else cared to notice.

"She wasn't using you." Levi sounded so sure, but how could he know? He hadn't been there. He hadn't seen how good Kate was at drawing information out of him. How she'd lured him into telling stories that she'd probably written up in the fucking article.

"Maybe she was using you at first," his friend acknowledged. "But that's not why she wrote the article. Have you even read it?"

No. He hadn't been able to stomach the thought of staring at her words. Words that had been taken from him without his consent.

His silence must've spoken for him because Levi nodded. "You really need to read it. Hell, it almost made me choke up."

"I can't read it," Jaden said simply. He'd read plenty of articles that had torched him, and he hadn't cared. But Kate's words would matter more.

"Guess I'll have to read it to you, then." His friend shifted and pulled his cell phone out of his pocket. "At least the good parts."

"No thanks—"

"'When I first met J.J. Alexander,'" Levi interrupted, "'I saw what the rest of the world had seen—a cocky, bitter, fallen hero—'"

"You can stop now." Pain roiled in Jaden's gut. He knew her words would sting.

"Sorry. I shouldn't have read that part. It gets better." Levi turned his gaze back to the phone. "'After spending a week with him, I realized I was wrong. We were all wrong. J.J. isn't bitter or closed off or arrogant. He's wounded, haunted by regrets just like the rest of us. In one split second, his board caught an edge, and that tragic accident didn't only change Kipp Beckett's life, but it also changed J.J.'s life forever. He hasn't been able to escape it. He thinks about Kipp every day.'" Levi glanced up at him. "See? She's obviously trying to help, to get people to see your side of the story."

"I don't need people to see my side of the story." He hadn't made excuses for any of it. The accident might not have been intentional, but it was still his fault. It was all on him. "The article will only make things worse." She'd put him back in the same spotlight he'd been running from for months.

"There's more." Levi bent his head and went back to reading. "'Instead of exposing Jaden as a disgraced athlete like I had intended to do in this article, I fell for him. I fell for his subtle wit and his thoughtfulness and his profound depth. I fell for the way he loves and protects the dog he rescued from abuse and neglect. And yes, I even fell for his emotional scars because they are what make him so real. In one week, I discovered that J.J. Alexander has more empathy and strength and compassion than I ever will.'"

Her words roused hope, but he couldn't quite hold on to it. "Maybe she wrote it that way on purpose." Everyone wanted a good love story. "Maybe she wanted it to go viral so she'd have a recognizable name." What if she didn't care about him at all? No one else except for Gram ever had. Not his parents or his teammates. When he had been competing and winning, everyone had wanted to stand by him, but after he had fallen, he stood alone.

Levi shoved his phone back into his pocket and glanced around, a sure sign he was changing his approach. "Growing up, you and I didn't exactly have the greatest example of what love should look like."

"That's an understatement." When your parents left, love pretty much looked like abandonment. Levi knew that as well as he did.

"I was like you for a long time," his friend said. "Happy with a hookup here and there. But everything was different when I reconnected with Cass. It didn't matter what she did to me. How angry she got or how many times she pushed me away. I couldn't let her go. Not because I wanted anything from her either. I just loved her."

Jaden stared out the window. Had he ever just loved anyone? He didn't know how.

"Look..." The first signs of frustration showed in Levi's narrowed eyes. "I'm not as good at this lecture thing as Lance is. All I know is, I couldn't picture my life without Cass. I guess you need to decide if you could have feelings like that for Kate. Or for anyone. Maybe not now, but someday."

The feelings were already there. That's why he hurt like this. Somehow, the last two days had been lonelier than all twenty-four years of his life before he'd met Kate because now he knew what he was missing. "I already screwed it up." Jesus...had he really told her she was the fakest person he'd ever met? It wasn't only the words he'd used, though; it was also the venom behind them. She'd never forgive him for treating her that way.

"Believe it or not, I have some experience in begging a woman for forgiveness." Humor returned to Levi's voice. "But before you can ask for it, you've got to get yourself in a better place so you don't need a distraction anymore. Or things will never change."

The words were like stones sinking into his gut. Nothing would ever change if he didn't work for it. He'd put too much on Kate. It couldn't be her responsibility to pull him out of the pit he'd been living in. It shouldn't be. She deserved more. "I did use her." He cared about her, too, but that didn't change the facts. He'd only wanted her there because she made him feel something. She'd given him the courage to face the mountain again. All that had mattered was what she could offer him.

"Well, my work here is done." Levi stood and gave Bella a good scratch behind the ears before he opened the back door. "We've got a poker night at my place next Tuesday if you're up for it."

Jaden simply stared at him. How could he think about next Tuesday right now?

"You can let me know after you get this shitshow cleaned up," Levi said with a grin. Then he slipped out the back door, leaving Jaden to sit and wallow in his own stupidity.

Seeming to sense his misery, his dog walked over, sat down, and laid her head on his knee.

"Damn, Bella." He rested his hand on her head. "How are we gonna fix this?"

* * *

The Craig Hospital gift shop was stocked with flower arrangements, stuffed animals, and inspirational books and plaques. Jaden wandered down an aisle past shelves of trinkets inscribed with clichéd messages: *Get well soon! Healing thoughts and good wishes!*

The sentiments turned his stomach sour. What could he say to Kipp? What could he bring him that would make any of this better? He'd been trying to figure that out for two days, and he still had nothing.

Hands empty, he ducked out of the gift shop, dragging three months of guilt along behind him. When he'd emailed a request to visit Kipp in the hospital, Jaden fully expected him to decline, but he hadn't. *Come on by anytime,* Kipp had written. *I'll make sure you're on the list.*

It was surreal walking down the hall now. He'd imagined this place would look like a dungeon—dark and depressing—but windows everywhere let in the bright sunlight. Two young women pushing themselves in wheelchairs rolled toward him, chatting and laughing like they were in the hall of a high school. They smiled as they passed, and somehow he found a smile too. They looked happy. Healthy. He hoped the same was true for Kipp.

Jaden continued down the hall, following the directions to the rec center where Kipp apparently spent most of his afternoons. The room looked nothing like he imagined. There were low Ping-Pong and pool tables and a huge television screen mounted on the wall with video game consoles lined up underneath.

"What's up, Cowboy?" Kipp wheeled himself over, a Ping-Pong paddle sitting in his lap. He looked…the same. From the bandanna tied around his head to the sturdiness of his broad shoulders to his confident grin.

The sight stung Jaden's eyes. "You look…good." He didn't mean to sound so shocked, but all of the mental images he had of Kipp were still from those first few days after the accident when the media had plastered pictures of him being loaded into the medevac.

"I feel good. Just kicked Jones's ass in a game of Ping-Pong." He gestured to another man in a wheelchair who'd moved on to the Xbox. "You want to be next?" Kipp asked with that signature spark in his eyes. Without waiting for an answer, he wheeled over to the Ping-Pong table and brought Jaden a paddle.

He almost didn't know what to do with it. "You want to play Ping-Pong?"

"Hell yeah. I'm undefeated." Kipp trucked to the other side of the table and got into position. "Zeros," he said one second before he nailed a killer corner shot that Jaden of course missed.

"I wasn't ready." He wasn't ready for any of this. He hadn't even told the man he was sorry yet.

"Better get ready, Alexander. Because I've had a lot of time to practice." Kipp found another ball on the floor nearby and rolled back to the table. "One–zero." He served another zinger that whizzed by Jaden's right shoulder.

"Wait. Hold on." Jaden set down his paddle. "I didn't come here to play Ping-Pong. I came here to tell you I'm sorry. I'm sorry you got hurt and not me. I'm sorry I'm not the one sitting in that chair." It could've been him. "You don't have to pretend this is easy." He got that Kipp didn't want his pity—Jaden wouldn't want pity either—but the man's life would never be the same.

Kipp rolled his eyes as though he'd been dreading this conversation as much as Jaden. "It's not easy," he acknowledged. "But I've had three months to process things. At first I was as pissed as hell about it. Some days I still am. But I've also learned my life isn't over. Hell, I've already been invited to be a commentator for the X Games next year."

He should've been competing in those games, though. Jaden didn't say it. Kipp already knew what he'd lost. Somehow he seemed to be on the road to accepting it. So why couldn't Jaden? Why couldn't he release the guilt? "You let me know if you ever need anything." Maybe that would help. If he could just do something for Kipp, maybe he could forgive himself. "I'll be there for you. I'll help you out however I can."

"You don't have to be sorry, J.J. I've seen the footage."

His old rival mocked him with a smirk. “It’s not your fault you’re not as good on a board as I was.”

Same old trash talk from one of the greats but this time Jaden didn’t return fire. He couldn’t. “I should’ve pulled back.” He’d been moving too fast, too recklessly. He’d wanted to win. That was the truth of it. If he’d backed off, the accident never would’ve happened.

“I would’ve been offended if you had slowed down,” Kipp said. “We competed. We’re athletes. That’s what we do.” The man’s expression sobered. “The last three months have sucked but I’ve got a lot going for me. That’s what I want to focus on now. The future.”

And that’s what Jaden would focus on too.

CHAPTER ELEVEN

"Welcome to the Chocolate Therapist." Kate greeted the older couple with the same enthusiasm as she had greeted every other couple and family group and friend group that had walked through the doors for the last nine hours.

Her feet, which were stuffed into her favorite pair of black Manolo Blahniks, ached like a mother, but even the pain couldn't dim the excitement of day four in her new life. All within less than a week of the big falling out with Jaden, she'd managed to fly home, pack up her apartment, and say farewell to everyone before she'd driven straight back to Topaz Falls.

When she'd driven into town, the sun was setting over the mountains in a fiery red welcome. So far it felt like this place had always been her home. Even with long days of learning the wine and chocolate business, the shininess of her new venture still hadn't dulled.

"Would you like a table?" she asked the couple, gracefully withdrawing two menus from the hostess stand. "Or would you prefer to sit at the bar?"

Darla appeared behind her. "I can take over, Kate. Your shift was over a half hour ago."

"That's okay. I'm having so much fun." Even with achy, swollen feet, this was better than going back to her room at the Hidden Gem to spend the evening by herself. Despite the homey decorations, loneliness echoed between the walls.

"All right." Darla drifted back to the bar. "But at least sit down after they're seated."

Ignoring her friend, she turned back to the elderly couple.

"We would love a table near the windows, dear." The woman appeared to be in her early seventies with white wispy hair and jewel-like blue eyes.

Her husband was a head shorter than her and just as adorable with a rim of frizzy gray hair around a shiny bald spot. "There's something going on down the street, and we'd like to see how it turns out."

"Of course," Kate sang. "Right this way." Ignoring the pinch in her toes, she led them to a quaint table for two that looked out on Main Street. Darla had been right. She was good at this. Good with people. They always smiled at her, and even though she'd only been working here for a few days, she'd managed to defuse three grumpy patrons' complaints and had them all smiling and laughing again within a matter of minutes.

"Here we are." She tucked the menus under her arm and pulled out each chair with a charming smile, patiently waiting until the couple had gotten situated before she handed them the wine and chocolate list.

Instead of opening his menu, the man craned his neck as though trying to see down the street. "Any idea why all that trash is piled onto the car out there?"

"It's not trash, Gerald," his wife corrected. "It's sweet. There are flowers and streamers and balloons..."

Kate choked on a gasp. Flowers. Streamers. Balloons. On a car...

She tried to keep her hopes smothered under practical logic, which had never been one of her strengths. Jaden hadn't returned any of her emails or calls. After a few days, she'd stopped trying.

"It's so pretty," the woman went on. "I saw the man fixing it all up nice. He was tying heart-shaped balloons to the door handles, the sweetheart."

Sweet Lord...

Those darn hopes threw logic to the wind and sent her heart sky-high. Bracing her hands on the table, Kate leaned forward as far as she could without bumping her forehead on the glass. Each beat of her heart thumped harder when she looked down the block to where she'd parked her car earlier. Sure enough, it was covered.

"Oh my God." It had to be him. No one else around here knew that story.

"Um...your waiter will be right with him...I mean you," Kate stammered to the couple. The happiness burning in her eyes made her voice all weepy. She steadied herself against their table once more and pulled off her shoes, letting them dangle from one hand as she hurried toward the door.

"Are you all right, honey?" the woman called.

"I will be." As soon as she saw him—as soon as she felt his arms wrap around her—she would be. Kate ran down the sidewalk barefoot, her pencil skirt surely making her resemble a waddling penguin, but she didn't care. It was such a lovely sight, her car covered in orange. There were gerbera daisies and orange hearts cut out of construction paper, and yes, even heart-shaped balloons. But she couldn't see the front yet. Would Jaden be there? Had he really forgiven her?

"Pardon me," she mumbled, bumping her way past people.

When she finally broke through the crowd that had gathered, her knees gave. Jaden was sitting on the hood of her car with the stem of an orange gerbera daisy between his teeth.

"Look at you..." She stumbled off the curb, nearly incapacitated by the tears and laughter, sure that the happiness of this moment could fill a whole lifetime.

"Hey, gorgeous." He somehow managed to annunciate perfectly, even with the daisy in his mouth.

The crowd around them grew, pressing in on both sides of the street. Both locals and tourists snapped pictures and selfies on their phones. He hadn't tried to disguise himself. No hat. No sunglasses. Just J.J. Alexander sitting on the hood of her car. None of the attention seemed to bother him, though. He stared steadily at her as she crept closer. "What're you doing?"

"I'm asking you on a date." He took the flower out of his mouth and dropped it on the hood and then reached for her hand. "Kate Livingston, will you go on a date with me?"

"Hell yes, she will," Darla called from behind her. "How about right now? We can set up a nice private table in the back."

Murmurs of approval went around the crowd. Someone even clapped.

Kate shushed everyone with a frantic wave of her hand. This moment was a scene straight out of her dreams, and she didn't want anyone to intrude.

"I'm sorry I was such an ass." He eased off the hood and stood across from her. "I'm sorry I didn't hear you out. I'm sorry I ripped up your article."

"Awww. I'll go on a date with you," some woman yelled from the other side of the street.

"No." Kate put her hands on his broad shoulders to make sure this was really happening. "I mean yes. Of course I'll go on a date with you."

Jaden lowered his face to hers, her favorite grin in the entire world flickering on his lips. "Now?"

"Now," she confirmed.

The crowds parted. Cell phone cameras followed their every move as they huddled together and hurried back to the Chocolate Therapist, ducking through the doors so they could leave the rest of the world behind.

"Back here, you two." Darla quickly ushered them down the hall to the room where they met for book club. She'd already had the waitstaff drag in a small round table, two chairs, and a vase with a single orange gerbera daisy she must've swiped from the car.

God, these women. They had the best and biggest and brightest hearts she'd ever seen. "Thank you." Kate brushed away her tears as Darla gave her a wink and disappeared, closing the door firmly behind her.

They both sat down.

"You're crying." Jaden took her cheeks in his hands, using his thumbs to wipe away the tears.

"You humiliated yourself out there." All for her. "That'll be all over the news by tonight." People were probably tweeting and Instagraming and Facebooking the pictures right now.

"I don't care." Something had changed on Jaden's face. The day she'd met him, it had borne the lines of tension and stress, but now his features seemed softer. Relaxed. "I'm tired of caring what everyone else thinks. Except you." He slipped his hand under hers and held on. "You were right. There is something between us. Something...special. Something I've never had with anyone else."

Kate closed her eyes, letting those words soak in to heal all of the wounds he'd inflicted before. She looked at him again, wanting him to cut away that last bit of uncertainty that still dangled from her heart. "What changed?" she whispered. "You were so angry..."

"Yeah." A sigh slipped out. "Levi pretty much put me in my place. Told me I'd better get my head out of my ass and figure things out before I lost you for good."

"Levi, huh?" She smiled, thinking back to Jessa and Naomi's secret little side conversation at Everly's café the day she'd told them what had happened.

"Yeah, Levi." His smirk confirmed her suspicions. "He reminded me that I had issues to work on too. So I went to see Kipp."

Kate tightened her grip on his hand. "That must've been hard. How is he?"

"Still in rehab." Jaden threaded his fingers with hers, and the power of it, the intimacy of that gesture, heated her eyes again.

"But I spent the afternoon with him. He's exceeding the doctor's expectations. He's even taken a few steps with a walker."

"That's great news." For Kipp and for Jaden. No wonder his appearance had changed so much. He'd been set free.

"I read the article too. Actually, Levi read it to me." Jaden brought her hand to his lips and kissed her knuckles, sending an electrical charge all the way down to her toes.

"I'm sorry I betrayed your trust." She'd been waiting to say those words for over a week, but before now, something told her they wouldn't have done any good. "I should've told you. Right away. But I was afraid you'd keep me out. And I loved being with you."

"I loved being with you too," he murmured, leaning over the table until his lips were nearly touching hers. "I think that's why I lost it when I found out about the article. It was an excuse to bail. I figured you'd turn out to be like everyone else." His gaze shied away from hers. "I haven't exactly had much commitment in my life."

She kissed him, hopefully taking away any lingering doubts about her feelings for him. "I meant everything I said in the article."

This time his eyes stayed steady on hers. "I know."

"Levi said you were thinking about moving away." God, when she'd heard that, she'd had to excuse herself so she could cry in the bathroom.

"I was seriously considering it," Jaden said. "Until he reminded me it wouldn't help. I want to stop hiding. I want to make you happy. I want to focus on the future instead of the past."

She rested her forehead against his. "Me too."

Just as his lips brushed hers, the door swung open.

"Don't mind us." Darla traipsed in, followed by Everly and Jessa and Naomi, all carrying something different. They set down truffles and a bottle of wine and glasses and small china plates.

"Carry on," Everly said, herding the others toward the door.

"Those truffles are strawberry-filled dark," Darla called, fighting Everly's hold on her.

"The perfect aphrodisiac," Jessa added before Everly shoved her outside.

"Happy date night!" Naomi said with a sly grin.

Shaking her head, Everly waved at Kate and Jaden once more before closing the door.

Jaden laughed. If she could bottle up that deep throaty sound and listen to it every night before bed, she totally would.

"Levi wasn't kidding about their persistence."

She leaned in to claim the kiss she'd never stop craving. "Sometimes true love takes a village," Kate murmured against his lips.

And they seemed to have found theirs.

ACKNOWLEDGMENTS

Thank you, dear readers, for spending more time in Topaz Falls. I hope you are enjoying this town and these characters as much as I am. It's impossible for me to express how grateful I am for your notes, comments, reviews, and mentions. Your support keeps me going.

As always, I am so thankful to the team at Forever for allowing me to live my dream and write more books. You all continue to amaze me! With each project I learn more from my brilliant editor, Alex Logan. Thanks for everything you do to make me look good.

I will never be able to thank my family enough for their patience and perseverance, especially while I was writing this book under such a tight deadline! Will, AJ, and Kaleb, you will always have my heart.

Champion bronc rider Mateo Torres has big plans to bulldoze his newly purchased acreage so he can turn it into a lucrative investment property. Unfortunately for him, his new tenant, Everly Brooks, isn't planning on going anywhere.

Please see the next page for a preview of *True-Blue Cowboy*.

In Everly's world, happy hour used to mean a little black dress, strappy heels, sapphire martinis, and schmoozing with the law firm's wealthiest clients in a private room at Saison. But she wasn't in San Francisco anymore, Toto.

Walking into the Tumble Inn, the heels of her worn, thrift-store cowgirl boots crunched against the peanut shells you weren't supposed to throw on the floor. She paused inside the door. Instead of the clean lines and sleek modern decor of her past, the place was a hodgepodge. Battered metal covered the bar. Concrete floors glistened with a generous coat of sealant. The heavy wooden pub tables bore the scars of endless games of beer pong, and maybe the occasional bar fight.

The place even sounded different than her old life. Instead of glittery laughs and muted tones of classical music and hushed murmurs of gossip, this place was as loud and rowdy as an off-color great-uncle. Country music blared from the speakers, and since happy hour had already started, it was accompanied by echoing laughs and loud chatter.

Okay. Deep breath. She raised her head with shaky confidence and waded into the crowd. Even though she loved it—wanted it to be hers—everything about this life still felt new. Like she couldn't fully claim it as her own. After being in Topaz Falls for over two years, there were still so many moments she felt like an outsider, a foreigner trapped between two worlds. Though she looked the part of the mountain cowgirl in her simple white sundress and worn leather boots, most of these people who raised their hand in a wave or bumped her shoulder lightly as she passed didn't truly know her.

That was her fault. Betrayal still lingered on the edges of her ability to trust people. Ever since she'd arrived in this town, she'd filled her life with animals and chores and cooking and baking rather than risk developing deep relationships again. She'd come out of her old life with none of them intact.

Everly made her way closer to the bar, clinging to the outskirts of the crowd along the wall. Now, most nights after getting all the work done around the farm, she was too tired to do anything anyway. Tonight was no different. She would've been happy just to curl up in her jammies on the couch. But Darla had stopped by and demanded she meet them for happy hour since Cassidy was back in town after a two-week stint of working as a nurse in Denver.

Obviously, Everly was the last to arrive. From the shadows, she spied Cassidy and Levi; Jessa and her husband, Lance; and Naomi and her husband, Lucas. Not far away, Darla stood in a small huddle with some man she didn't recognize and Ty Forrester, Charity Stone, and yes, ladies and gentlemen, Mateo Torres.

Nerves rolled through her before settling heavily in her stomach. Her new landlord had one elbow leaning on the bar top. Everything about him was dark—from his eyes to his clothes to the cowboy hat he wore tipped forward on his head. Mystery wrapped itself in the shadows of his face, hiding secrets she was sure he'd never share. Or maybe he would, but they just might kill her. The tattered jeans he wore hugged his lower body snugly, but somehow he still had room to swagger. And he didn't have to try. Mateo Torres was a man who could swagger without moving a muscle.

Studying him, she finally understood the Zorro thing. The lustrous dark hair, the tanned skin, and the seductive eyes made him downright dangerous, but his irresistible smile fooled his prey into thinking he was harmless.

Everly had yet to have any real conversation with the man, though she'd noticed that he'd parked his palatial fifth-wheel camper on the hill above the farm's stables like some kind of overseer. But she couldn't keep avoiding him. If she wanted to preserve the farm, she needed to win him over as soon as possible.

She smoothed her hands down her dress, wiping off the clammy feel of nerves, and raised her shoulders the same way she had before she'd walked into the courtroom. Whatever she did, she had to show him a capable, savvy professional who could be an asset to him instead of a burden. Maybe she wasn't yet, but she would be. Eventually.

Smiling like she believed it, she strode across the room to her friends.

"You're here!" Cassidy untangled herself from her husband's arms and captured Everly in a hug. "I didn't know if you'd make it."

"I wouldn't have missed a chance to say hello." Everly returned the embrace, feeling that pull again. She wanted this so much. Friends. Community. A place to belong. She pulled back and looked Cassidy over. "You look amazing."

Every time the woman came home for a visit, she looked even rosier, as though she glowed with happiness, especially when Levi happened to be nearby.

It only convinced Everly she'd done the right thing in walking away from her old life and an upcoming marriage that had seemed more like a business arrangement. Since she'd moved to Topaz Falls and met these amazing couples who were so in love, she'd decided that every marriage should be a romantic escapade. She wouldn't ever settle for anything else.

"How's work been?" Her smile came more easily with the warmth beaming from her friend.

"Crazy," Cassidy said. "And wonderful too. I'm busy and running all day, but instead of being exhausted, taking care of those kids energizes me, you know?"

Everly nodded. For the first time in her life, she did know. She knew how it felt to wake up every day and feel like there was purpose in what she was doing. "I'm so glad you love it."

"What about you?" Concern shadowed her friend's pristine blue eyes. "I can't believe Owen sold his land. Owen was such a fixture in this town."

"Yeah." And he was pretty much the only one who cared about the farm as much as she did. "I'm sure it'll be okay." She kept that chipper harmony in her voice. "I mean, once he sees how important the farm is, I think Mateo will leave it alone."

"Of course he will." Cass leaned in. "And even if he doesn't, Levi is one of his best friends, so I may have some influence in that department." She winked. "You let me know if you have any issues, you hear?"

Relief soothed the nerves stirring in Everly's stomach. "Thank you. I might have to take you up on that." Though something told her Mateo did what he wanted. He had that untamed air about him. She glanced over at the man again. Three women had officially invaded his personal space and were giggling with the force of high school cheerleaders at whatever he was saying. Tourists most likely, seeing as how she didn't recognize them.

"Oh, there's my mom. I'll be right back." Cassidy slipped away, but Everly didn't have time to feel lonely before the rest of her friends crowded in.

"Everly!" Darla, Jessa, and Naomi drew her attention away from the spectacle currently taking place around Mateo. Seriously, he stood in the center of those women like some mythical god…

"Here. I already ordered your drink." Darla handed her a dirty martini from the bar. Everly thanked her and threw back a gulp while all of her friends took a sip from their colorful frozen cocktails. Okay, so maybe she hadn't left San Francisco behind completely.

"I thought you were going to be here an hour ago," Darla said.

"Leave her alone," Naomi butted in. "She's a busy lady. Running a farm, serving breakfast and lunch. It's not like she has a lot of free time."

"And yet she still looks like that." Jessa appraised her with a look of mock jealousy. "Seriously. You look gorgeous."

"So do you." Her friends were all beautiful, strong women in their own ways. Darla with her sassy black pixie cut and chic clothes. Naomi with her long red hair and friendly girl-next-door manner. And then there was Jessa with her blond hair and adorably round, innocent face. Lately, Jessa seemed to be even more radiant than usual, too, though no official pregnancy announcement had been made.

Gratitude swelled inside of her, filling up the space her earlier insecurities had occupied. She may not have lived here long, but these women had made it their mission to welcome her into their circle. "I would've been here earlier but I got held up." Walter had broken out of lockdown, and she'd had to chase the duck around the chicken yard, slogging through the mud, which had splattered all the way up to her face, which meant she'd had to shower again. Just another typical day in her life.

"Well, I'm glad you're here." Darla leaned in and linked their arms together. "I've been dying to hear if you've seen your new neighbor in his underwear yet." Her eyebrows wiggled with hints of dirty thoughts. "Or better yet, without it."

Everly couldn't help but laugh. Her friend's greatest mission in life was to see all of the cowboys in town naked, but she didn't share that ambition. "When could I have possibly seen him in his underwear? Or without it, for that matter?"

The woman directed her gaze over Everly's shoulder. "I'm guessing he's the kind of man who isn't shy about showing off the goods."

"Definitely not," Jessa agreed, openly staring in Mateo's direction.

"I bet he walks around naked all the time," Naomi added, suddenly as rapt as everyone else.

As if he needed more attention. If the flirty touching was any indication, Mateo had his hands full at the moment. "I haven't seen him at all," Everly said to land their focus back on her. "Clothed or naked." Not for lack of trying. To see him clothed. All afternoon, she'd found excuses to zip past his trailer, but he hadn't been around.

"Well, you can see him right now." Darla slid her glance sideways, but Everly refrained from looking.

"Mateo doesn't do it for me," she lied. Actually, he did it for every straight woman. She simply couldn't let him do it for her.

"Well, he sure seems to be watching you," Naomi murmured into her margarita glass.

Jessa's eyes popped open wider. "Totally. Wait...he's coming over here!"

"What?" Suddenly panicked, Everly whirled around and lost the grip on her martini glass. It flew from her hand in a high arc and sailed right toward Mateo, hitting him square in the forehead before it fell and shattered on the floor.

A collective hush silenced the room.

Shock appeared to ice over Mateo's gaze as his hand rose to his head.

"Oh my God! I'm so sorry!" Glass crunched underneath her boots as she rushed over to him, vaguely aware of the stares and whispers following behind her. "I didn't mean to! The glass was a little slippery and it flew out of my hand and..." God, she'd hit her new landlord in the head with a martini glass!

"You're bleeding..." She snatched a napkin off the table next to her and went to wipe the trickle of blood from his forehead, but he quickly stepped out of reach, his stony expression brushing off her desperate apology. His eyes looked even darker than normal. And the trail of blood had now streaked down over his left eyebrow.

"Cleanup on aisle five," Darla called over to the bar. Leave it to her friend to deflate the tension in the room. With that one quip, the noise level rose again. A couple of people chuckled as they went back to whatever they had been doing before Everly had humiliated herself. Even without the attention of the room, Everly's face burned hotter than the heat coils on her commercial stove. Those damn martini glasses. They were too awkward to hold on to.

Gil Wilson, who owned the fine establishment, lumbered over with a broom. "Next time you want to start a bar fight with a cowboy, take it outside." Judging from the crooked grin on the old man's face, he said it in jest, but that didn't make this any better.

"I'm so sorry, Gil," she mumbled, unable to look up. "I can pay for the glass."

"Don't be silly. The look on Torres's face was worth every penny. He looked as shocked as a fox that had a rabbit swiped right out of his mouth." He swept up the mess in his slow, methodical way, chuckling the whole time.

It hadn't looked like shock to her. It'd looked more like anger. Everly took the dustpan from Gil and knelt to help him clean up the mess. Mortification still pulsed in her cheeks, made more potent by her own irritation. She'd apologized to the man and he'd simply looked down on her like she had no business talking to him. Well, that wasn't going to work for her. He didn't get to treat her like a second-class citizen because he was her landlord.

Everly rose to her feet to tell him so but Mateo was already gone.

ABOUT THE AUTHOR

Sara Richardson grew up chasing adventure in Colorado's rugged mountains. She's climbed to the top of a 14,000-foot peak at midnight, swum through Class IV rapids, completed her wilderness first-aid certification, and spent seven days at a time tromping through the wilderness with a thirty-pound backpack strapped to her shoulders.

Eventually Sara did the responsible thing and got an education in writing and journalism. After a brief stint in the corporate writing world, she stopped ignoring the voices in her head and started writing fiction. Now she uses her experience as a mountain adventure guide to write stories that incorporate adventure with romance. Still indulging her adventurous spirit, Sara lives and plays in Colorado with her saint of a husband and two young sons.

Learn more at:

www.sararichardson.net
Twitter @sarar_books
Facebook.com/sararichardsonbooks

Looking for more cowboys?
Forever brings the heat with these sexy studs.

COWBOY REBEL
By Carolyn Brown

After a brush with the law, rancher Taggart Baker has decided to leave his wild ways behind, especially when he meets a beautiful ER nurse worth settling down for. But before he can convince her he's a changed man, his troubled past comes calling—and this time he won't be able to walk away so easily. Includes a bonus story by Annie Rains!

Visit us at read-forever.com.

THE COWBOY NEXT DOOR
By R.C. Ryan

The last thing Penny Cash needs is a flirtation with a wild, carefree cowboy. Sure, he's funny and sexy, but they're as different as whiskey and tea. But when trouble comes calling, Penny will find out how serious Sam Monroe can be when it comes to protecting the woman he loves. Includes a bonus story by A.J. Pine!

HARD LOVING COWBOY
By A.J. Pine

Walker Everett has good and bad days—but the worst was the day that Violet Chastain started as the new sommelier at Crossroads Ranch. She knows nothing about ranch life and constantly gets under his skin. But when a heated argument leads to the hottest kiss he's ever had, Walker must decide whether he finally deserves something good. Includes a bonus story by Sara Richardson!